THE WEDDING OF THE WOLF

ANSLEY VAUGHAN

The Wedding of the Wolf
ISBN # 978-0-85715-422-4
©Copyright Ansley Vaughan 2011
Cover Art by Natalie Winters ©Copyright 2011
Interior text design by Claire Siemaszkiewicz
Total-E-Bound Publishing

Published in 2011 by Total-E-Bound Publishing, Think Tank, Ruston Way, Lincoln, LN6 7FL, United Kingdom.

THE WEDDING
OF THE WOLF

Dedication

To Nemone Thornes, who forces me to write.

Chapter One

In a bright room in Covent Garden, a woman worked at a keyboard, sighing occasionally. The computer was built into a mock eighteenth-century desk and at the flick of a switch could be hidden to create the illusion of a clear surface. Obviously, this was a place of business, but furnished in the manner of an elegant drawing room. Veneered cabinets concealed files and stationery, velvet curtains flanked the long windows and the smart carpet had a muted pattern. A chaise-longue and some imitation *Louis Quinze* chairs completed the furnishings.

The woman matched her surroundings. Beneath dark auburn hair pulled back into a chignon, her pale oval face was discreetly made up. She wore small pearls at her ears and throat and plain glasses masked green eyes under arched brows. Her suit of burnt orange toned with her colouring, the fitted jacket long on her hips, the knee-length skirt pencil thin. Slender legs and brown stilettos completed the outfit.

The door opposite her opened and a young man looked in.

"Eloise, I just got a call from Lady Connaught. She's on her way."

"Good. Thank you, Jamie. Though why she should phone ahead when she's already made an appointment, I don't know."

"Perhaps she wants to make sure we've got the red carpet out."

"Well, if I had one, I'd fling it down. There's a lot riding on this."

"I'll dig out the best china!" he said with a laugh and went out. Eloise got up and moved gracefully over to the window.

The view from the first floor room was of a narrow London street, clogged with cars and taxis. Throngs of tourists made their way to the Piazza, just visible to the left.

She stood with a hand on each of the velvet drapes. She could see her reflection in the glass and she sighed again, wondering what on earth she was doing in this parody of an eighteenth-century drawing room, waiting to butter up an appalling woman. And knowing that failure meant ruin.

Another door, concealed in the wall behind the desk, opened, not gently this time and in burst what looked like a very big cat. On closer inspection, Eloise realised it was a woman wearing cat ears and a painted face with a blackened nose and whiskers. A basque-like garment in tabby-coloured fake fur thrust her breasts upwards and outwards and her arms were covered in long tabby gloves. Her legs were encased in fishnet tights and her feet in high black heels and as she pranced into the room, visible behind her was a swinging tail. She looked startlingly out of place amid the restrained elegance of her surroundings.

"Miaow!" she said, clawing the air. "Yow! What do you think? Aren't I a pretty pussy?"

Despite her anxiety, Eloise laughed. "Stunning!" she agreed. "But you'd better get out, Lady Connaught will be here any minute and the sight of you would send her out into the street screaming blue murder."

"Fine." The other woman swished her tail behind her with one hand. "That's how I feel about her."

"God, Sammy, we need her. If I can land this contract we may just be able to save the business."

"Well the downmarket bit's doing okay."

"Nothing downmarket about *Show-Offs*. But if *Lace Dreams* goes down, it'll take everything with it."

Sammy patted Eloise's shoulder with a furry paw. "I know, darling. You'll be brilliant. But don't let her tell you she's got lots of other agencies bidding for this wedding. I met Mandy from *Brides' World* the other night and she told me *La Connaught* was impossible. They parted on bad terms. I know she's been doing the rounds."

From the door into the outer office they heard a loud female voice.

"That's her! Quick, get your pretty pussy out of here!"

The cat scampered off towards the hidden door, only just reaching it as Jamie ushered in a well-dressed blonde woman.

"Lady Connaught, how very nice to see you again!"

"Ah, Eloise," the woman drawled, and made a kissing sound either side of her cheek. "You know my husband Lyndo, don't you?"

"Of course." Eloise extended her hand. "Hello, Sir Lyndo."

Sir Lyndo Connaught was a bluff businessman, who had earned his knighthood by building a small engineering firm into a huge international conglomerate in the days when he was plain Lindsey Connaught. He ignored the hand and planted a smacking kiss on her lips. "Little Eloise! It's been a long time…"

"Indeed," his wife interrupted. "But we mustn't waste time. Sit down, Lyndo."

Eloise looked hopefully towards the door. "Isn't Tamsin with you?"

"No, she's got some frightful horsy thing to go to. Anyhow, she wants me to do all the field-work."

Eloise reflected that Lady Connaught was unlikely to let her daughter have much say in the arrangements for this wedding. She was pretty sure that her ladyship was taking her responsibilities as the mother of the bride so seriously that she'd been largely responsible for choosing the groom. She motioned Sir Lyndo to a chair and sat behind the desk, noticing out of the corner of her eye that the hidden door was slightly ajar and the tip of a tabby tail was protruding from it. The door opened slightly, the tail was whisked away and it shut again quietly.

Eloise suppressed a growing feeling of hysteria. She put on her glasses and opened a folder on the desk.

"If you'd like to give me an idea of your requirements, I'll take some notes. I think Tamsin showed you our brochures?"

"Yes, thank you. I should tell you at once, Eloise, that I am seeing several different agencies — rather grander ones than this, I might add," she added, looking critically around the room. "But I agreed to give you a chance since you and Tamsin were at school together."

"Thank you, I appreciate it."

"I will expect whoever takes this on to be responsible for every aspect of the wedding. Venue, ceremony, clothes, reception — everything."

"Of course."

"And I envisage a full-time commitment. This is a big society wedding — Lyndo has a reputation to maintain. We want it to go like clockwork."

"I understand. But having one consultant working full-time would mean considerable fees..."

Lady Connaught waved one scarlet-nailed hand, laden with diamonds. "That's not a problem. Lyndo will sort all that out."

Sir Lyndo opened his mouth to speak, then thought better of it and contented himself with nodding benignly. His wife patted her improbably yellow shoulder-length hair. "And of course, I'll be available for guidance and advice."

There was always a downside, Eloise thought but she nodded and smiled.

"Right, let's get down to business. First can I offer you something? Tea, coffee, wine, sherry?"

They both opted for sherry and when Jamie brought in the tray, Eloise took a glass herself, feeling she might need the fortification of alcohol.

"The first question is when and where?"

"We thought early June," Lady Connaught said. "That gives us about four months of preparation. And in Italy. That's why I need an organiser, because of the legal and logistical complications. You could handle that?"

Eloise resisted a desire to punch the air, but merely smiled politely. "No problem. I speak good Italian and I've organised weddings there before."

"The Allwood affair. I know. But nothing on this scale, I imagine."

"No, nothing on this scale. Did you have a particular place in mind?"

"Not really. One of those lovely hilltop villages in Tuscany or Chianti, thereabouts. Something wild and romantic. I want people to talk about this wedding for years to come."

"We'll make sure of that. Let me compile a list and then I can give you a rough costing in a few days' time. We'd be talking about a flat fee plus expenses and costs, obviously. Does that sound reasonable?"

Sir Lyndo gave a rumble of assent and Eloise realised he'd happily pay over the odds so long as he didn't have to think about the wedding himself.

They went through the requirements, with Eloise making meticulous notes. It took nearly an hour, during which Sir Lyndo consumed most of the decanter of sherry and resorted to staring out of the window at the passing tourists.

At last, Eloise put down her pen. "I think that's all clear. Except, of course, for the question about the venue. And that's really the most important." She pulled a file from the cabinet behind her. "Plenty of Italian hotels and other places are setting up for weddings now. I can give you some brochures to study."

Lady Connaught shook her head. "No. I don't want something that's in a brochure. Nowhere that's already been used."

Eloise was nonplussed. "But to find somewhere new, I'd have to go to Italy. Scout around."

Her ladyship gave her a sharp look. "So? Then that's what you'll have to do."

Eloise felt an acute moment of panic, quickly brought under control. "Of course. But although I'm happy to put a great deal of time and effort into this tender, I'm afraid the company wouldn't be able to underwrite a trip to Italy. The expense would be too great. And there'd be replacement costs and so on."

Lady Connaught frowned and clutched her bag with a determined air. "In that case, we'll say goodbye." She stood. "We're sorry to have taken up so much of your time."

Eloise inclined her head. Her heart pounded, but she couldn't give in. Not only would it make her seem too desperate and violate every rule of good business, but she knew the company couldn't afford it.

Sir Lyndo turned from the window, speaking for the first time in an hour. "Now, now, Bryony. The girl has a point. If you want to send her scouting round Europe, it's a service and we have to pay. I mean, there's no guarantee she'll get the job, but if she finds you a suitable venue, that's a big chunk of the work."

His wife sat down again. Eloise got the impression Sir Lyndo's interventions were so rare that they added impact when they did occur.

"If you say so, Lyndo," she said, without enthusiasm.

"Excellent. Eloise, we'll pay for a week's recce in Italy. Flight, hire car, living expenses. If you discover a suitable venue, regardless of whether or not you get the job of planning the wedding, we'll pay a reasonable finder's fee. How does that sound?"

"It sounds very fair indeed, thank you, Sir Lyndo."

"I think we could drop the Sir, don't you, if we're working together? And my wife is Bryony."

"Thank you. I'll arrange a trip as quickly as possible."

"Excellent. Well, come on, Bryony, time to go."

Lady Connaught stood. "I look forward to hearing from you Eloise — soon."

"Yes indeed, Lady Con... Bryony. Please give my love to Tamsin."

"I will." As they reached the door, Lady Connaught turned. "You've never married, have you, Eloise?"

"Not so far, no."

"Ah. I suppose in this business, it's a case of *'always the bridesmaid, never the bride'*." She swept out, followed by her husband who shot a rueful smile at Eloise before he went.

Eloise told Sammy about it later, when she was ensconced in their flat with a large glass of wine. "I wouldn't have minded so much, but it was that phrase *'you've never married.'* If she'd said, *'You're not married,'* it wouldn't have sounded nearly so insulting. It's what they put in obituaries, isn't it? *'She'd never married.'*"

Sammy lay on the other couch. She had changed out of the cat outfit into tight denims and a T-shirt which strained across her breasts. "You're not unhappy though, are you? Surely, you wouldn't want to be married just now? To Jake?"

Eloise laughed. "Oh, most certainly not to Jake! And I'm perfectly happy. It's just...sometimes I feel there's something missing. I mean, the work's fine, but it's hardly intellectually stretching. And it's such a strain, keeping our heads above water."

"Well, we've got a fighting chance if you can pull this off. And it sounds as if Sir Lyndo is on your side. Well, he would be, of course — he always had the hots for you, even when we were at school."

"Oh, Sammy!"

"Face it, Lois—you've always had that power over men. Pity you don't use it more." She reached for the wine bottle and topped up her glass. "What I don't understand is how Tamsin has grown up so normal, with that monstrous mother."

"Well, to be frank, she's not very bright. I think a lot of it just goes over her head."

"True. Who is he, this chap she's marrying?"

"Alistair Carew-White. Pronounced Carey, as Lady C told me about a dozen times. He's a cousin of the Earl of Langdon and he's the eldest son of a Baronet, so she views this as a big step up the ladder."

"What's he like?"

"I don't know. I haven't met him. But Jenny Pargeter has, and she says he's loud and hearty."

"Should suit Tamsin down to the ground."

"I hope so. I'd like her to be happy."

"Yes, and I'd like *you* to be happy. You've got me worried now."

Eloise smiled. "Don't be, Sammy. I'm fine. And if we can work out how to run the business while I'm away, then I've wangled myself a free trip to Italy, even if it comes to nothing."

"I've been thinking about that and I know just what we can do. I'll take over *Lace Dreams* again and we'll let Jamie have a bash at *Show-Offs*."

"Jamie? I suppose it would be all right. He's very bright and enthusiastic. But you're not keen on the wedding planning side."

"I don't mind it. You've only got a couple of them coming up, haven't you? And I bet you've already done most of the work. You always keep such good notes. I'll be able to recline in the office looking glamorous."

"Well, if you're sure… Great!"

They sat in companionable silence. Nine years earlier, when Eloise had lost her parents in quick succession, she'd moved into Samantha's tiny flat in Knightsbridge and they'd thought about starting a business together.

About that time, Eloise agreed to organise the wedding of another school friend, with great success. A second acquaintance from school also asked for help.

"Of course, I'll pay," she said. Eloise did it for cost and expenses. The day after the wedding, there were three more requests. And so the business was born. But it soon became clear that until they were firmly established, there wouldn't be enough work for them to live on all the year round. Not many people wanted elaborate ceremonies in the winter. They fell into their second string by accident. A businessman, misunderstanding the *Lace Dreams* advertisement in the paper, telephoned to order two brides to hand out leaflets publicising the opening of a travel agency in Camden. Sam took the call and instead of disabusing him, accepted the commission. She and Eloise turned up dressed in tutu-length bridal gowns with tiny veils and very high heels. It was a great success.

Show-Offs supplied demonstrators and exhibition staff. They could show you how to operate a steam cleaner, provide a bikini-clad girl to writhe on the bonnet of a car, men to dress as chickens and hand out Easter eggs, Father Christmases, cupids, dinosaurs. A number of people worked for them regularly, many of them out-of-work actors. Eloise met Jake, her current boyfriend, when he was impersonating a mushroom outside a supermarket.

"Shall I open another bottle?" Sammy asked.

"Why not? Though I ought to stay a bit sober, Jake's coming round later."

"Ah, Jake. I take it that's not serious?"

Eloise leant back. "What do you think? If you bumped into him when we've just made love and asked him who he'd been with, he'd probably have to think for a few minutes before he answered. He's the most self-centred man I've ever met."

"Why on earth stay with him?"

"Come on, Sammy, just look at him. He's beautiful. Witty and charming. And he's all I've got."

"And in bed…?"

Less open than her friend, Eloise wasn't comfortable with this intimate sort of talk. "It's fine."

Sammy raised her brows. "Only fine?"

Eloise was saved from having to reply by the arrival of the man himself. He was, indeed, beautiful — tall and blond, with broad shoulders tapered to narrow hips and long, straight legs. The shock of wavy golden hair surrounded his face. He had dark, lash-fringed eyes of the deepest blue. Brown eyebrows arched above them, giving his features startling definition. His face was like that of an angel in a medieval picture.

However, this was one very cross angel. As soon as he was inside he started. "Fucking philistines! I don't know why these people bother to go to the theatre. Bastards!"

He flung himself on the sofa. "For Christ's sake, get me a beer, babe."

She went into the kitchen and Sammy asked, "What happened?"

"You know I'm doing pub theatre in Camden? Well, the play's about this labourer who's dying of AIDS. And at the end, he's thinking about what he could have done, who he could have been. It's a long soliloquy, absolutely brilliant. Anyhow, some yobbos at the back had been a bit rowdy and halfway through, one of them yelled out, 'Get on with it!' Someone else shouted, 'You're too fat to be dying, mate.' Well, really! Fat? There's not one ounce of spare flesh on me."

"What did you do?" Sammy asked, trying to suppress her amusement.

"I ploughed on. Then some idiot threw a can on stage. It just missed me." He sounded, not unreasonably, querulous.

Eloise came back and handed him a bottle of beer. She sat next to him and smoothed the hair from his face. "Poor darling. It must have been awful."

"That wasn't all." He took a long draught of the beer. "The first lot started yelling, 'Poof, poof, poof...' I struggled to the end of the speech, cutting it a bit and then when the house lights came up, I got off as quickly as I could. No curtains," he explained to Sammy.

"Then you were all right?" Eloise asked.

"Not really. The bloody stage manager was sitting on the side of the stage crying. Crying with laughter. I mean, if you don't get loyalty from your own cast and crew, what hope is there?"

Eloise glanced reprovingly at Sammy, who now had a cushion pressed to her face. "No, indeed. Come to bed, you must be exhausted. You'll feel better in the morning."

At a time when things had been going well for their twin businesses, the two women had taken out a lease on prestigious offices in the West End of London. Included was a small flat on the top floor, where the servants had once lived. If they were not such good friends, it would have been a strain, working and living together, but so far there was no problem.

Sammy got up. "I'll leave you two in peace," she said, escaping to her bedroom where she could laugh without hindrance.

"And on Wednesday I've got an audition—Tynan Donaghue is doing a modern dress Hamlet with the prince as a drug-addicted rock star. I think I'm in with a good chance."

Once he got to bed, Jake calmed down a little, though his beautiful face was petulant. Eloise stroked his body, moving her hand down the golden flesh to his perfect penis, so in proportion to the rest of him.

After a while, he rolled on top of her and, without speaking, entered her. She lay in the classic position, her legs spread and knees drawn up either side of him and over his shoulder she could see the perfect globes of his bottom as it rose and fell. With a strange sense of detachment, she reflected that he performed in bed rather as he did in the theatre—with technical competence, but a complete absence of passion. She thought he was almost certainly viewing this as if seeing the rushes of a film— judging his performance, seeing it in terms of camera angles and his own appearance.

Shaking her head, she tried to make the thought go away, tried to stop thinking at all. She felt the familiar tingle, an intimation of a climax. But there was no time for it to develop, because suddenly he thrust hard into her, once, twice, and came with a grunt. He flopped onto her body, breathing heavily for an instant, then levered himself up again, looking deeply into her eyes.

It was that precious moment of intense intimacy, his cock shrinking inside her, their stomachs sticky, flesh moist.

"Eloise," he breathed, "I knew I had something important to ask you. Do you think I should have my hair streaked for this Hamlet audition?"

Chapter Two

It was surprisingly easy to sort out the business and by the middle of the next week, Eloise found herself collecting a snazzy little purple Fiat at the airport in Florence. She had compiled a list of hotels to visit, all old buildings in romantic locations, but after a few days she felt dispirited and tired. Even the magic of Tuscany failed to cheer her. At a farmhouse hotel near San Gimignano she went through her papers, trying to decide where to go the next day. The friendly proprietor brought her another pre-dinner drink and saw her furrowed brow.

"You have problem?" he asked in heavily accented English.

Eloise explained what she was looking for. He thought deeply and then suggested a number of places nearby.

She sighed and said, "I've already seen all of them."

The proprietor shrugged. "Then there is nowhere else. Unless..."

She looked at him expectantly. "Yes?"

"No, no, it wouldn't do at all."

"Oh, please tell me. I'm desperate. Anything."

He looked at her, frowning. "Well, there's a place... Lovely castle — partly ruined. Very old family, but it's just a cousin living there now, I think. It's got a bad reputation, but I heard they were trying to relaunch."

"Bad reputation?"

He made a face. "Mafiosi, wild goings on. Not respectable. But it is beautiful."

"What's it called?"

"Castel Rufina."

Eloise drove to the small town of Rufina the next day. She wasn't very optimistic, but thought it was worth a gamble. The castle was visible from miles away, perched up on one of those hills that rose suddenly and surprisingly off the flat Tuscan plain. She arrived at lunchtime and stopped at an ancient inn, in the shadow of the castle. Although it was February, the skies were clear and blue and the sun warm. Outside were a few round tables — there was a noisy American family at one, some elderly Italian men at another. She sat near the door into the inn and ordered a glass of wine, studying the usual choices of salad and pasta on the menu. A man came out, carrying a beer, and looked around. Hers was the only table with any space.

"Scusi, Signora... Permesso?" He indicated the empty seat.

"Si." Then, realising from his accent he was not Italian, "Yes, please do."

"Ah." He sank gratefully into the seat. "English. Thank God! My Italian is stretched to breaking point."

"I know what you mean!"

The man was in his mid-thirties, stocky, with straw-coloured hair flopping over a fresh, friendly face. He thrust out a hand. "Tom Sherwin from London. Tell me if I'm annoying you and I'll shut up."

"On the contrary, it's nice to talk to someone without having to conjugate all the verbs first. Eloise Lambert, also from London. How do you do?"

They conversed easily while their food arrived, salad Niçoise for her, pasta for him. When she'd nearly finished her wine, he leaned towards her. "I wouldn't mind a glass of white. Will you share a carafe with me?"

By the end of the meal, they were chatting like old friends. He explained he was a writer seeking inspiration and tranquillity so he could pen 'the great British novel,' while sustaining himself by selling freelance travel articles. And she told him about her quest to find the perfect marriage venue which no one had ever used before, after several glasses of wine probably revealing more about the perilous financial position of the company than she should have done.

He repeated what he knew about the Castel Rufina.

"It's owned by a very old family, headed by the Conte de Rufina. But he's lived outside Italy for many years and some sort of a cousin has run the place as a rather rackety hotel. There's a vineyard attached and a little winery." He held up his glass. "This stuff we're drinking probably came from there. It would be the perfect place for your wedding — so long as they've abandoned the Mafia connections and…the other things."

She knew she should pursue this last remark, but the last of the wine had clouded her judgement. "So, is it worth going up there?"

He looked thoughtful, but eventually said, "I think it is. You'd love the house. It's very wild and romantic—all grey granite and turrets. A lot of the towers and part of the walls are intact. Why don't you book in? See what you think of the place. If it feels right, you can take it from there. If not, you've lost nothing."

"But I don't want to risk it if there's anything dodgy. This is a big society wedding. I can't afford to have Don Corleone turning up at the reception."

He laughed. "I don't think that's going to happen. Look, go up and have a poke around. I'm staying here. I'll give you my mobile number. If anything worries you, give me a call. I can be there in five minutes."

About an hour later, Eloise followed a battered signpost off the main road and headed up a winding lane, at the end of which was an elaborate stone gateway. She stopped the car to admire its truly gothic magnificence. It looked like a tomb, one of the grand square edifices one sees in Florentine churches, and had clearly been built much later than the castle itself. There were three arches, the one in the middle large enough for a carriage or car to get through, the others a little smaller. On either side of the central opening was a greater than life sized statue. One was the poet Dante, the other Virgil. Both wore togas and stretched out an arm as if urging the traveller to enter. She put the car into gear and nosed it up the narrow drive.

Nothing had prepared her for the magnificence and strangeness of the Castel Rufina. Once through the stone gatehouse, a narrow and winding track led between bowing cypresses for some way. Then the road opened out as it emerged from the little wood. Ahead, she could see the castle.

The hill on which it stood had a jagged summit and the builders had incorporated the dramatic natural features into their structure. Great walls, crumbling in some places, surrounded the top of the hill, like an uneven crown. They were punctuated by semi-circular fortified towers—her research had told her there were five of these, giving the castle an unusual pentagram shape. Inside, the keep was visible, a solid structure rising upwards. To its left a smaller tower thrust into the sky. It was a campanile, she thought. Squinting through the windscreen of the car, she thought she could see a bell at the top of it.

The road led to a huge arched gate, an ancient portcullis still visible. Outside the walls, to the left, a sign indicated a parking area and when she pulled in, she gasped. At the edge of the gravelled car park, a sheer drop gave views across the Tuscan plain. It was a quiet, clear evening, and she could see the colours of the fields and vineyards stretching far below.

She got out of the car and walked back to the gate, crossing the wooden drawbridge, which spanned a brackish moat, scarcely more than a ditch. And so she entered the walls of Castel Rufina.

Inside was a large grassy area, dominated by the keep. It was immediately obvious to Eloise that generations of residents had been unable to resist the temptation to tinker with the place. To the right of the square tower was a sprawling structure, which was partly constructed, in the same dark stone. But as it had been built on to, the style changed, until at the far end, it took on the appearance of a villa, with white walls and larger windows. Eloise had bought a brochure about the place down in the town and she knew the castle had been begun in the twelfth century, but that an ambitious count had expanded the living quarters in the early fifteen hundreds and almost every descendant subsequently had wanted to leave his mark.

Oddly, although the place was so incongruous and the styles so mixed, it didn't spoil its brooding beauty. Eloise thought it was as if the whole history of Tuscany had been encapsulated in this one establishment.

She consulted a signpost inside the gates and saw one finger pointing to the white-painted part of the building read 'Reception'.

She entered a broad panelled hall, decorated with tapestry hangings. A wooden reception desk was unmanned, but there was a bell on the counter and after looking around, she gave it a tentative tap with the palm of her hand and heard it ping.

After a while unhurried footsteps sounded from a passageway to the rear of the hallway and a pleasant, motherly looking woman emerged wiping her hands on an apron.

So much for the Castel Rufina's louche reputation, Eloise thought. "Signora, good afternoon. I wondered if it would be possible to book a room for tonight and possibly for tomorrow?"

"I'm sure we can do that. Is it just you?"

"Yes. I'd like a double room for single occupancy—one with a view, if you have it."

"Certainly, Signorina. There's a form to fill out." The woman pushed a slip of paper over to her.

The room was upstairs at the back of the main building. The window had a small balcony, reminiscent of the one from which she imagined Juliet mooning over Romeo. On the left, she could see the stunning view of the plain she'd viewed from the car park. Below, gardens and terraces sloped downwards until they reached the lower walls.

Here, they were in ruins and a path was visible. Beyond them, the bright red roofs of Rufina gleamed. The housekeeper shaded her eyes and pointed. "You can walk into the village that way. It's faster. But quite a climb on the way back up!"

She showed her the large, old-fashioned bathroom and asked, "Would you like to dine here tonight?"

"Please. At about eight? Oh, and I wonder if there's someone I could talk to about holding a function here?"

"A function?"

"I'm organising a wedding. I'd like to get an idea of costs, expense, what would be available."

"A wedding?" The older woman looked surprised, almost shocked.

"Yes, the people would be coming from London. The bride's parents are quite wealthy, it's going to be a...what's the word? Very fashionable."

The woman's face cleared and she smiled. "Oh, yes, Signorina, I see. You would need to speak to Signor Ugo. The proprietor—the manager. I will ask him to come and talk to you after dinner."

* * * *

Much later that day—or rather, in the early hours of the next morning—in a cavernous underground room in Soho, two men sat on bar stools, drinking champagne. It was the end of the night's entertainment and the tables were littered with glasses and ashtrays. A couple of girls in cocktail frocks, incongruously covered by business-like aprons, were clearing up, chatting as they did so.

"It really does seem a desperate measure," one of the men observed. He was tall, slender and fair, clad in immaculate evening dress with blond hair flopping over his forehead. "I don't see why you can't just pay someone to take care of them."

The other man was dressed similarly, although his black tie had been undone, the ends hanging loosely down his shirt. He was as tall, if not taller than the first. Dark, wavy hair sprang back from his forehead and his face was pale, his black brows drawn together in a scowl. He took a swig of champagne, scarcely appearing to taste it. "I daren't. The thing is, Toby, they're out of control. Anything could happen. And because of the age difference, none of the problems is the same. They're into completely different things. I never know which direction the next blow is coming from."

The blond man took a cigarette from a pack on the bar and offered one to his friend before saying, "Oh, I forgot, you've given it up."

"Yes, but the worry of these blasted children is probably going to send me back to it. It's already driven me to drink." He examined the champagne bottle and poured the tiny drop left into the other man's glass. "Another one?"

"Why not? We're only drinking the profits."

The dark man got down from his stool and, walking round behind the bar, he retrieved another bottle from a chill cabinet and removed the cork with practiced ease. When he had settled again, he went on, "I know it's a real nuisance for you, Toby, and I'm sorry. But I've got to sort this out."

"Don't worry about it—you've got enough troubles. Larry can help me run the club and we'll get in the usual crowd for the music. The punters will be disappointed, but it can't be helped."

"Yes, thank God for Larry. He could practically look after the place single-handed."

"He more or less does. He'll keep me in order, anyway."

"Bless you, Toby. Once I've got them settled in, I'll look for some serious help. I just feel I need to get them away from the bad influences of inner London."

"Surely Matt is helping? After all, he is the oldest. What is he now...seventeen?"

The other gave a short laugh. "Matt? He's the worst of the lot. Out half the night, drinking and God knows what else. He's made a whole lot of new friends, most unsuitable. Last week we had a flurry when he thought he'd got some girl pregnant. He's one of the main reasons I want to get them away."

Toby laughed, flicking the ash from his cigarette. "Now who does that remind me of?"

"Christ, I hope I wasn't so immature."

"But he told you about it? The girl?"

"Oh yes, he told me. Full of trepidation, but he did tell me. Of course, it was a false alarm. But he shouldn't have put himself — or her — in that position. Idiot."

"Still, he did tell you."

"Damn it, Toby, I'd rather not have known."

"How's Jessica coping with all of this?"

His friend made a face. "How do you think? She does her best with them, but she's less than enthusiastic."

"You don't want to lose her."

He shrugged. "Oh, I don't know. Easy come, easy go."

Toby grinned. "Especially the easy come bit, I imagine."

The other man arched his brows. "A gentleman doesn't discuss such things. Anyway, the sooner it's sorted out, the sooner my love life can get back to normal."

Toby laughed. "Dan, your love life has never been normal."

One of the girls came over. "We've finished clearing up, Mr Rufin. Will you lock up?"

"What? Oh, yes, thank you, Deborah. All well?"

"No problems."

"Thank you. Goodnight, Deborah — 'night, Tricia."

When the women had gone, he poured himself another glass of champagne. Toby grinned at him. "I take it you're not driving?"

"Driving? Oh no. That's another reason I need this." He held up the glass, looking at the bubbles. "I sold the Alfa yesterday."

"Sold the Alfa? Oh, Dan!" Toby put his hand on the other's arm. "God, things must really be bad. I'm so sorry."

His companion gave a twisted grin. "Not to worry. By this time next year, I'll probably have a nice sensible people-carrier. Drink up!"

* * * *

The housekeeper told Eloise that guests could bring their cars inside the castle walls to a small area to the left of the keep and she had done so, carrying her suitcase up to the spacious room. When she'd freshened up, Eloise wandered round the castle grounds, relaxing in the warm Tuscan air. She experienced a feeling of rising excitement. The place was perfect.

From the outside, the keep was sturdy, mysterious and romantic. Obviously functions were held there and the main hall had been restored to its medieval splendour. At least, she thought it had been restored, given the air of neglect it was possible it had just remained like that since the Middle Ages. At the far end of the hall was a wide central staircase, in the distinctive local granite—perfect for the bride to make her entry into the reception. She climbed upwards. The chamber was surrounded by a covered gallery, with stone carvings and tracery and pillars supporting the canopy—again, very reminiscent of the Montagues and Capulets, she thought. There was no one around and so she opened one of the doors, revealing a large bedroom with a four-poster bed. She gave a sigh of contentment. Lady Connaught would love it.

A circular stone stairway, built into the wall, led upwards and she climbed it. There was a second floor of bedrooms. A further climb brought her onto the roof of the keep, a big flat square area bounded by castellated walls. From here, the view of the surrounding countryside was superb.

She spent a long time up there, looking at the view from every angle. Finally she squinted up at the flag, which flapped in the gentle breeze. It consisted of two horizontal bands of red, with one of white in between. In the centre, a circle of weapons picked out in gold. She recognised sabres and what she thought might be halberds. And right in the middle, in profile, a prowling wolf, its face turned towards the viewer, lips drawn back in a rather knowing snarl.

For some reason, Eloise shuddered. She felt cold suddenly and, looking at her watch, realised it was time to go back down.

Any doubts about the suitability of the place were completely dispelled by that night's dinner. She ate stracciatella, followed by a delicate Tuscan lamb and artichoke stew, succulent with prosciutto, sage and rosemary and served over polenta. Then a selection of fresh fruit and sorbet. The meal was simple and magnificent, Italian cooking at its best.

The dining room was in the old part of the main building, a room with low, arched ceilings and lit by flickering sconces. There were very few guests. A young couple, whom she assumed were newly married, had eyes only for each other. An older man and woman, obviously local, were having what she guessed was a celebration meal of some sort. There was a group she couldn't place. All men, noisy, clearly at home. One of them — thickset and middle-aged, with dark curly hair and a black bandit-type moustache — seemed to be the boss. At least, he was dominating the conversation, his loud, rough voice carrying across the room. Eloise couldn't make out much of it — the man had a heavy accent. There were four others with him and they seemed to be eating and drinking their way through the menu and wine list. Half-way through the meal, a tall, distinguished looking man with a shock of silver hair came to their table and a long conversation ensued.

Eloise was making notes in the book she carried in her bag, but she became aware that the occupants of the other table were looking at her. The silver-haired man came across.

"Signorina Lambert, is it not?"

His English was excellent, very correct and old fashioned.

"I am Ugo de Martino. I am the manager of this hotel — and a member of the family which has lived here for nearly a thousand years. I understand from Maria that you are interested in holding a function here."

"Oh yes, Signor de Martino, thank you for coming to talk to me. Won't you sit down?"

"If you do not object, thank you." He drew up a chair and sat opposite her. As he did, the waiter appeared with an ice bucket from which protruded a bottle of champagne. Eloise, who had been drinking one modest glass of wine, looked at him in surprise. "Oh, no, I didn't order that."

The waiter flashed a glance at de Martino. "No, Signorina. It is a gift. From Signor Petrela."

De Martino said, "Tolka Petrela. He's a local businessman, over at that table. Very generous."

"But I don't think I should…"

"There's no harm in it. And if you want to do business in this region, it is as well to be a friend of Mr Petrela. He has a great deal of influence." Ugo opened the champagne as he spoke and poured a glass before she could protest further. There was no help for it, so she took it and raised it in the direction of Petrela's table. The man nodded and smiled, raising his own glass in acknowledgement.

"Tolka Petrela — that's not an Italian name, is it?"

"No, Mr Petrela is Albanian. Or rather, his father was Albanian and I believe his mother was Sicilian. But he spends a lot of time here in Tuscany. Now, tell me what is this function you wish to hold here?"

Eloise told him the story of Lady Connaught's demands, omitting any mention of her own perilous financial position and making it clear that nothing had been decided at this stage.

"You see, I might go back with all the details and find she's gone off the idea. Or she might like the venue, but decide she doesn't want me to do the planning. Or she might want me to find somewhere else."

"She sounds like a very difficult woman."

"She is," Eloise agreed, with a sigh, then feeling a bit disloyal, added, "But of course, Tamsin is her only child and you can't blame her for wanting the very best for her."

"No, indeed. But let us suppose everything were to go ahead as you wish. What would that entail for us?"

"I anticipate that the bride's family, bridesmaids and so on would arrive about a week before the ceremony and, of course, would all require rooms. The groom and his party would probably turn up a couple of days before. And most of the guests would come on the eve of the wedding."

"And we are speaking of — how many?"

"How many rooms do you have?"

Ugo smiled. "It is a vast place. We can bring rooms into service that haven't been used for years, if we have sufficient notice. I should think we could probably make available more than one hundred and fifty rooms."

"I think that would be more than enough. And if Lady Connaught does go completely overboard, which is not beyond the bounds of possibility, I suppose there are places in the village and around where we could put people up?"

"Oh, certainly."

"Fine. Well, I'll need to do some research about the regulations in this part of Italy involving the wedding itself, but I'd favour a civil ceremony in a town hall — Siena, maybe, or perhaps in Rufina itself — followed by a religious blessing here. On the top of the keep, perhaps."

He nodded. "Yes, that would be possible. Or there's an ancient chapel which we could put at your disposal."

"That would be wonderful. But they aren't Roman Catholics."

"It doesn't matter. The chapel has been deconsecrated for many years. It is available for any denomination. I'll show it to you tomorrow, if you like."

"Thank you. That would be kind. Anyhow, after the blessing, there would be drinks and some food and then a break before a proper reception in the evening, with a sit-down meal. Is whoever cooked the meal this evening your regular chef?"

"Gianni? Yes, he has been with us for several years."

"Well, the food was excellent, so if he were to supervise I'd be very happy. There would be dancing, music, a big party going on into the night."

"Fine. And the next day?"

"The next day, all the guests would remain and it would be nice to do something more relaxed. Maybe a barbecue?"

"That could certainly be arranged. Around the swimming pool, perhaps?"

"You have a pool? Even better."

"At that time of year you would be almost guaranteed a cloudless, hot day."

"And then in the evening, perhaps an early meal, something light and some music—not dancing, but chamber music or something of the sort. Something relaxing. The next day I think we'd go for a champagne breakfast to send the bride and groom on their way and that would be it. Some guests would probably want to stay on, but that's up to them."

"We could certainly do all this. If you like, tomorrow, we can get together with Gianni and draw up some sample menus for you to take back to this lady. And I'll do some costing so you can get an idea of expense."

"That would be most helpful." She took a drink, then realising he had nothing, she said, "Oh, I'm so sorry, how rude of me. Please, do have some of this champagne. I won't be able to drink a whole bottle."

"If you are sure, Signorina. It is our finest vintage." Ugo smiled and clicked his fingers for the waiter, who was sent away for another glass. While they waited, chatting about the weather, Eloise studied the man. He was tall and slim and not as old as he first appeared. She thought he was probably in his late forties or early fifties, but the silver hair made it hard to judge. He had a fine patrician face, high cheek-boned and unlined.

"So, do you run this place alone?"

He nodded.

"That must be very hard work, such a big, historic building."

"It is, but it's a labour of love. As I mentioned, my family has lived here for about a thousand years. The castle is actually owned by my cousin, but he and his family have lived abroad—indeed, in London—for many years."

"The place must be very expensive to maintain."

Ugo sighed. "It is, punishingly so. Which is why I'm glad of any new business. If you can bring me this wedding, it will help to pay towards some essential renovations and improvements."

Eloise got up. "Well, I'll do my best. And of course, if it's a success, others will follow. Weddings in Italy are all the rage in London society at the moment."

He stood and bowed. "Signorina, we live in hope. I'll come and find you after breakfast and show you around."

As she passed Petrela's table, she said goodnight and the men scrambled to their feet. Petrela made an exaggerated bow and kissed his fingers at her. She went to her room, conscious of a slight unease.

* * * *

The next day, after breakfast, Ugo escorted her to the kitchens to meet the chef, Gianni. She'd been expecting someone wild and dark and temperamental. But Gianni was a calm, stocky young man, with his fair hair in a buzz-cut. He seemed pleased at the prospect of cooking for a large party and was full of ideas — though Eloise could see she was going to have to work hard to make sure that wild boar, the local delicacy, didn't feature in every course.

After their meeting with Gianni, Ugo took her on a tour of the castle, much more comprehensive than her own wanderings the previous day. The chapel was a separate building, near the walls to the left of the keep. It was small, with a weathered marble facing and an ornate belfry. Cypress trees surrounded it and a sunken path, fringed with flowering camellias, connected it to the keep. In her mind's eye, she could see the bridal procession moving up from the chapel, perhaps passing beneath arches entwined with roses.

She had a small camcorder with which she recorded every step, every view and every picturesque corner of the castle.

After they'd seen the chapel, Ugo took her round the walls. Where the structure was solid, there was a walkway high up, with a castellated parapet. He explained that the fortifications at the front of the castle were more or less intact, but that during a feud with a rival house in the fourteenth century, the enemy had infiltrated the town and unexpectedly attacked from the rear, which was why the walls there had been badly damaged.

In some places, he pointed out, the walls were so thick that there were rooms built into them and some of these had been converted into guest rooms. "So if you did bring a very large party here, we'd be able to accommodate some of them actually within the old stone of the castle."

He took her to the rear of the main building, where a bewildering series of terraces led down to the breach in the walls near the town. On the second of these levels, incongruously, was a large swimming pool. "We are hoping to extend, to build a fitness centre. This is the kind of thing which will set us above the rest." They moved round the back of the main house and Ugo pointed upwards. "There, where the balconies are, is your room. The hotel part continues until we reach the white-painted villa, where the private accommodations for the family are."

"And the family is—de Martino?"

He shook his head. "No, sadly, it's my mother who was one of the family and so I don't carry the name. The Conte—the Count—is the Conte de Rufina."

They walked on a little way. "I think you've seen everything now—except the dungeon."

"The dungeon?"

"Oh yes. No self-respecting castle would be without a dungeon. Come with me." He led her back towards the keep and to the left-hand-side and through a heavy door to where a flight of stone stairs led downwards.

They descended the spiral stairs until they got to a solid oak door, which Ugo unlocked. It was very dark and he fumbled until he found a switch. As the room was flooded with light, Eloise let out a gasp. It was a torture chamber out of an old Hollywood film. High stone arches, supported by pillars, formed the ceiling and the floor was stone-flagged. Around the walls, suspended on the pillars, everywhere, were instruments of torture and death. Racks, thumbscrews, wheels, spikes, wrenches, whips and chains, interspersed with suits of ornate Italian armour.

Ugo watched, enjoying her reaction. "Yes, it is rather startling, isn't it? I have heard guests compare it favourably with the Tower of London."

"And all this is…original?" Eloise was walking around now, taking in the exhibits.

"Absolutely. Much of it was here, accumulated over the centuries and my grandfather, Conte Umberto, became something of a collector. The armour is all local and some of it was almost certainly made here in the town. Although most armour-makers were further north, around Milan, Rufina also had a small armoury trade."

"Is that why you have weapons on your standard?"

"Yes indeed. And the wolf signifies the attributes of the count and his family. Swift, silent, dangerous and merciless. The family motto is *'Lupus est homo homini'*. How good is your Latin?"

"Well, I recognise wolf, of course. And man."

"Excellent. It means, *'Man is wolf to man'*. Not a very attractive tag, but I think our ancestors were more concerned about being feared than being loved. Please, do touch the objects. They are all in working condition."

She walked around slowly, occasionally stretching out a hand to feel the sharpness of a spike, or to let the lash of a whip pass through her fingers.

"This dungeon is used for parties which are...less reputable than the one you are hoping to arrange. It's a regrettable necessity for us."

"But we could use it?"

He looked surprised. "Of course."

"Because it would be a wonderful place for a stag party."

"Stag?"

"Sorry. For the prospective groom and his friends. Before the wedding. Men only."

"Ah, I see."

"Sometimes there are dancers, strippers. It's a very silly tradition."

"Indeed. I'm sure something could be arranged. Shall we go back up?"

She nodded and he led her up to the open air. At the top, he bowed. "Signorina Lambert, I hope you will do me the honour of lunching with me so we can further discuss the enterprise."

After a long and pleasant lunch, Eloise went to her room to write up her notes. She felt increasingly confident about being able to sell the idea of the Castel Rufina to Lady Connaught. And she reasoned that the more work she had done on the bid, the more likely it was that she'd be allowed to carry out the commission.

She forced herself to consider the negative aspects. The place was by no means a luxury hotel — but it was well run and comfortable, and she thought the romance and beauty of the setting would balance out any lack of amenities. Then there was the suggestion of nefarious goings on, the parties to which Ugo had referred and allegations of Mafia connections. Remembering Tolka Petrela from the previous night, she shuddered. She could well imagine the businessman being involved in some shady deals. But on the whole, there was nothing here which could upset the fastidious Lady Connaught—or, more seriously, mar Tamsin's wedding.

The phone on the bedside table gave an abrupt ring and Eloise frowned. No one knew she was here. She picked up the receiver.

"Eloise? Miss Lambert? This is Tom Sherwin. We met yesterday in Rufina."

"Oh, yes. Hello, Tom."

"Hi. Look, I don't mean to be a pest and do tell me if you're busy, but I wondered if you'd like to come out to dinner tonight. There's a nice restaurant out towards San Gimignano, and I'd be interested to know what you think of Castel Rufina."

"That's very kind of you. Actually, I'd love to come. I've been immersing myself in this place all day, taking photographs and writing notes and I could do with a break."

"Splendid. Shall I drive? I'll pick you up at about seven-thirty."

* * * *

They travelled for about half an hour. Despite the season, it was still mild and Tom had not yet raised the top of his convertible. The restaurant in a small hilltop village was already full. From the chatter all around her, Eloise realised these were all Italians. The décor was simple and the menu concentrated on basic Tuscan recipes. A plump, balding man came to the front of the restaurant to seat them, his arms open in welcome. "Mr

Tom, you have come back to us. Excellent. And the lovely lady too. This is Mrs Tom, no?"

"No." Tom laughed, shaking hands. "This is Miss Eloise Lambert from England. She's staying up at the Castel Rufina."

The proprietor made a comical face. "Ooh, plenty going on up there, I bet." He found them a small table in the centre of the restaurant and disappeared, then reappeared with two glasses containing a pinkish liquid, which he banged down in front of them. "On the 'ouse," he said before hurrying off to greet another customer.

Eloise regarded her drink with suspicion. "What is it?"

"It's Aperol. It's got…let me think…bitter orange and gentian and I think rhubarb, as well as lots of other herbs I can't remember."

"Rhubarb? Well, this is a first!" She sipped the pink liquid gingerly, then with more enthusiasm. "It's nice. A bit like Campari."

Over a simple meal of pasta, they chatted easily. Tom wanted to know what she thought of the Castel Rufina and she waxed lyrical about the setting and the beauty of the place. Tom was interested, attentive, pleased for her. But when she told the story of the champagne which had been sent to her table by Tolka Petrela, she saw him stiffen.

"He was there? Petrela?"

"Yes, he was there. I believe he keeps a suite of rooms in the castle. Ugo says he's a respected local businessman."

"Businessman, yes, respected, no. He's a member of the Albanian Mafia, well placed to do deals in Italy because of his Italian mother. We… It's not at all clear what he's doing here, but whatever it is, it will be bad."

She shrugged. "I'm not going to worry about it. After all, he was only having dinner."

Tom looked as if he was going to respond, but then he shook his head. "Do you want a brandy? Or a Grappa or something? I'm going to have one."

"You've got to drive," she said, only half reprovingly.

"Yes, why not? It's my last night in Italy."

"But you'll be coming back soon?"

"Well, it rather depends on Lady Connaught. If she takes me on, I'll have to spend a lot of time here." She held up a well-manicured hand. "Fingers crossed."

"Mine too!" He showed her. "Look, I'd really like to know what happens. If I give you my card, will you give me a ring when you get back? Then if you are going ahead, perhaps we can meet up."

Eloise gave him a sharp look. There was nothing she wanted less at this time than a romantic entanglement. She was still deciding what to do about Jake, and her concern for the business took precedence over everything else. And although he was a very attractive man, there was, as yet, no spark there. But nothing in Tom's manner suggested he wanted anything more than a friendship and the thought of having a friend in Rufina was very attractive. She took the card he offered and handed him her own.

* * * *

At about the same time, Dan Rufin was sitting by himself in a bar in Soho, looking morosely into his beer. It was Monday and the club was closed and for once, Matt was taking care of the others. Jessica was on a modelling assignment in Paris and he was at a loose end. A burst of feminine laughter came from a nearby table and he looked across, recognising a group of working girls who operated from rooms near the club. The club had a relaxed policy — the girls were allowed in, but the management wouldn't permit open soliciting. He was well known and popular with them.

The girls noticed him and waved and one of them broke away and came over to him. "Hi, Dan. All alone? Where's the supermodel?"

"Paris," he said, shortly.

"Aaah, how sad. Why don't you join us? We're having a night off."

"Thanks, Avril, but I don't think I will. I'm feeling a bit grumpy, wouldn't be very good company."

"Poor darling. Is it the kids?"

He sighed. It seemed as if the whole world knew about those blasted children. "Well, yes, they are a bit of a handful."

"Do you mind?" She eased her mini-skirted bottom onto the stool next to him.

"Oh, be my guest. Can I get you a drink?" He went across to buy her a gin and tonic, looking back at her as she had a laughing conversation with her companions at the other table. She was a good-looking woman, in her early thirties, he thought. The ravages of her profession had not yet caught up with her and she had smooth, evenly tanned skin, and extravagantly blonde hair piled up on top of her head. Dan had once intervened to stop an ugly scene between her and a punter and she had since been particularly friendly towards him.

When he got back, she touched his hand. "You look frazzled. I bet I could make you feel better."

He laughed. "I thought you were having a night off."

"This would be pleasure, not business."

"You're very kind, Avril, but…"

"I know," she said, with sudden savagery. "You don't want to fuck a tart."

"No, that wasn't what I was going to say. You're a beautiful woman and I can't think of anything I'd like more than to make love to you. But my life is a mess and I'm not the sort of person you want to spend your free time with."

"Dan, you're a musician, right? A professional musician."

"I do my best."

"So night after night you play and sing for the punters. Perform for money?"

"Yep, that's what I do."

"And when you're at home, do you ever feel like playing just for yourself? Or singing?"

"Often. I get more pleasure from that than from performing in front of an audience."

"Yes, well, just because what I do isn't particularly artistic, don't think I'm not exactly the same."

"But surely, if what you enjoy is solo activity, you don't need me!"

She aimed a mock slap at him. "Idiot. You know what I mean." Then, more seriously, "I've just had my monthly physical. All the tests. Completely clear. So if you want— it's the works. No condom."

"But, Avril, I…"

She put up her hand to stop him and he realised to his surprise that she was nervous. "Oh, for heaven's sake, Dan, if you don't want it, say so. But it must be quite clear to you that I've fancied the pants off you for ages. Hell, now you've managed to embarrass me. I'm a fool, why would a man like you with a model girlfriend want to go with a back-street whore like me?"

Not for the first time, he reflected on the thin veneer of confidence these girls possessed. They were so loud and brash and in your face, but underneath nervous and plagued with feelings of inadequacy. He felt a distinct stirring, and he tossed back the rest of his drink and stood up, holding out his hand.

"Nothing back-street about you, Avril, darling. You're pure class. And how could I refuse such an offer from a beautiful young woman? Come along, but it has to be your place, I'm afraid. Mine's been turned into a kindergarten, as you know."

They left the bar to a round of derisive applause from the other girls and walked the short way to the next street, where Avril had a room over a chemist's shop.

Upstairs, she turned to look at him. It was a smallish bed-sitter, with a separate bathroom and tiny kitchen area. Through the thin pink curtains, the lights of Soho winked and flashed. She pulled off her tight white jumper to reveal large breasts bursting out of a black bra. He stood against the door, breathing heavily.

She put her hands behind her back and deftly unfastened the bra, letting it drop to the floor and revealing her swinging breasts. Now she wore only her pink mini-skirt and high-heeled white stilettos. He moved forward, but she motioned him to stop and dropped to her knees in front of him. She took off his shoes and socks, unfastened his trousers and manoeuvred the zip down with practiced ease. She pulled them downwards, taking his shorts with them.

As his cock was revealed, already half erect, she let out a sigh of pleasure. "I knew it would be big," she said. "I told the girls."

"You've been talking about my…attributes?"

"But of course." Soft lips enveloped his cock, causing it to lurch to life. Then she dodged lower, licking his balls, sucking on them hard. Her tongue moved along the ridged vein under his cock, swirled around the rim and pressed into the slit.

She began a steady, firm suction, her head bobbing forwards, taking him deeper and deeper and he stood, his eyes closed, everything driven from his mind. Nothing mattered except the warm, tingling, exquisite feeling—the concentration of pulsing nerves and lubricious pleasure here, at the very centre of his being.

Finally he drew a breath and warned, "I'm about to…"

In response she took him deeper into her mouth, her hands reaching for his balls. He ejaculated copiously into her willing throat.

Later he fucked her savagely, letting all his recent rage and frustrations out in that one, animal act. Afterwards, he kissed her before he got up and dressed.

"Please stay," she said.

"I can't. The children."

"Oh yes, of course."

"I'm taking them to Italy on Thursday."

"You mentioned. But you'll come back?"

"I devoutly hope so."

She sat up in bed. "You were wonderful. I can't wait to tell the others."

He grinned and felt in his pockets for his wallet. "And so were you. Great therapy. I feel better than I have for weeks. Here, let me make a contribution…"

She got out of bed and put her hand over his, standing on tiptoe to kiss him again. "No, Dan. My treat. A thank you for rescuing me. Something I've been lusting after."

"Well, I hope I was worthy of your day off."

He walked the short way to his flat and let himself in. They were all asleep and quickly he did the rounds of his small domain. The two boys lay in bunk beds in one spare room and in the other, scarcely bigger than a cupboard, Laura slumbered, her face tranquil. In his own room, with its bold, masculine décor, the toddler was curled up in his cot-bed. He smelled warm and milky when Dan put his face down to kiss him.

"Oh God, has it come to this?" he murmured to himself, stripping off his clothes again. "A house full of children and the local tarts are giving me mercy fucks."

Chapter Three

The day after Eloise got back to London, she received a summons to the Connaught mansion in Lord North Street. To her great relief, Tamsin came to the door. After giving her a hug, Tamsin led her into the huge drawing room. Lady Connaught sat in state, looking rather like the Queen receiving someone to whom she was to present a minor honour. Sir Lyndo, lurking by the window, came forward to kiss Eloise and retreated again.

"Well, Eloise, you've been away for over a week. Did you manage to spot anything suitable at all?" Her tone suggested this was unlikely.

"I've prepared a report for you, Lady Connaught. Let me go through it and see what you think." Eloise had considered her options during a sleepless night and had come to the conclusion that if she presented her principal with the Castel Rufina from the start, Lady Connaught's natural cussedness would make her reject it out of hand. So she proposed to lead up to it by showing her all the other places she'd visited, hoping the woman would think she'd made the discovery herself.

"Very well. Show me."

Eloise got out her portfolio of pictures and details and went through the venues, San Gimignano, Radda and several other places—all beautiful and with nice hotels and facilities. Lady Connaught looked through them carefully but stony-faced, passing each document or picture on to Tamsin, who studied it, making encouraging noises.

Finally, Eloise opened the file marked 'Rufina'. "There was another place I went to, but I'm really not sure if you'd like it."

"Let me be the judge of that, Eloise."

Eloise described the castle and the surroundings, punctuating the narrative with caveats about the hotel itself and touching, in a fairly vague sort of way, on the slightly sleazy nature of the place and on the suggestion of Mafia connections. She reasoned that if she'd laid out all the problems at the beginning she couldn't be reproached later if anything went wrong.

Lady Connaught maintained her cool attitude, but Eloise could see she was interested. After she'd seen the still photographs, she said, "I believe you mentioned a video? Lyndo, would you...?"

Sir Lyndo opened what looked like an ornate cabinet to reveal a state-of-the-art television with DVD and video player below. He took the disk Eloise offered.

Eloise had edited her film quite professionally and in ten minutes had given them a complete tour of the Castel Rufina.

When it ended, Lady Connaught spoke sharply. "I really don't know why you thought this place unsuitable, Eloise. It looks ideal."

"I'm glad you like it. I've brought some sample menus, rough costing, details of rooms and so on. Would you like to look at them now?"

"Of course, my dear, of course."

They studied the documents and after half-an-hour, Lady Connaught sat back. "Well, I'm happy with this. It looks just right and so long as you can assure me it has never before been used for a society wedding—a British wedding—I think this must be the one."

"The manager told me there hasn't been a marriage there since the seventeenth century."

"Excellent. Leave all this information with me. Give Lyndo details of your expenses and he'll see a cheque is sent to you. Lyndo, Tamsin and I will discuss how we wish to proceed over the next few days. If we decide we want you to take on the whole commission, I'll phone you." She stood up, extending her hand. "Thank you, Eloise. Goodbye."

Tamsin, who had been mostly silent throughout, now said, "Oh, Mummy, I don't think there's any need for discussion. I know I want Eloise to do the job." She glanced at her father, who rumbled his assent.

"Absolutely. Little Eloise has done very well with finding the venue and I think she'll do a splendid job of organising the wedding. Let's make a decision now. It will be a weight off your mind, Bryony."

Lady Connaught looked rattled by this clearly pre-planned ambush. But she gave in with, for her, good grace. "Very well, if that is what you want, Tamsin. Eloise, Lyndo will talk to you about your terms and a contract. I shall want you here first thing tomorrow morning to start thinking about the dress."

Eloise felt faint with relief, but masked it with a cool, "Thank you, Lady Connaught. I'll do my very best for you."

"And now we're going out to lunch," Tamsin said, pulling at Eloise's arm. "Come on, Ellie, we'll go to Harvey Nicks."

They got a taxi almost straight away and arrived at the Knightsbridge store just after midday—early enough to get ahead of the hordes of wealthy shoppers clamouring for their salads and white-wine spritzers. Once they were seated, Tamsin ordered cocktails—a Manhattan for her, a Bloody Mary for Eloise. The latter came with a straw and she began sucking at it eagerly, feeling the need for alcohol after her stressful morning.

"I'm sorry about Mummy. She likes to make people sweat. But she always meant you to do it."

"Well, thank you for coming to my rescue."

"No problem. Daddy and I had it all stitched up days ago."

"So, tell me about Alistair. When can I meet him?"

"Oh, thank you for reminding me. We're having a little dinner party tomorrow night. Well, I call it a dinner party, but I'm not bloody cooking. In a restaurant. We'd love you to come. And bring...what's his name? The beautiful actor?"

"Jake," Eloise answered, without enthusiasm.

"Yes, of course. Bring Jake."

"Thanks,—I'd love to come. Jake may still be in a play, I'm not sure. Haven't spoken to him since I got back from Italy. But Alistair. What's he like? I haven't even seen a picture."

"Oh, he's fine."

Eloise didn't think this sounded like the passion of a prospective bride and perhaps Tamsin picked up on this, because she went on. "He's very good-looking. Tall and, er…everything. Sporty. He rows. Rides to hounds. Plays rugby. What you might call a rugger-bugger."

Eloise remained silent, just staring at her friend, eyebrows raised.

"He's a really nice man, and he's going to be a Baronet, and Mummy likes him."

"But do you love him? That's what matters."

"Oh yes, of course I love him. He's wonderful. You'll see tomorrow night." Tamsin turned the conversation to her horses, of which she had three — stabled in Hertfordshire, within easy reach of London.

"Poor old Smokey was really poorly and at one point, I thought I was going to lose him, but Arno pulled him through. Arno owns the stables. He's great, so in tune with the horses. I swear they talk to him."

"Arno?"

"Arno de Vries. He's Dutch. You'll love him. He'll be there tomorrow as well. He's brilliant and *so* sexy."

As she went home on the bus, Eloise wondered why Tamsin had spoken with more enthusiasm about the man who ran her livery stables than about her aristocratic fiancé. Tomorrow evening was going to be interesting, she thought.

In the end, she was relieved to find that Jake was 'resting' and able to come with her. It would be good to have an ally and she had to admit, as she admired his velvet jacket and ruffled shirt over tight black trousers, he did look good. What Sam vulgarly described as eye-candy.

The venue for the party was one of those smart chrome-and-glass restaurants that had sprung up in London, especially in the City. The other diners were already seated by the time Eloise and Jake arrived. Tamsin had said there'd be about twenty people there and with a sinking heart, Eloise could hear them as the waiter took their coats at the door. They had been placed at a long table in the window of the restaurant, with a view of the busy street outside. Loud, well-bred voices and braying laughter wafted across the room.

Tamsin stood to welcome them. A bold red dress with white polka dots emphasised her voluptuous curves and enhanced her shining blonde hair. She looked stunning. She air-kissed them both, reminding Eloise suddenly and sharply of her mother. "Darlings, welcome. Look, we've saved places for you. Jake, down this end near me. Ellie, you're sitting next to Alistair. Come and be introduced."

Alistair Carew-White was big and fresh-faced. He looked like a sportsman and when he got up to shake hands, Eloise could see how tall and broad he was, with wide shoulders and a muscled physique. Brown hair flopped over his forehead and he had a loud, confident voice as well as an extremely firm handshake. Eloise retrieved her hand, wincing a little, and sat down.

The people at the table were mostly his friends, either bankers or rugger-players or both, with wives and girlfriends. Alistair introduced Eloise to the man next to her. "This is Freddy — he's going to be my best man. Fred, this is Eloise, who is fearfully well-organised and is going to keep us all in order at the wedding."

Freddy was of similar build to Alistair, but with cropped hair and a bullet-shaped head. He subjected her to another crushing handshake. "Good to meet you. That's just what

I need, actually, keeping in order. I'm Laurence, by the way. Laurence Carson."

"I thought Alistair said your name was Fred?"

"It is," Alistair chipped in. "Fred by name and Fred by nature." Both men seemed to find this disproportionately funny and they fell about laughing. Eloise realised that, in terms of alcohol consumption, they were at least two bottles ahead of her.

"It's a nickname," Alistair explained, taking pity on her. "Everyone calls him Fred and no one knows why."

Fred began to tell her who the other guests were. "That's Simon—he works with Ali in the bank. Amanda is his girlfriend…" He went on round until he got to the end of the table where Tamsin sat. "I don't know that chap at the end with Tamsin—oh, it's the guy you came with. Husband?"

Eloise shook her head.

"Boyfriend then. Serious?"

"I don't think so," she replied, taken off guard.

"Good. I'm between girlfriends at the moment."

Eloise wasn't sure if the two observations were connected, but Fred went on, "Tamsin you know, of course, and next to her on the other side, that fair-haired character, he's called Olaf or something and he's Dutch. Looks after her horses."

Eloise regarded the famous Arno with interest. From this distance, she could see that he was tall with hair so fair it was almost white and the good deportment and carriage that comes from a life in the saddle. He was leaning back in his chair, taking in the conversation but not joining in— very detached.

Fred completed the circuit of the table, leaving Eloise's head spinning. Her companions continued drinking, their voices getting louder and louder, enough so that she looked round in embarrassment to see how the other diners were reacting, but no one seemed in the least bit bothered about the noise and hilarity coming from the table near the window.

Before they became too drunk, Eloise raised the possibility of holding a stag party in the dungeon at the Castel Rufina. The suggestion was enthusiastically received.

"Bloody hell, Fred! Floggers and whips and chains! Just like Eton."

"Sounds good to me, Ali, old chum. With a few...um...additions. You're right about this girl — she really is going to keep us in order. Will you spank me if I'm naughty, Miss?"

Eloise found this heavy-handed facetiousness exhausting and when they tired of their witticisms and got on to discussing the prospects for the England rugby squad in the Six Nations Championship, she made her excuses and went to the Ladies. This was at the rear of the restaurant, a room of futuristic lighting, smooth marble surfaces and stainless steel hand-bowls. She went into one of the cubicles, grateful to be alone at last. But not for long. Soon, she became aware that someone else was in the room. She assumed whoever had come in was using the mirror to check hair or makeup. No one entered the cubicles and when she had adjusted her clothes, she opened the door to go out. She stopped abruptly when she saw what was happening.

A woman bent, face down, over the marble counter in which the washbasins were set. Her dress was pulled up to her waist, revealing a naked bottom — white high-heeled shoes were planted firmly apart. A man stood behind her, a little to one side and Eloise could see his fingers busy between her legs, moving in and out rhythmically. The woman groaned, her head sideways, pressed onto the marble surface.

"Do it. Do it now! Fuck me, please fuck me."

The man unzipped and Eloise, trapped, prepared to retreat back into the cubicle when he looked up. Cold blue eyes met hers in the mirror and he gave a thin smile, as if giving her permission to watch. It was Arno de Vries, the man who was good with horses. Apparently, he was good with women too, because his companion thrust her bottom backwards at him crying out for his attention.

"First we lubricate," he said, in a voice with only a trace of an accent. Eloise could not avoid seeing his cock, large and hard, as he stroked it a couple of times then rammed it into the woman without further preliminaries. He fucked her hard for two or three strokes, making her squeal, then pulled out again. "Now, the arse," he went on conversationally and began to work his organ into his companion's anus. She groaned in a mixture of pain and pleasure as he forced himself right inside her. Only a few feet away, Eloise heard the slap of his balls against her flesh. At last, she managed to tear her eyes from the sight, went back into the cubicle and shut the door. She sat on the loo seat fully clothed and breathed heavily as the sounds of mounting passion filtered through to her. She was profoundly shocked and not just because she'd witnessed such a lewd display in a public place. What had really shaken her was the fact that the woman she had seen in such a compromising position was wearing a red polka-dot dress. There was no doubt about it—it was Tamsin Connaught.

By the time Tamsin had reached her agonising, noisy climax, the two of them had left and Eloise had emerged, shaking, from the Ladies, the party was breaking up. Some of them were going on to a club and as they spilled over onto the pavement, Tamsin came up to her, with Arno de Vries in tow. "Ellie, darling, are you coming to the club now?"

"I don't think so, sorry, Tamsin. Jake has an early rehearsal and I've got a few more preparations to make before my meeting with your mother in the morning."

"Oh, what a shame. I wanted you to get to know Arno."

He stepped forward, smiling that secretive smile. "Well, at least we've seen each other. Haven't we, Eloise? And I hope we'll do much more than that in the future." He took her hand and kissed it, giving her another enigmatic look, and added, "I am sure we'll have so much in common. Tamsin, I'll see you tomorrow. Au revoir, ladies." And he sauntered off towards Charing Cross.

Eloise walked with Jake to the underground and said goodnight to him, relieved he didn't want to stay.

Later, when they were in their dressing gowns and drinking cocoa, she spilled the whole story to Samantha.

Sam was agog, laughing and gasping. "So when you came out and saw them, what were they doing?"

"I told you, she was bending over and he was...fingering her."

"And then?"

"I've told you this already, Sam—he, er...made love to her."

"I know you've told me, I just like the refined way you say it. Then what happened?"

"Oh, really. And I thought you were making fun of me. Well, then he said, 'Now the arse,' and he took her anally."

Sam rocked backwards and forwards on the sofa, laughing in delight. "Well, things are really looking up now — we're going to be in the middle of a society scandal."

"Oh, God, I hope not, Sammy. We really need this job. But I just don't understand what she's playing at. She's getting married in a few months and she's fooling around with another man. And not discreetly, either. I mean, the ladies' loo, for heaven's sake. Anyone could have walked in."

"Well, she's her mother's daughter, all right."

"What do you mean?"

"Oh, darling, everyone knows Bryony Connaught's had a string of toy-boys. She's always got one on the go."

"Good heavens, Sammy, how on earth do you hear about these things?"

"Because I'm not sweet and good like you and I listen to gossip properly. Anyhow, if you were married to Sir Lyndo, wouldn't you stray?"

"Well, I don't know about the mother. But Tamsin! Doesn't it seem a bit off to be carrying on with another man at what was practically an engagement party?"

"I have to admit, it doesn't augur well for the marriage."

Eloise went off on another tack. "Do you really think I'm refined and sweet and good?"

"Of course. That's why I love you."

"But it's not very exciting, is it? My life is dull, my sex life is dull and I'm dull."

"Oh, Ellie, no, never that. You're just a bit...prim. Delicate. It's nice, it's rare. Don't knock it."

"Well, I'm sick of it. I'm tired of always being the sensible one."

Sam swung her legs around so she was sitting properly on the sofa, looking at Eloise. "Just how much did you have to drink tonight, Ellie?"

"Enough."

Her friend got up and took the mug from her. "Well, no more cocoa for you. You're out of control. Sleep well, darling."

Chapter Four

The next day, Eloise began a series of difficult meetings to discuss every aspect of what she was beginning to term the wedding of the century. Lady Connaught was meticulous about detail in a way which bordered on the obsessive, but oddly, Eloise, who had a tendency to be that way herself, found this comforting. She knew where she was, unlike with many clients she'd had to deal with who left things to her to decide, or changed their minds with alarming frequency. After a few days, the two women reached an unspoken understanding and had developed what could best be described as armed neutrality. It wasn't comfortable, but it wasn't war. It was agreed that Eloise should return to Italy to begin negotiations with Ugo de Rufina and to start the laborious business of getting the paperwork sorted out for the civil wedding. She also needed to find an Anglican clergyman for the blessing and to research local caterers, coach hire firms, florists, musicians, hairdressers, beauticians—the list was endless.

Tamsin had not been much in evidence, drifting in to answer questions, then disappearing. But on Friday, knowing Eloise was due to go to Tuscany at the weekend, she turned up in the afternoon and insisted on taking her for a drink.

"Now, if we can get a taxi, we'll go to Alfredo's—he does wonderful cocktails."

"No we won't," Eloise replied, quite brutally. All week she'd been worrying about what she'd seen in the restaurant and she felt she needed to clear the air before she spent any more of the Connaughts' money. "Let's go up towards Trafalgar Square. I want to talk to you."

They walked in silence, Tamsin tottering on three-inch heels. After a while, she said, "I don't care where we're going, but please can we get a taxi? I can't go much further in these shoes."

Eloise was very much on edge. "Oh, all right. And I don't know why you're wearing shoes like that. You never used to."

Tamsin would have been well within her rights to tell her to mind her own business, but at that moment, a taxi appeared, driving up from Millbank. As they sank into the back seat, she observed merely, "Arno likes me in them."

They stopped the taxi in the Strand and went into the first pub they saw. Eloise bought two glasses of white wine and dumped them down on the table.

"Ellie, whatever is the matter with you? I know mother's a pain, but surely…"

"It's not your mother. It's you I'm worried about."

"Oh." Tamsin looked down into her glass of wine, then at her friend, as if she'd been expecting this. "Arno told me you'd seen us."

"Yes I did, and I was very embarrassed and confused by it. For heaven's sake, Tamsin, here I am planning a lavish wedding for you and Alistair and what do I see but you and Arno cavorting in the loos."

Tamsin laughed. "Oh, Ellie, you are gloriously old-fashioned!"

Eloise was beginning to develop a complex about these references to her conventionality. "I don't think it's old-fashioned to believe that if you're just about to get married, you shouldn't be acting out pornographic scenarios in the ladies' lavatory with another man."

This made Tamsin splutter into her wine and then choke and it was a while until she could respond.

"Yes, well I'm sorry if what you saw offended you and it was a very silly thing to do. But when Arno wants it, Arno wants it, and I can't say no."

"But...if you feel like that about him, why are you marrying Alistair? Marry Arno instead."

This made her laugh out loud. "Arno's not the marrying kind. He just likes to control people from the outside. Besides, how do you think Mummy would react if I waltzed in and told her, 'Oh, by the way, I'm not going to marry the future baronet. Instead I'm going to rough it with a Dutch stable boy.'"

"He's hardly a stable boy."

"That's not the point. He's not husband material. He's something else, he's an entertainment. An absorbing, irresistible, compelling entertainment, but not the sort you marry."

"A bit on the side, is that what you mean?"

"Well, it's not how I'd describe Arno. It certainly isn't how he'd describe himself. But yes, in effect, that's what he is."

"But it doesn't seem very fair to Alistair."

Tamsin tossed her head. "Oh, Alistair wouldn't mind. He's got his own interests. We understand each other."

"Anyhow, isn't Arno very embarrassed? I would be."

Tamsin laughed again. "I know you would, darling, that's what's so sweet about you. But Arno thinks it's funny. He likes being watched."

"Oh, Tamsin, that sounds awful. Do be careful."

"Please don't worry about me, Ellie, dear. I know what I'm doing."

The two women parted friends, but Eloise was still uneasy about the situation in which she now felt, however accidentally, complicit. She was glad to be going back to Italy, but there she faced complications of a different sort.

* * * *

She arrived at the Castel Rufina in the early evening. She'd already messaged Ugo and he was waiting for her as she parked her car. With a slight feeling of misgiving, she noticed that Tolka Petrela's big black limousine was already in the residents' car park.

Ugo walked with her to the main building. "We've put you in the same room, I hope that is acceptable? And I thought we could have a quick drink now so you can tell me what stage we're at."

"Yes, fine, I'd like that. It's looking good."

In the bar — which was next to the dining room, with a view through stone-framed windows onto the sloping garden—he brought out a bottle and showed her the label. "This is our own wine. I'd be interested in your view."

The bottle was a dark green colour, with a heavy base and a distinctive chased pattern of grapes and vines etched in the glass. She sipped, relishing the flavour. It was white, delicate. "This is lovely. It would be so nice to serve this at the reception."

Ugo looked gratified. "We've worked hard at it and we have a small, but discerning clientele in England. We have a warehouse there and we export more every month, so orders can be despatched overnight. We bring the bottles in from Albania—they are made to our strict specifications. It seems to be working very well."

Eloise told him about her agreement with the Connaughts. "I now have their full authority to negotiate with you. So we just have to go through the expenses and costs, draw up an agreement and we've done it!"

They chinked their glasses together, laughing. Ugo said, "I should tell you that things here have changed slightly since your last visit. Nothing serious, but some members of the family are now in residence. It shouldn't affect you at all."

* * * *

Ugo had provided a tiny office for her, on the first floor, looking out onto the garden and the town, and she spent the next morning on largely fruitless calls to various officials, trying to sort out the complexities of the civil wedding. By lunchtime, she felt frustrated and tired and she decided to go into Rufina. At the back of her mind, she thought she might see if Tom Sherwin was around.

It was early March and the sky was clear and blue, a bright spring sun shining down on the Castel Rufina. Eloise decided to leave the car and walk down through the gardens, through the breach in the wall and into the medieval centre.

The path, which Maria had indicated to her on her previous visit, wound down from glass double doors at the back of the area where her room was. In places, it was level with the gardens on either side, built into terraces very similar to the ones on the other side of the hill, where the vines were growing. In others, it sank between rough-stone walls. To her left, as she descended, was the main garden of the hotel, the pool being on the far side. To her right were the smaller private gardens of the family residence.

She had been walking for a short while when she became aware of a furious row going on just below her. A female voice was shouting, in English, "How dare you tell me what to do? How dare you? You're a beast, a bully. Why don't you just leave me alone? My life is hell since you brought us to this god-forsaken place."

She looked over and saw, in a lawned area, a young girl in jeans and a crop-top, long dark hair rippling down her back almost to her waist. She was screaming up into the face of a much older man. He too was dark, very tall and just as angry as she was.

"Your life? Your life, you selfish little bitch! What about my life? Do you really think I'm enjoying this existence?"

"Oh, who cares? You just like being in charge. I hate you, I hate you and I want to go back to London."

"Oh Christ, Laura, you know why we had to move…"

"Yes, because you wanted to. Beast. Foul, brutal beast!"

There was a thump and a subdued exclamation and Eloise, who had stopped on the path, thought the man had hit her. She heard noisy crying and the girl broke away and ran towards the path, almost cannoning into her.

"Are you all right?" she asked, concerned. The girl's hair was wild and tears were pouring down her face.

"No, of course I'm not all right. He's ruined my life. It's over."

The girl ran up the path towards the house. Eloise wheeled round to look at the man. He was shouting something to a person on a higher terrace, out of her view, but he turned again and saw her and for a long moment, their eyes met. He came striding towards her.

"Can I help you?"

"No, no. I heard the shouting, that's all."

"Oh." He scowled, his dark hair falling over his eyes. "You're the woman from London, I take it? Ugo said you were organising the wedding."

"That's right."

"Bloody hell! In my day all that was done by an elderly madam from Naples. You do this professionally?"

"I…" Eloise was completely thrown. "Yes, of course."

"Amazing. And do you intend to perform yourself, or are you bringing in girls for that?"

She looked at him blankly and he went on impatiently. "Do you have girls? Employees? Staff?"

"Sorry, I don't quite…yes, I have staff, of course. But I supervise the whole thing from beginning to end, making sure everything runs smoothly."

"So it's an agency?"

"Yes, that's right. An agency."

"But you'll get involved? Hands on?"

"Of course. I would never ask an employee to do something I wouldn't do myself."

"Extraordinary. Well, I'm sorry if it spoils your business prospects, but this has to be the last one. I've told Ugo. And I'd very much appreciate it if you could be as discreet as possible. I don't want the children to be aware of anything going on."

"But why...?" He turned away and she could see she would get no sense from this surreal conversation. She felt a sudden blast of anger at his rudeness and as he walked off she said sharply, "Did you hit that girl?"

He faced her again and gave her a black look. "Hit her? Did I hit her? Most certainly not. In fact, she kicked me." He leant down and rubbed his shin. "It hurt."

* * * *

In the town, Eloise did some shopping and visited the baroque church, which dominated the central square, seeming almost too grand for its surroundings. Then she wandered up to the inn, which she now saw was called the Albergo Rufina. It was mid-afternoon and although she'd missed lunch, she wasn't hungry. She ordered a glass of wine and sat in the sunshine. Despite the season, it was strong enough to merit getting out her dark glasses. She was thinking about the strange conversation she'd had on the way down. The rude man could only be a member of the family. But he sounded English. And the girl—his daughter, presumably—she was English too. She wondered how Ugo liked this invasion into what had previously been his sole territory. And she puzzled over what the man had said to her. What possible reason could he have for keeping the children unaware of the wedding?

It was entirely baffling and, of course, impossible. She would have to talk to Ugo about it.

Just then, she heard an exclamation from the road and saw Tom Sherwin waving at her. "Eloise, how nice. I was wondering if you'd be back soon. How are things?"

He sat and ordered a beer from the hovering waiter. She told him about her deal with the Connaughts. "And I owe all this to you, so I really ought to buy you that beer."

"Oh, you can do better than that. Have lunch with me here tomorrow. Unfortunately, I've got an appointment now, or I'd suggest dinner. But why don't you come down early and we can have a leisurely meal and catch up on the gossip."

She agreed, reflecting that it was nice to have a friend in this strange place, particularly after her earlier odd encounter. She was on the brink of telling Tom about it, but then stopped. It was still unclear to her what it had been all about — she'd wait until she had some elucidation from Ugo.

She walked back the way she had come. Tom had offered to drive her, but she wanted the exercise. It was still pleasantly warm, although a little breeze had sprung up. She'd been glad of her lightweight suede jacket in the shady environs of the town, but up here, she really didn't need it. She walked through the gap in the walls, inhaling the fresh spring aromas. The path was steep and she began to flag, feeling the twanging of rarely used muscles in her calves. About halfway up, on the hotel side, there was a pond with an ornamental fountain — one of those circular stone ones with a large base from which grew a stem which held a smaller one and so on. It rose in six tiers and at the centre of the final basin, a fat stone cherub lay on his back, his disproportionately large penis rigid, spouting a chute of water into the air. This descended over the various basins until it was reabsorbed into the lily pond below.

A young man sat, facing the way she was coming, working at an easel. He looked up when he saw her.

"Thank God—a nymph come to rescue me!"

"A very hot nymph," she responded, laughing. "When you're walking down this hill, you don't realise how steep it's going to be on the way back up."

"Come and sit down," he said. "Look, I can even offer you a beer." He reached into a little cool box by the side of his stool and brought out a can. "No glass I'm afraid."

"Oh no, I couldn't really…"

"Please do. I could do with some company. And the muse has deserted me—unless you're the muse in human guise."

"I'm afraid not." She smiled, sitting with gratitude on the stool he had vacated. She held out her hand. "I'm Eloise Lambert."

"You're staying at the Castle?" He shook her hand. "I'm Matt."

She took a long draught of the beer and turned her attention to the canvas. "May I look?"

"If you must. I'm playing really, but there's nothing else to do here."

She peered at the easel. He had painted the view at an angle—in the foreground, the fountain, with the absurd little cherub; in the middle distance, the jagged fortifications, and in the background and below, the red roofs and bell-towers of the town. Half of the picture was composed of sky—the pale blue of a spring afternoon, interspersed with wispy clouds. She went very still. "This is wonderful."

"Oh, it's a daub. Watercolour isn't really my style — I like oils. But I think the medium lends itself to the subject somehow."

"You're a professional?"

He looked embarrassed. "Oh, no, far from it. Just a dabbler."

"Well, a very talented dabbler." Looking at him again, she realised he was very young, probably no more than eighteen or nineteen. "Do you sell them?"

"If I can find anyone mug enough to buy, yes."

"You should have an exhibition in the hotel. They'd go like hot cakes — all the guests would want one."

Matt blushed. "You're very kind." He looked at her speculatively. "Perhaps you could pose for me? You'd just need to perch on the edge of the pool there. And take all your clothes off, of course."

She grinned. "I don't really see myself as an artist's model."

She finished her beer and resumed her climb. When she reached the terrace where the altercation had been that morning, she saw the girl was there, flat out on a lounger, dark glasses in place, enjoying what was left of the sun. Her crop-top was pulled up to expose as much of her midriff as possible. As Eloise drew level with her, she heard the thwack of some hard object hitting flesh and the girl let out a terrible scream. At first, Eloise thought she'd been shot. But that fear was quickly dispelled as the girl leapt from the lounger. At the edge of the lawn, near where she was standing, trees and bushes had been planted over the years to separate the private garden from the open area of the castle. One of these was a fine and ancient plum tree and the girl scrambled up the trunk with the grace of a cat and disappeared into the branches, which were cloaked in leaves and nascent blossoms. There was a brief and violent struggle, during which the whole tree shook. Then a cracking sound as part of a branch broke loose and fell to the ground, followed by a small boy and then the girl. Without any pause to check if they'd hurt themselves, they continued with the fight. The girl yelled, "You foul, foul little beast. I'm going to kill you this time, I really mean it." The boy alternately shrieked and laughed. "Stop it, Laura. That hurts! Ow!"

"Will you two please stop that at once?" It was the man she'd seen earlier, walking down from the house. This time, he had a toddler on his hip. The child had his legs wound round the man and was kicking his feet against him as if he were a horse—at the same time clapping his hands and shouting, "Kill, kill, kill!"

The man put the child down. "You're a bloodthirsty little bastard as well." He waded into the fight, pulling the two combatants apart. "Now what the hell is all this about?"

"I was resting on the lounger and this loathsome reptile started firing fruit things at me with his catapult. Hard fruit."

"Marc?"

The boy was panting, his dark hair ruffled and full of twigs and blossoms. He looked about ten. "Well, it's her fault. Lying there with her big fat tummy showing. Just like a bulls-eye."

The man held out his hand. "Give it to me?"

"Oh no, please, Dan…"

"It's confiscated. You can have it back when you've behaved yourself for a bit. Now, hand it over and go and find Matt. It's supper time."

Reluctantly, the boy surrendered a homemade catapult and scampered off down the path, giving Eloise a cheery grin as he did so. The girl pouted. "It's too early for supper."

"Yes, I know it's early, but I want Charlie to get into a routine. When he's more settled, we can eat a bit later."

"Why do we have to eat with him anyhow? It's like being in the zoo."

"Because it's good for him – and all of us – for us to eat as a family. Come on now, Laura." The man looked round. "Now where the hell is he...?"

The baby had toddled over to the path and, finding Eloise there, flung his arms around her legs and hugged her. The man made an impatient sound, walked swiftly to her and began untangling the child. "I'm sorry," he said. "He's like a little limpet."

As soon as he'd got him away, the child began to scream, a startling, high-pitched sound as if he were being tortured.

"I hate you, I hate you, I hate you!" he raged.

"And I hate you as well," the man responded equably. "Come on, it's time you had something to eat and went to bed."

He picked the boy up under his arm and began to walk away, so that all Eloise could see of Charlie was his wildly thrashing legs.

"I hate you and I want my mummy."

Abruptly, the man stopped and put the child down, crouching in front of him. "I know you do, darling. We all do. But we've got each other. We'll be all right if we stick together." He enfolded the little boy in a hug and Eloise, suddenly feeling she was intruding, moved on up the path to the hotel.

Chapter Five

Ugo had gone to Florence on business, so she wasn't able to ask him about the odd reference to the wedding. She was disconcerted, that evening at dinner, to find Tolka Petrela and his entourage in their usual place. Another bottle of champagne appeared at her table and this time, she took the bull by the horns and went across to him.

"Really, Mr Petrela, this is most generous, but I can't accept."

"Nonsense. Is good for pretty ladies to have champagne. Ugo says you fixing a wedding party here, no?"

"Yes, for later in the year."

"And we have our own wedding party as well. A bit different to yours though. You know about it?"

"No, I'm afraid I don't."

"Well, one day I tell you. The Wedding of the Wolf. You must come. You are invited." He made an observation in what she assumed was Albanian and the other men laughed.

"Now, if you have problems, you tell me. I know everyone. The mayor, the chief of police. Everyone. You tell me."

She smiled her uneasy gratitude and went back to her table, realising that with a man like Petrela, it was best just to go with the flow.

In the morning, she caught the housekeeper, Maria, as she bustled through the main lobby, clearly very busy.

"Oh, Signora, could you tell me who the man is who's living in the family quarters?"

"The man? Oh, Signor Dante." She corrected herself hurriedly. "I mean, of course, now he is the Conte. The Conte de Rufina."

"Well, he was very rude."

"No? He's a bad boy. But he does have a lot on his mind, Signora. Perhaps we could talk about it later? Just now I have to check the rooms."

Eloise again took the path through the garden down into the town. It was more peaceful this time, although she did see the girl Laura and the boy called Marc — they had set up a table-tennis table and were playing happily together. She realised the girl was much younger than she'd first thought — probably only about fifteen or sixteen. Presumably, these were the children of the bad-tempered Conte. She thought she'd heard Marc call him 'Dad' the previous day. She wondered what the story was, where their mother was and resolved to get the information from Maria later on.

Tom met her with a kiss. He was casually dressed, in a thin jumper, shorts and sandals, dark glasses pushed back onto his head. As he ushered her into the Albergo, he said, "I hope you don't mind, but I thought we'd eat here.

They've got an excellent lunch-time menu, as you've seen, and Carlo has tables set up in the garden—it's very pleasant."

An arch from the main street led to the side of the inn into a small courtyard which overlooked a pretty walled garden. Tables were set out on the flagstones, covered by a green awning. He showed her to a table near the side door and the innkeeper himself came through to serve them, smiling when he saw her.

They ate a simple but enormous meal, starting with terrina di fagiano con pure di castagne—a pheasant and chestnut puree—which came with walnut bread and a salad. This was followed by a mushroom soup—zuppa di funghi misti e porcini. For their main course, they had duck with fennel seeds and artichokes, and after that, a pear tart. All washed down with the local white wine. By the time they got to the coffee and brandy, Eloise groaned, "I don't think I've ever eaten as much in my whole life."

"We didn't really over-eat. It's just that there were so many courses."

"God knows how I'm going to get up that hill. All I want to do is sleep."

"Well, I'll take you back, but I think I ought to wait a bit before I attempt to drive. Why don't we have a wander round, try and walk some of it off?"

In the late afternoon sunshine, they ambled round the little town, chatting and comfortable in each other's company. On the far side, away from the castle, were some further walls, called the Bastion, which looked over a sheer drop onto the plain below. They strolled along there, enjoying the view. At the farthest point was a circular tower where the authorities had placed a telescope and Tom put one Euro in the slot and swung it round for her to view. She put her eye to it and he stood behind her, his arms on hers, moving it around, pointing out distant objects of interest. They had moved three-quarters of the way across the plain when the money ran out and a black shutter came over the viewfinder.

She exclaimed. "Oh, it's gone."

"I've got another Euro."

"No, I've seen enough, thanks," she said, laughing, and turned around in his arms. And they kissed. It was as simple as that. It was a sweet kiss, warm tongues probing and as she felt his hardness against her, a throbbing commenced deep inside her.

They broke the kiss gently and no words were exchanged, but as they walked back to the inn it seemed natural that they were hand in hand. When they got there, he asked, "Are you ready for another drink? Or do you still feel exhausted?"

"I feel comfortably tired. I'd just like to rest before I make the attempt to go back."

"Well, why don't you come to my room and lie down for an hour? I won't bother you, of course," he added hastily.

"That's a pity," she said, demurely, then, "I'd like that, thank you."

The room was one of a row in a wooden-built block on the ground floor, with a low veranda and French windows opening onto the garden. He led her there silently. On the way, Eloise wondered what had made her come out with that provocative phrase. It was quite unlike her to be so bold. Over the course of the past few days, she'd been thinking again about Jake, about her sterile love life and the fact everyone viewed her as so conventional and boring. But here in Italy she felt as if the normal constraints of her life were absent. There was no doubt that the affair with Jake was teetering to a close. And here was a good-looking, charming man who obviously liked her.

"Just this once," she told herself, "I'll go with the flow. I won't over intellectualise. Try and be a bit more like Sammy, just enjoy it."

Once inside, he fiddled with the blinds until the room was filled with dappled half-light. Then he turned to her, indicating the big double bed. "It's all yours."

With a sense of disappointment, Eloise slipped off her sandals. He'd chosen to ignore the bait. She climbed onto the bed and lay down, her head propped up on the pillows.

"Don't you want to get under the covers?"

"No, I think it's warm enough, thank you." Now that it seemed he was not interested in her, she realised she'd worked herself up to a fine state of arousal. Her breasts felt heavy and swollen, the nipples tingling, and between her legs was wetness and warmth. Little lightning flashes of desire were playing along her spine. "What are you going to do?"

"Oh, I'll just sit in a chair and doze. Unless…"

He paused for so long that she had to prompt him. "Unless what?"

"Unless you meant what you just said. About me bothering you."

She took a deep breath. "Oh, I meant it."

"In that case, I think I'll join you." He took off his sandals and sat on the side of the bed. With one hand he smoothed the wisps of auburn hair from her forehead and then let his thumb delineate the curves of her cheekbones and brush her lips. "You know, you're absolutely beautiful."

"I don't think so."

"Well, you are." He lowered his face and they kissed again. Eloise could feel her whole body suffused with an anticipatory glow. He climbed onto the bed and they carried on kissing, his hands roaming across her body through the thin material of her green dress.

His hand slid down the front, inside her bra, finding the stiffening nipples. He extricated one breast and lowered his face to it, his tongue flickering over the small, erect bud. He pulled at the skirt, stroking her thighs, moving inexorably up towards the triangle between her legs. As he started to caress her vulva through the thin material of her panties, she was aware of an increasing wetness, of a throbbing inside her and little fluttering contractions in her sex.

"Can we take this off?" he demanded huskily, and she eased herself forward to allow him to pull the dress over her head. He got off the bed and stripped off his jumper and shorts.

At this stage in a new sexual encounter, it was usual for Eloise to keep her eyes closed — partly in maidenly anticipation, partly out of embarrassment and fear. Now, she felt emboldened to look. She liked what she saw. Tom was solid, chunky, and his equipment matched. His cock was not inordinately long, but it was thick and at the moment, rearing strongly out of a patch of brown fur. Breathing heavily, he hooked his fingers round the waistband of her pale blue panties and pulled them downwards. He made a little sound as the triangle of hair was revealed, trimmed, reddish brown. He fumbled with the fastening of her bra and drew it from her, then sat back on his heels to admire her slender form. Then he lowered his head and kissed her before moving downwards, lips and hands feather light on her breasts and down her flat stomach. She trembled slightly and the light pressure on her thigh was enough to make her spread her legs to allow him to slide his fingers up and down her slit. He lowered his face between her legs and inhaled deeply.

She longed to feel his tongue and she wriggled her hips a little, thrusting upwards. Jake was not particularly keen on giving her oral sex. But she was too shy, too sexually timid to tell Tom what she wanted and after a while, he moved up her body and kissed her again, rolling on top of her and manoeuvring himself into position. Then, with great gentleness, he entered her.

He fucked her with care, almost reverentially. She moved against him and pushed her hips upwards, wanting him to go harder, faster, but not quite confident enough to tell him so. And just as she felt the beginnings of the tingle, the warmth, which heralded her orgasm, he thrust a little harder and, with a sigh of contentment, came himself.

Afterwards as they lay in each other's arms, she was conscious of a faint sense of disappointment. She wasn't quite sure what she'd expected. Eloise was far from being a sexual ingénue, but she was conscious of some undefined longing in her, which had never been fulfilled. Lovemaking with Jake had been pleasant, no more than that. With this man, with Tom, she had hoped for something else. She felt as if her sexuality were an unopened bottle, waiting for the right person to get the top off it. It might be champagne, or fine wine, or perhaps just beer. But all she'd tasted so far was lemonade.

Flat lemonade.

It was late in the evening by the time they were dressed and respectable and Tom drove her back up to the Castel

Rufina. He drew up in front of the residential area and came round to her side of the car to help her out. It was dark, still quite warm, the area inside the walls of the castle bright with floodlights.

"Shall I walk you to your room?"

"No, thank you. I'll be fine now. Thank you, Tom. Thank you for a lovely afternoon."

"Thank *you*. I haven't felt this good for ages."

They were awkward with each other, but in a pleasant way. "I feel good too. Thanks."

He pushed her against the bonnet of the car and kissed her, a deep, long, passionate kiss. Then he broke away. "I'll phone you in the morning."

The car crunched off over the gravel and she watched it as it navigated the narrow arch and disappeared into the night. Then she set off towards the entrance to the hotel.

There was a dark strip between her and the door where the floodlighting didn't reach. As she drew nearer she could see a little glow of red in the still night.

Someone stood there, smoking a cigarette. When she got close, she realised it was the bad-tempered Conte. He was leaning against a stone mounting block and holding a glass of dark liquid.

"Well, good evening. Nice to see you've taken it upon yourself to entertain the locals."

Eloise was level with him now and became aware of the distinctive smell of whisky. She decided to ignore this sally and walk past. He said, "Actually, I need to apologise to you."

This made her stop.

"It's been explained to me that the wedding you are organising is absolutely legitimate. Totally respectable. I'm sorry."

Irritation welled up in Eloise. She wasn't going to let this go. "Thank you. But why preface your apology by insulting me again?"

"Oh, dear, have I offended you? So sorry. I suppose that bloke who was mauling you is just an old family friend."

"It doesn't matter who he is, it's nothing to do with you. I mean, you haven't even had the courtesy to tell me who you are."

"Indeed." In the darkness, he sketched an elaborate bow. "I'm Dan Rufin. And you…"

"I'm Eloise Lambert. And, according to Maria, you're actually the Conte de Rufina."

There was a moment's hesitation. "Yes, I suppose I am, but I try not to think about it."

"Well, you're not going to help the family business if you go round insulting the guests."

As if he hadn't heard this last remark, he stepped forward and took her chin in one hand, examining her face. "Eloise Lambert," he said. "Silly mistake — you're far too uptight to be a madam. Shame really. If you'd really been in the business, I was thinking of saving up to avail myself of your services."

She took a sharp intake of breath. But he was just mischief-making and in any case, he wasn't entirely sober. Nothing would be achieved by getting into a slanging match. She wrenched away from his grasp and walked on towards the hotel.

"Never mind," he called to her retreating back. "I can see you've already got your hands full with your pal from the village. If 'hands' is the right word." He watched her until she got to the door, then threw away his cigarette and walked slightly unsteadily back towards the family quarters.

* * * *

Eloise didn't see Dan Rufin over the next few days, although the children were much in evidence, playing and squabbling in the garden. She was preoccupied with bureaucratic problems. Each Italian region had different regulations governing the marriage of foreigners. Although she had originally intended to arrange to hold the civil ceremony in Siena, she now thought it might be better to have it in the town hall here in Rufina. But she needed to talk first to the Mayor, and making an appointment was proving impossible. Every day came a new excuse—he was busy, he was out of town, he was entertaining a visiting delegation. She expressed her exasperation to Ugo. "It's just that so much hinges on what he has to say. If he'll agree to us holding the ceremony here and we can agree on a date, everything else falls into place. And if he can't, we'll find somewhere else. But I just need that conversation."

Ugo nodded. "He is very busy. A man with a finger in many pies. Let me see what I can do."

The next day, when she made her now routine morning call to the Mayor's office, his normally sharp secretary took on a different tone. "Ah, Signorina Lambert. Yes, the Mayor will see you today. Can you be here by three-thirty?"

She hadn't seen Tom since their afternoon tryst, although he had telephoned her several times. She wanted to get that first, awkward meeting over with, so she called him and suggested lunch. "But it will have to be pretty restrained and abstemious," she warned him. "I have an appointment with the Mayor afterwards."

"From what I hear of the Mayor, he doesn't know the meaning of the word abstemious."

She drove down to the town, parked the car in the square and walked to the Albergo. Tom was sitting outside, but he leapt to his feet and gave her a chaste kiss. They ordered a small carafe of wine and a pizza each and she told him about her days of research into flowers and food and clothes and all things matrimonial. When they were having coffee, he reached over tentatively and took her hand. "I know you're very busy, but I wondered if you'd like to come on an outing. We could go to Pisa or Florence, perhaps stay the night. It would be a break for you. And...after the other day... Well, I don't want to push you, but I'm longing for a repeat performance."

"We shouldn't have done it."

"Oh I know that. Is it...is it a problem for you? There's someone else?"

"Sort of. Oh, I don't know, Tom. It's too complicated to go into now. Let's have that day out and we can talk about it."

Chapter Six

The meeting with the Mayor went surprisingly well. He was a big, powerful man, with a loud voice and a commanding presence. He was happy for the civil ceremony to be performed in the town hall and thought the date Eloise suggested would be all right. He promised that his secretary would make a list of the papers she would need to submit.

"Also, the prospective bride and groom need to come before the Ufficiale de Stato Civile here in the town and file their intention to marry. And that has to be well in advance of the ceremony."

Eloise nodded. "I anticipate that happening in late May."

"Excellent. Well, Signorina Lambert, if you like to call in before the end of the week, we will have those details for you. Don't hesitate to contact me if you require more assistance."

They shook hands and Eloise said, "Thank you very much for making the time to see me, Signor, I very much appreciate it."

"Oh, it's nothing. For a friend of Tolka Petrela, nothing."

As she drove back to the castle, a little worry nagged at her. Ugo had clearly used Petrela's name to secure the appointment, and she felt uncomfortable about being beholden to the man in any way, though he had never given her cause.

She tried to express her unease to Ugo, but he just laughed, "Oh, there's nothing wrong with using a little influence. It's how things work."

"And also, Ugo, Mr Petrela told me something about a wedding party, something about it not being respectable. I think you ought to tell me what he's talking about."

They were walking along the battlements and he stopped, looking out across the countryside. "Very well, I will tell you the story. In the latter part of the fourteenth century, the de Rufinas were engaged in a vicious feud with a neighbouring noble family, the Cascaris, whose lands were over towards Pisa, not very far. Insult followed insult, outrage followed outrage. The then-Conte was a violent and uncouth man…"

"Not unlike his present-day descendant," Eloise muttered under her breath.

"…and when he heard his rival was to be married, he was determined to disrupt the ceremony. The bride was called Isabella d'Empoli and she came from another noble family which had, up until then, been neutral in this quarrel. The Cascaris were celebrating, not expecting anything so underhand as an attack on the wedding day itself. But Conte Rodolfo got together a huge band of men and ambushed the bride's procession as it crossed the plain and neared the Cascari stronghold. Isabella, in all her wedding finery, was snatched onto the Conte's horse and brought here to the castle."

Fascinated, Eloise asked, "What happened?"

"He told Isabella she must marry him instead. Naturally, she refused. So with great cruelty, he raped her repeatedly in front of his cheering men."

"How dreadful!"

"Yes. Of course, the Cascari family was incensed and demanded her return. After several months, an envoy was allowed into the castle to see her. Rodolfo told him to ask Isabella if she wanted to go home. And she said no. She insisted on staying with Rodolfo. Admittedly, by this time, she was heavily pregnant, but I like to think she had actually fallen in love with him."

"But surely the Cascaris didn't leave it at that?"

"No, of course not. The battles intensified and that is how the damage came to be done to the walls nearest the town. But whatever stage the hostilities were at, Isabella refused to leave and she ended her days here, the mother of six children. Both the present Conte and myself are her direct descendants."

They had begun walking slowly along the pathway again. Eloise said, "It's an extraordinary story. But I don't understand the relevance to what Tolka Petrela was talking about."

"I'm getting to that. Much later, probably at the end of the eighteenth century, the story of Rodolfo and Isabella was incorporated into an annual festival, which became known as the Wedding of the Wolf. We think it was instituted by one of the most dissolute of the family, Pietro, known as the Conte Negro, the black count. He would gather his court together and re-enact the rape of

Isabella. At that time, it's believed the woman chosen was a virgin from the town. As you can imagine, this was not popular amongst the townsfolk, but was much enjoyed by the retainers and hangers-on."

"You mean they just snatched some poor girl?"

"I think it was probably a bit more business-like than that. Certainly the girls did all right afterwards—if they survived. Some accounts say the party could get a little rough."

"Ugh." Eloise could not suppress a sound of disgust. "But surely nothing like that happens now?"

"Oh, now it is almost a tourist attraction. But it does take place, every year. We use the dungeon that I showed you and now a woman, a prostitute, is paid to take the part. Not so different from the eighteenth century really."

"And who...who takes the other part? That of the Conte?"

"It rather depends on who attends. Sometimes it is performed by an actor—sometimes a patron will wish to do it himself. In the past, it has been enacted by a member of the family."

"And this is ending now?"

"Yes. This one will be the last, unless... Dante wants it to stop, I don't know why."

Eloise went back to her room in a thoughtful mood. She knew this was only one of the dark secrets of this place. She hoped no more would emerge to threaten her arrangements.

* * * *

Now that she had a potential date, she was able to begin work on the plan in earnest and she spent an hour or so getting things in order before venturing out for a pre-dinner drink. The bar terrace was a long, narrow paved area at the rear of the main building, near the path down to the town and, at the far end, overlooking the swimming pool. She was alone and when the barman brought her drink, he lit one of the tall patio heaters. She relaxed in her steamer chair and contemplated the darkening sky.

The peace of the evening was shattered by a blood-curdling scream. She started upwards, then relaxed. It must be one of the children. The noise went on and on, unremitting, ear-splitting. Eventually, she could stand it no longer. It probably was just a childish tantrum, but if something dreadful had happened and she ignored it, she would never forgive herself. She got up and crossed the path, walking down a little way to the gap in the hedge that led to the family area.

On the other side of the lawn, the bad tempered Conte seemed to be trying to disentangle something from the plum tree. Under one arm he held the toddler, who was the source of the screaming. Dressed in an all-in-one pyjama suit, Charlie was red in the face, his feet thrashing and his fists flailing. The man stopped what he was doing and held the child up in front of him. "Look, you little bastard, will you stop making that noise? I'm trying to get it for you. Please, Charlie, give me a break."

Looking across the grass, he saw Eloise, but instead of being irritated, his face showed relief. "Oh good. Will you take him, please, just for a moment? Every time I put him down he disappears."

"Of course." She walked across to him and held out her arms. She couldn't help adding, "Should you really be calling him a bastard?"

"Believe me, that's the mildest thing I can call him. I'm exercising enormous restraint." He handed the screaming toddler over to her. Charlie put his legs around her waist, his arms round her neck and his head on her shoulder. And went blissfully quiet.

"Thank God for that. He's been at it for about an hour."

"I only heard it start up ten minutes ago."

"That's when we came outside. He'd been yelling his head off in the house."

"What's the problem?"

The Conte returned to the plum tree. "Earlier on he was playing with his kite and it got tangled in the tree. I told him I'd sort it out for him later. He came in and had his supper and bath and everything was fine, then just as he got into bed, he started demanding the kite. And screaming. The others are out and when I left him in the house to come and get it, he just followed me. If I put him down, he disappears. I'd no idea toddlers could move so fast."

Without the encumbrance of the screaming child, he soon got the kite down from the tree and roughly rolled the string into a ball. Charlie gave every appearance of being asleep.

"I'll take him now, thank you."

Eloise detached the arms from round her neck and began to pass the child over. But immediately the garden was filled with ear-splitting screams again.

"Look, Charlie, I've got your kite!" The flimsy scrap of cloth and wood was dangled in front of him. More screams.

"No, want to stay with her." Charlie fastened his arms round Eloise's neck with renewed determination.

The Conte regarded them both with a helpless expression. "Look, would you mind very much bringing him into the house and seeing if he'll let you put him to bed? I'm afraid he'll make himself ill if he goes on like that."

"That's fine. He's pretty sleepy, I think."

The Conte led the way into the house. Wide French windows led into an untidy sitting room. He crossed it, irritably kicking toys and games out of his way and through a door into a corridor. "This is his room."

It was a large, whitewashed room with a cot-bed, opened up. She laid the child on the bed and immediately he opened his eyes. "Story!" he demanded.

"I don't think so, Charlie, it's well past your bedtime," the Conte said. "Go to sleep now."

"Story."

"Oh, God, I suppose I'd better read him one. He's the most consummate blackmailer I've ever met." He examined a bookcase by the door and pulled out a book. "*Fairy Tales* by Hans Christian Andersen. This'll do."

"Aren't they a bit old for him?" Eloise asked.

"Are they? He seems to like them."

The Conte opened the book and Charlie scowled. "Not you," he insisted. "Her."

The man shrugged. "Sorry," he said, handing the book over. "The dictator has spoken."

She read a few pages of 'The Emperor's New Clothes,' and could see that Charlie was battling to stay awake. Eventually, he could fight it no longer and went off into an untroubled sleep. The Conte took the book from her and put it away. He pulled the covers over the sleeping child and kissed his forehead gently and together they tiptoed out of the room.

When they got into the sitting room, he said, "Thank you so much. He's not usually such a little beast, but I think the move must have unsettled him."

She moved towards the French windows. "Look," he said, "I was going to open a bottle of wine. Will you have a drink?"

"No, really, I've already got one on the terrace."

"I'll get it for you. I have a feeling I need to apologise for my apology the other evening. Just give me a few minutes? Please. Why don't you make yourself at home, I won't be a moment."

Outside the window stood a large patio table and some comfortable looking chairs. The Conte had disappeared in the direction of the bar and Eloise, intrigued, sat down and waited for him. After a while, he returned with the remains of her spritzer and then busied himself with a bottle and glasses. "You can have some of this when you've finished." He poured himself a large glass and sat down wearily.

"Right, now, where was I? Oh yes, that apology. I have a hazy impression that it was rather more insulting than the original insult. I'm sorry. There's no excuse, but it had been a hellish day. Once the little devils were asleep, I rather hit the scotch. And then I had this terrible craving for a cigarette. I've given them up, you see. And of course, I won't allow smoking around Charlie. But I had to have one, so I nipped out and pinched one from the office. That's when I saw you coming back. Was I very rude?"

"Yes, you were rather. But let's forget it."

"Sometimes those children wind me up beyond endurance."

"Do you mind me asking where their mother is?"

He said shortly. "Their mother is dead."

"I'm so sorry. How dreadful. You must miss your wife terribly."

"My wife? I've never been... Oh, I see, you think... No, they're not my children, thank God. Well, I suppose they are now. But I sort of inherited them."

"Inherited them?"

He gave a wry smile. "Yes, they come with the title and this magnificent pile of rubbish. Actually, they're my siblings."

"Your brothers and sister? Charlie is your brother?"

"Unfortunately, yes. Being the eldest means having all the responsibility and none of the authority."

"I'm sorry, but the age difference..."

"I know, it's ridiculous, isn't it? I'm thirty-six and Charlie is two. Do you want to hear the story?"

She nodded, genuinely interested now, and he poured her a fresh glass of wine.

"My father, as you might expect, was born here. My grandfather was a real old-fashioned aristocrat, a bit of a martinet. My dad was easy-going, cosmopolitan, artistic. He wanted to be a jazz saxophonist, which his father viewed with abhorrence. So Dad walked out. In Florence, he met my mother, who was studying art. She was English and just eighteen. They fell helplessly in love. When I was already on the way, and to the fury of both sets of parents, they married. They settled in London, where I was born. My father played in various bands, my mother painted and taught art. It was a very happy childhood — bohemian, perhaps, but loving and fun."

"It sounds wonderful," Eloise said.

"I was an only child for a very long time. I think there were several miscarriages, but of course, no one mentioned that sort of thing to me. Then when I was eighteen, along came Matt."

"Weren't you jealous?"

"Not at all. After all, I'd had my parents' exclusive attention all the time I was growing up. At eighteen, I'd just gone up to University and after that I moved into a bedsit. I was very fond of Matt. Then came Laura and after a gap of six years, Marc. When he was five, my mother became very ill."

"I'm sorry."

As if he couldn't bear to hear the words, he went on abruptly. "Breast cancer. She died. My father was absolutely lost. But he wasn't the sort of man to be without female company and about a year after that he remarried."

"Was that difficult for the children?"

"Surprisingly, no. Jane was a darling. She fitted in wonderfully and we all loved her. Then Charlie came along and the rest of the family doted on him."

He drained his glass and poured himself another. "Late last year, Dad was invited to perform at a jazz festival in Penzance. The other children were farmed out to stay with school-friends and he took Jane and the baby—thought it would be a little holiday for them. On the way back..." He took another long drink and briefly moved the palm of his hand across his eyes. "On the way back, a lorry crossed the central reservation. The front of the car was completely flattened. They were killed instantly. The rescuers found Charlie in his baby seat in the back, completely unscathed, but screaming. I sometimes wonder if that's why..."

Eloise reached out and touched his hand. "I'm so sorry. There's nothing one can say."

"No, nothing. Well, after the initial shock, I started to sort out Dad's affairs. They were in a terrible mess. The house was mortgaged up to the hilt, the insurance wasn't enough to cover his debts and everything had to be sold. Social Services came to see me. They said Matt was old enough to fend for himself and the two other older children would be taken into care. They couldn't guarantee them being kept together. An elderly aunt of Jane's offered to take Charlie."

"How awful." Eloise said, horrified and fascinated by the drama of his story.

"And I'd been living this wonderful, hedonistic bachelor life."

"What do you do?"

"Oh, I'm a musician too, of sorts. Jazz pianist. I sing. With a partner I run a nightclub in Soho. Drinks, dinner, entertainment. It's doing all right. With a flat within walking distance. Perfect."

"What a terrible dilemma. Were there no other relatives to help?"

"No. My mother's parents are dead and they wouldn't have been much use in any case. He was a gentleman farmer, country squire type, frightfully old fashioned. A bigot. He never got over having grandchildren who were half Italian. And of father's immediate family, there's only Ugo and a great-aunt in Rome."

"But you couldn't let them be taken into care?"

"No. If we'd been able to hang onto the house, things would have been better. But with Dad's debts just about squared, there was nothing I could do but move them all into my flat."

"And Charlie?"

"I told myself he'd be happier with the aunt. But then I thought about him growing up alone, in that sterile environment, without experiencing the love and fun the rest of us had. And I couldn't bear it. So Charlie moved in as well."

"Quite a dramatic life-style change for you."

"You're telling me! And they didn't settle down as a loving little family. Oh no, not my brothers and sister. They immediately started playing up. Dad lived in Camden, so when they moved to Soho, they had to go to new schools. Matt decided he didn't want to study any more — he's seventeen, for God's sake! I had endless battles with him. Then he was out all night, hanging around with most unsuitable people. And getting into trouble with girls."

"He's very talented, though," Eloise interposed. "I saw one of his watercolours the other day."

"Isn't he? I thought he should get some formal training, but he doesn't seem to care. Laura hooked up with the son of a chap who runs a Chinese restaurant near me and they vowed undying love. Which is why she won't speak to me except to heap invective on my head. And Marco...well, I thought I'd got off lightly with Marco. Then he got into a fight at school and a knife was involved. I don't think he was carrying it, but it put the wind up me."

"Marco?" she asked.

"All our names are Italian. Matt is Matteo and Marc is Marco. Laura's just Laura."

"And you? Dan?"

"It's Dante. Dante de Rufina at your service." He grinned at her. "So that's when I decided to move them all over here. Dad wasn't really interested in this place, but we used to come for holidays. And to visit my grandfather when he was alive." He shuddered. "Ugo's been running it for as long as I can remember."

"Will you stay?"

"I was rather hoping to get back to my own life. I want to settle the children in new schools here, find someone to look after Charlie and keep an eye on the others and get Matt into some form of further education. Then I can go back to my flat and my job."

"You said you're not married. Girlfriend?"

"Yes. Not at all happy. She's not very keen on children."

"I see." Privately, Eloise thought that a girlfriend who was unable to rally round in these extraordinary circumstances was not worth having.

He looked at his watch. "Oh my God, look at the time. If you're eating in the restaurant, I'd better let you go. Unless you fancy taking potluck with me here?"

"No, thank you." She got up gracefully. "I'll just have a quick bite, then I've got things to do."

"Right." His dark eyes clouded again. "Thank you for rescuing me from the child from hell."

She touched him gently on the shoulder. "Cheer up. It does get better."

"Only a large injection of money could improve my life. That would solve all my problems."

Chapter Seven

The next day, Eloise was walking to her car when a taxi drew up in front of the hotel and from it stepped a stunningly beautiful woman. She was black, very tall and elegant, with hair swept up onto the top of her head. Eloise thought she was vaguely familiar. Unlike Sammy, Eloise wasn't a voracious reader of celebrity magazines, but she rather thought that's where she'd seen her. While she was pondering this, Dante de Rufina emerged from the house and went swiftly across to where the taxi driver was unloading suitcases, bags and vanity cases from the car. "Jessica, I didn't expect you so soon."

"I got an earlier flight," she said, moving towards him with feline grace. "Darling!" They fell into a passionate embrace, leaving the taxi driver gawping at them with frank amazement.

Ah, the girlfriend who doesn't like children, Eloise thought as she got into the car.

She had accepted Tom's invitation to spend a couple of days in Florence and the next day he drove up to Castel Rufina to collect her. As they drove along the almost empty motorway, through the rolling Tuscan countryside, she told him about her encounter with Dante de Rufina.

"Oh, Dante's turned up, has he?"

"You know him?" she asked, surprised.

"Only by reputation. A very shady character."

"Is he?"

"Well, let's say that since he inherited the castle the dodgy dealings there have become more…blatant."

She shook her head, perplexed. "He didn't seem like that to me. Bad tempered, perhaps, and rude. But not a crook."

"Oh, come on, Eloise, he's the owner of a club in Soho. And now an associate of Tolka Petrela?"

"Well, that doesn't mean he's up to something illegal. I mean, the story about the children seemed genuine."

"Yes, but what wonderful cover for other nefarious activities."

She was silent for a while, then she asked carefully, "What sort of activities? I keep hearing these dark mutterings about the place, but what are we really talking about?"

He glanced at her for a moment before turning his attention back to the straight road ahead. "Apparently drugs are frequently smuggled from Albania through Italy to other European Union countries. There are many routes, but one is through Northern Italy. There is some suggestion that the Castel Rufina is a clearing house for these drugs."

"That's appalling."

"And also women. Girls are brought in from the east—some willing, some not. There's plenty of opportunity for cheap labour in the brothels and bars of Western Europe."

"But surely, Dante de Rufina couldn't be involved in that sort of thing?"

"Why not? He owns a business in Soho, at the heart of the sex trade. A convenient base to run the London end of such a business."

"You seem to know a lot about all this."

"I like to know what's going on. And then there are the parties. Very wild gatherings which degenerate into orgies."

"But that's not illegal?"

"No, but it tells you what sort of a man you're dealing with."

She wanted to tell him that Dante was stopping the parties, but that would have meant explaining their original misunderstanding and for some reason she didn't want to do that.

They were silent for a while and when they spoke again it was about Florence and what they planned. Tom said diffidently, "I wasn't sure what you wanted to do about rooms. So, being an optimist, I booked a double and if that's not what you want, I can ask for another one."

She was still thinking about the Conte de Rufina, but she smiled at this. "Let's see how it goes."

Florence in the spring was glorious. The height of the tourist season was months away and the streets were relatively uncluttered, although every now and again, a giggling party of Japanese schoolgirls would pass by, eyes glued to the windows of every expensive shop.

They had drinks at a bar restaurant overlooking the Arno and lunch in one of the smart cafés in the Piazza della Signoria. Afterwards, hand in hand, they strolled around the Uffizi, admiring old masters they had previously only seen in art books. When they emerged, Eloise said, "Let's go and see the David. It's at the Accademia, the other side of the Duomo, and we can have a look at the Baptistery Doors on the way back."

"Well, I'd like to look round the Duomo again. But if you don't mind, I think we should save David for tomorrow. I don't want any comparisons if we…"

This made her laugh out loud. "Oh, I wouldn't worry. I've already seen and approved your equipment and in any case, Michelangelo was surprisingly ungenerous with poor David."

They spent a pleasant few hours and finished their sightseeing by walking across the Ponte Vecchio, peering into the windows of the goldsmiths' shops. Eloise admired a pendant which consisted of the masks of tragedy and comedy, linked together, one mask in yellow gold, one in white gold, and he insisted on buying it for her. They dined at the Enoteca Pinchiorri in the Via Ghibellina. It was known as one of the best restaurants in Florence, if not in the whole of Italy, and they had a magnificent, leisurely meal. Afterwards, they strolled along the Arno, taking a last brandy at the café in the Piazza della Republica. Finally, it was time to return to the hotel in the Via Cazaiuoli, in the heart of the city.

As they walked through the narrow marble hallway towards the reception desk, Tom said, "Well, this is it. If we need another room, speak now."

She turned to him, laughing, slightly tipsy. "I think I need you to help me upstairs before I attempt to speak again."

The lift was tiny and on the way to the fourth floor, he leant forward and kissed her. When the lift door opened, it was on the other side to where they'd entered, which confused them, and by the time they got to the room, they were laughing helplessly.

They made love comfortably, like old friends. Tom had a fine, muscular body and he treated her with great gentleness and respect. Perhaps too much so, Eloise thought, lying next to him as he slumbered deeply afterwards. But she still wasn't sure what it was she wanted from him, let alone how to ask for it.

* * * *

They drove back to Rufina the next day and she threw herself into the business of arranging the wedding with renewed vigour. In the evening, she went to the bar terrace for a pre-dinner gin and tonic. She relaxed, thinking about the conversation she'd had with the florist and the negotiations over the cost of rose arches on the path to the chapel. She became aware of a tugging at her skirt and, looking down, saw Charlie smiling up at her. Having got her attention, he clambered onto the lounger and sat astride her, patting her face with his hands. "Hide," he demanded. "Want to play hide!"

"Hide and seek? I don't think so, Charlie, not now. What are you doing here anyhow? Where's your brother?"

The child waved his arm expansively in the direction of the family quarters. "Story!" he demanded.

"Well, all right, just a quick one, then I'd better take you back." Eloise improvised a story about talking bears that went to live in London and she'd just got to the denouement when the girl, Laura, appeared through the gap in the hedge.

"Oh, God, I'm sorry," she remarked, taking in the scene. "He's an awful pest." She turned back towards the way she had come and, without warning, bellowed in a foghorn voice. "Dante, it's okay, he's here." She flopped down in a chair next to Eloise and said, without rancour, "Little bastard."

Eloise smiled. Obviously Dante de Rufina's colourful language was catching. "Would you like a drink?"

"Oh, yeah. Thanks. Coke please." Laura scooted round to gesture at the barman, who came and took the order. When he'd gone, she lowered her voice and muttered, "Actually, I'd really like a beer, but they won't serve me. Dante lets me have beer and wine."

"Does he? How old are you?"

"Nearly sixteen," she said. "Are you the wedding lady?"

"Yes, I suppose I am."

"Oh. You're going to put the hotel on the map."

"Am I?"

"That's what Ugo told Dante. He said he had to be nice to you because you were going to put a lot of business our way."

"Well, that all depends on how well this first one goes."

Laura swung round in her seat so her legs were over one of the arms and reached out to grab a handful from the bowl of nuts supplied with the drinks. "You live in London?"

"Yes, in Covent Garden."

"Wicked. We were in Camden, then Dante moved us to Soho. That was great. Now he's decided we have to live in this dump."

"You don't like it?"

"There's nothing to do. No one here. No shops, no friends, the television is terrible. I hate it. And now I can't even spend time in our own flat."

"Why not?"

"Oh, because of Her Highness. Ordering us around all the time."

"Is that your brother's girlfriend?"

"Yep. Jessica Anthony. International supermodel. She says."

"I thought I'd seen her somewhere before. She's very beautiful."

"She's a pain in the butt," Laura remarked, no doubt again borrowing from her brother's vocabulary.

At that moment, Dante de Rufina appeared, looking cross. "Oh, there you are, Laura. Come along, please, and bring the brat with you. Dinner's ready."

"Oh, it's dinner now, is it?" his sister replied, sarcastically. "Now Madam is with us we don't have supper anymore."

"Come on, Laura, we don't have time for this."

"You know it'll be a disaster. Like last night. I thought her ladyship was going to have hysterics when Charlie threw spaghetti all over her."

"Yes, well Charlie ought to be made to eat in a glass box to protect everyone within a five mile radius." He clicked his fingers at his little brother. "Come on, monster, and stop annoying Miss Lambert."

"Oh, he's no trouble. I was rather enjoying our cuddle."

He grinned at her, suddenly looking much younger. "Yes, we're all good at cuddles. You should try my technique some time." He scooped the toddler off her lap and swung him round onto his shoulder. "Laura!" he said. "And don't forget we're going to Pisa tomorrow."

"Oh, I can't come with you."

"Why not?"

"Because…because I promised to go shopping with her." She pointed at Eloise, giving her a look of entreaty.

"With Miss Lambert? Really? Are you sure, Miss Lambert?"

Unable to resist the look in the girl's eyes, Eloise nodded. "Yes, I was thinking of going to the outlet shops. You know, Gucci, Dolce e Gabbana, Fendi… There are things I need to get for this wedding and I might as well have a look around myself."

He looked dubious. "Well, if you're sure. She'll be an awful nuisance. But I suppose if she's in the shops annoying you she won't be in Pisa winding Jessica up."

"Of course I'm sure. We'll have a great time. Why don't you meet me in front of the hotel tomorrow at eight, Laura? We have to start early because apparently there are always queues."

"You bet. Thank you very much!" As she walked away with her brothers, she was saying excitedly, "Can I have some money, Dante, please? You must give me something. I can't go to Dolce e Gabbana without any money."

Eloise smiled a little guiltily, but she'd been planning a visit to the famed retail outlets and this seemed a good opportunity to go. She felt sorry for Laura, at an awkward age and surrounded by a variety of unsympathetic males. Such a pity she couldn't have got on with her brother's girlfriend. Eloise wondered if there was an element of jealousy involved.

The next day, when they were in the car, she said, "I thought we'd take the scenic route over the mountains, rather than go nearly all the way up to Florence on the motorway. Is that all right?"

"Oh yes, fine."

"I would have thought looking at the smart outlet shops was just the sort of thing your brother's girlfriend would like. Didn't she want to do that instead?"

"Oh no, for heaven's sake, she wouldn't be seen dead in a retail shop. She has to go to the real thing in Milan or Rome, darling, where all the men fawn and slobber over her."

Eloise couldn't help asking. "And does your brother fawn over her?"

"Dante? He doesn't do fawning. He used to pant a bit— well, that's what Matt said. But he's past that now. It's funny, because she's suddenly decided she's keen on him again, now she realises he really is a Count. Though Dante says he's the only skint aristocrat in Italy. But he's seeing she's got—what's that thing you say—feet of clay. She nearly slapped Charlie yesterday and I thought he was going to explode. It's all right for him to go on and on about Charlie, but no one else is allowed to."

"He does yell at him."

"He yells at all of us. You can't blame him really," Laura added, with surprising fairness. "We make his life hell." This was said with a certain amount of relish.

"So you think Jessica is impressed by the title?"

"Impressed! She can see herself in the papers already. 'The Black Contessa.' Well, that's what Matt thinks."

"He doesn't like her either?"

"No. None of us do. Charlie was sick on her yesterday."

"Oh dear. And your brother doesn't seem very pleased about being the new Conte."

"Well, up to now it's always been a bit of a joke. But here they take it really seriously."

"Did your father use the title?"

"Dad? He used it professionally. You know, 'Count Enzo and his Syncopated Sound.' Every now and again there'd be an article in one of the papers, 'Count Enzo—a real aristocrat of Jazz'. He just laughed and was pleased with the publicity. But that was it. I think..."

She became silent and Eloise waited, watching the winding road ahead.

"...I think Dante's really shocked by the responsibility. Of the Castel Rufina, of us, all of it really. The weight of history, Ugo calls it. Poor Dante."

They drove over the hills, chatting as if they had known each other for ever. At Gaiole in Chianti, an enchanting little town, they stopped for a quick coffee. "I thought we could go to the Prada outlet a little further along at Montevarchi. Then we'll find somewhere for lunch and go on to the Mall."

"Is it in a town?"

"No, it's weird. Just a strip of shops out in the country."

"Oh, I know. Dad took us to the outlet shops in Street once—you know, in Somerset. I don't suppose this will be like that though."

"No, but the idea is the same. You can sometimes get as much as seventy-percent off real designer items. Did your brother give you some money?"

"Yes, he gave me a hundred and fifty Euros."

"That was nice of him."

"Well, he made a terrible fuss about it. He's always saying we've got to economise. Apparently Dad screwed up the family fortunes."

She sounded bitter and Eloise said gently, "I expect he'd have sorted things out if he hadn't had the accident."

"You didn't know my dad! He believed in living for the present. Everything was fun. He was insanely generous."

"He sounds like a wonderful father."

"He was."

They drove on to Montevarchi, to the Prada shop. There had been a queue there since early morning but by the time they arrived it had thinned out a little—and so had the goods in stock. They browsed for an hour and both bought some sunglasses at a greatly reduced rate, but saw nothing else that appealed to them. In the town of San Giovanni they stopped for lunch and to visit Dolce e Gabbana. Laura found some flat black ankle boots in the softest leather and fell in love with them. They were reduced from two hundred and fifty Euros to fifty, they were in her size and they were the last ones in the shop. She emerged, flushed with triumph, the prized D & G bag clutched in her hand.

"Brilliant." Eloise was pleased for her. "You've really got a bargain. Shall we go on to the Mall now? There's a Gucci shop there, so we can give this one a miss."

The Mall was, as Eloise had explained, a row of designer shops in the middle of the Tuscan countryside. They wandered from shop to shop, trying things on, holding fabrics up to show each other, laughing at some of the more outrageous styles. They tried the shoes in Sergio Rossi, fondled the softest cashmere sweaters in Loro Piana and modelled bags for each other in Fendi. In Agnona, Laura found a belted black leather jacket, which would go perfectly with the boots she'd bought earlier. It was an amazing one hundred Euros. They went outside and she surreptitiously counted her money. "I had the one hundred and fifty Dante gave me and about thirty Euros of my own. I spent twenty on the sunglasses and fifty on the boots. So I've got, what…a hundred and ten left. I could get the jacket and that would be it. Oh dear, Eloise, what shall I do? It is gorgeous."

"Why don't you think about it for a while? You might see something you like better. I've got to go to La Perla to get something for the friend whose wedding I'm arranging. We could look round there, then go to Gucci and we can come back here if you decide that's what you want to do."

In La Perla they wandered around, admiring the wispy lingerie, lacy knickers and revealing bras. "What is it you have to get?" Laura asked.

"I need to buy a strapless basque for Tamsin—my friend—to wear when she's being fitted for her wedding dress. I volunteered to get it here because it should be a lot cheaper."

"Oh, look at this!" Laura was holding up the flimsiest of bras. Two bits of green lace, in the shape of vine leaves, supported the cups. They were cut low, so they would scarcely cover the nipples and were dark purple, representing miniscule bunches of grapes. The attached panties were thong-like. Two scraps of green material met in bows, which would sit on the hips. In the middle, a tiny triangle of purple grapes would do very little for modesty.

Eloise gasped. "That's gorgeous!" she exclaimed. "I want it!" But she wondered who she would be pleasing if she bought it. The gentlemanly Tom Sherwin, or the self-obsessed Jake Matthews? She sighed and turned away.

"It's the sort of thing Dante really goes for!" Laura said, betraying rather more knowledge of her brother's taste in female underwear than was proper. Eloise had a sudden vision of Dante de Rufina, lounging against the mounting block outside the castle, whisky on his breath, saying, *"If you'd really been in the business, I was thinking of saving up to avail myself of your services."*

For reasons she couldn't have explained, she wheeled round. "I'm going to have it."

For Tamsin, she bought a simple basque in white silk, but with enough support to hold her large bosom and constrain her waist. Next, they went to the Gucci shop. Here, Laura found a man's wallet for forty Euros. She hesitated for only a moment before saying, "I'm going to get this for Dante. It's his birthday in a few months' time."

"But that means you won't be able to afford the jacket."

"I know. But he'd love this."

She went off to pay for it and Eloise reflected that it was a very sweet, unselfish act. Laura was an interesting, complex girl and she hoped Dante appreciated her.

Having blown her chances of buying the jacket, Laura seemed content to spend the rest of the money on presents for her family. She bought some more sunglasses—this time for Matt, *"For when he's painting"* —a baseball cap for Marc, a cuddly clown toy for Charlie, perfume for Maria and finally a key ring for Dante. "That's for now—the wallet's a birthday present."

By now exhausted, they repaired to the café for tea and cakes. After a while, Eloise excused herself. "I'll be back in a minute." She returned to find Laura examining her purchases. Eloise sat down and handed over a bag, bearing the distinctive Agnona label. "Here you are. My gift."

Laura looked surprised. She peered into the bag and gave a shriek of joy. "My jacket! Oh, Eloise, thank you, thank you so much. I love it!" She pulled out the coat, scattering the tissue paper in which it had been so carefully wrapped a few minutes before. It was beautiful, soft leather falling from slightly gathered shoulders. Laura gazed at it with joy before thrusting it back in the bag and rushing round the table to hug her benefactor. "Thank you, you're so kind."

They drove home a different way, stopping for dinner at a small trattoria. By the time they got back, it was nearly ten and Eloise felt a little nervous about having kept Laura out so late. She walked with her round to the side of the house, where the front entrance to the private quarters was. Laura's vigorous knocking soon brought the Conte to the door. He seemed unconcerned about their lateness.

"Oh, there you are. Good. Did you have a nice day?"

"Wonderful! We've bought loads of stuff, haven't we, Eloise?"

"We certainly have."

"I'm glad you enjoyed yourselves. Miss Lambert... Eloise, won't you come in and have a drink? Everyone's still up, I can't even persuade Charlie to go to bed."

"I won't, thank you."

"Oh, Eloise, please come in. I want you to see them get their presents."

With some reluctance, she agreed. In the sitting room, she was introduced to the glamorous Jessica Anthony. The model, reclining on a sofa, nodded, but that was all.

Laura handed out the gifts. "This is for you, Matt, and for you, Marco. Dante...and look, Charlie, I got this for you." She glanced at Jessica and Eloise saw her face freeze for an instant. Quickly, she reached into her own carrier-bags and produced some upmarket bath crystals she'd bought for herself. "Here you are, Laura. You forgot you gave me Jessica's present to carry. Just because it was the heavy one!"

Laura flashed her a look of gratitude and handed the gift to Jessica who opened the little bag and raised an eyebrow in surprise. "Thank you, this is quite good stuff."

Eloise glanced up to see Dante regarding her with a steadfast look. "I ought to go now," she said, beginning to gather up her parcels.

"Oh no, you must stay for the fashion parade." He grinned. "Anyone who goes on a shopping spree has to model the loot for the others."

Laura had already pulled on her boots and she paraded round the room in them. She put on the sunglasses and then the jacket, which was admired by all, even Jessica. "Eloise bought it for me," she said. Eloise saw Dante's brows fly up, but he said nothing, except, "Let's see your purchases now, Miss Lambert. Eloise."

Eloise smiled and pulled out the pretty green mules she'd bought in Dolce e Gabbana and the bag from Fendi. They were duly admired and she began to pack them away, but Laura burst out impulsively, "Show them the thing you got in La Perla."

"That's not for me, it's for the bride — at this wedding."

"I didn't mean that. The grape thing."

Eloise blushed, remembering the strange urge that had caused her to buy the underwear. "Oh, they don't want to see that."

"Yes we do," Dante said, a gleam in his eye. "Come on, we have to examine it all."

Eloise opened the bag and pulled out the bra and knickers set, still on its little hanger. Identical whistles came from Dante and Matt.

"Wow," Matt exclaimed. "I like that."

"Me too," Dante chipped in. "Are you going to model it for us?"

Jessica's eyes narrowed for a second before she smiled sweetly. "Yes, it's quite pretty in a garish kind of way."

Eloise heard a sound from Laura and saw her face, furious with indignation. She put out a hand to stop her before she could vocalise it and reminded her gently, "Laura, don't forget we bought sweets for everyone. Probably too late to have them now, but you should give them to your brother for tomorrow." Laura began digging about in the bags again and the tense moment passed.

That night before she went to bed, Eloise tried on the two tiny strips of material. She stood in front of the long mirror and examined herself carefully. Her breasts were not large, but they were rounded and firm and the green and purple bra lifted them up, accentuating her cleavage. Her nipples were just visible, nestling among the lacy grapes. The thong was minute. The purple motif just covered her mons and stretched flat across it, leaving very little to the imagination. Her legs looked impossibly long in the high-heeled green shoes she'd bought.

She looked at herself full on, then turned, sucking her flat stomach in even more and pushing her auburn hair provocatively above her head.

"Yes, perhaps it is a bit vulgar. But I like it. It's me — the new me."

But as she got into bed she wondered again who she was thinking of when she bought the outfit. And her sleep was troubled by visions of Dante de Rufina, his hand edging forward to unfasten the bows that held up the lacy panties.

Chapter Eight

Perhaps it was because of the dreams that, the next day, she phoned Tom and invited him to dine at the hotel. He accepted with alacrity.

"And Tom," she added. "Bring your toothbrush."

She took him out onto the terrace for a pre-dinner drink. It was dusk and Frederico the barman had turned on the lights that spanned the area. She'd half expected Laura to turn up and she did, carrying a sleepy looking Charlie. Trailing behind them was Marco, playing with a football, alternately banging it against the flagstones and trying, without much success, to bounce it on his head.

It wasn't ideal for a couple trying to have a romantic tryst, but Tom was charm itself when he was introduced to the children. They sat down without being asked and accepted the offer of drinks. Charlie scrambled up onto Eloise's knee.

"Jessica's going," Laura volunteered, with some satisfaction. "She's got some modelling thing in Rome."

"Yes," Marco chipped in, his voice muffled because he'd gone under the table to retrieve his ball, "but she's coming back. Worst luck."

Tom asked them about their schools and they began telling him about the trouble they were having settling in, the superiority of British schools over Italian ones and general moans about having to leave friends behind. They didn't really give the impression of being too unhappy. Eloise was impressed by the serious way Tom was talking to them. He began to ask about their plans. "So will you go back to England?"

"It depends on Dante." Marco was now sitting at the table drinking his Coke. "He says he needs to be a millionaire to afford us."

"And if he was a millionaire?"

"Then he'd buy a posh house in a smart part of London and ship us all back there. Roll on that moment."

Tom went on questioning them about Dante until the man himself arrived. He took in the scene at once and Eloise thought his eyes glinted as they rested on Tom.

"So, Miss Lambert, you've hijacked my family again."

"I think it was the other way round," she said mildly.

"And who's this?"

"This is Tom Sherwin. He's a writer who's staying in the town."

Neither man offered to shake hands, and there was a moment of palpable tension as they faced each other. Dante spoke crossly, "Laura, Marco, please come now. It's our last meal together before Jessica goes to Rome." He reached for the toddler, who immediately began to wail.

"Oh, Dante, can't we stay a bit longer?" Marco wailed.

"No, you can't," his brother said sharply. "Can't you see you're intruding? Miss Lambert wants to be alone with her friend."

Laura looked at Eloise, distress etched on her face. "That's not true. She was pleased to see us."

"Yes, of course I was. I'm always pleased to see you."

"Well, the party's over. Home, you kids."

Marco and Laura got up reluctantly and Eloise gave Laura an impulsive kiss. "I'll see you tomorrow."

When the two older children had gone down the path towards the gap in the hedge, Dante turned back. "By the way, Miss Lambert, I believe I owe you some money. Do let me know how much that jacket cost. And the lunch and dinner and any other expenses."

She stared at him for a moment in blank astonishment. Then she recovered herself enough to say, "Don't be ridiculous, Conte. I enjoyed Laura's company and the coat was a gift."

"We don't need charity, Miss Lambert."

"No indeed. And if I had intended to dispense charity, I'd have looked for someone who deserved it. For heaven's sake, if it makes you uncomfortable, give me a bottle of Castel Rufina wine."

He looked embarrassed. "Well, if you're sure. Thank you." He moved towards the path then again turned back. "By the way, Mr Sherwin, I think you're going to be the luckiest recipient of the big shopping trip."

"I am?"

"If she's going to model the grape outfit for you, then I think there's no doubt about it. You've hit the jackpot."

He marched away, a sleeping Charlie draped over his shoulder.

In any event, Tom didn't get to see the provocative green and purple bra and panties. After dinner, they drank coffee and grappa in the lounge. Eloise explained that Tolka Petrela usually held court in the dining room and in the lounge afterwards. "Thank goodness he wasn't here tonight. He makes me feel so uncomfortable." Through the open doorway to the lobby, she could see Dante de Rufina. He stood for a moment, looking at her, a sardonic smile on his lips. Then he turned and spoke to someone who was out of view. A few minutes later, the other person moved across and she saw it was Petrela himself. He, too, stood in the doorway for a moment and when he saw her, blew an elaborate kiss.

Eloise stood up abruptly. "Come along, Tom, it's time for bed."

He gazed up at her, amused. "What's all this cave-woman stuff?"

"You'll see. Upstairs. Now!" She took his hand and pulled him towards the door and as they climbed the stairs, she could see Dante de Rufina, still talking to Petrela, his mocking eyes watching her until she disappeared from view.

In her room, she took control. Tom was shocked, amused and obviously incredibly aroused. She stripped him swiftly and, still dressed in her clinging red dress, sank to her knees and took his bloated erection in her mouth. She had not fellated him before. She was aware of him watching her fixedly as she worked on him, taking his length into her throat, ducking underneath to taste his balls. It was as if a devil possessed her as she worked her way around his body, lapping at his flesh, his thighs. When he was at the height, the last level before the complete abandonment of control, she stopped, pulled away and began to remove her own clothes, leaving him panting and desperate.

"Lie down," she instructed, pushing him back onto the bed. When she was naked, she got astride him, kneeling so that his rampant erection fitted into the cleft of her buttocks. With a flourish, she pulled the fastening from her hair, letting it cascade down.

"Please," he groaned. "Move upwards...over my mouth. Let me taste..."

She shuffled her knees on either side of him until her slit, puffy now and moist, was just above his mouth. He began to explore her folds, skimming the surface before plunging more deeply. At last he concentrated on her clitoris, agitating the very tip of his tongue while she writhed in delight. She arched her back as a burst of pleasure struck her somewhere near the base of her spine and released liquid into his eager mouth.

Her vagina still throbbed, opening and contracting. Desperate to regain the wonderful sensation, she moved down again and lowered herself onto him. For about a minute they were still, savouring the intimacy, then Eloise began to move slightly, varying the angle, causing him to stir her insides. She rode him, rising upwards and falling back, getting him as deep as possible. Tom thrust his hips and cried out with exertion, his hands blindly caressing her breasts.

At last his hips jabbed upwards. She felt him grow, pulse and empty himself inside her. And as he did so, she worked her clit furiously with the middle finger of her right hand, so that her climax followed his and she collapsed limply on top of him as he softened and left her.

They made love a second time that night and again in the still air of the early morning, although Eloise never recaptured that feeling of abandon, of approaching some sort of a goal.

Afterwards, Tom rolled off her and lay on his back. "Eloise, you're a very special woman. Very special." He swung his feet out of the bed, sitting with his back to her. "I've got something to tell you."

"Oh? This sounds serious."

"It is. I'm afraid I haven't been entirely honest with you."

Eloise's heart sank. He was going to tell her he was married, or bisexual, or that he'd tired of her.

"I told you I was a writer and it's true, I'm trying to write a novel. But I also have a job." He swung round so he was sitting sideways on the bed, looking into her face. "I'm a police officer. I'm sorry."

She was bewildered. "But why...why not tell me? There's nothing wrong with being a policeman."

He sighed. "I'm not supposed to tell anyone. I shouldn't have mentioned it now. I have to rely on your discretion. Because I'm working, you see. I'm undercover."

It all seemed strangely overdramatic to Eloise. "What are you working on? What's the case?"

"For some time now we've had our eye on Tolka Petrela. The British police, the Italians and the Albanians. There's no doubt he's a big-time gangster, but he's clever. And since he's started to take an interest in this place, we've managed to get closer. I mentioned before the traffic in drugs and women coming from Albania and moving to Western Europe. We're pretty sure that Petrela is the supplier. This castle is the hub of the operation in Italy. Someone here organises the shipments."

She listened intently. "And then?"

"We believe that the importer, the distributor in London, is your friend Dante de Rufina.

"No!"

"I'm sorry, Eloise, but all the evidence points that way."

"But he's broke. That's why he's brought the children here."

"That's what he says. And in any case, didn't you tell me he was desperate for money to get his life back on track?"

"I don't believe he'd do anything to endanger the children."

"He may feel it's worth a few years of getting his hands dirty to secure their future."

She was silent for a while, thinking it through. "And is this why you struck up an acquaintance with me? To get a foothold in the Castel Rufina?"

He reached out his hand to stroke her shoulder. "No, of course not. Once I'd seen you, I couldn't keep away."

"But now. You're using me to get close to Dante de Rufina."

"No, Eloise. It's just coincidence."

"Last night, on the terrace. When the children were there, you interrogated them. I thought you were just showing an interest. But you were questioning them about their brother. That's pretty low, isn't it?"

"It wasn't intentional. But let me tell you something, Eloise. The drugs that are smuggled into Britain are the focal point for crime, misery, disease and death. And those poor girls who travel from Albania — some of them are hoping for a better life, away from grinding poverty. Others are kidnapped, taken against their will and forced into prostitution. They're worked almost literally to death. They're controlled by being hooked on drugs — they work for no pay just to enrich their pimps and the men who traffic in them. If I can put a stop to that I'll use whatever method I can, even if it does mean questioning children, however unethical you may think that is."

In her heart, she knew he was right, but she still felt uneasy, as if he had used her. And now she felt the beginning of a gnawing fear about the de Rufina children. If Tom was right about the involvement of the Conte then their little family, which had held together despite all the odds, was about to face its most intractable threat yet.

"I'd better get dressed." He leaned over her. "Are we all right? You forgive me?"

"Of course," she said and returned his kiss. "But I think you're wrong about Dante de Rufina."

After breakfast, she went through the lobby to get to her little office and found Dante in deep conversation with Ugo. He broke off and gave her a sardonic smile. "Ah, Miss Lambert. I trust you had a...satisfactory night?"

"Very, thank you."

In a different voice, he called out as she climbed the stairs. "Oh, by the way, in your travels, would you keep an eye open for Charlie's little tricycle? He was playing with it out in the grounds somewhere and came back without it. Now he's inconsolable. If you spot it, please just shove it inside the French windows."

Chapter Nine

Eloise needed to deliver some papers to the Town Hall and she walked through the gardens after lunch. Afterwards, she visited the pharmacy and a couple of other shops. She was careful to avoid the inn — she needed time to digest what Tom had told her. On the way back to the castle, near the place where Matt had been painting, she noticed a flash of red in some undergrowth. Charlie's trike. It looked as if he had crashed it into the bush and just got off and abandoned it. She pulled it out and carrying it by the handlebars, walked on upwards.

The garden was very quiet and Eloise remembered the children saying something about Maria taking them to visit her sister. She came to the entrance to the family garden, hesitated and went in, meaning to leave the tricycle up by the house. When she got to the top terrace, she stopped dead.

On the patio area, a man and a woman were entwined. Both were naked. The woman was partially sitting on the table, her legs and arms wrapped around him. His head was on her breasts and from what Eloise could see he was biting and sucking at the nipples. Visible below the tight embrace of her legs, muscled buttocks moved to and fro, the effort rippling down through long legs defined by dark hairs.

Dante de Rufina. It had to be. She knew she must move. For the second time in recent days she found herself cast in the role of Peeping Tom. But something compelled her to stay, her eyes focusing on the strong torso, the narrow waist.

Suddenly, he stopped and whispered something to the woman. Then he pulled out abruptly, standing back. Of course, it was Dante, his hair wild, his chest heaving with effort. He turned slightly and Eloise could see his cock, massive, heavily veined and slick with the woman's juices. He grabbed her hair and spun her around so she was spread-eagled on the table on her stomach. Then, as if instinct told him they were being watched, he looked up. Eloise was frozen, she couldn't move, she couldn't turn away. He looked straight at her, his eyes locking onto hers.

There was a moment when no one moved. Then the girl, her head down on the table, gabbled something and he replied, "Si, pronto." Without ever breaking the eye-contact with Eloise, he took his cock in his hand, running his fingers along its length a couple of times and then entered the dark girl very slowly. When he was buried deep inside her, he waited a while before starting to bang into her. He drove on, harder and harder, until the force was so great that the heavy table began to edge across the flagstones. The girl shrieked with every thrust. And still, he looked into Eloise's eyes and still she could not break away.

Her face burned with shame, but she was totally unable to tear her eyes from the spectacle, couldn't stop watching this animal performance. Her legs felt weak and the place between them throbbed and spasmed with a thrilling urgency.

Dante slapped the girl's buttocks—deliberate, open-handed blows which made her shriek in ecstasy. Then he put his hands on her shoulders and speeded up still more, pounding into her. Every time he drove inwards she gave a gasping inhalation.

Suddenly he stopped dead. Still looking at Eloise, he gave a final, savage thrust—then, and only then, closed his eyes in release as the woman climaxed noisily beneath him.

The spell was at last broken and Eloise hastily put the tricycle down against the hedge and hurried to her room. She shut the door and sank down on the bed, noting she was shaking.

The man was disgusting. Shameless. Any normal person would have stopped what he was doing when he'd realised they had an audience. Any normal person would have spoken out.

Any normal person, she acknowledged, would have got the hell out of it as soon as she'd understood what was going on.

She lay down, her eyes closed, her face burning. All she could see was the muscled back, the narrow hips, the jutting penis. He was foul. Lewd. Vulgar. And at that moment, she wanted him more than she had ever wanted any man before. She could only think it was her enforced loneliness in a strange place which made her reaction so extreme, so uncharacteristic. Because Dante de Rufina was a monster. Her hand reached under her skirt and hot tears scalded her eyes as she gave herself release, her mind's eye seeing him gyrating in front of her.

That night, on the terrace, she found Laura subdued and a bit sulky. She wondered if Dante had made some remark about her which had upset his sister. However, after a while, Laura said, "Eloise, can I ask you something?"

"Of course."

"You know your period? Well, when it doesn't come...on time, how long is it before you know you might be...you know?"

"Pregnant?" A bolt of alarm shot through Eloise. "Why do you want to know?"

"Oh, Eloise..." She could see the girl was trying hard not to cry. "It's six days. And I'm so scared. Dante will kill me."

Eloise got up and crouched by the frightened child, putting one arm around her. "Don't worry, Laura, we can sort this out. Just tell me what happened."

"When I...? Oh, it was Xiaoming. My boyfriend. Just before we left London. I was so angry with Dante for taking us all away and so unhappy about leaving Xiaoming. We went to his room when his parents were at the restaurant and we did it. But now I'm afraid."

"Well, the best thing would be to find out straight away if you really are pregnant."

"I won't see the doctor. I can't."

"No, but we can get a pregnancy test. And I think you should tell your brother."

"No, never! He wouldn't understand."

"But if you are pregnant, he'll have to know."

"I won't tell him."

Eloise was faced with a dilemma. Clearly, Dante de Rufina, as the closest thing Laura had to a responsible guardian, ought to know what was happening. But she couldn't break the girl's confidence. She decided to worry about Dante after they had found out if Laura really was pregnant.

The next day, she bought a pregnancy test in the pharmacy in the town and met Laura in the garden to hand it over.

"The instructions are in the box and they look pretty simple. Just go and do it as soon as you can and then come and find me."

"I'll do it straight after school. I've got to go in this afternoon for some stupid exam thing."

As it happened, it wasn't Laura who came to find her that evening, but Dante de Rufina. Eloise had dined and moved into the large sitting room for coffee. The hotel was filling up and there were several couples there, as well as a party of German walkers. She was sipping her coffee and glancing through an Italian bridal magazine, when she became aware of the Conte striding across the room. He stopped right in front of her and flung something down on the table.

"What the fuck is this?"

Around them, conversations stopped, eyes turned towards them.

"I imagine you know what it is."

"Yes, it's a pregnancy test. Which you bought."

"Can we talk about this in private?"

"Why? What can you possibly want to say to me in private?"

Suddenly she was very angry. "Nothing. I have nothing to say to you either publicly or privately." She lowered her voice. "But since it seems you want to make a scene about a very intimate issue involving your teenage sister—it would be just as well to do it without an audience."

He nodded abruptly as if he couldn't bear to continue the conversation and wheeled around, marching from the room. Eloise followed him, her heart sinking. If he was as angry as this with her, heaven knows what he had been like with Laura.

They went out onto the bar terrace, empty now, and he turned, leaning against the stone balustrade.

"Right. Perhaps you can explain to me what you thought you were doing, buying something like this for a child, a child like Laura. She's only fifteen, you know."

"Indeed. And she thinks she's pregnant. She asked for my help. I told her to talk to you, but she was too afraid. I thought we should find out if she really is pregnant first."

"But why didn't she come to me? She hardly knows you."

"If you were a fifteen-year-old girl in this sort of trouble, I think you'd probably want some female advice."

"Well, Jessica was here. She could have asked her."

There was silence while they both reflected on the unsuitability of this suggestion. He went on, "And who is it? Who's she been... Jesus, was it that boy of Fan Liu's? He must have forced her. I'll kill him."

"That wouldn't help much. How old is Xiaoming? About the same age as Laura? And she was entirely willing. You'd do much better to think of the future and how you're going to support her if the worst comes to the worst."

"Oh fuck!" He collapsed suddenly onto one of the steamer chairs. "What a mess. What a bloody awful mess. I can't seem to get anything right with them."

More kindly, Eloise said, "Look, this isn't your fault. But how you handle it could dictate your future relationship with your sister."

"But she didn't come to me."

"As a matter of interest, how did you find out?"

He made a face. "While she was out this afternoon I went to her room to get her dirty washing. One of the many unglamorous tasks I find myself doing these days. I put her nightdress in the basket and then checked in the drawer to make sure there was a clean one. I found this." He picked up the box containing the pregnancy test. "Oh Christ!" He weighed it in his hands, then squinted at the brief instructions on the packaging and gave a sigh. "Well, since you've got yourself embroiled in this, I suppose you'd better come now and supervise it. I'm afraid she's a bit upset."

The invitation was far from gracious and he set out towards the family quarters without looking back to see if she was following. But she was sufficiently concerned about Laura to put her pride behind her and she followed him into the flat and across the cluttered sitting room.

The bedroom was large and airy, with two long windows overlooking the terrace and the garden beyond. Laura lay face down on the bed, but she got up when she saw Eloise and ran to her, flinging herself into her arms. "I'm so sorry, so sorry, but he *made* me tell him where I got it from. He's been absolutely beastly."

Eloise smoothed her hair. "I'm sure your brother didn't mean to be beastly. He was just a little shocked, but all he wants is what's best for you."

"Oh yeah," Laura said bitterly. "If that was what he wanted, he'd never have dragged us away from our home and everyone we loved."

"Yes, and it's a pity I didn't do it a lot earlier. If I'd known what you were getting up to…"

Eloise held up a hand to stop him. "Please, Conte, this isn't very helpful just now. Laura, are you ready to do this test now?"

The girl pulled away from her arms and nodded tearfully.

"I'll come to the bathroom with you and make sure it's set up properly."

The Conte had gone to one of the windows and stared out into the darkness, his shoulders hunched. As she moved towards the door, Laura said in a small voice, "Dante, I'm sorry."

He turned and regarded her with a dark expression, then shook himself and walked swiftly across the room, pulling her into his arms. "Laura, my darling, don't worry. Whatever happens, we'll sort it out."

"But if there's a baby?"

"Well, there are ways to deal with it. You could have an abortion…"

Laura stiffened. "No, I couldn't do that."

"Adoption then."

"I don't think I could give a baby away."

"Well then. I suppose… I've got the hang of Charlie now and I guess another one wouldn't make much difference." Over the top of his sister's head, his eyes, wide with horror, met Eloise's. She smiled.

"Let's find out first." She led Laura away and shortly afterwards came back into the room. He was sitting on the bed, head in hands.

"That was a kind and brave little speech."

"Totally mendacious and driven by terror. I can see my life disappearing. Nothing in front of me but nappies and screaming brats."

"But if there is a baby, you'll let her keep it?"

He shrugged. "What else can I do? I'm like the Pied Piper, acquiring children I don't want from all over the place."

Laura came back into the room, carrying a jar full of yellow liquid in one hand and the rest of the kit in the other. She shook. "I can't do it," she sobbed.

Eloise took the long, thin packet from her and tore it open. She removed the cap from the stick inside and, after consulting the instructions again, dipped it in the jar, counting to twenty. Then she got it out and held it steady.

"How long?" Dante asked.

"Two minutes."

No one spoke, but as the time went on, three heads moved inwards to look at the white stick. After a while, a line appeared and some writing.

Eloise read. "Non incinta."

"What does it mean?" Laura whispered.

Eloise breathed out slowly and with relief. "Negative. You're not pregnant."

At first, she thought the girl was going to faint. Laura staggered a little and made a moaning sound. Then she fell into her brother's arms and burst into tears.

When they'd calmed her down and got her into bed, they both kissed her. Dante said, "Settle down now, Laura, and don't worry about it. Eloise will have a talk to you in the morning and tell you what to do to make sure nothing like this ever happens again."

Eloise looked at him with raised eyebrows, but he shrugged, "Well, I can't do it." After they had moved into the sitting room, she looked round curiously. "Where are the other children?"

"Matt's got them in his room playing computer games. I told him not to let them out on pain of death." He shot a glance at her. "Look, thank you. I'm sorry you got dragged into my family's intimate affairs again."

"I'm happy to help Laura. Of course, if her period hasn't started in a week she ought to do the test again. But it's probably just because she got so worked up about the move."

"Fine."

Suddenly there loomed between them the spectre of the incident in the garden. He said a little awkwardly, "I hope you've recovered from the rather personal scene you witnessed yesterday."

She turned her head sharply, conscious of a blush rising across her cheeks. "It's no business of mine how you choose to spend your leisure hours."

He'd been quite apologetic but this seemed to infuriate him. "Oh, I do so agree. So it was odd that you were in my garden, in a private part of the grounds."

Eloise glared at him. She was furious with him for embarrassing her and for the unjust accusation that she'd been trespassing.

"Of course I know this part of the garden is private. But you told me, if I found Charlie's tricycle, to bring it up to the house and put it through the French windows."

His expression didn't alter. "And you found the trike?"

"I did, down by the fountain. I brought it back."

"So, where is it?"

"What do you mean, where is it? Do you think I'm making it up? Do you think I need to find some excuse for having accidentally witnessed your...your animalistic activities? It's where I dropped it, down by the hedge."

"Animalistic, eh? I noticed you spent rather a long time deciding just how affronted you were. Couldn't take your eyes off us. I think you need to question your motives, my dear. There's a fine line between seeing something by mistake and being a voyeur."

"I was stunned. Absolutely shocked and disgusted. I left as soon as I could." She knew she shouldn't sound so defensive, but somehow she couldn't help it.

He moved towards her, face dark. "I'll tell you what, Miss Iceberg. I think you were really turned on. What happened afterwards? Did you run and find your bucolic swain from the town? Or did you have to fend for yourself?"

Instinctively she reached out and slapped his face, hard. "You absolutely disgust me. I've tried to help you and your sister and all you can do is insult me. However private your garden is, no man with any sense of responsibility would have behaved like that, in full view of the house. What if one of the children had seen you?"

"The children were all away, if it's any of your business."

"And what about Jessica? How would she feel knowing you were...cavorting with other women like that?"

"I should think Jessica would be glad someone was dissipating my lust, so she wouldn't have to be the recipient of it."

"Oh!"

He rubbed his cheek. "You know, that really hurt! Why are women always hitting and kicking me?"

"Because you're impossibly rude." She made as if to leave by the French windows, but his hand shot out and gripped her wrist.

"Wait a minute. I have some advice for you. Loosen up. Let yourself go. Inside that frosty exterior is a real, live, sexual being."

She wrenched her arm away. "How dare you. Let me go."

He grabbed her again, by the shoulders and pulled her towards him. His head was bent, his face close to hers. Against her stomach she could feel the hardness of his arousal, warm and throbbing. Without warning she felt liquid welling between her legs and a desperate, aching desire shot through her sex.

"Perhaps, instead of being a spectator, you'd like to be in on the action this time? What do you think — shall I help to release the animal in you? After all, thanks to that scene in the lounge, everyone in the hotel thinks you're carrying my child."

For the briefest of moments she felt as if she was losing consciousness, abandoning the will to think for herself. She stared into his dark eyes and very, very slowly their mouths edged closer. She could hear her heart thudding and felt an insistent twinge deep inside her. Her lips moistened, parted slightly.

With a supreme effort, she wrenched herself away.

"You disgust me. Your touch revolts me. How dare you try to involve me in your nasty erotic games? I'd rather die. Now let me go."

She plunged out through the French windows and into the night.

Chapter Ten

She didn't see him again for several days, although the children were often around. They'd now discovered the location of her office and were always dropping in—Charlie demanding stories, Laura wanting a chat, Marc sitting on the windowsill, drumming his heels against the wall and asking her disconnected and complex questions.

Matt came in the evening and sat on the terrace. "I want to paint you," he declared, "and since I despair of getting you to take your clothes off, I'll have to sketch you fully dressed. Unless you want to slip into that outfit you bought when you went shopping with Laura?"

She laughed, thinking, with a twinge, that he was very like his brother. So, he settled down with a sketchpad and charcoal to do some preliminary drawings. Dante seemed to be avoiding her, for which she was grateful, and he always sent one of the children to round the others up, or shouted irritably from his part of the garden.

* * * *

Soon, it was time for her to return to London. Arrangements there would take several weeks—the final decisions on wedding dress, bridesmaids' outfits and so on. But everything else, from flowers to food to the cake, would come from Italy. On her first week back in Britain the invitations went out. From here, there was no going back. But they had to be sent out exceptionally early so guests could plan in advance for the trip abroad. Over a hundred-and-fifty people were invited and somewhat to her surprise and irritation, this included Jake.

"You won't be able to come though, will you?" she asked, hopefully.

"Don't worry, babe, I'll be there. That television commercial I did took the financial pressure off for a while. Anyhow, I'd like to see this place where you spend so much time. And if I get a cheap flight, I can shack up with you, so it shouldn't cost much."

"I don't think so, Jake," she said doubtfully. "I'll be working, on duty. It wouldn't be very professional." Unbidden, there came to mind the sardonic pleasure Dante de Rufina would derive if she took yet another man into her bedroom.

"Whatever," he said, carelessly.

* * * *

When Eloise returned to Tuscany, Tamsin and Alistair were due to come with her to have a look at the venue and to file the necessary papers with the Mayor. She was relieved to find that Lady Connaught was too busy with her various social engagements to accompany them, but disconcerted when Tamsin informed her that both Arno de Vries and Alistair's friend, Fred, were joining them.

"Won't Alistair mind Arno being there?"

"No, he likes it, because Arno keeps me occupied and he and Fred can do their own thing."

Not for the first time, Eloise reflected that this was a very strange match.

She arrived with her odd travelling companions in the evening. Separate rooms had been booked for each of them and if Eloise was surprised that Alistair and Tamsin weren't sharing, she managed to conceal it.

On that first night, she arranged for them to have drinks with Ugo before dinner so they could discuss what arrangements had been made so far. She could see he was vastly taken with Tamsin, who flirted with him shamelessly.

"I wish I could do the grand tour with you tomorrow, but sadly, I'll be away on business. But my cousin, the Conte, has agreed to take you round. He doesn't usually do this, so it's a special occasion." He beamed at them and Eloise cut it quickly.

"There's no need to trouble the Conte. I think I know enough to show them round."

Tamsin spoke at the same time. "That would be wonderful. I'm so looking forward to meeting the Count."

Yet again, Eloise was forcibly reminded of Lady Connaught.

Ugo smiled blandly. "He'll meet you in the reception area at ten o'clock."

Dante was smartly dressed in black slacks, a white shirt open at the neck and a black leather jacket. His eyes flickered briefly over Eloise, but then he ignored her. To the others he was charm itself, flirting with Tamsin, chatting about sport with Alistair and Fred. She thought he would have nothing in common with Arno de Vries, but it was as if the two of them recognised each other at once, or what they were. Nothing was said, but there was a strange sense of wary mutual respect.

The tour was even more thorough than the one she'd made with Ugo, and Dante was surprisingly well informed about the place, given how much he professed to dislike it.

One consolation to Eloise was that they were all clearly very impressed. Tamsin exclaimed and fluttered her eyelids at Dante, Alistair and Fred clowned around like schoolboys and even Arno exuded a quiet air of satisfaction. This was much in evidence when Dante showed them the dungeon.

As he ushered them in, he told them, "And this is where Miss Lambert thought you might have the stag party."

"Oh yes!" Fred exclaimed. "Cool! Look at this rack, Ali."

Arno padded around like a large wild animal, examining the restraints and the whips, his eyes alight. "Most satisfactory," he murmured and held out his arm to Tamsin who went straight to him and took his hand. "Look at this flogger. Antique. Beautiful."

"Mmm!" Tamsin responded, letting go of his hand and moving hers down his back and onto his buttocks. "Very nice."

For the first time, Dante looked straight at Eloise, his eyebrows raised questioningly.

Arno said, "You must sometimes use this place—for what it was intended?"

"What, to torture people?"

"I imagine that whoever made this collection had another purpose in mind."

Dante sighed. "My great-grandfather. Yes, you're probably right."

"And if one wanted to use the...artefacts for that reason?"

"Oh, I'm sure that could be arranged," Dante agreed carelessly and then with a slightly apologetic grin at Eloise he added, "If you've seen enough here, I'd like to invite you to lunch. Our chef has prepared a few courses to give you an idea of what you can expect at the reception."

The lunch was a success. Gianni had surpassed himself and Dante was the perfect host. In the course of the conversation, Tamsin asked Dante why he spoke like an Englishman.

"Because that's what I am. I've lived in London all my life."

"And you work there?"

"Yes, I own a club. Play the piano."

"Oh really? What's it called?"

For the first time since she'd known him, Eloise thought he looked a little embarrassed.

"What do you think? Inevitably, I'm afraid, it's *The Inferno. Dante's Inferno.*"

Tamsin squealed excitedly. "Ooh, we've been there. Haven't we, Ali? And Fred." She put down her knife and fork and stared at the Conte. "I know who you are, you're Dan Rufin!"

"So I am."

"We saw your act. Loved it. But why...?"

He anticipated the question. "I thought the Italian name sounded a bit phoney. But in fact, I use the two variations more or less interchangeably."

"You don't use the title?"

"The title is fairly recent and I still find it rather strange. My father was a musician too and he used it in an ironic sort of way."

Tamsin was off on another tack. "Aren't you engaged to Jessica Anthony?"

"No, not engaged," he replied, a little too hastily. "She's a girlfriend. Miss Lambert's met her, haven't you, Miss Lambert?"

"I have indeed," Eloise said flatly.

"She's very smart. I do hope she'll be here at the time of the wedding. And you as well, Conte, of course. Mummy will be so pleased."

Eloise bowed her head, willing someone else to intervene to stop Tamsin wittering on. But another thought had struck her friend. "Why do you call Ellie 'Miss Lambert' all the time?"

"Oh, we were on first name terms once, but there's been a bit of a cooling off," he answered, grinning at Eloise again. "I did call you 'Miss...' something else for a bit, didn't I?"

She remembered him addressing her as 'Miss Iceberg' just before he'd asked her if seeing him *in flagrante delicto* in the garden had driven her to masturbation. Fear, embarrassment and a bolt of intense excitement shot through her. Swiftly, she moved the conversation to a discussion of the honeymoon plans and to her great relief the moment receded.

At the end of the meal, Dante announced, "Incidentally, Ugo is holding a small cocktail party tonight, to which you're all invited. You met Ugo, of course. He's my cousin—well, my father's cousin, and he runs this place. It's in the library, next to the dining room."

In the afternoon, Eloise dragged Tamsin off to her office to talk about menus and flowers, while Alistair and Fred lay on the terrace with a drink and Arno mooched around in his mysterious way. After they'd done some useful work, Tamsin flopped back in the armchair in the tiny room. "Whew, that's enough wedding stuff for today. I was hoping to get away from it here—Mummy is driving me round the bend."

"Well, Tamsin, it's getting closer. There's quite a bit to do."

"Do you know, you're even beginning to sound like Mummy? Don't be so stuffy, Ellie, and tell me what's going on between you and the gorgeous Count?"

"Nothing. He's a very rude man."

"Oh, Ellie! The atmosphere between you is just crackling with sex."

"Really, Tamsin!"

"Well, it is. Do tell me what's been going on?"

Before Eloise could construct an evasive reply, the man himself tapped at the partially open door. "Ah, Miss Lambert, you are here. Your...er...friend from the town is here. Shall I show him up?"

"My friend...? Oh, you mean Mr Sherwin. Yes, please do, Conte. Thank you."

He looked around the room. "It might be a little crowded in here. Perhaps you'd like to take Mr Sherwin to your bedroom? I mean, he's been there bef—"

"Yes, thank you very much."

When he'd gone, Tamsin leant back in the chair, glee etched on her face. "Another one? Oh, Ellie, you have been busy."

Tom edged round the door, smiling at Tamsin. "Eloise, I'm so sorry to come up here without phoning. But I'm on my way back from Siena and as I was driving right past the gates, I thought I'd pop in. You got back yesterday?"

Eloise had come round the desk and she let him kiss her, aware of Tamsin's simmering amusement. "This is my friend Tamsin Connaught, whose wedding I'm arranging. Tamsin, this is Tom Sherwin. He's a...he's a writer."

They shook hands. Tamsin said, "Well, Tom, it's nice to meet you. Any friend of Ellie's... Why don't you stay? We've been invited to a drinks party and you could have dinner with us."

He beamed. "Thanks, I'd like that."

"We're all going to swim. Do you have trunks? If not, I'm sure some of Ali's would fit you."

"As it happens, I've got some in the car. I'll go and get them. Terrific!" He leaned over to kiss Eloise again, whispering something to her as he did so which made her blush and giggle a little.

"No, I don't think so, Tom. Not tonight."

When he'd gone, Tamsin regarded her friend with amusement. "Well, for such a good little girl you seem to be playing a very dangerous game."

"I'm not playing any game at all," Eloise replied, trying to be cool.

"Oh? We've got the handsome writer chasing after you with his tongue hanging out and the dark and enigmatic count striking sexual sparks off you every time he comes near. And we haven't even mentioned the beautiful actor back in London."

"Oh, don't be ridiculous," Eloise said, putting her glasses on and attempting to look severe.

"I'm beginning to think this demure manner of yours is all an act. In fact... Well, let's see what Arno says."

The weather was warmer now and the pool had been open for several weeks. Tom had changed into his swimming things and he and Tamsin were joined by Alistair and Fred, splashing around and shrieking in the sunshine. Eloise sat on the terrace, dark glasses masking her eyes, going through lists. She became aware of someone watching her and looked up to see Arno de Vries sitting elegantly opposite.

"Hello, Eloise. Am I disturbing you?"

"No, not at all." She put down her pen and notebook. "I'm glad of a break."

"I brought you another drink." He put a gaudy looking cocktail down in front of her.

"Thank you."

"You don't want to relax in the pool?"

"Not at the moment. I still feel I should be working. Don't you want to go in?"

"No. I do not swim." He said it with a great deal of finality, then leant back in his chair and regarded her steadily, until she began to feel uncomfortable.

"Tamsin tells me this man" — his eyes flickered towards Tom — "is your lover."

Eloise was flustered. "Well, I really don't know why she should…"

"Of course he is. The body language is unmistakeable. And this is in addition to that narcissistic boy you had with you in London?"

"You mean Jake?" She felt as if the day was getting completely out of control and she might as well go with it. "Yes, I suppose it is."

"And the Conte? Has he had you yet?"

"Of course not!" She spoke with indignation, partly to mask the fact that the suggestion had sent another jab of arousal through her centre.

He leant forward, searching her eyes. "Eloise Lambert, you are a most interesting young woman. I think you have depths. Hidden depths. Tell me, when you saw me with Tamsin in that restaurant, when you witnessed our coupling, what did you feel?"

"I..." Eloise faltered and took a long drink. "I really don't want to talk about it. It was nothing to do with me."

"But that's where you're wrong, my dear. Sex and the response to it, is universal. I think you were interested, intrigued, turned on even."

"Please, I really don't want to have this conversation."

He continued to stare deeply at her, his compelling eyes burning into hers. "I imagine that despite the fact you're running two men at once, you are fairly sexually inexperienced."

This was too much for Eloise, even in the relaxed state engendered by the cocktails, and she began to get up. "I'm sorry, this is just not acceptable."

His hand snaked out across the table and grabbed her arm. "Sit down!" he said, in a quiet voice. She sank down again, mesmerised by him.

"Now listen to me, Eloise. I think you have potential. And if you wish to discover yourself, to expand your sexual identity, to become a fuller, rounder person, you will do what I tell you."

"I don't understand." Her voice was close to a whisper.

"Later. I will come for you later." He got up in one sinuous movement and walked back into the house.

Eloise thought afterwards that it was from this time onwards that her life descended into chaos. She was still sitting on the terrace, unnerved by her encounter with Arno, when Tom bounded up, dripping wet and laughing. "Eloise, is it all right if I use your room to change? I could do with a shower."

"What?" She shook herself. "Oh, of course. I'll come up with you."

In the room, he stripped off his trunks, still laughing and turned to her, half erect. "You're very quiet. I hope you don't mind me staying? Your friend did say."

She smiled. "Of course I don't mind."

"Then come and shower with me."

Her initial reaction was to pull away. But that's what the old Eloise would have done. And she was slightly tipsy. So she stripped off her clothes and followed him into the bathroom. The shower was a big glass cabinet, with old-fashioned chrome fittings, and Tom got the water just right before venturing in and turning to offer her his hand. He pulled her under the spray and into a kiss.

His lips were warm and tasted of chlorine and his hands stroked softly, everywhere. "Oh, God, Eloise," he murmured, moving her round to push her against the glass wall. He kissed her breasts, pulling back to watch as the water defined their contours, then returning to lick and bite gently at the nipples. His hand went down between her legs, the fingers entering her strongly. He lifted one of her legs, bent his own knees until he was in position, and thrust into her hard.

Perhaps because of the strangeness of the day she began to climax immediately. She kissed him greedily as he thundered into her, the water falling all around them and before long she shook and pulsed around him. That triggered his own orgasm and he ejaculated hard into her.

They took the towels and spread them on the bed, where they lay, wetly embracing.

After a while, Eloise said, "You know Tolka Petrela will almost certainly be at this drinks thing?"

"Yes, I'm looking forward to meeting him."

She got up and dried herself. "He doesn't know he's being watched?"

"He must know someone is keeping an eye on him. But he doesn't know who."

"Tom, be careful. He gives the impression of being a very violent man."

Chapter Eleven

Violent he might be, but at the party, Tolka Petrela was charm itself. He held court, surrounded by his entourage, shaking hands with local dignitaries like the mayor and the doctor. Eloise was surprised to see the priest there as well. She'd just introduced Tamsin to the florist who was supplying most of the wedding flowers when she saw a nervous-looking Laura making her way across the room. She hugged Eloise. "Oh, thank goodness you're here. What boring people."

"Shh! You don't want them to hear you. Are you all here?"

"No, only me and Matt. Dante thought it would be good for us. He's bribed Marco to look after the brat."

Tamsin had been half listening to this conversation and now she made her farewells to the florist and turned her full attention to Laura. "So, who's this?"

"This is Laura de Rufina. The Conte's sister." She saw Matt approaching them through the throng. "And here's Matteo, her brother."

"Gracious, you're very young!" Tamsin exclaimed.

"Wait till you see Charlie," Matt replied, grinning. "Eloise, I need you to pose for me again, please. I'm nearly ready to paint, but something strange has happened to your neck. And it's such a lovely neck."

"Yeuch!" Laura said. From some way away, Dante's voice boomed. "Laura, Matt, come and meet Capitano Verdi who's in charge of the police in Rufina. I want him to know who you are when he comes to arrest you."

The two grimaced and, promising to see Eloise later, they went to their brother.

"So," Tamsin said. "The plot thickens. You hardly speak to the brother but the children adore you. Curiouser and curiouser."

"Oh, do stop being so ridiculous."

"And Arno had a word?"

"Did you tell him to do that? It made me very uncomfortable."

"That's what Arno does, make you uncomfortable. He gets under your skin. Makes you do things you'd never dreamed of. Things that drive you wild."

"Well, he's not doing it to me."

"Wait and see." Tamsin laughed as Eloise broke away, plunging through the throng. She felt a hand on her arm and stopped, looking into the dark face of Tolka Petrela.

"Ah, Signorina Eloise…" He pronounced the name as 'Ellouse' which made her think of some nasty bug. "I'm glad I have found you. Are you enjoying yourself?"

"Yes, thank you, Signor Petrela." She sounded a little breathless.

"Good, because I want to ask you something. Next week we go on a little trip in my boat."

"I didn't know you had a boat." There was no reason for her to know anything about him, but it was something to say.

"Yes, indeed. She is called '*La Donnina*.' You know what that means?"

"I think it's what we'd call a loose woman."

He laughed heartily. "That's right. Your Italian is very good. Better than mine and my mother was Sicilian."

"Your Italian is perfect. Sometimes I find the accent difficult."

He laughed again, revealing teeth white against the black of his moustache and his swarthy skin. For a moment, Eloise thought he looked rather attractive, in a brutal sort of a way. She chastised herself mentally, *Dear God, what is the matter with me?*

"Now, what I want to ask you, my dear Ellouse, is if you will do me the honour to be my guest on board *La Donnina*."

Quickly she said, "Thank you so much, Signor Petrela, but I'm afraid I can't. As you see, my friends from England are here. And of course, I'm working. So I really can't go away."

"No indeed, my dear. But your friends won't be here forever?"

She was silent, trying to think of her next escape route.

"When are they going back?"

"Well…they're here for five days."

"Aaah!" he gave a shout of triumph. "Then we will have our holiday in a week's time. Next weekend. An Adriatic cruise."

"No, really, Signor Petrela, I can't…"

"Now then, Ellouse, I think you are working too hard. Taking things too seriously. It is important to you that this wedding should be a success?"

"Very important."

"Then you must stop worrying. Because I can help. I will act as an insurer, a guarantor. So long as we work together, nothing will go wrong. And you can relax and enjoy a weekend of sailing on *La Donnina*."

He put his arm around her and hugged her to him, so hard that it hurt, then lifted his hand to wave to someone on the other side of the room and disappeared.

Eloise went in search of Tom, finding him deep in conversation with Matt. Once she'd dragged him away to a far corner of the room, he listened to her story of Petrela's invitation attentively. He looked grim, but there was a light in his face which he couldn't hide.

"Well, I can see why you're concerned. But it's a wonderful...it would be great if you could go. We've been trying to establish what happens on that boat for ages."

"You actually want me to go?"

"I'd rather it wasn't you. But what an opportunity!"

"Tom!"

He looked apologetic. "Darling, I know. But we think that's the vessel they use to bring the drugs and girls from Albania. To get someone on board would be a real advance in the investigation. Absolutely stunning."

"I'm not a spy."

"No, of course not and no one would expect you to do anything dangerous. But just to be there, to keep your eyes open — to be able to tell me about the crew, where the boat sails, what the interior is like, if there are any no-go areas."

Although she understood that his professional enthusiasm had kicked in, Eloise was piqued by Tom's apparent lack of concern for her personal safety and when, after dinner, he slipped his arm around her and enquired, "What about a rematch tonight then, my lovely Eloise?" she found it easy to say, "Not tonight, Tom, if you don't mind. I missed a whole lot of meetings and phone calls today and I'm going to have to work hard tomorrow to catch up."

He went at about ten, a little crestfallen, but promising to call her. On her way back from seeing him off in the car park, she met Arno de Vries and Tamsin standing outside the front entrance, almost as if they were waiting for her.

"Ellie, there you are. Come with us."

"Why, where are you going?"

In answer, de Vries, who hadn't yet spoken, stretched out his hand and took hers. "The dungeon."

"Oh no!" She laughed, backing away. "Not me, I don't like that place. Did Ugo give you the key?"

"No, the Conte promised me he'd leave the place unlocked." Arno smiled his silky smile. "I think he understands, that one."

Tamsin dragged at her arm. "But hurry, we have to be out by one o'clock."

"What are you going to do?" Eloise knew she sounded fractious.

"What do you think?"

"Well, you don't need me then," Eloise said, literally digging her heels in as the two of them took her arms and began to draw her towards the keep.

"Oh yes we do, Ellie, because…because I want to talk privately to Arno and of course, if you're with us, Alistair won't be suspicious."

"No, I won't play gooseberry." If Eloise hadn't had rather a lot to drink that day it might have occurred to her that it would take more than his prospective bride spending half the night in a dungeon with a sinister Dutch riding master to make Alistair suspicious.

"Oh come on, Ellie, don't be so stuffy. Just for an hour."

There it was again, that word — stuffy.

Arno stopped and put a hand on her shoulders, holding her away from himself, his strange blue eyes looking deep into hers. "Eloise, are you afraid of me?"

She returned his gaze steadfastly. "No," she lied.

"I'm glad. Then understand that I mean you nothing but good. But you have deep-seated problems, severe inhibitions, which will damage you and your relationships again and again unless you take steps to conquer them."

"This is rubbish. Look, if you two want to play in the dungeon, go ahead. I'm going to bed."

"All in good time," Arno murmured, reaching forward to smooth a stray wisp of hair from her forehead. "If you're not afraid of me, what is it that's scaring you, Eloise?"

"Nothing. Nothing scares me. Please, this is an absurd conversation. I want to go to my room."

"But your friend is asking for your help. Dear Eloise, come with us for a while."

She couldn't say at what point she gave in, but with his eyes boring into hers, it suddenly seemed churlish not to agree to such a small request. She sighed, swaying slightly. "All right, just for a few minutes."

He gave her cheek a gentle stroke. "Good girl. Come along, Tamsin."

They walked unsteadily to the steps to the dungeon and went down. With great confidence, Arno opened the door and after a pause, switched on the lights.

"Tamsin, light the candles."

She moved over to the first of the giant candelabrum and began to light the altar candles on them, moving all around the great chamber. Arno found the main electrical panel and dimmed the illumination, leaving only a soft glow around the x-frame he'd admired the previous day.

"Now, Eloise, we'll show you some of the things you're missing."

"I don't want to see anything. You said you were going to talk."

"Oh, Ellie, don't be so ridiculous. You must have known that was just a euphemism." Tamsin pulled her green sundress over her head as she spoke.

"For heaven's sake, Tamsin, this sort of thing should be private. And you know I don't approve."

"I know, darling, and it's irresistible. Isn't she adorable, Arno?"

"She's more than adorable." He looked closely at her, his eyes glittering. "Eloise, we're just trying to help you."

"But there's nothing wrong with me. Suppose I don't want to be helped?"

"Then look on this as what the Americans would call an intervention." He broke his gaze and went to a small bag he'd placed on the solid oak table in the middle of the chamber. "Well, there's no point in getting upset. Let's have a drink."

From the bag he produced a cylindrical leather-covered flask and a set of stainless steel cups. He poured something out and handed one to Tamsin before offering another to Eloise. At first, she refused to take it. Then, with an effort of will, she made herself relax. After all, Tamsin was her friend. They had known each other since they were ten. Tamsin wouldn't let anything bad happen to her. In any case, the more she resisted and protested, the more she seemed to confirm their view that she was uptight. Though why they should care, she couldn't imagine. She accepted the silvery cup and took a drink. It was strong, aromatic. "What is this?" she asked.

"It's a special concoction of my own. Helps you relax,"

On top of all the alcohol she'd had already, it made her feel very relaxed indeed and she sat without protest and watched Tamsin strip off her bra and panties. She'd never seen her friend naked and now she looked with interest at the big breasts, a little pendulous, with large brown aureoles topped with long nipples. So very unlike her own. Her vulva was covered with coarse blonde hair.

Tamsin went to Arno and held up her arms, as if offering a sacrifice. He led her to the x-frame—a wooden St Andrew's cross—and with spare efficiency fixed her to it, face forward, wrists and ankles fastened by leather straps.

When she was tethered to his satisfaction, Arno walked up and down the wall on which the whips were hanging, taking his time. Every now and again he would take one down, swish it about, test it on the palm of his hand, or slash it against a piece of furniture. Eloise watched Tamsin, admiring her naked body from the rear. Tamsin was a big woman, with an old-fashioned hourglass shape. A muscled back narrowed into a lean waist, then her figure flared out again to wide hips and a full bottom. She wore only the high-heeled black mules that Arno liked so much. Eloise noted that although Tamsin was standing very still, one leg trembled insistently as the Dutchman made his selection. Her head was turned to one side and her eyes were closed, her long eyelashes fluttering against her cheeks.

He came back and stood behind her, carrying a shortish, flat piece of black leather. He flicked it into his hand and, leaning over Tamsin, held it in front of her face. Eloise thought he looked like a head waiter showing a diner the label on a particularly fine bottle of wine. Then he turned and proffered it to Eloise as well. "It's called a devil's tail tawse. Look." With his fingers, he showed her how the tongue of the strap split into two. At the end, the leather came to a triangular point.

"Touch it. It's soft."

She reached out a finger and stroked the leather thong. It was indeed silky against her skin.

"Now!" He turned back to Tamsin. He watched until the trembling extended from her leg to the whole of her body. Then he placed the tip of the tawse at the top of her spine and with a feathery touch, drew it right down until it reached her coccyx. He pulled the little strip of leather back and slapped her, very deliberately, on her buttocks.

Eloise watched as Tamsin undulated on the frame, letting out a gasp of what sounded like pleasure. Now Arno began to beat her, each stroke strategically placed, never in the same place, never with the same firmness. Every time the strap made contact with her flesh, she made this noise, something between a howl and a deep exhalation, until all the sounds joined into one and she was letting out a continuous low moan.

Suddenly, he stopped and dropped the tawse, then undid her arms and legs. She turned round and slithered downwards until she crouched in front of him, getting herself in a kneeling position. She scrabbled at his fly, an air of desperation about her, but he pushed her hands away.

"Wait. You wait until I tell you." Very slowly, he unzipped and withdrew his penis, only slightly inflated. Tamsin made a grab for it and he stood back, causing her to fall onto her face. "I told you to wait. Be polite." He turned to Eloise, who watched in horrified fascination. "Our guest should have the first refusal."

Eloise could have sworn that Tamsin, now on her hands and knees like a dog, made a growling sound as Arno took his limp member in his hand and offered it to her as if it were a canapé at a cocktail party.

"No, no thank you," she breathed, turning her head away.

"Then it is all yours, my dear," Arno said, offering his delicacy to the woman on the floor.

Eloise watched in horrified fascination as Tamsin licked and sucked the cock into adamantine hardness. Then her friend turned around and offered up her ample bottom, wiggling it seductively. On his knees and still fully dressed, Arno took her hips in his hands and plunged into her, fucking her hard and without any apparent tenderness for a while before pulling out and going straight into her anus. Eloise winced, thinking it must hurt, but perhaps Tamsin was used to it, because she arched her back and stretched her neck in clear enjoyment, until she came, shrieking like a banshee.

Arno withdrew, his cock glistening and still hard.

"Now, little Eloise, let's see what we can do for you."

She must have shrunk away from him, like a maiden in an old B movie, because he added kindly, "Don't worry, Eloise, you know we won't make you do anything you don't want to. Look, I'm just going to hold you. We love you, Eloise." He wrapped his arms around her, pulling her backwards. She was still dazed, drunk—high, perhaps. She registered the hardness of his cock, pressed into her bottom and the thought of him, of anyone, entering her anus made her shudder with a mixture of fear and prurient excitement.

In front of her, Tamsin was on her knees again and her hands were working their way up under Eloise's short cotton dress.

"Tammy..." she said, using a childhood nickname long since abandoned.

Arno pulled her face around and began kissing her, his tongue probing. She could feel hands on her legs, her thighs, reaching for her knickers, pulling them downwards. She tried to break away from Arno to protest, but he was too strong for her. One of his hands was now moving down the front of her dress, his long fingers on her breast, stroking the nipple.

Now she felt the lightest of breaths on her vulva and gentle fingers pulling at the lips of her sex, spreading them out with a wet sound which even in her parlous position she found embarrassing. And then a tongue — Tamsin, her childhood friend — worked its way along the slit, around the whorls of her labia and despite her resistance, she began to move, hips swaying upwards.

Tamsin worked her way downwards, the tip of her tongue glancing over the perineum. She came up for air and looked at Arno and, as if they had spoken, he stood up and pulled Eloise back onto the table, so her torso was on it, her hips at the end, her legs open and available. He sat sideways on the table, resuming his examination of her breasts. The tongue went on downwards, grazing across her anus. Eloise writhed, trying to get away from its probing intensity, desperate for it to stop, frantic for it to go on.

Back up and finally the warm, wet instrument of torture made contact with her clitoris, now hard and throbbing. Back and forth, round and round. Arno kissed her, his tongue probing ever deeper and his hands everywhere on her breasts.

Something entered her vagina. A finger. Tamsin's finger. And another, then a third. The hand moved rhythmically and Eloise's back arched, her hips thrusting. She felt another hand massaging her perineum and circle her anus, then something — it had to be Tamsin again, perhaps her little finger — penetrated the tight ring. And Eloise climaxed as she had never done before, liquid pouring from her, her vagina spasming around her friend's hand, her voice strangulated until Arno removed his mouth and let her cry out in wonder and anguish.

Then there was another voice, speaking coolly from the other side of the room. "I'm so sorry to interrupt, but I do have to lock up now. Such a bore, but it's the insurance, you know."

Arno and Tamsin looked towards the door without embarrassment. Eloise, coming down to earth after her orgasm, was aware of a feeling of panic. Dante de Rufina.

"Oh dear, what a pity. We were just getting going," Arno said.

"I see. But I must lock the door."

"But you could lock it with us inside?"

Dante thought about it. "I don't see why not. There's a door at the back, which leads to a dressing room and bathroom. And if there were any problems you could get out through the fire-door into the keep."

"Excellent. I thought you would understand, Count."

"Oh, I do. Only too well."

Eloise struggled to sit up, pulling her dress down, feeling groggy and embarrassed. Dante went up the short flight of steps to the door, but at the top, he turned.

"By the way, Miss Lambert, will you be staying, or would you like me to walk you back to your room?"

She got to her feet, resisting the pressure of Arno's hands on her shoulders.

"Yes, please, Count. Thank you," she managed to say in a shaky voice.

"Oh, Eloise, do stay with us." Tamsin remained on the floor, unconcerned about her nudity.

"Yes, Eloise. We've only just begun your re-education."

Dante said. "It's up to you, Miss Lambert."

With a tremendous effort she moved away from the table and straightened her skirt. She patted ineffectually at her hair, walked to the steps and mounted them shakily. At the door, she turned.

Arno bowed. "It isn't over, my dear," he said. "We have unfinished business here." He began whispering to Tamsin, giving her new instructions. They seemed to have forgotten her already.

Dante stood aside to allow her to go through the door and she stumbled up ahead of him. When the cool air hit her, she staggered and nearly fell and he swiftly put out his arm to steady her. But as soon as she recovered her balance, she pulled away and walked unsteadily along the path towards the hotel entrance. He stood still, gazing after her.

"Well, Miss Lambert, you do have the most unexpected depths."

"I could do without your comments, please. Just let me get back to my room."

"Whatever you say," he replied equably and began to follow her again. "I hope you had a very pleasant evening."

She rounded on him. "I did, actually, and I resent your interference. How do you know I didn't want to stay?"

"I'm so sorry. Of course. Come on, I'll take you back there. I'm sure your creepy Dutchman will be delighted."

"No, it's too late now."

"Really? It looked to me as if you'd already got what you needed."

She stopped dead. "How long were you watching?"

"About ten minutes."

"How could you? You should have left. Or said something."

"I was shocked, disgusted, stunned," he said, in a falsetto voice. "I spoke as soon as I could."

This paraphrase of her words after the episode in the garden infuriated her.

"That was uncalled for."

"Yes, perhaps it was. But absolutely irresistible. As I mentioned, you have quite unexpected depths. I shan't be able to call you Miss Iceberg any more. In fact, I don't know what to call you. Miss Lambert is too formal. Eloise is too proper. Ellie is too familiar. Miss Orgasm would just be rude." He thought for a while. "I think I'll call you Lola. Lola, that's good. It seems to fit your new image."

She stalked on a little further then her heel turned in the thin sandals and her legs buckled. He was there in a second, holding her up. "I think you're a bit pissed," he said, amused. "What have you been drinking?"

"Cocktails. Wine. Some funny drink of Arno's."

"Oh really? What a delightful man he is. You're shivering. Here, take my jacket."

He took off his linen coat and put it round her shoulders. They walked on in silence to the hotel entrance and she climbed the stairs, Dante a step behind her. At the door of her room, she struggled with the key until he took it from her and let her in.

"Well, you seem to have had a great night of experimenting. I suppose you don't want to take it a step further? I don't mind being a guinea pig."

"Most certainly not," she responded, rather too vehemently.

"Fine, fine." He held his hands up as if in surrender. "By the way, I understand your bold new image has extended to accepting an invitation from Petrela to spend a weekend on his boat."

"No. I didn't accept. He just told me I was going."

"Oh. And will you?"

"I don't know. I don't want to. But he made it sound like a threat."

"Yes, I know what you mean. Well, don't worry, we'll sort something out." He lounged in the doorway. "Incidentally, I suppose tonight makes us even."

"Even?"

"Well you caught me in the garden and I've just…"

"It's not the same thing at all," she answered crossly. "You shouldn't have been there. You shouldn't have watched."

"I might say exactly the same thing about you. But somehow, I can't find it in my heart to score points off you tonight." He leant forward, very close, until their faces were only inches away from each other and she felt a moment of panic when she thought he was going to kiss her. But after scrutinising her intently, he withdrew suddenly. "Oh hell, you look all in. Time for bed. We'll talk about this in the morning. Goodnight, Lola."

Something stirred in her brain. "Wasn't Lola a man? In the song?"

"In the song? Oh, I know what you mean. But don't worry, my darling, after tonight I'm in absolutely no doubt as to your sex."

Once the door had shut behind him, Eloise realised she still felt rather dizzy. She went over to the windows and opened them, then stepped onto the balcony. As she looked out into the garden, she was surprised to see the Conte making his way down the path. Instead of taking the connecting door from the hotel part of the building, he was obviously going to his apartments via the gap in the hedge and the French windows—the long way round. She leaned on the balustrade to watch him, enjoying the cool night air.

At the gap, he stopped and looked up at the window. In the moonlight, she could see his face break into a smile and he blew a kiss. She could hear his voice, faintly. "Goodnight, Lola," he called before disappearing.

Chapter Twelve

Waking the next morning, she was surprised at how calm she felt about what had happened. Of course, she was embarrassed and not looking forward to facing Tamsin again. But she didn't have any of the feelings of dread and shame she would have expected. After all, she'd been stripped, examined and manipulated by a man she hardly knew and she'd been brought to a shattering orgasm by an old school-friend. But all she really regretted was the involvement of Dante de Rufina and the fact that he'd seen her in a moment of acute vulnerability and lack of control.

She breakfasted alone and afterwards went to her office. She'd been there about half an hour when Dante came in without knocking and shut the door.

"Well, little Lola, how do you feel this morning? Hung over? Satiated? A new woman?"

"None of those," she replied coolly. "What can I do for you?"

"Now that," he said, his eyes gleaming, "is what they call a leading question."

"Please, Conte, I'm very busy."

He moved over to the window and perched on the sill, his face becoming serious. "I've been talking to Ugo about the invitation from Tolka Petrela."

Now she gave him her full attention. "Yes? What did he say?"

He scowled. "That Petrela is...interested in you. Very interested."

She looked at him in shock. "Interested? You mean personally?"

"I mean sexually."

"But I've never given him any encouragement."

His expression lightened. "You don't need to, Lola, my love. You just have to walk about the place being your own sweet self."

She thought hard. "Well, that settles it. I just won't go."

He sighed. "I'm afraid it's not as easy as that. What did he say to you, when he invited you?"

"Well, he mentioned he had this boat, *La Donnina,* and he asked me if I knew what it meant."

"And do you?"

"Of course. And he wanted to know if the wedding was important to me. He said something about helping me, being a guarantor. It was...I think he said if we worked together, nothing could go wrong."

Dante sighed, briefly covering his eyes with his hand. "I thought so. It's the crudest form of blackmail. 'You do what I want or I'll ruin things for you.' "

Eloise's face, already pale and drawn after the events of the previous day, got whiter. "But what could he do?"

He shrugged. "What couldn't he do? Get his people to put laxative in the food, send a biker gang into the ceremony, kidnap the vicar, unleash rats at the reception. Believe me — men like Petrela don't mess about."

"Surely you can stop him? The police..."

He held up a hand. "A gangster as big as Petrela can do more or less what he wants. And although the police would love to send him down for a long while, disrupting a wedding is hardly what they're looking for."

She thought briefly about involving Tom Sherwin, but realised this was hardly the sort of thing for which he would break cover. "So what on earth do I do?"

"Well, if you spend the weekend with him on *La Donnina*, you'll be alone, with only his guests, his crew. And at his mercy."

"Oh, for heaven's sake, don't be overdramatic."

"You think? He's already having fantasies about what you're going to do in bed."

"Oh God! But if I don't go and he ruins the wedding, my business will go under."

"And it won't do this hotel any good either. Just as we're beginning to pull up again." He thought for a long while and then lifted his head. "Well, there's only one thing we can do. You'll have to go with him..."

"Thank you very much!"

"...and I'll come with you."

"I'm sorry! What good will that do?"

"If he thinks we're together, he won't touch you."

"But that would mean us...pretending..."

He shot her a look of irritation. "Well, it would only be for a few days. And don't worry, I won't bother you. I know now your tastes lie in a different direction."

She winced, but went on. "But would he invite you?"

"He'd be fine. We're in the middle of a business deal. It would make sense."

She was silent, thinking this seemed to confirm Tom Sherwin's suspicions.

He moved to the door. "Well, do you want me to ask him or not?"

"Oh God, oh God, what a mess. I suppose...yes, you'd better. If you don't mind those arrangements. It seems to be the only way." As an afterthought, she added, "Thank you."

He bowed, his face inscrutable. "A pleasure, Miss Lambert."

Her meeting with Arno and Tamsin was less painful than she'd anticipated. They'd stayed out of sight—she presumed they'd returned to their rooms once Dante had unlocked the dungeon in the morning—and when she went onto the terrace at lunchtime, Tamsin was lying on a lounger by the side of the pool, dark glasses masking her eyes. Arno was at a table, a khaki sun-hat on his head, coolly reading the previous day's *Times*. Alistair and Fred had unearthed an old croquet set from somewhere and were on the lower lawn playing noisily with Laura and Marco while Charlie dodged between their legs and got in the way of the shots.

Tamsin reached out a languid hand. "Ellie, darling, there you are. Come here."

Eloise went over and took the proffered hand and Tamsin pulled her downwards. "You're all right? Not completely spooked?"

"Only mildly spooked."

"Good. Give me a kiss." She lifted up her face and, as Eloise moved towards her, snaked an arm around her neck and pulled her down into a full on-the-mouth kiss.

Eloise began to resist when Tamsin's tongue forced its way past her lips, but she was too late to stop it. When she emerged from the clinch, Tamsin laughed. "Still not quite cool with it, then?"

As Eloise pulled away, she saw Arno looking at her over the top of his sunglasses. "My dear Eloise, you are a very good pupil. But there's more, so much more for you to learn. It's sad that we're going back to London tomorrow. But next time, we'll do things properly."

"Next time you're here, it'll be for the wedding," Eloise reminded him, trying to inject some normality into the conversation.

"Indeed," Arno agreed, his blue eyes glittering. "And what a great opportunity that will be."

* * * *

She was heartily relieved to see the back of them. As the taxi disappeared down the winding drive, she sighed with relief. Now she could get on with the job. And perhaps at some point she ought to sit down and mull over what had happened with Tamsin and Arno.

Dante waited for her outside the hotel entrance. "Sorry to see your little friends go?"

"Not really. They were a terrible distraction."

"I noticed. It's a...er...novel set-up."

She was not going to be dragged into discussing Tamsin's odd engagement with this man, so she said coldly, "Did you want me for something?"

He grinned. "Sweet Lola, I want you for absolutely everything. But on this occasion, I have news. Petrela has agreed to me coming on your trip. He's not very happy to discover we'll be sharing a bed, but he's prepared to put up with it in order to see you in a bikini. You do have a bikini?"

She ignored the question and went straight to the part of his speech that had grabbed her attention. "Sharing a bed?"

"Well, yes, that's what lovers usually do." He saw her recoil and his cheerful mood vanished swiftly. In a cold voice, he added, "Oh, don't worry, Miss Lambert, I am aware you think of me as the lowest and most sexually incontinent of men. I'm not going to touch you or look at you or bother you in any way. I'm just doing this because it's the only way I can protect my business."

She nodded, still surprised at the vehemence of her own reaction. "I know. Thank you."

That evening she telephoned Tom and arranged to meet him for lunch the next day. Despite his recent revelations, she still thought of him as normal and reliable and she felt she needed some stability. He sounded pleased. "Why don't I come up there, we could eat in the restaurant?"

"No!" She realised she sounded abrupt. "No, I've got some bits and pieces to do in the town. I'll see you at the Albergo. Oh, and Tom—something light. I can't afford to eat any more lunches like that last one, or I won't be able to get into my outfit for the wedding."

She walked down through the gardens, enjoying the quiet now her guests were gone. Matt was in his usual place, painting.

"Oh, thank God, a welcome distraction. Come and sit down, have a beer."

"I can't, I've got an appointment in the town. How are you getting on?"

"Very slowly. I can't concentrate."

"May I look?"

He hesitated. "Well, just a glance. It's not really ready for public consumption."

"Is this the landscape?"

"No, it's a portrait. Not yours, though. That's coming on very nicely."

She moved over to look at the canvas. It was a nude, a small, slight female figure seen from behind and at an angle. Dark hair veiled her face. One foot was raised, placed on the basin of the fountain and she was touching her ankle with a hand. The curves of her body were soft, the light playing off the planes of her flesh, giving the figure subtle radiance.

"So you did get someone to pose for you! It's lovely, Matt, you really are very talented."

"Thank you." He sounded gratified. "It's one of a pair. I'm going to do her full frontal next." He grinned, blushing slightly and looking suddenly more boyish. "I'd still prefer it to be you, though."

"Oh no, you'd need so much more paint for all the extra rolls of flesh I've acquired since I've been here."

She walked on down and when she got to the inn, Tom was outside waiting for her.

"I thought we'd eat here." They sat at one of the pavement tables on the other side of the main door, separated from the others. He ordered some wine and she began to study the menu, but looked up as she became aware he was staring at her intently.

"What is it? What's the matter?"

"Eloise, you do know that I'm falling in love with you?"

She put her hand up to her cheek and made a little sound of distress.

"No, you mustn't…"

"I'm afraid I can't help it."

"But you mentioned someone else."

He made a dismissive gesture with his hand, as if brushing something away from him. "Nothing. It means nothing. If you felt the same about me." He looked at her sadly. "But I don't think you do, do you?"

She looked straight at him, her eyes serious. "I don't know. Everything is very strange, things are changing so much. I'm changing."

"Is it that chap you told me about? The actor, what's his name?"

"Jake. And no, I don't think he's the love of my life."

"Then who…"

"No one. I'm just in a state of flux. Confused. And so preoccupied by this job I can't really think about this sort of stuff."

He lowered his eyes to the menu. "Fine, sorry, I shouldn't have mentioned it. But bear it in mind will you?"

"Of course. And, Tom, thank you so much." Feeling she had been harsh, she reached out and touched his arm. But even as she did so, irritatingly, visions came into her head of Dante de Rufina.

When they had finished their meal, they took a turn around the Piazza arm in arm, and as they got back to the hotel, he asked, "What are you doing next, have you finished your errands?"

She nodded. "I've got nothing pencilled in for the next few hours. I thought you might be able to think of a way to pass the time."

His face broke into a smile. "I can indeed."

In the heat, their lovemaking was sweet and languorous. Afterwards they both dozed for a while and when Eloise got up, Tom was still sleeping, his face clear and untroubled. As she dressed, she looked at him with affection, reflecting that that was what she felt for him. Deep affection, but not love.

She took the climb back up the hill very slowly. No sound came from the fountain terrace and she thought Matt must have gone in. But when she got level, she could see his painting kit still out. Then she saw two figures entwined near the pond. The girl faced her, naked. Behind her, his arms around her, was Matteo. He was stripped to the waist, his tee shirt flung down at his side. One hand caressed a heavy breast, pulling at the long nipple—the other worked up and down her slit, the middle finger extended. His eyes were closed as if in bliss as he nuzzled the curve of her neck.

The girl looked straight at Eloise and smiled. Without a doubt, she was the model in the painting. But this wasn't the first time Eloise had seen her in the flesh. She was also the woman with whom she'd found Dante in an even more compromising position on the terrace. Swiftly, she walked back to the house.

When she emerged from the dining room after dinner he was waiting for her in the panelled hallway, lounging against the reception desk.

"Ah, Lola, there you are. I'll buy you a drink and we can discuss our plans."

"We have plans?" she asked, irritated, then as he ushered her towards the bar, "I wanted a coffee."

"Well, you can have coffee later. What you need now is strong alcohol." He settled her at a table by the open French window and disappeared behind the bar, returning with two large balloon glasses of brandy. "Here you are, my little Lola." He sat opposite her and raised his glass. "Now then, I hope you're all organised, because Petrela tells me we're sailing tomorrow."

She gasped. "But it's only Wednesday. I thought we were leaving on Friday."

"So we were, but Tolka has some business to conduct and it's had to be changed. So pack your bikini. We leave at midday."

She clutched at her brandy. "Oh, God, I'm not...there's so much to do. And I'm still not sure...are we really going to have to share a cabin?"

His face darkened. "You know, Lola, this maidenly reticence would be a lot more convincing if I hadn't seen that clodhopper from the town put his tongue down your throat and then caught you with the Dutch pervert mauling your tits and the prospective bride's fist in your cunt."

Eloise's face flamed at the crudity of his language and in her embarrassment, she lashed out. "Well, at least I wasn't doing it in public. Unlike you, cavorting about in the garden—and with your own brother's girlfriend."

His eyes widened and he sat back in his chair, nursing the brandy glass, now nearly empty. "The thing I love about you, Lola, is your ability to come up with something completely unexpected. But I have to confess, I'm absolutely baffled. Which brother? I suppose you mean Matt. Or possibly Marco. Though coming from you, anything is possible. Perhaps I'm going to discover that Charlie has developed a secret passion for one of the hotel maids."

"That girl you were...were making love to in the garden. She's modelling for Matt. And they were...it looked as if he was in love."

Dante's eyebrows shot up. "So Matt is enjoying the charms of the lovely Ginata now, is he? I shall have to have a word with that boy — that is not what I pay him his pocket money for."

"Pocket money?"

"Yes, obviously I'm giving him too much. Ginata is the local tart."

"A prostitute? But you were..."

"Yes, well, I was feeling a little frustrated after Jessica... But never mind that. I'm sure you're delighted to have caught me out again. No, I'm not guilty of seducing my brother's girlfriend, but I have been fucking a whore." He got up and tossed the remainder of the brandy down his throat. "You're absolutely right — I'm a most unsavoury character. So let's just get this little charade over as painlessly as possible. I'll come to your room and collect you at midday."

He walked swiftly from the room, leaving her puzzling over his changeable temperament and anticipating the following day with some trepidation.

It occurred to her she ought to tell someone where she was going. Of course, Tom knew, but he, too, was an unknown quantity. It might seem melodramatic, but since she was going on a cruise in strange waters with a Mafia Don and under the protection of a man of dubious morals and uncertain probity, she thought she should err on the side of caution.

Luckily, Sam was in when she called. She could have tried the mobile, but the kinds of places Samantha frequented in the evening were usually far too noisy for her to hear the ringing of a phone.

"Lois, darling, I'm so glad you called. I need to ask you about the Poole-Graves wedding. About the centrepieces.

Your notes say peonies and lilies, but Pam Graves insists it's pansies. It sounds a bit weird."

"It would be weird. Peonies. I think you'll find Pam Graves doesn't know her flower names very well. Show her a picture of a peony then she'll be happy."

They talked about the business then Sam asked, "How are you getting on? All well?"

"Yes, more or less. I'm going to be away for a couple of days—one of the regulars here has invited me onto his yacht in the Adriatic."

"His yacht! Wow, you really are moving in the right circles. Is he gorgeous?"

"Well, not really. He's actually very dodgy—involved with the Mafia. It's something to do with a protection racket. That's why I need you to write this down."

"What? What did you say? Bloody hell, Ellie, I think you'd better get on the next plane out of there."

"You know I can't do that. But just in case I disappear without a trace, will you jot down that I'm going on the yacht *La Donnina*, owned by Tolka Petrela."

There was a long interval where she had to spell out the names, with lots of grumbling and fussing from Sam, who eventually demanded, "Surely you're not going to be alone with this character?"

Eloise hesitated. "No, not exactly. There's a party. And I'm being…escorted…by the man who owns the castle here. You'd better write him down as well, because I think he might also be involved in something shady."

Not joking this time, Sam said, "I really don't like the sound of this. Do you want me to come out?"

"No, for heaven's sake! What would happen to the Poole-Graves do?"

"So who is he, this dodgy castle owner?"

"Oh, yes. The Conte."

"You're going on a cruise with a Count?"

"Yes, but don't get excited. He's a real bargain basement Count and he's the rudest man I've ever met."

"Well, you'd better give me his name."

"He's the Conte de Rufina. Dante de Rufina."

Sam wrote it down laboriously and, as an afterthought, Eloise added, "He sometimes calls himself Dan Rufin."

"Dan Rufin? Dan Rufin? But he's the man who runs that nightclub in London. He's always in the gossip columns. You must be imagining things. I think that Tuscan sun has driven you potty, Ellie. Or perhaps it's all the Italian wine."

"No, it's the same man. He's a singer or something, isn't he?"

"He certainly is. Engaged to Jessica Anthony."

Automatically, Eloise corrected, "No, they're just going out together."

"And you're really going on a yacht with Dan Rufin? My golly, you've fallen on your feet. He's gorgeous."

"Gorgeous is not how I would describe Dante de Rufina. He's grumpy, badly behaved and incredibly rude."

However, when he stepped into her room the next day, his mood had changed again and he was cheerful and pleasant. He looked at her luggage with amusement, noting the suitcase, holdall and large shopping bag piled up by the door, a green sun-hat on the top.

"You do realise we're only going to be away for a few days, not several weeks, don't you, Lola, darling? There's enough stuff here to sink *La Donnina*."

"Well, I didn't really know what to pack." She sounded defensive. "I presume I'll need a few smart clothes."

"Yes, Tolka likes to flaunt his wealth. There'll almost certainly be some formal occasions."

"Well, there you are then." She retrieved the sun-hat and watched as he picked up the bags. "How are we getting there?" She realised she'd allowed him to take complete control of the expedition. "I don't even know where the boat is."

"It's moored at Rimini. Tolka wanted to ferry us there in one of his limos, but I thought it better to go independently. We'll take my car. Well, Ugo's car, really."

He led her to an old Fiat Estate parked round the side of the house. As she climbed into the passenger seat, she asked, "Who's looking after the children?"

"Maria's keeping an eye on them. She's got one of the maids doing the housekeeping."

"They like her, don't they?"

"Yes, a lot. I'm hoping to persuade her to look after Charlie on a full-time basis. For a while, anyhow."

"And then what would you do?" she asked curiously.

He shrugged his shoulders. "I don't know. I just want to get back to London and see if I can salvage anything from the ruins of my career. Perhaps if this deal with Petrela comes through…"

They drove in silence for a while and Eloise took the opportunity to study her companion. His hands rested lightly on the wheel and his eyes, masked by wrap-around dark glasses, were fixed on the Strada Provinciale. His dark hair sprang from his forehead, some strands flopping forward. His face was lean, with high cheekbones, a firm chin and a determined mouth, looking, in repose, rather grim. The green open-necked shirt suited his colouring and just for a moment, he looked conventionally handsome—like a male model, she thought. A handsome, bad-tempered criminal, if he was, as Tom believed, a crook.

He turned his head suddenly. "So, I suppose we need to get our story straight. About how we got together. Make sure we say the same thing."

She blushed, bowing her head and contemplating her hands. "What did you tell him?"

"Well, more or less what did happen. I mean, I told him how we met, in the garden, through the children. I just pretended we actually liked each other."

"Oh!" Although it was no more than the truth, she felt as if he had hit her.

"So all you need to do when we're in public is look feminine and loving and resist your natural desire to slap my face."

"I still think this is ridiculous. Petrela's not really interested in me."

His hands tightened on the wheel. "One day when we know each other much better I'll tell you what his comments were when he discovered we were an item. Believe me, he's interested. Obsessed, even."

After that, they drove in silence until just before Bologna. He glanced at his watch. "Half-one. We ought to get some lunch. I'll pull off — there's a place in Marzabotto."

The restaurant was just off the main piazza, small and homely, the food excellent. Eloise thought she ought to try to be pleasant — after all, they were going to be living in each other's pockets for the next four days. But Dante was quiet, almost sullen, and after a while she gave up attempts at conversation and they ate in silence. When they left the restaurant and walked out into the Piazza

Vente Settembre, she could no longer contain her irritation.

"Really, if you're going to sulk like this for the whole trip, it's going to be hell for us both."

He shook himself. "Oh, God, I'm sorry. I'm not sulking, really. Just thinking about what happened here."

"What did happen?"

"In 1944, the Nazis rounded up the people from Marzabotto and the surrounding villages and killed every one of them. More than eight hundred men, women and children. There were lots of children. Some of them Charlie's age."

"How dreadful."

"It was. There's a memorial over there." He waved his hand. "This place still has the power to cast a shadow. Puts our little problems into perspective, though, doesn't it?"

They drove onwards, making desultory conversation. But after a while the effort was too much and they fell into a silence, which lasted until they were approaching the port of Rimini. Then she spoke again.

"I was just wondering...do you think you could ask for us to have separate cabins? I mean, even if he thinks we're together, we don't necessarily have to sleep in the same room, do we?"

He wrenched the wheel over and pulled the car in to the side of the road. "Well, Lola, you're a grown up woman and you must make your own decisions. But if I tell you that one of Tolka's fantasies is to bugger you until you scream for mercy, you may decide that it would be a good idea to accept my pathetic offer of protection. Or you can choose to be by yourself in a cabin on a yacht where every crewman is Petrela's and every key belongs to him."

"But that's disgusting…"

"Petrela is disgusting. And we've got to spend the next four days pretending he's the most charming man we've ever met."

La Donnina was the kind of vessel for which the epithet 'floating gin palace' had been coined. She was white, wedge-shaped and gleaming. "A hundred-and-sixty-four feet," Dante told Eloise. "Must have cost a small fortune. Who says crime doesn't pay?" He pulled the car into a marked parking space, next to Petrela's Mercedes. Before they'd even got out, Petrela's crewmen were there, resplendent in white uniforms with gold braid. The bags were taken from the car and one of the men said, in fractured English, "Please, you come on board now."

Together, they walked up the narrow gangplank and boarded *La Donnina*.

Chapter Thirteen

The young sailor who had spoken to them pointed towards the bow. "Mr Petrela is by the pool. We take your bags to the stateroom."

They made their way along the deck until they reached the open bow area. In the centre was a large Jacuzzi, raised a little above the boards and surrounded by handrails. Petrela sat in it with two others, a man and a woman. His barrel chest, visible above the bubbles, was thickly covered in dark hair. He waved a greeting. "Ah, the noble Conte and his beautiful friend. Welcome to *La Donnina*. This is my legal adviser, Fatos Dibra, and his companion Delanna Lancione." The man was dark, heavy-set and probably in his early fifties. The woman was younger, very slender and elegant, even in these circumstances, with heavy blonde hair piled up on the top of her head and impenetrable sunglasses.

"We're enjoying ourselves here. Go and change. Have a soak before dinner."

It was more a command than a request. The sailor led them back the way they'd come. "You're in the VIP cabin," he said.

"What does that mean?" Eloise whispered.

"On this kind of yacht there's a master cabin, very luxurious and then the next one down is called the VIP cabin. We're honoured."

Their cabin was, indeed, rather smart. Even so, it was small and Eloise noticed with a sinking heart the double bed which dominated the room. There was a beautifully fitted en suite, with a toilet, hand basin and shower. Their bags were already there. The sailor spoke again, this time in Italian, "Will you be able to find your way back to the Sundeck? If not, just ring the bell and I'll come and escort you."

"No thank you, I think we'll cope." Dante shut the door behind the man and contemplated the room. "Not bad at all. And plenty of cupboard space, Lola, so you'll be able to fit your extensive wardrobe in." He took off his jacket and flung it on the bed, then started to unbutton his shirt. Eloise looked at him in horror.

"What are you doing?"

"I'm changing into my trunks."

"But…can't you do that in the bathroom?"

He glanced into the tiny room. "I think I'd do myself a serious injury if I tried to change in there."

"Well I'll go in there then. Just wait."

He sat on the bed, groaning, as she opened her suitcase and then the other bag, pulling things out and throwing them aside. At last, she found what she was looking for and went into the bathroom, sliding the door shut behind her. She looked around. It was minute and she noted that the sliding door and the wall of the shower, which adjoined the bedroom, were both of frosted glass, allowing very little privacy. With a sigh, she began to remove her clothes.

It was rather like undressing in an aeroplane lavatory and after knocking her elbows several times and nearly falling over as she hopped on one foot, she realised they'd have to come to some other arrangement. At last she was ready and she slid the door open and stepped out, depositing the pile of abandoned clothes on top of the open suitcase. Dante stood up, wearing plain black boxer-style swim shorts. His skin was pale, dark hair in a V shape covering his chest and tapering away towards his navel and then thickening and broadening again at the point where it disappeared beneath the waistband of his shorts. She thought he looked magnificent—but his voice was irritable.

"Come on, Lola, for heaven's sake, it'll be dinner time before we get..." He broke off as he registered her appearance, his eyes wide. "Oh fuck!"

She had been brushing her hair, bending down to look at her reflection in the dressing-table mirror. Now as she straightened up and turned towards him, she twisted it into one auburn braid and secured it on top of her head. "What's the matter?"

"You're not really going out there like that?"

"Why, what's wrong with me?"

He looked her up and down. Her bikini was absolutely plain, emerald green. The top consisted of two half-cups, which barely concealed her nipples and pushed her rounded breasts upwards and together. The bottom was brief, high cut and set off her long legs and flat stomach to advantage. She wore the green mules she had bought on her expedition with Laura.

179

"Nothing," he replied, shaking himself. "There's absolutely nothing wrong with you at all. You look stunning. I should think you'll give old Petrela a permanent hard-on. It's just... don't you have anything a bit more...conservative?"

"Well, there's a one-piece costume. But I don't think it's..." She held up something that looked like two broad silk ribbons, fastened together at the bottom. "I thought the bikini was more suitable. You don't think it's too much, do you?"

"No, Lola, my love, the very last thing it is, is too much. Too little, perhaps. Anyhow, it doesn't matter. Shall we go?"

She fussed around, collecting dark glasses, sun cream and her hat. When she was ready, he said, "Now listen, Lola. Stick close to me. I know you think I'm being ridiculous, but if we're to get through this unscathed, it would be as well if you're never alone with Petrela. Understood?"

"Understood."

Apart from the two they had already met, the guests consisted of three other Albanians, all associates of Petrela's and men who'd been frequent guests at his table in the dining room at Castel Rufina. There was another couple, an Italian banker and his wife, a much younger Croatian woman and a dazzling handsome young German, who was apparently an actor in a Croatian soap opera which was also popular in Albania.

When they had made each other's acquaintance in and around the Jacuzzi, it was time to dress for dinner. Eloise said, "I'll take a shower first, if you don't mind – then I can dress while you're in the bathroom."

"Are we really going to have to go through these contortions every time we change our clothes? It's rather silly, I have seen a naked woman before, you know."

"I'm only too well aware of that. But just because your standards are so low, it doesn't mean that mine have to be."

Even to her own ears, this speech sounded impossibly priggish, but she gathered together her things and enjoyed a leisurely shower, washed her hair and came out, wrapped in a towelling robe which she found in the cabin.

Dante lay on the bed, still in his trunks. He gave her a sweet smile. "Nice shower?"

"Very, thank you."

"Good. I'll go in now." He got up and moved towards the bathroom. "By the way, Lola, if you want a laugh, keep an eye on that glass wall. I think you'll like what you see."

Furious and not wanting to comply, she was nevertheless drawn to look at the glass partition. With a gasp of fury, she realised she could see him clearly, if a little blurred. He was in profile, holding his head up to the shower, washing his hair. When he'd finished, he looked downwards. She could see his cock, rigid and hard, rearing upwards. His hand moved down and stroked it. He stopped, turned towards her and gave a thumbs-up. Then he wheeled round so his back was to the glass. Finally, he pressed his bottom onto the glass, two pale ovals clearly visible. She watched for a while as they moved and shook, then with an effort, dragged her eyes away and went on with her makeup.

When he came out, he had a towel wrapped round his waist. His hair was damp, sticking up spikily from his head—and as he grinned at her, he looked like a naughty little boy. "So then, lovely Lola, did you enjoy the show?"

She turned on the dressing table stool and gave him a look of loathing. "For a so-called aristocrat, you're really amazingly vulgar."

"I'll take that as a no. Never mind, I enjoyed your performance. You have a fantastic body. What a pity you have the soul of a virgin school mistress, circa 1950."

She didn't deign to honour this with a response, but went on applying mascara with a savage vigour. Behind her he turned his back, dropped his towel and reached for his jockey shorts. In the mirror she had another view of his naked rear, the long, strong legs, the pale buttocks and the shapely back. And furious as she was, she felt a totally unbidden bolt of desire, which was gone as quickly as it had arrived, leaving her shaking and hot.

They went on dressing in silence and only when she was completely ready did she stand up and look at him. She drew in an involuntary breath. In full evening dress he looked stunning—the well cut suit sitting elegantly on his tall frame and the white of the shirt illuminating his face and throwing the dark wavy hair into sharp contrast.

"You look very nice," she remarked, in a prim understatement.

"And so," he replied, with rather more enthusiasm, "do you."

She wore a cocktail dress in a deep rose-pink silk. Narrow straps tied in a halter-neck and broadened out over the bust, creating a deep V, the swelling globes of her breasts visible on either side of the thin strips of material. The bodice was tight at waist and hip, flaring out into a petal-shaped hem at the knee. Her shoes were stilettos in a matching rose and her hair was piled in soft curls on her head. From her ears dangled earrings of delicate gold and diamond, matched by a pendant and ring.

They stood together in front of the mirror and for a second, he put his arm around her, his hand gently touching her bare shoulder.

"We look good together," he said.

Tolka Petrela certainly thought they looked good together — the minute they appeared in the main salon, he fussed over them. "Look, everybody, my aristocratic friend and his beautiful English girlfriend. Quick, drinks for the Conte and Ellouse."

The evening was surprisingly pleasant. They dined under a canopy on deck, the air still warm. On one side of Eloise was the Italian banker, who was courteous and chatty, and on the other the entertaining German actor, his English fluent. Afterwards, they moved back into the salon for coffee and Eloise found herself sitting on one of the cream leather sofas with Delanna Lancione, the elegant Italian partner of Petrela's lawyer.

"So," the woman said, without any preamble, "have you and the Conte been together long?"

Taken aback, Eloise took her time to answer. "We met at the beginning of the summer," she replied, eventually.

"Ah. So it is not a deep-rooted attachment." The woman was looking appreciatively at Dante, who was standing on the far side of the room talking to their host and the young Croatian woman.

Eloise couldn't believe anyone could be so blatant, or so rude, but Delanna went on. "He's very handsome. I imagine he lives up to his appearance in bed?"

Fortunately, this appeared to be a rhetorical question. Delanna got up and moved towards the other group, looking like a predatory cat. At that moment, Petrela called for quiet. "Ladies and gentlemen, as you all know, our talented friend, the Conte de Rufina, is a professional musician and I am delighted to say he has agreed to perform for us."

Dante made a self-deprecating face, but he moved across to sit at the baby grand piano in the corner of the salon. He strummed a few chords before moving into the Fats Waller standard, *Ain't Misbehavin'*. His voice was deep and pleasant—his hands swift and sure on the keyboard. Eloise watched him exhibit this new side to his personality with great interest. He went through a repertoire of songs, light jazz and from musicals, all familiar. Then he stopped. "Well, ladies and gentlemen, I'm going to do something very foolhardy now and attempt to sing you a number made famous by the great Eda Zari."

There was a burst of applause and Eloise turned, puzzled, to Petrela, who was sitting next to her. "Eda Zari is a very wonderful Albanian singer," he told her. "Your man is good."

Dante sang a haunting melody, a ballad with a syncopated, difficult beat, about love and longing and regret. Eloise watched him in fascination—the laughing, facetious tease had gone. He was solemn, concentrated, even melancholy. At the end, there was a burst of spontaneous applause, which he acknowledged modestly.

"Thank you, you're very kind," he said, getting up. "And that's about enough from me."

"No, no, encore!" The enthusiasm was undeniable. Reluctantly, Dante sat down again. "One more then. What's it to be?"

"More Zari," Petrela rumbled.

Dante thought for a while, then went into another number, more upbeat than the first. Eloise saw that

Delanna had got up and was leaning over the piano in such a way that he would have a direct view down her cleavage. Uncharacteristically, Dante didn't seem to have noticed it.

He finished the song to more applause and stood up. As he moved away, Delanna stopped him, leaning towards him, asking him something, her manicured hand resting on his arm. Eloise felt a twinge of irritation, but Dante's eyes scanned the room and as soon as he saw her with Petrela, he murmured an excuse, broke away and came over and perched on the arm of the sofa. His hand went to her neck, smoothing the little curls on her nape and for a second Eloise saw, flashing over Delanna's face, a look of pure malevolence.

When they got back to the cabin, she sat down at the dressing table to take off her make-up. "That Italian woman scares me. She looks at me as if she hates me."

"Well, I think she has hopes of a relationship with Petrela. And it's quite clear he's obsessed with you."

"It's not Petrela she's got her eye on. At least, he's not her first choice."

"Really? I thought she was pretty blatant."

"You missed the signals she was beaming at you? Really, you must be slipping."

"Really? No, I didn't notice. I was watching you all night."

He fiddled with his cuffs, moving over to the dressing table to put a pair of cufflinks down in front of her. "Do you mind if I leave these here? I don't want them to get lost, they're very precious."

"What are they?" She picked up one of the objects, two gold shapes linked by a fragile chain. "Oh, how lovely. Are they dogs?"

"No, wolves. A family heirloom. The de Rufina standard, you know."

"Oh yes, the wolf. So very appropriate for you."

"So you think the Delanna woman is interested in me, do you?"

"I do. The little Croat girl was giving you the eye as well."

"That's professional interest."

"Professional?"

"Indeed. That's what she is. A pro."

"You mean Petrela has invited a prostitute onto his yacht?"

"Absolutely. I was given to understand that she's one of the facilities. Available to all. You too, of course, if you want to practice your newly discovered lesbianism."

A frosty silence ensued and Eloise went into the bathroom, keeping well away from the glass partition. She came out clad in a black nightdress and he murmured in appreciation. "Silk, I like that." He was dressed only in his boxers and as she got into the big bed, he glanced at her. "I usually sleep in the nude, but I suppose…"

She gave a theatrical shudder. "Oh please do keep your underwear on." And as he climbed into bed beside her, she said in a bright voice. "I'm rather glad that tart is on board. At least you'll have someone on your own level to consort with."

They were quiet as they settled down and Dante switched off the light. After a while he turned to her, lying with her back to him, and laid his hand on her side. She stiffened.

"I was going to say that we're here and we're grown-up and it seems a waste…"

She turned around, shaking off his hand and sat up.

"For heaven's sake! What is the matter with you? 'It seems a waste...' That's all sex is to you, isn't it, a meaningless animal activity you try to fit in as often as possible? Nothing to do with love or affection or mutual respect. Just a snatched act of gratification that means nothing."

He lay back on the pillow, sighing. "And for you it's a dirty, unpleasant chore. I can see you in a few years' time, married to some crashing bore, someone like that deadly dull writer beau of yours. Once every two weeks, with the lights out and the curtains drawn, you'll let him lift up your winceyette nightdress and fumble about with his half-erect cock while you lie in the missionary position, rigid with disgust, and think of England."

She was stung into replying. "What rubbish. Of course I like sex, I just don't want it with you. Ever. Anyhow, only a short while ago you were taunting me about what happened with Tamsin and Arno. You can't have it both ways."

"Oh, the business in the dungeon. But that was so out of character, it hardly counts. I think the creepy Dutchman had you mesmerised, so you hardly knew what you were doing. And of course, once the spell was broken, you wanted out."

This was so close to the truth she couldn't reply.

"Well, settle down now, Lola, and don't worry—I'm not going to trouble you again tonight. But one day I will teach you that pure sex, no strings, no entanglements, can be a wonderful and liberating feeling. I'll give you an experience that you won't get from anyone else, not from your Dutchman, or the bore, or any others you may have up your sleeve. Naked, uninhibited lust." He rolled over so he was facing away from her. "I'll say goodnight now, Lola."

She didn't reply, but at that moment, another wave of desire emerged from nowhere and raced through her body. As she lay there, hearing his even breathing, she could feel twinges of arousal starting at her centre and making their jagged way to her extremities. She was aware of wetness gathering between her legs and her nipples hardening.

This infuriating, beautiful man had equal powers to arouse and irritate her. Perhaps he was right. *Everyone keeps telling me I'm too prim, too uptight.* She wondered if here she was being offered the sexual awakening she craved. But she swiftly dismissed the thought. He was an unprincipled, lascivious oaf and quite probably a criminal. She knew she must keep well away from him. Nevertheless, she turned to face him, thinking she'd say something so they didn't go to sleep quarrelling. But he was already asleep, lying on his back, his face, in repose, looking young and innocent, the dark lashes fluttering gently against his pale face.

Chapter Fourteen

At breakfast, Petrela announced, "Now, my friends, while you have been asleep, our engines have been working overtime. We're now on the other side of the Adriatic and cruising through the islands of Croatia. The idea is to go as far south as Durres, one of the main cities of Albania and my home town. But this morning, we thought we'd stop at a secluded cove and have a swim in the sea."

It was a glorious day and by mid-morning the yacht was moored near the lovely island of Hvar. The party had gathered aft, where the swim platform was available for the braver to dive from, while a broad ladder led down to a raft for the more cautious.

"Come on, Ellouse," Petrela said jovially. "Let's see you dive."

She was wearing the green bikini, her fair skin a little pink from exposure to the sun. "Not me!" she responded firmly. "I can't really swim properly. I may scramble off the raft where I've got something to hold on to."

"You shouldn't give way to your fears." Delanna Lancione moved to the platform. Her sleek costume in black and silver looked impossibly elegant. When she was sure all eyes were on her, she walked out onto the edge, posed, stretched and executed a perfect, straight dive, entering the blue water below like a knife. There was a round of applause and after a while she came up the ladder, her blond hair sleek around her head. "There you are, Eloise, it's not difficult. Come, I'll show you." She held out her hand in a deceptively friendly gesture, but Eloise was not convinced.

"No, thank you. I really don't want to."

"I'm not going to make you do anything. Just come and watch. Then you can practice from the raft, if you like."

"Yes, go on, Ellouse. I would love to see you dive."

Reluctantly, she went and stood with the Italian woman on the narrow platform. Delanna stepped forward, turned to smile at her audience and positioned herself again. Just as she was about to launch herself upwards and outwards, her foot appeared to slip and she staggered back, crashing into Eloise. Delanna managed to steady herself and recover, but Eloise teetered on the edge and then, with a faint scream, disappeared, falling, arms and legs flailing, into the water below.

Delanna put her hands over her face, gasping in feigned shock. Dante sprang out onto the platform. In the water, Eloise surfaced briefly and sank again. "She can't swim," he explained shortly, and dived into the sea close to where she'd disappeared.

The shock had confused Eloise and she splashed wildly, her panic growing. She'd swallowed a lot of seawater and was going down for the second time when strong arms surrounded her and she was manoeuvred into the classic life-saving position. Dante's deep voice said, "It's all right, I've got you."

She felt instantly calm. One hand held her firmly beneath the chin the other was wrapped round her body, holding her rib cage.

"Are you all right?"

"I'm fine. Fine, just a bit surprised."

"It looked as if you took on a lot of seawater."

"I did." She remembered what had happened. "That wretched woman pushed me on purpose."

"I know." He moved his hand up so it cupped her breast.

In her hazy, relaxed way, she registered that something wasn't quite right. Then she realised. "Oh, my bikini top…I've lost it."

"Yes, it's floating over there. I'll get it in a minute."

"You should move your hand," she said, faintly.

"I dare say I should. But I think I'm entitled to a small reward for my heroism."

They reached the raft and, looking up, could see the assembled guests looking down anxiously. One of the sailors began to descend.

"It's all right," Dante called up. "No need for assistance. She's just a little waterlogged."

He left her facing the raft where she could cling onto the submerged steps, the blue water concealing her modesty, while he swam to where the little strip of green material bobbed around and brought it back to her. Deftly, he put the bra top around her and tied two bows at the neck and at the back, fumbling a little. "I'm sorry, I'm more used to undoing them than doing them up." When it was done, he turned her around in the water and lifted her up onto the platform. With his feet on the steps he leant forward between her legs and pressed his open lips to hers. She pulled away at once.

"What are you doing?"

"The kiss of life? No, actually, they're all watching. And we are supposed to be lovers." Seeing her hesitate, he added, "It'll really annoy Delanna."

Without speaking, she stretched out her legs, wrapped them around his lithe body and pulled him close to her. Her arms went around his neck and their lips met. It was not a kiss, but it was warm and intimate and she felt the blood begin to pound and the familiar tweaks of desire between her legs. She could feel the hard evidence of his arousal. From above came a few ragged cheers. Dante pulled away, his face contorted. "Got to stop now, sorry. Even my self-control has a limit."

He helped her up the ladder and onto the deck. Delanna ran forward, full of apologies, carrying a towel. Eloise thought she detected an element of irritation – the Italian woman's plan to make her look foolish had misfired.

"Another towel for the Conte!" Delanna demanded, causing one of the stewards to hasten forward. "You're shivering."

"Yes," Dante acknowledged, his arm around Eloise. "But not from cold."

He took her back to the cabin and got her to lie on the bed, spreading her dressing gown over her. By now she was fine, embarrassed by the fuss. "Just give me half an hour. Let my stomach settle and I'll be back to normal. Please, Dante, it's all right."

He looked at her seriously and gave a curt nod. "I'll come back to check on you in an hour."

In the warm atmosphere of the cabin, she fell into a light doze and was only just aware of his return. Someone was with him and in her sleeping state she half heard the conversation.

"She's asleep." Dante straightened the robe which was covering her.

"She looks all right." The dismissive tones of Delanna Lancione.

"I think she's fine. It was just a bit of a shock."

"You seemed pretty shaken too."

"Not really. I was just surprised at having to move so fast."

"And is that something you don't often do? Move fast?"

"It depends…"

She reached out a hand and stroked the front of his trunks. "It looks as if you could do with some pretty instant relief to me."

He took a sharp breath. "Let's get out of here."

Disturbed, but still not entirely conscious, Eloise turned over in the bed. She wasn't aware of anything else until she felt a hand on her shoulder and a soothing voice asking how she was.

She mumbled something, taking time to wake up. The robe was pulled downwards and she felt a hand smoothing her midriff, moving up towards her breasts. Now she was fully awake, her nerves screaming. Tolka Petrela. She remembered Dante's warning about being on a boat where all keys belonged to Petrela and she sat bolt upright. He was sitting on the side of the bed, his fingers stroking, moving now to her face, her neck.

"So, my little Ellouse, you are recovered now?" His hand swept downwards, cupped her breast for a second before moving on towards the place where the bikini bottoms met the soft flesh of her stomach.

She thought quickly. "I'm better, thank you, Tolka, but still full of seawater. I feel very nauseous. In fact... Oh, I'm so sorry!" She leapt from the bed and raced into the bathroom, retching so convincingly that in the end she genuinely brought up some bile. She took her time and when she emerged she was clutching one of the big white bath towels to her mouth.

"I'm sorry, Tolka. Still a bit dodgy, as you can see. I should be fine by dinner time."

He raised a hand and smiled. "No problem, my dear. I shall go back to my guests and we will resume this...discussion later. Meanwhile, rest, little Ellouse."

After he'd gone, she felt wide awake. She dressed quickly in white shorts and a loose black top. Remembering Tom Sherwin's interest in *La Donnina*, she thought she'd take the opportunity to scout around the boat. Having checked that most of the guests were still with Petrela at the rear of the vessel, she moved down the carpeted passageway. The cabin she shared with Dante and the master cabin occupied by Petrela, was on the upper deck, the rest of the guest cabins could be reached via a small central staircase. The deck below contained the crew's quarters, storage space and the engine room.

Starting at the lowest point, she made a cursory examination. At the end of a narrow passageway there was a large communal room. The walls were lined with bunks, three deep, and there was enough room, she reckoned, to house about eighteen people, although they'd be very cramped. But it was empty, each bunk with a neatly folded blanket and no signs of recent occupancy.

Up one floor and she was in the corridor occupied by most of the guests. As she moved along the thick carpet, she heard a groan. It sounded female. Instinctively, she moved towards the source of the cry, remembering Tom's account of girls being shipped across the Adriatic. Silently, she turned the handle on the door and peered in. At that moment, she heard the unmistakeable voice of Dante de Rufina.

"You really are a filthy little bitch, aren't you"?

They were naked on the bed—Delanna Lancione on hands and knees, her blonde hair wild about her face. And Dante, curved over her like a dog, thrusting, his arms either side of her, his eyes closed in ferocious concentration.

Eloise shut the door quietly and went back to her cabin.

When he came back, she was ready for dinner, dressed in a strapless black dress with petal-shaped cups just containing her breasts.

"Ah, Lola, you're ready. How are you feeling?"

"Fine, thank you." Her voice was unmistakeably cool. "I trust you had a satisfactory afternoon."

He shot her a glance, but didn't speak and went in to shower. When he came out he tried chatting to her but her answers were monosyllabic. Eventually, he said, "Look, despite the fact that I leapt over the side of an ocean-going yacht to pull you from the jaws of death, I don't expect you to fawn over me. But I did think you would manage at least to be civil to me for the space of one day."

"Oh? Then you underestimated your own ability to spoil things?"

"Really? And what have I done to offend you this time?"

"Delanna Lancione," she said succinctly. "That's what you've done."

"Oh really?" His face was expressionless. "Because I speak to her civilly?"

"No, because you've been doing a lot more than speaking to her this afternoon."

He gave her a long look and then shrugged his shoulders. "So you know about that, do you? I don't see the problem. You don't want me. Don't be a dog in the manger."

She stared back at him, icy in black and diamonds. "You don't see the problem? This vicious woman didn't even have the courtesy to conceal her interest in you — she pushed me off the yacht to make me look ridiculous. And what do you do? What you always do — let your penis do the thinking."

"But you don't care about me," he repeated, stubbornly.

"That's not the point. She doesn't know that. You've made me look pathetic and inadequate. She doesn't know this is all a sham. Now she's going to be triumphing over me, pitying me, even."

"I'm sure she won't. I didn't think…"

"No, of course not. You don't think, do you? How could you be so cruel?" Her eyes glittered with tears, but she didn't wait for an answer, sweeping out of the cabin ahead of him.

She spent the evening largely ignoring him, but her fury gave her a febrile energy. She was lively, exciting, sparkling, the centre of attention. Once when he spoke to her directly, she leaned close to him, whispering in his ear as if in shared intimacy. Thrusting her hips forward a little, she could feel his arousal, growing by the minute.

"You're magnificent," he whispered.

"And you are pathetic," she mouthed into his ear, her hand creeping about his neck. "You're like a teenage boy — completely without self-control."

"I don't know, Lola, be fair. I'm being subjected to a certain amount of provocation."

Her cheek rubbed against his. "Yes, well, if it wouldn't spoil our cosy little act, I'd bring my knee up very sharply between your legs."

He winced. "Lola, I didn't mean to hurt you. I didn't realise..."

"Don't worry about it. I'm no longer surprised by your insensitivity." She kissed him lightly on the lips and then went off to dance with the German actor.

After a few lively dances, they were both hot and Andreas led her out onto the deck. It was a perfect summer night; a gibbous moon hung over the water and the lights of the Dalmatian coast twinkled in the distance. They leaned over the rail, Eloise regarding her companion covertly. He was tall and very blond, his hair almost white in the moonlight. He was conventionally handsome, high cheeked and aristocratic, with a typical actor's voice, mellifluous and lilting, his English impeccable.

They talked about his profession and the strange life he led as a soap star in Croatia.

"It must be wonderful to be in regular employment though," she said. "My boyfriend is an actor and he's out of work more often than not."

Andreas looked startled. "The Conte is an actor?"

"Not Dante." She was flustered, but recovered swiftly. "I meant my former boyfriend. In London."

"And you and the Conte — is it serious?"

She gave a silvery laugh. "No, I don't think so. He's rather too shallow for me."

"Does that mean..." He had turned towards her in the moonlight and now he stretched out a hand to smooth a strand of hair back from her forehead. Then with the timing which had guaranteed his position as a Balkan heart-throb, he moved his head downwards very slowly until their lips met in a long kiss.

His hands were on her bare shoulders as their tongues joined in a warm, thrilling encounter. She could feel the jabs of passion, never far away since this adventure had begun, starting in her centre and causing her vaginal muscles to clench.

He broke the kiss and looked into her eyes. "It's up to you."

It wasn't necessary to ask him what he meant. "Yes," she breathed. "Your cabin."

Andreas was in one of the single cabins on the lower deck. It was much smaller than the VIP cabin, but still luxurious. They were scarcely inside before he pulled her into a fierce kiss. His hands tugged at the top of her dress and he wrenched it downwards, exploring her breasts. He stepped back for a moment to look at them, muttering something in German, then his head went down and he began to suck on the pink nipples.

All her pent up frustrations were coming to the fore now and she scrabbled at his shirt and got to work on his trousers. His cock wasn't large, but it was thick, uncut and very hard. He pulled the dress up and tugged at the flimsy panties, wrenching them downwards and making her step out of them. His hand went between her legs, feeling along the slit, pressing inwards. She was already wet and sensitive and she began to move her hips in the same rhythm as his hand, as his fingers entered her. He kissed and bit her neck as his thumb circled her clitoris, his other hand pulling at her nipples making her moan softly. Electric signals shot through her — there was something wanton and out of control about what she was doing, with a man she hardly knew. She could feel herself moving towards a peak and as she continued stroking his erect cock, she sensed that he was close as well. She put her head back, thrusting out her breasts and grinding her pelvis against his hand, feeling the tingling warmth spread throughout her body. And just as she had built up to that wonderful moment on the very edge of the climax, a furious voice spoke.

"What the fuck do you think you're doing?"

As Eloise felt her promised satisfaction ebb away and Andreas stepped back, trying ineffectually to zip himself up, the voice continued. "No, don't bother to tell me, I can see perfectly well what you're doing. Eloise, you'd better come with me."

Dante de Rufina had come into the cabin and shut the door behind him. He reached out and grabbed her arm, pulling her roughly towards him. She wrenched herself away. "How dare you, how dare you! Get out! This has nothing to do with you."

"Sorry, my dear," he said, through gritted teeth, "but as your boyfriend, I think it does." He placed particular emphasis on the word boyfriend and it was enough to remind her of their deception. He took her arm again. "You'd better adjust your dress, unless you want to give Tolka's sailors an unexpected floorshow.

In silence, she pulled her skirt down and stood mutinously while he drew the top of the dress back up over her breasts. Andreas had retreated to the other side of the room.

"Conte, I am so very sorry. She told me..."

"I can guess what she told you. She goes through these phases. She has incipient nymphomania, that's why I have to keep an eye on her. Don't worry about it."

He looked around the cabin and spotting her skimpy panties on the floor, snatched them up and thrust them into his pocket. Then he bundled Eloise out into the corridor and frogmarched her back up the steps to their own deck. Once, she began to protest, but he silenced her in a voice of repressed fury. "Not now. Wait till we get back to the cabin."

When they had reached the sanctuary of their own cabin, he flung her down on the bed, his face like thunder. "You stupid, selfish little cow! Do you want to ruin everything?"

She sprawled on her back. The top of the dress had slipped to reveal one heaving breast and her face was flushed. She pushed herself up on her elbows.

"Just a minute, why is it all right for you to go waltzing off with that Italian bitch, but if I attempt to have a little fun, you play the heavy Victorian father?"

"For heaven's sake, Lola, the only reason I'm here is to protect you from Petrela. If he gets to know you're so easy you'll fuck anything on the boat, of course he's going to move in."

She lay back on the bed, still smarting and twitching from the effects of having her orgasm snatched from her at the last minute. "I wish you'd make up your mind what you think of me—one minute you're attacking me for being too prim and the next you're accusing me of nymphomania."

"Well, I wish *you'd* decide if you're a nun or a whore," he responded shortly. "Now, if you don't mind, I'm getting ready for bed. We're going ashore at Durres in the morning. Here, take your fucking underwear!" He took the panties from his pocket and flung them at her, making them slither across her exposed breast.

They went to bed in sulky silence. Eloise, sobering up, was appalled at what she'd done. But overriding that was fury against Dante. How dare he tell her what to do? And even deeper was an aching longing for satisfaction, a desire so deep it was all she could do to stop herself reaching out for her loathed bedfellow.

Chapter Fifteen

The next day they went ashore at the port of Durres. Eloise was still furious with Dante, even more so when she saw him in deep conversation with her German would-be lover as they waited on the quay for cars to take them into the town.

"What did you say to him?" she hissed.

"Oh, various things. That you had bursts of mild insanity when you thought you were a vampire and needed new sexual conquests to keep you alive."

"You bastard! Surely he didn't believe such rubbish?"

"I don't know, but he rubbed his neck and thanked me profusely. I don't think he'll bother you again."

Her fury was more painful for being suppressed. He followed her into the black limousine, grinning cheerfully. "Try not to gibber, Lola, darling, it's very unbecoming."

Durres was Albania's second largest city and a very ancient one. Always the gateway to the west, it had seen desperate attempts to leave the country after the fall of

Enver Hoxa. There had been rioting and killing during the pyramid selling scandal in 1997. But today it looked quiet and peaceful under the hot summer sun. Their convoy drove along the coast, a rough looking line of rocks and gun emplacements. Petrela, in the car with Dante and Eloise, was quick to reassure them. "This centre is not so good. But further out, there are beautiful beaches. This will be the new Spain, you'll see."

He took them on a lightning tour of the city, pointing out the theatres, gardens and the ancient Roman amphitheatre. Then the caravan of cars swept up to an anonymous looking concrete building, with a fine view across a lawned garden to the sea.

"This is a restaurant owned by my cousin," Petrela said. "Now you will learn about the best of Albanian food."

There was a wonderful buffet spread, astonishing for such a poor country. There were fried, mint-flavoured meatballs, a dish of boiled chicken with walnut sauce. There was liver, eggs, tomatoes, mutton, yoghurt and more walnuts. There was beer and brandy and the potent raki to drink.

It looked as if the meal would go on for the rest of the afternoon. After the first few courses, people began getting up, wandering from table to table. Eloise saw Dante in deep conversation with one of Tolka's Albanian friends. Petrela himself had been pursuing her, at one point cupping her buttock in his huge hand. Looking round for sanctuary, she noticed that Andreas was by himself and went over to him and sat down.

"I'm very sorry about last night."

"So am I." His handsome face was solemn.

"What did he say to you?"

"What do you think?"

"Oh, he told me he'd frightened you off with some rubbish about me being unbalanced—thinking I was a vampire. It's not true, you know."

A smile briefly lit his face. "Of course I wouldn't believe anything like that. But it's not what he said. No. He told me the truth—how much he loves you, how he is always there for you, how every time you are unfaithful to him, he waits for you, picks up the pieces, takes you back, cares for you and cherishes you."

"But it's..." She stuttered in her indignation. "None of it's true."

He looked at her kindly. "I don't think you can say that, Eloise. The man adores you—that's perfectly plain. If you were just ordinary lovers, I wouldn't hesitate. But this is something pure, something special. You have a good man there, you should be grateful."

As she made her way across the room to where Dante de Rufina stood, it was not gratitude that was in her heart, but murder. Just as she got there, he finished his conversation with the Albanian. "Ah, Lola, there you are. I've got to go out for an hour or so. You'll be all right here, won't you?"

"What? No, I don't think I will. Petrela's been mauling me."

"Oh, God, well he does that," Dante said, seeming distracted. "Can't you go and cosy up to the soap star? He'll protect you."

Irritation swelled in her so intensely that she longed to hit him again. "No, unfortunately I can't. Not since you gave him a sob story of your noble love for me and my constant unfaithfulness."

"Oh that. Well, yes, I decided that extreme sentimentality was the only language he understood. He lapped it up—I think you can expect the theme to be all over Croatian television in a few months' time."

This time she actually took a swing at him, but he caught her hand, kissing the palm and looking over her shoulder as he spoke. "Careful, Lola, both your beaus are watching us."

"You make me sick!"

"Then why are you insisting on coming with me?" he asked, reasonably.

"Because if I stay here I'll be pestered by your disgusting friend and you promised to look after me."

He sighed, hunching his shoulders for a moment. "Look, I've got business to conduct. Private business. You'd be in the way. Embarrassed."

"I don't care. I'd rather be embarrassed than be fondled by Petrela and patronised by Andreas."

He scowled. "No, Lola, this is really not a good idea. It's private. Personal."

She wondered what possible business he could have here in Albania and at once remembered Tom Sherwin's theories about Dante's involvement in smuggling. Her face was hard.

"Well tough. You should have thought it through earlier. You can't pick me up and drop me according to a whim. You insisted on coming on this trip to protect me and your grubby little business deals have to take second place."

His jaw tightened and he appeared to make a decision. "Oh, all right then. You'll just have to wait outside. It's all your fault anyhow."

He hustled her out of the restaurant and through the streets into the main part of the town, occasionally consulting a scrap of paper. He strode ahead of her, going so fast that sometimes she had to run awkwardly on her high heels. His anger was palpable. Eventually, to her relief, they reached what looked like a rather seedy bar and he looked at the piece of paper again before plunging through the door.

They were indeed in a bar. It looked as if its clientele was drawn from the port and there were noisy groups of sailors at several of the tables. Dante went up to the bar and spoke to the moustachioed barman in rapid Italian. He nodded, his eyes flickering curiously over Eloise, and gestured towards a beaded curtain, which led to an inner room.

Any doubts she'd had about the place before were instantly confirmed. It was furnished rather like an airport lounge, with chairs grouped around low coffee tables. A flight of linoleum-covered steps led to an upper floor. Young women in various stages of undress were ranged around the wall, their eyes wary, flickering over the new arrivals. Towards the back of the room, a middle-aged man was pawing a girl whose muttered endearments and automatic response was at odds with the deadness in her eyes.

Dante stopped dead and Eloise cannoned into him.

"Oh my God," she exclaimed. "You've brought me to a brothel."

"I didn't bring you, you insisted on tagging along." An elderly woman moved towards him, a cigarette hanging from the corner of her mouth, her wrinkled face a testament to years of intemperate living. They spoke briefly and she gestured to the girls around the room as if offering him a choice. Her eyes slithered to Eloise and she fired a question at him. He shrugged, saying clearly in Italian. "She wanted to come. It doesn't matter—she can wait for me here.

Shocked to the core, she spun round towards the exit, but before she could make move, the bead curtain was thrust aside and a noisy party of sailors came in from the bar. One of them approached her, leering drunkenly and only staggered back when she stepped back directly in front of Dante.

"How could you, how could you bring me to a place like this? You are unbelievably foul."

"So you keep saying, but I did tell you it was private business."

"There's absolutely no way I'm staying here alone," she said. He pulled her backwards and she could feel his breath on her neck. She was also aware of his growing arousal, a hard length slotting neatly into the small of her back.

He spoke into her ear and she was suddenly and sharply aware of the smell of strong alcohol on his breath. He must have consumed rather a lot of the Albanian brandy which had been so freely dispensed at lunch. His arms were on her shoulders, the thumbs digging in slightly.

"Well, since you insist on being involved, you can choose for me."

"I...what did you say?"

"You choose. They all look the same to me."

"I think you're absolutely disgusting!"

"Oh I know that, darling, you've made it perfectly clear. But all you have to do here is pick a girl for me. Then you can just sit outside in the corridor for a while—a very short while, the way I feel now."

She turned her head to one side, trying to ignore the pressure of his erection and trying not to acknowledge her own surging excitement. This was so outrageous, so totally foreign to her. She was painfully aware of the hardness digging into her and as if he read her mind, he murmured, "Unless you want to do something about this yourself?" He thrust his hips forward.

"I...do...not!" she whispered, not wanting the rest of the people in the room to realise they were quarrelling.

He put one hand flat on her stomach, the fingers splayed. It felt as if it would burn right through her and she had visions of having a mark in that shape on her body forever. She was furious with him for placing her in this position, but overriding this was a pulsing excitement. One of the Albanian sailors, bolder than the rest, stepped forward and put his hand on her chin as if to pull her face towards him for a kiss, mumbling something as he did so. Dante spat out some rapid Italian and the man fell back, abashed. In a gentler tone, he added, "Unless the lady wants to, of course. Well, Miss Iceberg, do you want to go upstairs with this nice man? No? Then for fuck's sake, choose me a girl and let's get out of here."

Surrendering to the inevitable, she began to look at the women waiting around the room. She knew she should just pick one at random and let him get on with his disgusting tryst, but something made her drag it out. Part of her had to acknowledge that she was enjoying the experience.

On the extreme left, draped over a plastic looking armchair and dressed in an ill-fitting negligee, was a thin black girl with short, spiky hair. "Well," Eloise said, "She'd do. But Jessica is so very much more beautiful, I think we'll pass on this one. I rather fancy the tarty blonde for you. Well, of course, she would be tarty, how silly! And the next girl, the one that looks like a Russian shot-putter. Now that is exactly the kind of girl I'd like to see you with."

"Oh really, Lola!"

He sounded amused and his hand had now travelled downwards a little so it cupped her mound. It wasn't moving or encroaching but it still felt to her as if it were burning and now she could feel the moisture gathering between her legs. She wondered if he could actually feel the little pulse that was causing her vagina to contract, sending delicious vibrations deep into her sex.

"That skinny one seems a bit unhealthy and the plump redhead looks as if she'd literally eat you alive. Not that I'd care if she did."

His other hand, which had been on her shoulder, now made its way around her waist and moved sinuously upwards until it cupped her breast. She thought she was burning up. He must be aware of her throbbing need.

"Well, little Lola, you're bubbling away nicely there. Shall we dispense with all of this and go back to our stateroom?"

For one glorious moment she thought about agreeing. Complete capitulation, get it over with. Then her brain cut in and overruled her body, as it so often did. "No, I don't think that would be a very good idea. I wouldn't want to shut myself in a small space with a dangerous weapon. Let's see if we can find you something suitable for target practice."

He sighed and moved both hands until they were just clasped around her waist. "All right, go ahead."

She shuddered, her body still revolting against her brain, but managed to pull herself together and looked down the line of girls, who had now been joined by an elfin waif and another plump blonde. She drew in a breath.

"Well, you asked me to choose. I go for the shot-putter."

His arms tightened momentarily. "Thank you, my sweet."

There was a pause and then he urged. "Point her out. You have to point her out to the Madame."

"It's nothing to do with me."

"Oh but it is. Your choice. Do it, Lola, or we'll be here all night."

The elderly woman was looking at them enquiringly and Eloise straightened up and pointed. "My...my companion would like to choose this young woman — if she can bear it. Tell her it won't be pleasant. Not a lot of fun."

"She is not paid to have fun," the Madame retorted, in execrable Italian.

The girl smiled, showing large, slightly discoloured teeth. She was big — Eloise estimated that in Britain, she'd be a size twenty-two or twenty-four. Mousy brown hair reached to plump shoulders and she wore a travesty of a cowgirl outfit, in browny-orange suede, with a tattered fringe at the hem and on the bulging bikini top. Dante muttered, "Our hostess says she has hidden talents."

"She'd need them."

The girl led them up the stairs, Dante shepherding Eloise in front of himself. The sailors gave a ragged cheer as the party disappeared onto the upper floor. There was a long corridor, lined with wooden doors and the large young woman took them towards one at the end. Before she entered, she muttered something incomprehensible to Dante and gestured to a couch against the wall at the end of the hallway. It was empty except for an ancient, wrinkled man in a grubby white robe, who seemed to be asleep. The Conte took Eloise's shoulders and pushed her towards the seat. "Off you go, sweetheart. I won't be long."

Reluctantly, Eloise moved towards the couch and sat down. Almost immediately, the elderly sleeper woke up and jabbering in words she couldn't understand, but whose sense was all too obvious, he flung himself at her. Eloise screamed, pushing him away and averting her gaze from the scraggy penis, which he had dragged from beneath the hem of his garment, holding it tight in a grubby fist.

The girl had opened the door of the room, but they hadn't yet entered. Dante was at Eloise's side immediately. The old man had bounced back from her push and had fallen across her, his toothless gums seeking out her breasts. Dante picked him up and gently deposited him at the end of the couch. "Not today, Grandfather. She's mine."

He held his hand out to Eloise, now panting and ruffled. "Come on, you'd better come in. I hope you know what a nuisance you're being."

"I hope you know what an insufferable pig you are."

"Oh, very sophisticated and witty. Come along." He ushered her into the small room, saying something to the girl. She responded in heavily accented Italian. "You can sit over there." He gestured towards a tatty armchair by the narrow window. The room was like a cell, furnished with a wooden double bed with a thin cotton cover, a side-table against a wall with a small mirror and a stark hand basin.

Now Eloise was inside and the enormity of it all began to sink in. "For heaven's sake, Dante, this is absolutely outrageous. I can't..."

"What can't you do?" he growled roughly, propelling her across the room and making her sit in the chair. "You insisted on staying with me, now sit there and close your eyes until I've finished. Unless, of course, you want to watch. I forgot that you get your kicks from watching."

A furious denial rose to her lips, but then she recalled his performance in the garden and before that, the scene in the ladies loo involving Tamsin and Arno. She didn't think being the innocent viewer of these episodes made her a voyeur, but the delay was fatal and by the time she'd thought of a response, he had turned away and was addressing the shot-putter.

She couldn't hear this exchange, but saw the woman glancing at her a little dubiously. Dante turned. "Well, thank you very much, Lola. Because of you I have to pay extra."

She'd recovered herself by now. "I don't give a damn. I hope she takes you for all she can get. You disgust me."

"I know," he said, turning away pointedly. "That's why we're here."

Dante and the shot-putter faced each other at the end of the bed and in response to a few words, the girl reached behind her and fumbled with the cowgirl top. When she'd unfastened it, she peeled it away from her breasts, revealing them in all their magnificence. They were huge. Eloise, her eyes drawn to them, thought that although it was a truism to describe such orbs as being like melons, that's undoubtedly what they resembled.

Dante regarded them in awe, then stretched both his hands out and hefted them gently, as if weighing them. He lowered his head and used his tongue to touch the nipples—large brown protuberances the size of thimbles. His hands worked and kneaded and after a while his body shuddered suddenly and he pulled back and began to remove his clothes. He stepped out of his beige canvas deck shoes, quickly removing his dark red tee shirt and white cotton slacks and stood, naked, running his hand up and down the magnificent cleavage.

Eloise had been sitting with her eyes shaded but now she again felt compelled to look. She thought if he glanced at her, she could soon feign sleep, but now she could see he was totally unaware of her presence.

He was transfixed by the huge breasts. But Eloise herself had eyes only for Dante and she drew in a breath at the sheer magnificence of his physique. His pale body had coloured a little in the sun, but not much. His whole torso was covered in black fur, in a sort of egg-timer pattern— broad across his chest, narrowing to a strip down his flat tummy and broadening out again over his genitals. His penis jutted out and from her vantage point she could see its hardness and even witness the slight throbbing in the massive veins that supported it. His long, strong legs were slightly apart and he rocked slightly as his hands blindly manipulated the giant mammaries.

After a while, the girl removed the skirt, revealing huge thighs and a bottom inadequately clad in a tiny black thong. She sank to her knees and took the purple head of his cock between her lips.

Eloise watched in fascination as the big, red-lipsticked mouth formed a stretchy O shape around his shaft and began to move up and down it rhythmically, progressing further down at each thrust. Despite her recent experiences, Eloise had never seen anyone deliver a blowjob and she'd never really been sure she was doing it right. It wasn't the kind of thing you could ask a girlfriend about—well, Eloise wouldn't, anyhow. And now she had a ringside seat while an expert, a professional, performed.

Dante stood still, his hips a little thrust forward, letting the girl do the work. She took it slowly, swaying slightly.

From her armchair, Eloise could hear the sticky sound of lips on flesh. As the red mouth reached his pubic hair, she could see the swollen balls bounce with each steady slide.

She was so close she could see when they began to draw inwards and up. The shot-putter must have been aware of it as well, because she pulled back and swiftly pinched the head of his penis just below the glans, with her other hand pulling his balls downwards slightly. It looked painful and he reacted like someone coming out of a trance. The girl murmured something to him and she moved over to the bed, Dante following her like a priapic sheep.

The shot-putter lay down slightly at an angle across the bed, her head towards Eloise. She murmured to Dante as she writhed seductively, squeezing the massive breasts together. Still transfixed, he clambered onto her, kneeling astride her body. Eloise reflected that it was only because he was such a tall man that he was able to straddle her at all.

Now she watched with open fascination as he moved up towards the woman's head. With a jab of revulsion and excitement, she thought he was going to ejaculate over her face. But the shot-putter had other ideas. She pushed her breasts together again, urging him on. With a groan, Dante leant forward and thrust his cock into her cleavage.

From her vantage point, all Eloise could see was the heaving mass of flesh that was the shot-putter and the dark form leaning over her. The mounds of her breasts were pressed together like a huge, white blancmange. Then she saw the purple head of Dante's penis emerge from the cleft, like some primeval animal coming out of a cave. It was one of the most titillating things she had ever seen.

After a few minutes of thrusting, Dante jerked as if electricity had been run through him. She could see white liquid welling up at the centre of the purple tip and at that moment, he pulled upwards, letting his semen spray over the massive breasts and the woman's willing face.

It seemed to go on for a long time and when he had finished, he reached forward and massaged the liquid into the swollen flesh, his fingers circling those extraordinary nipples.

He loomed over the girl, his head hanging, black curls wet with sweat. Eloise felt herself getting hot all over, a flush that rose from her stomach and spread outwards. She was appalled and disgusted, but her overriding feeling was one of extreme arousal.

The woman sat up, her hand going to his cock and she said something which Eloise couldn't hear. She scrabbled in the bedside drawer and presented him with a condom packet. Then she got on her hands and knees, presenting her bottom to him. Dante climbed onto the floor and put on the condom. Eloise couldn't drag her eyes from the girl's large, moist slit, as he braced his feet and put the head of his cock against it. He made a few little jabs, then drove home, making the massive buttocks shake. He fucked her hard for what seemed like ten or fifteen minutes, the sweat pouring from him. The woman was grunting like a pig, her face red and shiny, her mouth a wide O shape of lust and pleasure.

Eloise saw the moment when he came, saw his balls tighten and lift and his buttocks contract. He thrust hard into the shot-putter and she gave a high-pitched scream as she climaxed herself, wobbling like jelly in an extreme of ecstasy. They lay together, shuddering for a while, then Dante got up. He dressed swiftly and took some notes from his wallet. The girl had rolled into a sitting position and now she shook her head. "No, you pay the madam. Downstairs."

"I know. This is for you." He took her hand and kissed it in an incongruously old-fashioned gesture, then folded her fingers round the money before turning towards the window. "Come on, Lola, I think you've had enough excitement for one day."

Downstairs, Dante conveyed to the bartender that they required a taxi and within a short while a battered saloon car arrived outside. Eloise got in first, still quivering with a mixture of shock, disapproval and arousal.

* * * *

They managed to get through the remainder of the trip without talking to each other at all, except for the occasional grunted instruction in their cabin.

On the last night, as they approached the Italian coast, there was a grand farewell dinner. Eloise was down to her last outfit, a stunning green sheath dress, strapless and knee-length. She danced with Andreas, who seemed to be regretting his earlier distancing of himself from her.

In the corner of the room, Petrela patted Dante's shoulder, his eyes fixed on Eloise's flushed, laughing face.

"God, Conte, she's beautiful. You're a very lucky man."

Dante had been drinking solidly all evening. "Yes, she is wonderful."

"I would give anything to be in your shoes — to be in your bed. Anything."

"I don't think you would, really, Tolka."

"Oh, but I would. Perhaps, when we finalise this business..."

That night, when they were in bed and the light was out, Dante rolled over and reached for her. "Lola, please…"

"Please what?" Her voice was tight and sharp. "I suppose you haven't exercised your libido for at least fifteen hours. Why don't you go and find someone who cares? I bet that Italian bitch would give you a quickie on the sun-deck."

He sighed, rolling onto his back. "You really are a sour little person, aren't you? What a rotten trick nature played on you—loading so much sweetness and beauty into one package, then giving it such a bitter, uptight personality."

"How dare you? How dare you criticise me? You are quite disgusting—your behaviour is beyond anything remotely acceptable. How could any man justify taking a respectable woman to a brothel and performing in front of her?"

"Yes, but you liked it, didn't you? I saw you. You really got off on it."

She turned away from him. "I was revolted. I don't want to talk about it, or to you, any more."

The drive home the next day was accomplished in silence. The wedding was now less than a week away and Eloise was immediately plunged into frantic last-minute planning. She only saw Dante in the distance, for which she was glad, but he filled her dreams in the most obscene manner.

"It must be because I'm under stress," she told herself.

Chapter Sixteen

On the Wednesday before the wedding, Ugo found her in her usual place on the terrace. "Ah, Miss Lambert. I just wanted to remind you that for the next few days the hotel is given over to a private function. You might want to...perhaps it would be as well to stay in your room in the evenings."

"Oh, yes, Maria mentioned something. It's that re-enactment you told me about, isn't it? The wedding of Rodolfo and Isabella?"

"That's it." His eyes slid away from her face. "The last one, if Dante gets his way."

"I'm surprised he's not all for it," she replied in a brittle voice.

"Yes. But he insists that it stops. It's ironic, he's been away all his life and now he comes here, demanding... Anyhow, the place will fill up with a different sort of clientele. Men...of a certain type. Associates of Tolka Petrela. We would not normally allow anyone who wasn't connected with the event to remain in the hotel. So I must ask you to be discreet—for your own benefit. It's only for two days and then we'll be able to turn our full attention to your own function."

"What about the children?"

"The children? Oh, the offspring of the late Conte. I believe Dante is sending them away to our aunt in Rome."

Eloise was totally preoccupied with preparations, faxes winging their way to the office in London. She was in the office putting together a final menu when the door opened and Dante came in, shutting it quietly behind him. He seemed awkward, not his usual confident self.

"Lola. How are you?"

"Well, thank you," she answered cautiously. They had not spoken since the trip on *La Donnina*.

"Everything under control?"

"I hope so."

"Good, good." He moved to the windowsill and perched on it. He seemed distracted and his face was pale. "I'm afraid I have a problem that I need some help with."

"Really?" She spoke coolly.

"It involves the children...well, Laura."

She turned round to face him more fully. "All right, you have my attention now."

He drew his hand across his face. She thought he looked exhausted.

"You know they're holding this ridiculous pantomime the day after tomorrow...the wedding? Well, I didn't want the children around with all the Mafiosi and others. So I sent them off to my aunt's apartment in Rome. They went yesterday—I drove them to the bus, they were going into Florence to get the train."

"What happened?" She was alarmed now.

"Matt called me late last night. He said that as they got off the bus, two men approached them. They told him I'd sent them to collect Laura, that she had to come back to the Castle."

"Surely he didn't let her go?"

"He said he thought it would be all right, but in any case, it was over before he could do anything about it. One of the men grabbed Laura and bundled her into a car. The other told him not to worry — they'd take care of her. Matt recognised them, he'd seen them around the hotel."

"Petrela..." It was scarcely more than a breath.

"Of course, Petrela." He bowed his head, covering his face with his hands, then straightened up again. "This morning Fatos Dibra came to see me. You remember him, from the boat?"

"I remember his girlfriend," Eloise said dryly.

"Yes, well. You know how they talk. That elliptical way, hinting, not actually stating things outright? Well, he made it clear that they have Laura. She's being held somewhere near here."

"Oh God, she'll be so scared."

"I know. Christ, I know. Anyhow, Dibra indicated that she'd be given back to me, without being touched, but only if..."

"What? What on earth does he want?"

Dante sighed, shifting his feet. "He wants to change the arrangements for the ceremony of Rodolfo and Isabella. He wants me to take part."

There was a silence and she said, "He wants you to perform? To be Rodolfo? The rapist?"

"That's right."

"Well...I can see it might be embarrassing. But for you... I mean, you're not a shrinking violet, are you? Horrible to give in to blackmail, but surely it would be worth it to protect Laura?"

"But of course. I'll do anything—anything to make sure my sister is safe. But that isn't all they want."

"Oh?"

"No." His voice was grim. "There's more. The real reason for snatching her, what this is all about. They want someone else to take the part of Isabella. And that's you. Petrela wants you to be the star of the ceremony."

There was a long, horrified silence.

At last, she spoke. "Petrela wants me...me...to submit myself to a pornographic performance in front of a whole lot of gangsters?"

He nodded, his eyes fixed on her face. "That's just what he wants. He doesn't care about me of course. He wants to see you naked and penetrated. He thinks we're together— that's the only reason I'm included."

"But...it's outrageous. You must go to the police."

He sighed. "Lola, have you any idea how strong Petrela's influence is around here? The police chief is going to be a guest."

"Well, get the police in Rome onto it then."

He got off the windowsill and stood up. "It was made quite clear to me that any attempt to bring in outside help would cause immediate punishment."

"What sort of punishment?"

"I don't know. But as he left, Dibra said, 'I assume your little sister is a virgin?' I think the inference is clear."

"Dante, that's...you can't allow this. There must be something you can do, someone you can turn to. You mustn't submit to blackmail."

"What happened to, 'Anything would be worth it to protect Laura'? Oh, of course, that was just when it was me who was required to make a fool of himself."

"I'm sorry. But you're a man—it's different. In any case, I was wrong—you can't let him get away with this. You must get help."

"No!" His voice was urgent. "At the moment I'm not interested in some abstract notion of justice. All I care about is getting Laura back unscathed. For God's sake, Lola, she's a child and I brought her here. I removed her from London and brought her to Italy because I thought she'd be safer. This is my fault."

"I don't get it. I thought you and Petrela were friends. Associates. You're doing deals with him."

He waved his hand dismissively. "You don't understand how Petrela works. He won't see this as damaging any relationship he might have with me. It's just how he operates. He wants something, he uses leverage, he gets it. He sees it as the natural order of things. Afterwards it will be as if it never happened." Dante moved forwards, his gaze fixed intently on her. "So, are you going to help me?"

She regarded him through narrowed eyes. "This is all so unlikely. Are you sure it isn't just some elaborate plan to get me into bed? Because you don't like to be thwarted?"

"For fuck's sake, Lola!" he exploded. "Do you really think I'd play that sort of game with my sister's life? What sort of a monster do you think I am?"

"I don't know," she admitted. He seemed entirely sincere. "I just don't know."

"Christ, you really do despise me, don't you? Well, look, you don't have to like me to do this for me. In fact, it might suit your weird puritanical mind. This way, you'd be sacrificing yourself for a noble cause. And getting what your baser nature really wants at the same time."

She was irritated now. "God, you are so smug, so over-confident. What makes you think my baser nature wants to go to bed with you? Even my baser nature is more refined than you are."

"Well, that's not quite what I meant. But actually, when you look at it, we are an unlovely couple. I'm sexually incontinent—is that how you would describe it? And you're an impossibly self-righteous prig."

Icily, she stood up. "I think you should leave now. And try to find a more conventional way to get yourself out of this mess. I'm sure you're over-dramatising the situation and when you're capable of rational thought you'll see there's a better route to take."

He was furious, white with anger. "So you refuse to help me?"

"I refuse to be dragged into your ludicrous games, that's correct."

At the door, he turned and spoke with an effort. "Lola, I'm going to ignore everything you've just said. I'm sure when you reflect on the situation, you'll change your mind. You must change your mind. I'll be in the office. However you feel about me, you have to think about Laura. Concentrate on her. Please."

When he'd gone, she walked over to the window, looking blindly at the Tuscan landscape spread out before her. She put her hands up to her mouth, then moved them away to examine them, noting they were shaking.

The most shocking thing was that Laura was being held, that she was in danger, that she might be afraid. She ran through the options. The police? But Dante thought they'd be slow to act because of Petrela's involvement. They mustn't do anything which would endanger Laura any further. What about Tom Sherwin? She'd spoken to him on the phone to give an account of the voyage on *La Donnina*. But she felt instinctively that this wouldn't be the sort of incident for which he'd be prepared to abandon his cover. Not even to save the honour of a kidnapped teenager. Especially as he thought Dante and Petrela were working together.

But all the time, her concern for the girl was obscured by thoughts of Dante de Rufina's proposition. Now the man himself had gone, she was able to consider it. She had no idea why Dante made her so cross, but once he was no longer in her presence, her irritation dissipated as if by magic.

What had he said? "You'd be sacrificing yourself for a noble cause. And getting what your baser nature really wants at the same time." And he wanted her to perform, to act out an ancient rape—a rape that had led to love. He wanted to make love to her in front of Petrela and his cronies—to bare her flesh and expose her most secret places in that dark dungeon to a group of sweaty, excited men.

She moved a hand swiftly to her breasts, trying to contain the insistent twinges of desire. The nipples were hard and prominent through the thin fabric of her bra and dress. Between her legs she could feel the pulse beginning, that steady thrumming of her body which Dante so often evoked. And which she'd always managed to resist.

She sat down, forcing herself to confront her deepest feelings. What was it about Dante that turned her into the icy prude he so despised? She'd been ready to go to bed with Tom when she scarcely knew him, and with Andreas on a few days' acquaintanceship. "I'm not hung-up sexually," she told herself. "I may not be a wild woman, like Sammy. But I'm fairly adventurous."

But she had shared a bed with Dante de Rufina and he had propositioned her nightly. All she had needed to do was to reach out a hand and he would have been hers. But she had resolutely turned away from him, even when her flesh was crying out for his touch.

She shook her head. Perhaps it was because of his arrogance, his high-handed attitude. Or perhaps, she admitted, she feared getting any closer to him. Because any woman who fell under his spell would be doomed to unhappiness and disappointment.

But here it was, an opportunity to be as wild and uninhibited as she liked, without any ties or commitment on either side and the bonus of it being all in a good cause. And she would never again be able to characterise her sex life as boring. She stood up again, smiling a little secret smile to herself and then, as if to pacify the prudish side of her nature, she said out loud, "For Laura. I'll do it for Laura." And she made her way to Dante's office.

He was sitting in a high-backed leather chair, watching the open door, and when she appeared he let out an audible sigh.

"Thank you, Lola," he said, without waiting for her to speak. "I'm beyond gratitude. I won't forget this."

She sat down. "You'd better tell me what it involves."

"You know the story?"

She nodded. "Ugo told me."

"Basically, this strange little playlet is the culmination of a day of excess. They come in the morning, they eat and drink for hours and after the performance has got them in the mood, there are girls to keep them happy."

She made a small sound and he looked up quickly. "Oh, I won't let anyone touch you. That's absolutely understood. No, Ugo brings in a busload of girls, usually from Florence. One was due to play the part of Isabella, so she might be a bit pissed off."

"But what do I have to do? You called it a playlet—does that mean I have to learn lines?"

"No, nothing like that. We just improvise—your Italian is good enough for that."

"So talk me through it."

"Right. There's a costume, of course—a white gown, veil, the works. Hardly authentic, but the whole thing has become very standardised. They know what they like to see and they want it year after year. You'll walk in a procession towards the keep..."

"A procession? Who else?"

"You have attendants. Ugo's tarts."

"Oh."

"At some point I'll sweep down and carry you off to the dungeon. The girls will take you onto the stage—there's a rough set on there, a bed, chairs, a little prie-dieu. They leave you and you kneel down to pray. They love that, for some reason. Then I...Rodolfo...come in. And we playact a rape."

"What...what...?"

He guessed what she was trying to say. "Everything. Rodolfo makes Isabella fellate him and then he, er...fucks her. It's quite rough, they want to see violence. There's blood. Because he's taken her virginity. Fake blood, of course. Afterwards he goes down on her and finally takes her anally. At the end, the suggestion is that she's beginning to enjoy it."

"No!"

He smiled humourlessly. "Why, because you could never enjoy sex with me?"

"No, I meant the anal sex. I don't… I've never…"

His demeanour had been very calm, as he tried not to alarm her, but now she could see a faint line of perspiration break out on his upper lip. "All the better," he said, his voice not quite steady. "It will lend verisimilitude to your performance."

"I'd rather not do it."

"I'm sure we'd both prefer not to do it, but it's tradition. They're expecting it."

"But I don't see why you have to stick slavishly to tradition. After all, you're going to stop it altogether."

"That's true, but while we're doing it, it has to be done properly. If Petrela thinks we're short-changing him, he might let his goons take it out on Laura."

"True, but…"

"And don't forget, it was his ambition to bugger you into unconsciousness. This is just what he wants to see."

She made a muted sound, which was partly fear, partly irresistible and rising excitement. She tried hard to bank it down, but at that moment, Dante had never seemed so big or so masculine. And oddly, what increased the sexual tension was that he didn't seem particularly interested in her, or the act they were about to perform, so preoccupied was he about his sister.

He looked at her seriously. "You ought to prepare. I think I've got something in the flat…and Vaseline."

"Prepare?"

"You've heard of a butt-plug?"

She nodded, reddening slightly.

"You should use one this afternoon."

"You've got one? Used?"

He laughed. "Not by me. It's Jessica's. She's into that sort of thing."

"But used!"

"Oh, for God's sake, Lola, I'll boil it if you like. Dip it in disinfectant. Why don't you come with me now?"

They walked silently to the apartment and he disappeared into his bedroom, reappearing with a bulbous purple object in some smooth material. "Come into the kitchen, you can watch me doing it."

He put the plug in a pan and set it to boil. "You know what to do?"

"I expect I can manage," she said dryly.

He smiled, eyes sparkling suddenly. "Do you think we ought to have a rehearsal now? So we won't have any nasty surprises?"

She gave an involuntary shudder—the core of her sex contracting at the thought of what he was going to do to her. But she wanted to wait—if she was going to do this thing, she might as well get the benefit of anticipation. "No! No, let's just deal with it when it happens."

Too late, she saw his face change and realised he'd misunderstood the shiver that had convulsed her body.

"Look, I know you find me repulsive, but it's nothing, it's just sex. Just a casual encounter. Try and imagine I'm your boring writer friend. I won't hurt you and I won't let anything bad happen to you. It doesn't mean anything and by this time tomorrow it will all be over."

She nodded, turning her face away, so conscious of the contractions inside her, the wetness gathering between her legs that she couldn't look at him.

More gently, he said, "Why don't you go and get some rest? I'll find you a bag for this and for the grease and I'll send someone to you with the dress at about seven."

She nodded and he held out a hand, taking hers. "Thank you. If we can just get Laura back…"

She bowed her head, feeling a thrill like a bolt of electricity as he touched her.

"And, Lola…next time we meet, I'll be in character. It's a ridiculous charade, but if we're going to do it, we should do it properly."

"In character. Yes." She turned to go then stopped. "Can I ask you one thing? You've never lived here, but seem to know a lot about this ceremony. Have you taken part in it before?"

He regarded her solemnly. "When I was seventeen before I went up to university, I spent six months here, staying with my grandfather. He made me play the part of Rodolfo. In his day, it was even wilder than it is now. Something approaching an orgy."

"Did you enjoy it?"

"Believe it or not, I was rather a shy youth. I was horribly embarrassed. But it turned out to be something I was good at." He made a face. "My grandfather was impressed — for the first time ever he was proud of me."

"That explains a lot," Eloise remarked, as he let her through the connecting door into the hotel.

Chapter Seventeen

When she got back into her room, she stripped off her clothes and clambered into bed, aware of the throbbing inside her, trying to make sense of why she was so excited. In the end, she abandoned her introspection and got out the purple butt-plug.

What she'd told him was true: she'd never been penetrated anally before. Of course, boyfriends had inserted a finger—just the tip—but that was all. If she thought about it at all, it was with disgust.

Now, she contemplated Dante de Rufina and the prospect of her anal deflowerment and it made her shake with longing. She got out the tub of grease he had purloined from somewhere and liberally coated both the purple plug and her own bottom. Then she placed the point onto her anus and began to push gently but firmly. After a while, the sphincter stretched and the head popped inside. She felt a momentary, stretching pain, then a blissful feeling of fullness. She lay on her side, thinking about what was going to happen to her and managing, with difficulty, not to anticipate events with an eager finger. In the end, despite her state of arousal and her nervousness about the evening's prospects, she fell into a dreamless sleep.

She was awakened by a knock at the door, which made her lift her head up abruptly, her brain scrambling to remember what was going on. The door opened and a woman entered. She was probably in her late twenties, with that thick dyed blonde hair which was so fashionably Italian.

"You are Signorina Lambert?"

"Si,"

"I am Rachele. I have been told to help you prepare for the ceremony."

Without an invitation, she walked in, depositing a garment wrapped in polythene on the bed.

"Do you wish to have a bath?"

Eloise was still confused and shocked by the way the woman had entered the room. She sat up, rolling sideways to accommodate the butt plug protruding from her bottom and pulling the covers up to her naked chest. "Yes, I'd better. Would you just pass me that dressing gown please? It's on the chair."

The woman had retreated to the window and now she gave her a scornful look. "Please, Signorina, didn't they tell you? I am a puttana, a whore. You have nothing that I haven't seen before."

"Yes, but still, I'd rather…"

"And by the end of tonight, about half the men in Rufina will have seen it too. Come along, please, we don't have a lot of time."

Reluctantly, Eloise got out of bed, acutely aware now of the butt-plug protruding from her behind. Somehow, as she edged towards the bathroom, Rachele saw what she was trying to conceal and gave a raucous laugh.

"Aaahh, you do well to stretch yourself there—I hear the Conte is hung like a horse. But of course, you'd know all about that, wouldn't you?"

Eloise thought about it, the feeling of unreality engulfing her. "Well, I do actually—but not for the reason you suppose."

"Oh?" Rachele raised her eyebrows, looking sceptical. "I thought that was why the arrangements had been changed. Would you like me to run your bath for you?"

"No, thank you..." Eloise was edging towards the bathroom door. "I'd just like to..." She made a dash for the sanctuary and hastily removed the butt plug. Sitting on the lavatory, she put her head in her hands. "I can't believe this is happening," she said out loud.

The door, which she had shut, was pushed open and the blonde girl came in and went to the bath, turning on the taps. "We have to get on, we don't have much time."

"Please, for heaven's sake. Let me have some privacy."

"Darling, if you'd wanted privacy, you shouldn't have agreed to let your boyfriend fuck you in front of a crowd of dirty men.

"He's not...not my boyfriend." Eloise got up from the loo and moved with as much dignity as she could muster over to the bath, having decided that getting under the water would be slightly less embarrassing than standing around naked.

"Whatever." Rachele managed to convey a supreme lack of interest, but she gave a searching look at Eloise's body as she clambered into the bath. "You'll have to take all that fur off; they won't like it at all."

"I'll have to what?"

"The peli pubico. The...what's the expression...muff? You'll have to shave it off."

In the bath, Eloise crossed her arms across her breasts. This was a step too far and she started to shiver uncontrollably, despite the heat of the water. Tears welled up. "No, I won't do it. I won't!"

"Oh Christ!" Rachele raised her eyes to heaven. "Save me from bloody amateurs. Look, you wanted to do this, you're taking their money, you have to give them what they want to see."

"Hang on a moment. Taking their money? What money?"

"Jesus!" Rachele was clearly irritated. "Their money. The money I'm not getting, thanks to you and your aristocratic boyfriend deciding to do some sexual slumming."

"I don't know anything about money."

"No, of course." Rachele's voice dripped with sarcasm. "You're doing it for luurve...amore..."

"No, I'm not." Eloise was in a state of complete agitation and the other girl's hostility was more than she could bear. "And money doesn't come into it. How much are we talking about?"

"We're talking about six-hundred Euros, on top of the ordinary fee. It would have paid my rent and given me a shot at settling some of my debts. Pin money for you and your fancy-man, no doubt."

"Well, I don't want it. As far as I'm concerned, the money's yours. And the Conte is not my fancy man, I don't even like him. And he hates me."

"Well why are you doing it then?" Rachele asked reasonably. "You must be kinky, right? You like it rough? With an audience?"

This was too much for Eloise and sitting in the warm water she put her face in her hands and began to sob.

"Oh come on. Come on." Rachele lifted her face up and started to sponge it quite roughly, but her tone was not unkind. "You'd better tell me what this is all about."

"It's just..." Eloise's mind worked furiously—she wanted to confide but she daren't say anything that might put Laura in more danger. "Have you heard of Tolka Petrela?"

"I have indeed. I suppose you might describe him as my employer." The voice was grim.

"Well, he wants to see me being... It's his idea."

"That doesn't surprise me—he's a disgusting old pervert. But you're not one of us—you don't have to do what he says. Go back into your room now, pack your things and bugger off back to England. You're lucky, you can get out."

"It's not quite that simple." She told the story of the wedding, her desperate attempts to save her business and of Petrela's pursuit. "And now he has something...he's blackmailing both me and the Conte. We have to do what he says."

"Huh, nothing can be worth submitting to Petrela if you don't have to. Just walk away."

"I can't. Someone else is involved. A child."

Rachele's eyes narrowed. "Oh, it's that sort of thing, is it? He's got a hostage. Bastard." She had been sitting on the closed toilet lid and now she stood up briskly. "In that case, we'll just have to make the best of it. Will you shave yourself, or do you need help?"

Eloise really didn't want any more of this enforced intimacy, but when she held up her hands, they were shaking.

"I think I'd better do it. Stand up. Have you got a razor?"

"The one I use on my legs. In the cabinet."

She stood self-consciously in the warm water as Rachele returned with the razor. "Now then, come close. Where's the soap? Good."

The Italian woman lathered her hands and then spread the foam across the heart-shaped patch of pubic hair. With firm, impersonal strokes, she began to strip it away. "Good job you keep it short, makes it easy."

Eloise stayed silent—waves of terror competed with flashes of extreme excitement as she submitted to these preparations.

"Put your foot up on the side of the bath so I can get between your legs. Yes, that's it." Rachele worked methodically, going back over the soft flesh a second time until she was satisfied. "Good, you can sit down to rinse off now."

Later, when she had dried herself and they were back in the bedroom, the Italian positioned her in front of the long mirror. "Now look!" she exclaimed, pulling the towel away from her.

Eloise contemplated her new appearance. "God, it makes me look younger!"

"Of course. The younger the better, that's how Petrela likes them."

Eloise thought of Laura and was glad that while Petrela was at the Castle watching her degrading performance, he wouldn't be near the girl. Rachele had unpacked the garment bag and now she held up a white lacy basque. "I think this should fit you, you're not very big.

Eloise wriggled into the skimpy outfit, which pushed up her breasts and left the pale, freshly shaved area of her mons starkly revealed. "It's not very authentic, is it? Did women in the middle ages wear this sort of thing?"

"I wouldn't worry about it—they didn't wear white lace hold-ups either," Rachele said, handing her the stockings. Eloise pulled them on and added her own white high-heeled shoes. Checking her appearance in the mirror she was astonished at how alluring she looked. The effect was at once titillating and surprisingly innocent. The sight of this underwear and the knowledge that in it, she would be on display to a crowd of men, set off Eloise's fears again and she sat abruptly on the bed.

"Come on, dear, pull yourself together. You're not really scared, are you? Fucking is the most natural thing a woman can do. I mean, no one has to teach you how to do it, do they?"

"No…" she whispered.

A thought struck Rachele. "You're not a virgin, are you? Surely not!"

Eloise managed a wan smile. "No, not a virgin. I'm just quite private. Modest, I suppose you might say."

"And you really haven't slept with this Conte?"

"No…well, I've shared a bed with him. But we haven't…fucked."

Rachele shook her head at the strangeness of human nature. "Well, what you need to do is to relax. Do you have anything to drink?"

"There's a bottle of wine in the mini-bar."

"Excellent." Rachele retrieved the bottle and two glasses, swiftly removed the cork and poured out the pale liquid. She watched Eloise down hers in several nervous gulps.

"Next the little panties, then the dress. But first, I think I'm going to try to calm you down. Just lie back."

The wine had gone straight to Eloise's head and she felt a little dizzy, but the alcohol had dulled the edge of her anxiety. Obediently she leant backwards, resting on her elbows.

"Spread your legs."

She hesitated and Rachele spoke again, more sharply, "Spread your legs. I want to make sure we got all that hair."

Reluctantly, Eloise opened her thighs more widely. Rachele dropped on her knees between them and ran a hand over the smooth mons, then down the naked slit. Eloise shifted a little, feeling the pulse start up again deep inside her.

"Have you ever been with a woman?"

"I have, actually," Eloise said, noting this was one taboo that she had conquered without too much pain.

"Oh," Rachele sounded surprised. "You are a lesbian?"

"No, definitely not. I didn't mind, though."

"Good." The finger which had been smoothing the fleshy lips now pushed forward, causing them to separate with a slight squishing sound. It explored gently, smoothing the whorls of her sex, eliciting the beginning of a tingling need. Then Rachele leant forward and began to nuzzle the spread thighs, not kissing, but touching them with her lips and then with the very tip of a moist tongue.

Eloise forced herself to relax, bending her knees slightly to allow the other woman access. One long finger was now inside her, curling upwards, feeling for her G-spot. It was joined by a second and then a third and fourth. She loved the sensation of fullness and began to thrust her hips upwards, trying to get the hand in deeper and harder. Rachele allowed her tongue to graze across the top of the clitoris before beginning to lick it steadily, listening to the growing crescendo of moans and using the sounds as a guide for minute alterations in pressure and angle.

Eloise's anxieties slipped away — there was no room in her brain for anything but an intense awareness of her sex, the hard thrusting of the hand contrasting with the soft strokes of the tongue. Her passion built up until she felt a finger enter her anus, slipping in with ease. And she exploded, yelling with abandon, liquid welling from her.

She laid back, panting, little aftershocks convulsing her vagina and Rachele stood up, brushing her hands together with the air of one who has just done a good job. "Feel better?"

"I do! So relaxed. Thank you."

"Good. Pity we don't have time for you to return the compliment. Now you must finish dressing and I've got to get into my blasted outfit as well."

"You have to wear a costume?"

"Oh yes," she said dryly. "We dress as bridesmaids. They like to tear the frocks off us afterwards."

Chapter Eighteen

A casual observer, viewing the little procession that set out from the main door of the hotel and made its way along the path to the keep, might have thought it the most charming sight. Two young women, in long dresses of virginal white, were at the front. Behind them, walking with slow, elegant steps, the bride, heavily veiled, her gown long and trailing. Two attendants walked after her, carrying the heavy train. Six other women brought up the rear.

The path was lined with well-wishers, who pressed forward to look at the spectacle. The observer might have been surprised to see that all of these were men.

Eloise was almost beyond fear. Her heart thundered and her hands clutched tightly at a large bouquet of lilies. But she kept her head up and her face was inscrutable beneath the lace veil. The dress was a heavy satin, in a simple style, almost medieval in appearance. It had a deep V-neck and long sleeves that fell away from her wrists in petal-shaped folds. Shaped in to the waist and fitting over her hips, it flared out below the knee. Rachele, looking at her critically before they left the room, smiled. "Signorina, you are absolutely beautiful. Ravishing. Now relax, enjoy. He's a good-looking man."

Eloise, fortified with most of the bottle of wine, nodded tremulously.

The procession was about halfway between the house and the keep when they heard the thundering of hooves and a man came from behind the massive stone edifice, mounted on a fine-looking black horse. Through her veil, Eloise could see very little, but she knew this must be the Conte. He was accompanied by a ragged group of men dressed in an approximation of fourteenth-century costumes.

He brought the animal to a halt on the path ahead of them and called out, "Isabella d'Empoli! I am Rodolfo de Rufina and I have come to escort you to your fate."

Now the pageant had actually begun, Eloise found she had an unfortunate desire to giggle. Dante was nearer now and she could see he was wearing a white shirt with full sleeves gathered at the wrist and a black leather jerkin over baggy trousers tucked into knee-length boots. On his head was a dark red velvet cap—square, the sort of thing she'd seen in paintings of medieval kings of England. She thought he looked like the principal boy in a pantomime, though not, of course, a very feminine one.

Fighting down rising hysteria, she drew herself up and replied, in her best Italian, "Thank you, Conte, but we do not require any company. We are on our way to the house of the Cascaris where I am to be married. We need not detain you."

He gave a harsh laugh, dismounted from his horse, thrusting the reins at one of the attendants and strode towards her, pushing the two flower girls out of his way. Any tendency to giggle was abruptly stifled—he was genuinely alarming, exuding authority and menace.

"You are indeed to be married—or at least to undergo some sort of rite of passage—but not with Pietro de Cascari. No, I have much more interesting plans for you. Now then, my lady, let me see your face. I'd like to know what I'm getting."

He lifted the veil and folded it back over her head, covering the circlet of flowers and pearls and for a moment, he seemed to slip a little out of character. "My God, you're absolutely beautiful."

"And intended for another!" she said, replacing the veil with trembling hands. "Please stand aside, sir, and let us get on."

"There is often a yawning chasm between what is intended and what transpires, madam. You will come with me."

"You'll have to kill me first."

"No, I don't think I'll kill you just yet. Having seen your face, I have quite another fate in mind for you. Come along, my lady—let's get you on this horse." He gestured to the man who held the bridle and then turned and picked her up, his hands around her waist. She struggled and kicked a little, but he had the advantage of surprise. She was forcibly reminded of how strong Dante was, of the power which lay below his carefully cultivated air of indolence. He placed her sideways, on the horse's shoulders, then with ease swung up behind her. "Bring the other women," he shouted to his attendants. "They shall all experience the richness of our hospitality."

He galloped at speed in the direction of the keep, veering off to the right at the last minute and taking the path between the house and the fortress. "I think we'll take the scenic route," he muttered. His arms were tightly wrapped around her, which was just as well, she thought, as otherwise she would certainly have fallen from her precarious perch. When they reached the area behind the tower, he reined in and put his lips to her ear. "Are you all right?"

"I was. This is a bit scary though. I wasn't expecting a horse-ride."

"Oh, don't worry. Bernardo is a pussycat. You okay about the next bit?"

"Not really. But I'll be fine. I've had quite a lot to drink."

His face contorted briefly. "That's nice — the only way you can bear to let me touch you is by the liberal use of alcohol." He urged the horse on and they came out of the little wood on the far side of the keep and rode between that building and the church, having done a complete circuit and ending up at the main door. Dante dismounted and then pulled her down so she fell across his shoulder in a sort of fireman's lift. His ragged army of attendants, now restraining the bridesmaids, were ahead of them and he strode up the stairs and through the crowd into the keep.

Eloise had been vaguely aware that there must be another way into the dungeon from the building itself, rather than the external entrance she'd used up until now. At the back of the main hall, a door led into a dank passage and another opening gave onto a circular stairway, which took them down into the cavernous room.

The dungeon was laid out as a theatre, with seating on three sides of the small platform at the end. The rows were filling up and from her odd position upside down over

Dante's back she thought she saw one or two men she recognised from the village. There was a buzz of excited conversation and on the far side, near the steps to the outside, a bar had been set up. The drinks seemed to be flowing.

On the platform a bedroom set had been erected, with a large divan, a chair, a mirror and a small kneeler with space for a prayer book. Dante flung her down on the bed and turned to the women who had followed him onto the stage. "Get her ready!" he instructed and then exited via an opening in the leather screen which spanned the rear wall.

"My lady!" Three of the women helped her to her feet and began fussing over her, straightening her head-dress, smoothing the dress.

"What does he mean, get me ready? Ready for what?"

The women exchanged glances over her head. One — Rachele — replied, "Who knows, my sweet? He probably wants to talk about a ransom. About arrangements for your return."

"Yes, that will be it. That must be it, mustn't it?"

"Yes, darling, yes," Rachele said, soothingly. "Now just wait quietly until he comes back."

"I think I should pray. Pray for release from this terrible imprisonment."

"That's a good idea."

The women helped her to the prie-dieu and arranged her dress and veil as she knelt, hands clasped, face lifted in a parody of piety. The three of them moved downstage, whispering.

"You should tell her what he's going to do."

"No, what's the point? She'll find out soon enough."

"The poor lamb, she's such an innocent. Rodolfo will tear her in half."

"I think he'll kill her."

The women made their exit, leaving Eloise alone. She kept her eyes closed, beneath the veil, waiting for Dante, and it wasn't long before she sensed he was close to her. She got up and turned to face him.

"Conte, I insist that you release all my people immediately. If you don't set us back on our route again at once, you will answer to my father and my husband-to-be."

"Oh, I'm so alarmed. Your ancestors and those of the idiot Cascari have been sniping at my family for hundreds of years. And yet look, Castel Rufina is still standing."

"Please, Conte, I beg of you. If you let us resume our journey now, I can still get to the ceremony."

He looked at her thoughtfully. "My dear Lady Isabella, I find it very difficult to talk to you when your features are obscured by that veil. If you were to show me your face, I might find conversation much easier."

"Sir, I put on this veil with the expectation that the man to take it from me would be my husband. You have already stolen one unauthorised look. I will not remove it for you again."

"Oh, but I think you will." He was swiftly at her side and with one firm movement, he tore the veil from her face.

"Count Rodolfo!" she said in tones of outrage. "My fiancé will…"

He cut across her. "Madam, it's no use you bleating on about your fiancé. Things have changed — you will not be marrying Cascari now."

"I don't understand you."

"No, my lady, instead you are to have the delightful honour of marrying me."

"Marry you? I would rather die."

"Indeed, that might perhaps be the eventual outcome. But first we will marry. The priest awaits us."

She looked at him with what she hoped was aristocratic hauteur. "Count, I have heard my father say there is insanity in your line and I see it is all too true. I will not marry you, now or ever. You will let me go at once."

He stepped up to her, very close, and took her chin in his hand, forcing her face up so she looked into his eyes. "Madam, either you agree to immediate nuptials, or I will be forced to do things to you which would mean no one, not Cascari or even the humblest peasant on your father's estate, would ever contemplate matrimony with you."

She wrenched her face away. "You would not dare."

He smiled. "I think you'll find I dare to do most things, my lady."

Abruptly, he crossed the stage and picked up the little wooden kneeler, bringing it across and banging it down in front of her. "Please, my lady, say your prayers. You're going to need them."

"I thank you—I have already prayed."

"I said, on your knees!" His hands went to her shoulders and forced her down on the embroidered cushion. Then, as she knelt, her hands grasping the small lectern, he began to unbuckle his belt.

"Tell me, Lady Isabella, is this a function you've performed before? I have a very displeasing vision of you servicing the brutish Pietro in this way. Still, I'm sure it's not very taxing—I don't expect you had to open your mouth very wide, did you?"

This got a laugh, reminding Eloise they had an audience.

"I don't know what you're talking about. What are you doing, Sir? For God's sake, stop!"

Dante had removed his boots and jerkin and now stripped off his trousers. She tried to get up and he used one hand to thrust her down again before pulling the shirt over his head so he was naked. His cock was at half-mast, but still it looked very big. Eloise felt a thrill run through her, starting at the very centre of her sex and radiating outwards.

He came towards her. "Now then, my dear, I'm sure you know what to do. If you haven't performed for Cascari, I expect you've serviced your straight-necked papa or your oh-so-righteous brothers."

"Really, Conte! This is intolerable. Disgusting. Please cover yourself up."

"My dear lady," he said with a silky voice, "if you think this is disgusting, wait until I've finished with you. For now, take this between your lips. I'll tell you what to do."

"I will do no such thing…" His hand shot out and fingers entered her mouth, keeping her jaws apart. "Now listen, my lady. If you attempt to bite — if there is the slightest touch of teeth on my manhood — I will get your handmaidens in here and allow my men to deflower them, one by one, and afterwards cut their throats. Do you want your wedding bed to be awash with blood?"

She tried to turn her head, his fingers tasting salty on her tongue.

"No? A little blood we understand, indeed, we hope for. But a charnel house would rather spoil the atmosphere. Now please, in your mouth. Suck. No? Which of your women shall I send for? Which would you like to see die first? I mean it, you know."

She made a strangulated sound which he took as assent. "Good, you're going to be sensible. Now open wide."

Eloise shut her eyes and opened her mouth. She felt the head of his penis on her lips and knew she would have difficulty accommodating it. Instinctively, she touched it with her tongue, tasting pre-ejaculate. Suddenly she experienced a flaring in her nerve ends, a reawakening of excitement and lust, a hot sensation spreading from the small of her back and along her spine. Not knowing how to play this, she began to fellate him normally, feeling his cock stiffen and grow in her mouth. She was dimly aware that he was talking her through it — or rather, that he was issuing instructions to Isabella — but she ignored him, her whole being focused on the object in her mouth. He held her head, crushing the headdress against her skull, moving her backwards and forwards, penetrating deeper and deeper until she could scarcely breathe. He seemed to read her distress, because suddenly he withdrew. Her ears were ringing, but she became aware that he was holding his penis up, offering her his sac. Now she heard his words.

"Suck them. Suck them! They are called balls, Madam. Take them in your mouth and taste them — but gently."

She did as he instructed, inhaling one shuddering breath before she took the swollen globes into her mouth, one at a time. Her whole body seemed to be infused with his odour — the musky, slightly leathery aroma that was sending little thrills down the back of her neck.

He pulled away suddenly. "Well, my lady Isabella, I've been very remiss, since you are a guest in my house, in not offering you any refreshment. But now I am ready to supply you with some nourishment."

His penis was back in her mouth, very hard and very hot. He let it move backwards and forwards against her tongue for a minute, then she felt it convulse, jerking, spurting liquid into her throat. He pulled back and sprayed her face with the stuff. Finally, drops fell on her hands, still clasped on the wooden bar of the prie-dieu as if in prayer. From the forgotten audience she heard raucous cheers and a smattering of applause.

"Now," he said, his hand on her chin, guiding her face towards the crowd, "show them. Show my men the evidence."

She shook her head mutely, her eyes big with terror.

"Open your mouth, Isabella."

She did so, exhibiting the white, viscous liquid in ropes around her tongue.

"And now swallow it. Take all the goodness of de Rufina nourishment into your supercilious d'Empoli body." He held up her chin, watching her, stroking her exposed neck with the forefinger of his other hand.

"Swallow, swallow it all, Isabella. Good girl. There's plenty more of that for you."

At last, he let her go and her head flopped forward onto her hands. Eloise's heart thudded and she felt as if her womb itself throbbed and contracted. The taste of him, the smell, struck a chord so deep inside her that feigning disgust and reluctance was near impossible.

"I suspect that was your first time—but you show distinct promise. Soon, with practice, you'll be an expert. Now, madam, get up. Let me see what I've got. We'll have that dress off now please."

"No, oh no, please, let me keep it. Leave me my modesty."

"You won't have a shred of modesty by the end of this. Get up!" He pulled her up roughly and held her so she faced the audience. "The gown, my lady, take it off now."

Eloise began to sob, wrapping her arms around herself. He turned her round a little, forced the arms apart and put both hands inside the v-neck of the dress. She thought he was going to touch her breasts, but instead, he gathered up the silky material and gave it a firm tug. The dress tore from neck to hem and he pulled the remaining tatters from her arms while she let out a genuine howl of outrage. "Oh no! My beautiful dress!"

"Very nice. Very nice indeed. The idiot Cascari is going to rue the day I took you from him." He twirled her around and then reached to the top of the basque, where white lace barely covered her nipples. "Let's have a look at these. You'll need good, lusty breasts to feed de Rufina brats."

She let out another wail, but his hands were inside the lace, lifting each breast so it rested on the edge of the garment, pushed upwards and outwards.

"Ah, splendid," he said, smoothing the two globes. "A little on the small side, perhaps, but vigorous suckling will soon sort that out. I'll start the process myself."

He lowered his head and began to flick his tongue across her exposed nipples. Shafts of aching pleasure shot through her, linking her breasts with her throbbing sex. She turned her face away from the audience, so that only the swift rise and fall of her chest gave an indication of her state of extreme arousal. He drew each little nub into his mouth, sucking hard and then pulled away.

"Well, Lady Isabella, you're rather more responsive than a nice well brought up young lady should be. Are you sure you haven't done this before?"

"No, never! This is for my husband, only my husband."

"Well, I'm your husband now. So, now we've seen what's on the top storey, let's look at the basement. On the bed, girl, hurry. I've been very patient with you, but I can't go on molly-coddling you much longer."

He pushed her backwards until she fell with a scream onto the divan. With one hand, he ripped her skimpy panties from her, stepping back as he exposed her naked mound to his eyes and those of about forty others.

"Well, indeed." His voice had subtly changed. "You are very smooth and shaven there, my lady. Hardly the appearance of a virtuous woman."

"Please, Conte, my maids did it. For my wedding night."

"Perhaps. We shall see. But first, I am going to taste this little flower. Spread your legs."

She reacted by moving them closely together. His hand went to her neck and he used one strong knee to force her legs apart. "Don't make me hit you, Isabella. I will if you persist in annoying me, you know."

"You are a disgusting, foul bully. God will punish you."

"Indeed he may, but I hope to have had a great deal of pleasure before then."

He stood back, savouring the view. She lay on her back, knees apart. Her hair was still up, but straggly now, the flower headdress slightly askew. The basque was round her waist, her breasts exposed. At the bottom, it came to a point, which finished just above her mound, pointing to her naked slit, now wet and glistening. Below this, the tops of the white stockings provided a lacy frame.

"Let us get rid of these," he said, tearing the stockings from her legs and tossing them one after the other into the audience. Eager hands caught them. With the thumb and forefinger of each hand, he spread her vaginal lips wide, exposing the pink slit to his own gaze and that of the onlookers. His finger circled the whorls and folds of her sex then he pulled back.

"We need to get you in position, my dear."

He dragged her unresponsive body to the end of the divan, so her bottom was on the edge. Then he climbed on the bed himself, kneeling near her face. She thought he was going to move into a sixty-nine position, but he didn't move on top of her, but stayed alongside, pulling up her legs so her knees were bent and wide apart. She was now completely exposed to the men in the audience, with nothing to interrupt their view. The knowledge sent a bolt of fear through her and precipitated a new surge of wetness, which glistened in the bright stage lights.

He lowered his head and swiped his tongue the length of her slit, setting her nerve endings twanging. Then he began to kiss and lick, pausing every now and again to drive his tongue into her. His lips were soft and hot and Eloise could feel the warmth of impending orgasm gather in her pelvis. She thrust her hips upwards, exposing herself still more shamefully to the audience, trying to manoeuvre his probing tongue onto her clitoris. But he suddenly pulled away and sat back on his haunches, leaving her panting and mewling slightly.

Without speaking, he dragged her around so she lay across the bed, her head hanging over one side. Then he knelt on the floor between her legs and pushed them up and over his shoulder before resuming his ministrations. Now, at last, he touched the throbbing bud of her clitoris, making slow, sure circles with his soft tongue. She was utterly helpless as he pushed her towards her climax. The bizarre circumstances, the pretence, her ambivalent feelings towards him were all forgotten as her back arched and a feeling of warmth and ecstatic fulfilment swept through her.

The audience, watching rapt, were in no doubt that after years of faked orgasms, here they were seeing the real thing. And as her spasms subsided and Dante sat back on his heels, they erupted into applause. Some of them exploded in a more tangible way, since many were masturbating openly.

For Eloise, there was no respite. Dante got to his feet and grabbed her hands, pulling her upwards.

"Now then, my lady, we get to the *res*. The ultimate act that seals our union."

He held her close and as she strained to get away, her head stretched backwards, exposing her long neck. Dante pulled at the pins which restrained her hair and it fell in shining tresses down her back, the little pearl and lace coronet still in place, giving her a sweet and virginal appearance.

"Now, now, my lady. I take my prize." His fingers moved down and felt their way along her slit, parting the lips slightly. His performance was absurdly melodramatic and although tingling with anticipation, she remembered her role and began to scream, pulling away from him. Catching him by surprise, she managed to slip from his grasp and she ran around to the other side of the bed, but he caught up with her in seconds, grabbing her roughly by her shoulders.

"It is very foolish to attempt to delay the inevitable."

Eloise concentrated on Isabella and what she would have done. Alternately crying and loading him with imprecations, now she attempted to kick him. Somehow, he evaded the blow, but used her movement to thrust his knee between her legs and topple her backwards onto the bed.

"Let's get rid of this confection; I want to see everything." He began tearing at the laces of the basque, wrenching it away from her. Now she was completely naked and both as Eloise and as Isabella she felt horribly exposed. There was nothing left to do but beg.

"Please, please, Conte, by all that is holy, spare me this. Leave me my honour. You are taking away everything I hold dear, my hopes, my prospects, everything. I beg you in God's name, stop now."

"My dear, not even God could stop me now." His fingers entered her again, more roughly this time. "For a woman who so vehemently professes to want to preserve her virginity, you are very receptive, very wet..."

Her fists beat against his chest. He grabbed her wrists and forced them above her head, where he pinned them easily in one large hand. His other hand pushed her leg upwards, bending the knee. For a few, short seconds, he looked her straight in the eye. She felt his cock nudge between her legs, was intensely aware of it pulsing at her opening. Then he drove it home with great force, penetrating her to the hilt, filling her exquisitely. She let out a great sound, which began as a theatrical scream of violation and ended up in a great cry of fulfilment and satisfaction.

He paused, buried deep inside her and scrabbled beneath her with his free hand, finally pulling out the ruined remains of the white wedding dress, which he waved aloft. Eloise could see it was stained with drops of a bright red liquid.

"See, gentlemen," Dante called to the audience. "Virgo intacta. Again, we triumph over the House of Cascari."

And then it began. For a while, he just thundered into her, driving hard. He'd let go of her wrists to rest his forearms either side of her and her knees involuntarily bent upwards and outwards. His slender, muscled body pistoned away. She could see the sweat on his brow, a lock of his dark hair flopping over his brow, a half-smile on his face, his eyes unwaveringly fixed on hers.

Eloise had given up any pretence of resistance. The best she could do was to keep her hands off him, meanwhile she moaned, rolled, thrust upwards, her back arching as she climaxed over and over again.

Then he pulled out of her abruptly and as she began to whimper at the sudden void, rolled her over and took her from behind. She could hear herself moaning as his hands moved underneath her, one caressing her swinging breasts, the other firmly manipulating her clitoris.

Now she'd forgotten about the audience, forgotten about the reason why they were doing this. She'd even forgotten who she was. Nothing mattered except the intensity of the experience, the shattering, constant friction of his cock, thrusting into her, widening, stretching, taking possession of her. She was aware of him pulling her about, taking her in various positions, exhibiting her to the audience. But the changes of angle meant only a brief period of anxiety before he came back to her and filled her again. At last he rolled her onto her back and she could feel his rhythm changing. He pushed right into her, his balls, sticky with her juices, squashed against her bottom. He was still. Then she felt him swell inside her and he jerked once, twice. She sensed his seed flood into her and she gasped, flat out on the bed, as he laid his head on her sweaty breasts.

Applause rolled over their heads as they stayed, panting and spent. Eloise closed her eyes, oblivious to the watchers, feeling exhausted and truly satisfied.

Apparently, this signified a break and she was aware of the audience getting up, moving around and going to the bar for drinks. An air of excitement and of anticipation permeated the room. The two of them lay, naked and sweaty. They didn't speak.

The audience was seated when she was aware of Dante pulling at her again.

"Get up, my lady, get up! There's one more rite you have to undergo. On your hands and knees."

She was floppy and unresponsive and he dragged her upwards, turned her round and pushed her slightly so she fell into a crawl. From the corner of her eye, she saw him dip his fingers into a bowl on the night table and then felt them applied to her anus. Shuddering in delicious anticipation and apprehension, she lifted her head, the flowery coronet still crookedly in place and looked at him over her shoulder with feline grace.

Perhaps he thought she was being too bold, even if by then Isabella had been warming to her violent lover, because as he continued to work his fingers into the narrow channel of her anus, he used his other hand to slap her hard on her rump, making her squeal and adding a new and shocking source of pleasure. However, she took the cue and began to speak in a voice made shaky by passion and by the constant encroachment of his hands.

"Conte, please, you have done enough. You have degraded me, deflowered me, spoilt me for any honest man. Please don't subject me to this ultimate humiliation."

"My dear girl." his voice was silky as he got himself into position behind her. "You will soon learn that there is no humiliation you can escape. I will do everything and anything to you. Your only function now is to give me pleasure. And believe me, this is going to give me a lot of pleasure."

She braced herself nervously, fearing he was going to lunge into her as he had before. But this time, he took things slowly, pressing his cock very gently onto her tight hole and easing it in, while stroking her flank with the hand that wasn't visible to the audience.

Because of her preparations with the plug and his liberal use of oil, there was surprisingly little pain. But the sheer bulk of him took her breath away as he eased his way inside her. When he was deeply in, she thought with relief that it was all right, it was uncomfortable, but she would survive. And then he began to move.

At first she just concentrated on managing the odd feeling of having such a large object moving in and out of the core of her being. Then incredible sensations began to obtrude—her insides felt as if they were on fire—the sensation of warmth and pleasure radiating outwards from the narrow channel into which he was thrusting with increasing vigour. As her sex began to pulse, her muscles tightened against the invader and then relaxed and she heard him groan. His hand reached underneath her, feeling for her breast and began pulling at the right nipple. The other, snaking round her a little lower down, cupped her vulva and a strong finger stroked her clitoris.

Just for a second, Eloise had a vision of the scene as the audience was viewing it—the couple locked together in the most intimate of embraces—the sweaty, pornographic sight of herself with only the little headdress as evidence of her recently lost virtue. She exploded into a shattering orgasm. Liquid poured from her—her legs and arms were consumed by a sweeping sensation of warmth and overwhelming consciousness, as if his hands were touching every part of her body.

She screamed—a long, tortured sound of pleasure, satiety and utter, complete surrender. And as the violent spasms of her climax communicated themselves to Dante, he came as well, swelling inside her and then firing his seed deep into her bowels. She fell forward, completely spent, and he went with her, still inside her. They lay together while the audience went mad with approval.

After a little while, he clambered off her and, pulling her by the arms, got her to her feet. She was exhausted and so dazed by the intensity of the experience that she could hardly stand. Dante, realising this, picked her up, putting her over his shoulder again.

"Gentlemen, I hope you have enjoyed watching me claim the ancestral rights of the de Rufinas. Though our enemies are powerful and vicious, our cunning is so great that nothing they hold dear is safe. I have taken this woman in every orifice—she is ruined for Cascari or any other noble suitor. Let no one doubt my strength and potency."

She felt him pulling at her buttocks, spreading them apart, and realised he was opening her up, exhibiting to the audience the two gaping holes, both running with his semen. She began to convulse again as another orgasm took her.

"But I would remind you all now, that she is my wife in all but name—my betrothed and a guest in this castle. You will treat her with the same respect and duty that you owe to me, now and forever." His eyes swept around the crowd of sweaty, excited men and he raised his right arm, his hand balled into a fist. "Lupus est homo homini!"

Chapter Nineteen

The sound of cheering and lewd shouting rang around the stone walls of the dungeon as Dante bowed and, walking a little unsteadily, carried her through the screen exit at the back of the stage, down a short flight of wooden stairs and through an open door behind it. Kicking the door shut, he put her down, letting her body slide against his until her feet touched the floor. He was starting to get hard again, the unmistakeable evidence wedged between them as they clung together.

Eloise felt as if she were no longer a person, but simply a mass of sensations, a bundle of agitated nerve-endings. As if from a long way off, she heard him say, "My darling, darling Lola, I've wanted you for so long."

They performed the one act that had been too personal, too private to exhibit to the mob outside. Their lips met in a long, passionate kiss. His arms went around her, pulling her tightly against him. The kiss went on and on. It was like nothing she had ever experienced before—it was as if they were truly merging, becoming one intensely sexual entity. They paused for breath then resumed the kiss, his tongue strong in her mouth, his hands now on her buttocks, fingers reaching below, entering her sore channels. Her hand snaked down between them, cupping his sac, as he lifted her leg, shaking with renewed desire. Without his mouth leaving hers, he pushed three fingers inside her and then he bent his legs slightly and manoeuvred himself into position. He was just about to enter her when there was a thunderous knocking on the door and it was immediately flung open. Petrela, flanked by several of his men, with Ugo in discreet attendance, strolled into the tiny dressing room. He had a fat cigar clamped between his teeth and he was applauding.

"My dear Conte! Ellouse! What a truly magnificent performance. One could almost believe you were coming together for the first time, but of course, the finesse, the — what's the word — choreography could only have been achieved by lovers."

The two of them sprang apart and Dante snatched up one of the hotel's towelling robes from a chair and wrapped it around her.

"Thank you, Tolka — I'm glad it pleased you."

"Now, we will party. Ellouse, you are a woman of immense talent. I hope I too will be permitted to experience some of your skill!"

Dante spoke quickly. "We'd like to join in the fun, Tolka, but as you can see, Eloise is quite worn out. I think she should have a rest."

Petrela looked disappointed, but Ugo murmured something in his ear and his good humour was restored. "Ah, your cousin has reminded me that the girl called

Anna is here again this year. She can do some really amazing tricks, Conte, you must see."

"Perhaps another time, I'm afraid I'm also feeling a bit exhausted at the moment."

"But of course, of course you are, my boy." Petrela clapped him on the shoulder. "A truly memorable performance. And later, perhaps you'll see your way to lending me some time with your beautiful girlfriend."

He was on his way out when Eloise called out. "Mr Petrela!"

"Ellouse?"

"The girl, Laura. The Conte's sister. She's all right?"

"But of course. She's just been visiting some mutual friends."

"We need to know when she'll be back."

"Oh." He looked around vaguely. "Some time before the morning, I should think."

As soon as the door shut, Dante said, "Let's get the hell out of here. Where are your shoes?"

"In there," she said, gesturing. "I think you kicked them under the bed."

"Oh yes. I can't go back now, or I'll be caught up in their orgy. I'll get them for you tomorrow."

"It's fine, I don't need them. Let's go."

Dante shrugged himself into another of the robes and put on some leather sandals. They walked as far as the main entrance to the keep. Outside, she took one step on the white gravel and let out a yelp. "Ouch! That hurts."

"Hang on, I'll carry you." He swept her up in his arms, this time with one arm supporting her torso and the other her legs—a slightly less humiliating method than the fireman's lift—and he carried her through the deserted hotel and the connecting door into his apartment.

In the sitting room, he put her down, but this time there was no lingering embrace. He took a step back, seeming embarrassed.

"Well, that was an extraordinary experience. Absolutely…extraordinary. Are you all right? It got a bit rough."

"I'm fine. Bruised, sore. I won't be able to walk properly tomorrow."

"Oh God, I'm sorry."

"Don't be." Now she, too, was embarrassed. They had just explored each other's bodies with the utmost intimacy, but she didn't know what to say to him.

"Would you like a bath? Or a drink?"

"Both please. Drink first. Something strong."

She sat on the settee and watched him move into the kitchen to get glasses. Between her legs, a pulse started. She wanted him again. What they had done had pushed her over the line from attraction to obsession. All she wanted was to smooth his hair, to touch his lips. She longed to run her fingers over the contours of his chest, to tease out that magnificent penis, to hold him in her arms and to have him make love to her without the distraction of a room full of observers.

She gave herself a shake. What was it he'd said? "It doesn't mean anything and by this time tomorrow it will be all over." A man like Dante de Rufina wasn't going to turn into a lovesick youth just because he'd been allowed to fuck her in the arse.

Even thinking the coarse words made her wriggle, the longing for him to do it again so intense that she felt he must be aware of it. She tried to compose herself, knowing that to preserve her dignity, she must be cool.

He came back into the room with two full tumblers of amber liquid. "Scotch," he said. "I think we both need it. And when you've finished, you can be first in the bathroom. Unless you want to go back to your room."

She didn't really want to leave him just yet. "No, if you don't mind, I'd like to stay until I know Laura is safe."

They drank their whisky in silence, beginning to relax and to come down from the sexual high. At last, he said, "We are going to have to talk about it, you know. Sometime."

"Talk about what?"

"What just happened."

She nodded. "I know. But not now."

He got up. "Why don't you come into the bedroom?" He saw the quick widening of her eyes and misinterpreting it, added, "Oh, I'm not trying it on. I don't think I could, actually. Just thought you'd like to relax, bath, perhaps have a sleep. I promise I won't touch you."

She sighed and followed him into the bedroom.

"Lie down if you want. I'll run you a bath."

Suddenly realising how tired she was, Eloise clambered onto the bed and lay back. The whisky had joined the wine she'd had earlier and her head was spinning. "No, don't bother with the bath," she said sleepily. "I haven't got the energy." She turned over on her side, falling asleep even as she spoke. "In any case," she murmured, "I rather like the feeling…"

She was out cold almost before she'd finished speaking and so failed to see the look of gratification flicker across his face. Dante took the folded blanket from the end of the bed and laid it gently over her, smoothing her hair back from her forehead. She muttered a little and rolled over, pushing the blanket away. The robe had fallen open, exposing one breast, the pink nipple looking rubbed and sore from his earlier attentions.

Dante sat in an easy chair by the window to watch and wait and ponder about his life, his past, his future. His reverie was interrupted at about four-thirty in the morning by a thunderous knocking at the outer door. He was there in seconds, Eloise behind him. When he flung open the door, there was Laura, framed by two of Petrela's heavies.

She ran into his arms, sobbing, and over her shoulder he glared at the men, his face dark with rage. "If you've touched her..." he said, but he was speaking to their retreating backs.

Laura lifted her head, saw Eloise, and quickly transferred to her embrace.

Much later, when they'd got her to bed, Dante went to make a pot of tea. As he left Laura's room, he whispered to Eloise, "Find out...find out if they did anything to her. Please. I can't..."

Eloise questioned the girl gently. Laura sat up in bed, sipping hot milk, her hair brushed back from her face and looking very young.

"No, they didn't touch me, but they scared me. I heard one ask the other if he thought I was a virgin — I thought they were going to rape me."

Eloise kissed the child and went out to the kitchen. "It's all right. They frightened her, that's all."

Dante's face was dark. "I won't forgive this."

She placed a hand on his arm, even now feeling heat shooting into her body. "She seems calm enough now. I'm going back to my room to get some sleep. The first of the wedding guests arrive tomorrow. Later today, I should say."

"Oh God, Lola, I'm sorry. I'll walk you back."

"No, it's all right. I imagine all the revellers have passed out by now. You stay with Laura."

At the door into the hotel, he put his hands on her shoulders.

"I'll never be able to thank you enough for what you did. To submit yourself to such an ordeal—for virtual strangers. I can't tell you how grateful I am. We must talk about it properly when you have more time. But if there is anything I can do for you—though I can never repay the debt—anything at all, you only have to ask."

He leant forward and placed a gentle kiss on her forehead before turning away.

Back in her own room, Eloise lay on the bed, eyes closed, too tired even to get under the covers. She ran through the events of the previous day—the shock of Dante's request, the shame of her encounter with Rachele, the fear, pain and humiliation of her performance in the dungeon. Her whole body ached and he had made such an impression in both her anus and vagina she could almost conjure up the illusion he was still there. She was too tired to subject the experience to very deep analysis, but she knew, from the sense of satisfaction and residual excitement, that she had enjoyed the ordeal, even relished it. And she knew she wanted Dante de Rufina again—needed him. But, she told herself severely, that didn't mean that she'd changed her opinion of him. He was still a man without morals or manners. But her perception of him had changed radically. The strength, the intensity of his performance— his sheer animal sexuality had rendered her helpless. He had obtained an awesome power over her.

"Damn the man!" she muttered to herself. But having once experienced what he had to offer, she needed it again — Dante de Rufina was like an insidious drug. She turned over again, remembering she hadn't washed or cleaned her teeth, nor removed her makeup.

She'd deal with Dante once the wedding was over. But whatever happened, it had to be on her terms; she wouldn't put up with being yet another of the women he amused himself with and then abandoned.

She sighed, opening her eyes for a second and remembering their cool farewell. How could a man who displayed such passion, demonstrated such a capacity for lust, have left her with that dismissive kiss on the forehead? And to describe himself and his family as strangers. Clearly, he wanted to distance himself following their intense sexual experience.

She could foresee nothing but trouble ahead. But as her hand moved down to stroke her swollen vulva, revelling in the unexpected smoothness — she thought with satisfaction that her world had changed forever. The sort of dull, conventional lovemaking she'd experienced with Jake, and even with Tom, simply would not do. Dante had finally got the bottle open, accessed the vessel which represented her sexuality. And it had, after all, contained vintage champagne.

Chapter Twenty

Alistair and his cronies were the first to arrive. The stag party was that night—Tamsin and her friends had gone to Florence where they were to have a statelier hen night with a meal in a smart restaurant.

The first of them roared up in a taxi in mid-afternoon. Eloise had been watching and hurried outside. She felt calm, if slightly hung-over and surreal. It was as if the previous day's dramatic events had never happened. She hadn't seen Dante, but Ugo, encountered in the lobby, had greeted her with his usual detached courtesy. She would have thought the whole business had been some lurid sexual hallucination of her own, if it were not for the physical evidence of the soreness in her orifices and the fact she was having trouble maintaining her usual elegant gait.

Alistair, Fred and four other men she vaguely remembered from the restaurant dinner party spilled out onto the gravel. As Alistair swooped on her and pulled her into a clumsy embrace, it became clear they had started the celebrations early.

"We had champers on the plane," Fred declared, expansively. "Lots."

"You don't say," she said with a grin.

As she led them towards the house, another taxi pulled up and a familiar figure got out. Jessica Anthony. One of the male hotel staff rushed across to help the taxi driver with her luggage as she sailed into the hotel, ignoring Eloise and her little group.

Eloise felt a sharp pang of something—she wasn't sure what. Irritation? Disappointment? Jealousy?

When she'd delivered Alistair and his friends to reception and promised to meet them for lunch, she went in search of Ugo to make sure the arrangements for the evening were in place. She herself was going to Florence for the meal with Tamsin and staying overnight, so she was keen to make sure everything was ready.

He was in the office. "Yes, it is all in hand. Food is hearty and basic. We've bought in extra imported beer and lager."

"And the entertainment?"

"All booked. There are dancers, striptease artistes. And some of the girls who were here last night will act as…hostesses."

She looked up sharply. "They won't mention…"

He understood at once. "They will be entirely discreet. Their jobs depend on being able to keep secrets."

She was still doubtful. "I'm really not sure about employing prostitutes…"

He raised his eyebrows. "Who said anything about prostitutes? They are hostesses, that's all. Any arrangements they may make with individuals are entirely private."

She was still shaking her head, wondering what Lady Connaught would say.

Ugo said, a little chidingly, "Really, Eloise, I would not have expected you, of all people, to be prudish."

It was his first reference to the events of the previous day and she felt a flush spread across her cheeks. At that moment, as if on cue, Dante appeared in the doorway. Eloise was unprepared for the wrenching movement of her heart when she saw him, but she managed to greet him coolly.

Dante seemed distracted. He nodded at Eloise and launched into questioning Ugo about a booking that had gone astray. Eloise, feeling herself dismissed, got to the door just as Dante moved forward and they collided, face to face. In the split second their bodies were touching, she felt his semi-hard state and knew it wouldn't take much to finish the job.

"Sorry," he said, giving her a tight little smile and pushing gently past her into the room.

* * * *

Driving to Florence, Eloise again tried to sort out her feelings. She had to admit she'd been hurt by his indifference. "But of course, just because what we did was so intimate, it doesn't mean he feels anything for me. Or me for him," she told herself severely.

The dinner was at the Enoteca Pinchiorri near Santa Croce, where Eloise had once eaten with Tom. It was a sedate affair, presided over by Lady Connaught. There were fourteen of Tamsin's friends, some old schoolmates known to Eloise, others members of her horsy set. Afterwards, to their relief, Bryony left them to their own devices and the girls went off to a nightclub.

"Poor Daddy," Tamsin told Eloise, as they walked across Signoria Square. "He's sitting in the hotel watching CNN. She wouldn't let him go to the stag do—said he'd only embarrass himself."

"She could be right," Eloise replied, remembering Ugo's hostesses. A thought struck her. "By the way, where's Arno? He hadn't arrived at the castle when I left."

Tamsin gave a little giggle. "Oh he's not going to the party. Not his style at all." She looked round to make sure none of the other girls was listening. "Actually, he's in my hotel room. A little something to go back to."

"Tamsin!" Eloise was genuinely shocked, but glad to be relieved of her guilt about Alistair. Whatever he got up to, she thought, it was being more than matched by his prospective bride.

The next day, she had cause to think she might be wrong. They left Florence early, Eloise leading a convoy of cars and taxis and arriving at the castle mid-morning. A wedding rehearsal was scheduled for midday—not ideal on the day after the stag parties, but it had been the only time the English chaplain was available to go through the ceremony of blessing.

Eloise escorted Sir Lyndo and Lady Connaught to their grand room in the keep and was rewarded with cautious approval from Bryony. "I suppose it's quite nice," she said, glancing at the superlative view and casting her eye over the ancient four-poster and the rich tapestry hangings. "If you like the old-fashioned look."

Eloise went to look for Alistair. His room was in the main building and the maids were working along the corridor, making up the beds. Eloise asked them if they'd seen the occupant of Room 203 and was told they hadn't been there yet. She knocked tentatively and then more firmly and finally, thinking he was still in a deep and hung-over sleep, she tried the door and looked inside. The bed was smooth and tidy and had clearly not been slept in. Puzzled, she went downstairs, thinking she'd check if he had been in to breakfast. But Maria, who'd been on duty in the dining room, shook her head. "The man who's getting married? No. I'll look at the list of room numbers if you like, but I'm sure he wasn't here. Such a handsome boy. I expect he's nursing a headache somewhere. I believe they had a very good night last night."

Eloise made her way to the office to see if Ugo knew anything about Alistair's whereabouts. He wasn't there, but Dante was, working on the computer. He scowled when he saw her.

"No, I haven't seen him, but if he was in the same condition as his pals in the early hours of this morning, I should think he's lying face down in a ditch somewhere."

Eloise paled, too worried about Alistair's disappearance to care about the awkwardness between them. "Oh, God, you don't think he's out in the grounds somewhere? Lady Connaught will never forgive me if I've lost him."

Dante got up. "Well, he can't have gone far. Let's go along the route he'd have taken to get back to his bedroom. He's probably in with one of the others. Did you think to look?"

She shook her head and followed him up the oak stairs to the second floor. The maids were just finishing and, after a quick conversation, Dante said, "No sign of him and one of the other rooms hasn't been slept in either.

Someone called... Laurence Carson." He looked at her questioningly.

"That's, Fred. You met him. The best man."

"Fred?"

"Don't ask. Where on earth can they be? I mean...Ugo was getting in — um — hostesses for last night. If they were with a couple of girls, where would they have taken them?"

"Well, I would have thought they'd bring them back to their rooms. But perhaps..." He set off down the stairs again. "I didn't lock up last thing, the night receptionist did. So it's just possible..."

They walked along the path to the keep, checking either side and peering into the little outcrops of stone and gun emplacements along the way. When they got to the place where her mock bridal procession had been stopped by his appearance on Bernardo, she couldn't resist a glance at him, but his face was expressionless and they walked on in an unfriendly silence.

Eloise could no longer bear the silence, so, just to make conversation, she said brightly, "I see Jessica's here."

"Yes," he replied shortly. "She's around for a few days then she has to go to Milan for some fashion shindig."

A little hesitantly, she said, "Well, if she is going to be here the day after tomorrow and she could be persuaded to come to the wedding, that would be wonderful. I mean, it would please Lady Connaught and it would be great publicity. For *Lace Dreams* and for Castel Rufina."

"It would, wouldn't it? Okay, I'll make sure she's there."

They lapsed into silence again for a while.

"How's Laura?"

"She's fine. Slept for hours then demanded food."

"Good."

Another pause.

"Well," Dante said, "he hasn't fallen by the wayside along here. But he could be anywhere — they were trundling him all over the place last night."

"They were...what?"

"In a wheel-barrow."

"Oh dear."

By now, the searchers had reached the keep and Dante brought out a bunch of keys, selecting a large iron one. "Well, here we go. No one should have been left here, but as we know, it does happen." He gave her a quick glance before opening the first door and plunging down the spiral staircase. At the bottom, he opened the second door and stood back courteously to let her go through. She stepped onto the ledge at the top of the short flight of steps that descended into the room and then pulled up so suddenly that, Dante, following behind her, cannoned in to her and put his hands on her waist to steady himself.

"Really, Lola, you must stop this business of rubbing yourself up against me all the time."

"Shh!"

He froze as he saw what had caused her to stop so abruptly. In the centre of the dungeon below them, brightly illuminated, Alistair Carew-Wright was stretched, naked, on a wooden X-shape. His hair was a startling red and green and his bottom, what they could see of it, was bright blue. And between his legs, dressed only in a red T-shirt, his best man was thrusting his penis between the garish buttocks, while the groom yelled, "Yes, Fred, yes! Fuck me! Fuck me! Harder, harder, harder!"

One of them must have made a slight sound, because for just a moment, Fred glanced in their direction. His eyes were glazed and there was nothing more than a slight smile of recognition before he turned back to his task, hands clasping blue buttocks, muscled legs apart.

Chapter Twenty-One

Somehow, they got out of the room and up the stairs, Dante in the lead. Outside, he put his arm around her, steering her to the place on the path to the house where a bench faced the gatehouse.

"Well, Lola," he said, when they had collapsed onto the seat, "your career as a voyeur is really taking off."

"Don't laugh." She shook with distress. "It's dreadful. Dreadful. What on earth am I going to do?"

"I don't understand why you're required to do anything."

She stared at him in astonishment. "You did see what was happening in there?"

"It looked as if the groom had rather pre-empted the wedding night, but with the best man instead of the bride."

"Yes and that's just the point. I can't leave Tamsin in the dark about a thing like that. And once she knows, she'll probably call the whole thing off."

He looked at her with raised eyebrows. "I strongly suspect she knows about it already."

"But…"

"Look, Lola, even you have to admit that the set-up is really weird. I mean, Alistair and the other guy are running round practically hand in hand, whereas your friend is clearly into some strange master-slave scene with the creepy Dutchman."

"He looks after her horses," Eloise said, lying loyally.

"If that's a euphemism for something very kinky, I'm sure you're right. The point is, it's not a normal, loving relationship, is it? Well, is it?"

She shook her head miserably.

"So my advice is to leave things well alone."

"But I can't. Surely you must see if there's the remotest possibility she doesn't know… I can't have a disastrous marriage on my conscience."

"Even though it may fatally damage your business and mine?"

She nodded slowly. "I have to. She's my friend."

Dante sighed then turned towards her and took her hands. "Lola, my darling, may I make a suggestion?"

"If you must." She drew her hands away, trying to ignore the shafts of excitement racing up her arms.

"Don't go blazing in to talk to your friend. Have a word with Alistair. If she really doesn't know what's going on, he ought to be the one to tell her. And it would be less embarrassing for you. But I think you'll find the whole lot of them are locked into some strange sexual conspiracy."

She nodded. "I think you're right. About talking to Alistair, I mean."

He grinned. "I bet you never thought you'd be using me as an agony aunt." He stood up. "We'd better go back to the house, unless you want an embarrassing encounter with the lovers when they come out." They began to walk along the path and he laughed. "I don't think that dungeon has seen so much action since my great-grandfather's day. You're having an interesting effect on this place!"

In the foyer he stopped and turned to face her. "Lola, my sweet, I know this isn't the right time to speak, but I haven't been able to stop thinking about this—about us. And there's no other way to say it. I know we're never going to be bosom buddies, or friends even. But what happened the other day was amazing. I've had my fair share of sexual experiences, but nothing like that. Nothing even approaching it. It was…incomparable, exquisite, sublime, if that doesn't sound too over the top."

Eloise bowed her head, not wanting him to see the sudden glow of pleasure that suffused her face, and he put his hands out and placed them gently on the tops of her arms. "I think when this is over, you and I should spend some time making love…"

She moved a little, making a small sound.

"Oh Christ, I didn't mean that. I know we're not lovers. But I want us to have sex, to experience it in its best and highest manner. Almost as an art form. And to do it privately, with all the time in the world and no pressures at all."

Eloise opened her mouth and he laid a gentle finger across it. "Don't yell at me! Don't say anything at all now. Think about it for when this wedding is over. I can't believe you didn't feel something special as well."

Eloise was so shocked and surprised, she couldn't have spoken even if she had wanted to. Dante leant forward and kissed her forehead before disappearing down the corridor to his office.

The main players in the wedding party had gathered in the library, where they were drinking coffee—Bryony Connaught making small talk to the chaplain, while glancing at her watch in increasing irritation.

"Ah, there you are, Eloise, we've all been waiting for you."

It could only have been about five minutes, Eloise thought, but she apologised. "I was looking for Alistair. He's been a little delayed, but I'm sure he'll join us as soon as he can."

"Well, there's not much point in doing it without Alistair, is there? It's rather like Hamlet without the prince."

Eloise laughed. "Yes, it would be. But we don't need him for the first bit, the procession down to the church. And I'm sure he'll be with us by the time we get to his part."

"Well, I hope nothing untoward has happened to him. I did warn those boys not to do anything foolish."

Eloise started organising the bridesmaids. The dress had a long train, but for today they were improvising with a heavy bedspread and she got the two maids of honour to tie it around Tamsin's waist, while she fixed a piece of lace on her friend's head.

"Where is he?" Tamsin whispered, seeing her mother was occupied with the clergyman. "Is he totally wasted?"

"You don't know the half of it," Eloise said with feeling.

"Oh, bless his little cotton socks!" Tamsin seemed unconcerned.

Rearranging Tamsin's hair reminded Eloise of Alistair's and she felt a jolt of horror. She turned to the Matron of Honour, "Barb, can you do this for me? I've just remembered something I have to do." She slipped from the room, running down the corridor to the office. Dante was there, standing at the window staring out.

"Dante, please will you do me a huge favour?"

He turned. "But of course, my love."

"Can you find Alistair and make sure he comes down to the chapel. And I've just realised, you must make him cover his hair up. We'll have to do something permanent about it tonight—but if Lady Connaught sees it, she'll have a fit."

"God knows what seeing his nether regions would do to her then. Don't worry, I'll sort it out. He's probably back in his room by now."

"And could you possibly send someone to get some hair dye? Brown."

The civil ceremony would take place first, in town, and Eloise had decided not to rehearse it, since it should be fairly straightforward. Afterwards the whole party would be brought up to the hotel by coach and would move from the main hotel building down to the chapel for the blessing.

The procession threaded its way from the house, in a disturbing echo of the Rodolfo and Isabella scenario. It was headed by one of the older bridesmaids, whose thankless task it was to lead the page boys and flower girls, six of them in all, including Alistair's nephew and Tamsin's five-year-old cousin. The children were playing up, fooling about, falling out of line and generally being pests.

Behind them came Tamsin, walking in a stately and unperturbed fashion, her arm linked through her father's. More bridesmaids followed then Lady Connaught and Alistair's parents. Those of the guests who'd already arrived had chosen to explore the grounds or the town, so their sole representative was Arno de Vries.

They walked under bare wooden arches — the florist was due in the late afternoon to fix the roses. At the chapel, the procession came to a halt. There was no sign of Alistair or Fred.

Eloise made a quick decision. "It doesn't matter too much about Alistair — the real purpose of this is to make sure the bridesmaids can cope with the train and don't fall over each other." She looked around. "Arno, would you mind standing in for Ali and I'll be the best man. Just so we get the positions right.

Lady Connaught rolled her eyes, but in the presence of Sir Alec and Lady Catherine Carew-Wright, there wasn't much she could say about Alistair's non-appearance.

The chaplain was taking them through the order of service when the door at the back crashed open and Alistair came in, panting slightly, closely followed by Fred. They were dressed in dark suits and open-necked shirts and incongruously, Alistair wore a woolly purple ski hat.

"Frightfully sorry, everyone. I was…er…looking for something."

He strode to the front of the church, where Tamsin and Arno stood hand in hand.

"That's a very fetching sight," he remarked, as Arno moved aside to let him take his place. "Cutting me out, Arno?"

"If only I could," the Dutchman said, bowing courteously.

Eloise wasn't sure, but she thought she saw a look of amused complicity pass between the two men. She gave up her place to Fred and moved gratefully to the back of the church, and the rest of the rehearsal passed without incident.

Afterwards there was a buffet lunch in the library. Eloise had taken a glass of wine and some food, meaning to eat quickly and then get on with the thousands of chores which seemed to have piled up while she was searching for Alistair, when the man himself appeared at her side. A lock of brown hair, striped with green, was escaping from his ridiculous bobble hat and he had a rueful grin on his face.

"Sorry about that, Eloise."

She wasn't sure if he was apologising for being late for the rehearsal or for the lewd display in the dungeon. She waited.

"Freddy told me you saw us."

"I did."

"Sorry. Shouldn't frighten the horses and all that."

"Well, I don't mind. Not my business. But I'm really worried about Tamsin."

"About Tamsin? I don't quite see…" Understanding dawned on Alistair's ruddy face. "Oh, I get it. You think she'd… Look, don't let it bother you — she's cool with the whole thing."

"You mean she knows?"

"Um, yes, well… Look, Ellie, I think you'd better talk to Tamsin about this. I'm not sure how much I'm…"

He broke off, looking confused. Remembering Dante's advice, Eloise pressed on sternly, "But first, you've got to tell her what happened."

"Okay." He didn't seem unduly concerned.

"What you and Fred were doing and that I saw you. Not just me, the Conte as well. Will you do that, please, Ali? Now?"

It was like negotiating with a four-year-old, but eventually he flashed his lovely smile. "Okey-dokey, Ellie. Will do." He put a huge hand on her shoulder. "I understand. You're being a good friend to Tamsin. I like that. Thank you."

"And, Ali…"

"Yep?"

"Where on earth did you get that hat?"

His face broke into a broad grin. "Dante found it for me. Said it belonged to his little brother. He's a good bloke, Dante." He wandered off into the throng, leaving Eloise shaking her head in confusion. When she'd finished her brief meal, she went out into the lobby. The first thing that greeted her was a familiar voice, speaking in loud, clear, well-modulated tones.

"Yes, well I'm not sure I need a room, actually. I imagine I'll be sharing with my girlfriend. She's already staying here."

"The name is Jake Matthews?"

"That's right."

"And your girlfriend is…?"

She sped to the reception desk, getting there in time to see Jake leaning carelessly on the wooden surface, while on the other side Dante tapped letters into the computer.

"Ah, here she is now. Hello, Ellie, darling. Will you explain to this fellow about the sleeping arrangements?"

As Eloise was swept into Jake's embrace, she saw an unholy grin of delight spread across Dante's face.

"Yes, please do, Miss Lambert. You really are a source of constant surprise."

It was fortunate that Jake was too self-absorbed to pick up on the atmosphere.

"Jake, darling, I did explain that I'm working. And I need the space in my room for all the papers and clothes and things. I'm sure we can find you a nice room somewhere."

"Oh, I'm positive we can," Dante said, wheeling round to look at the racks of keys behind him. "In fact, this one would be ideal. North Wall five. It's built right into the fabric of the castle, you'll love it."

Eloise repressed a laugh, recognising this as one of the old guardrooms, which had been hastily brought back into service because of the large number of guests. Dante presented Jake with a little map of the grounds and marked his room with a cross.

"Sounds good. So, I'll see you later then, babe." Jake looked down at his small suitcase and then at Dante. "You'll bring that over for me, will you?"

Eloise exploded, "Oh for heaven's sake, Jake, it's only a little bag. Carry it yourself."

Unabashed, he picked up the case and disappeared through the great oak doors into the grounds, nearly cannoning into someone coming in, laden with clothing bags.

A muffled voice complained. "Oh, don't bother to help me, Jake, will you?"

"Sammy! Oh, Sammy, thank God you're here!"

Eloise ran forward and relieved her friend of some of the bags.

"Bridesmaids' dresses," she said, shortly. "Where do you want them?"

She turned to find Dante behind her. "There's a small cloakroom near the office that's not in use. We can put them there if you like."

Gratefully, she piled the dresses into his waiting arms. "Brilliant, thanks. I'll come out to the car with you, Sammy. Leave the rest of the stuff on the desk."

Samantha had driven the smart little van from London. It was pink, with the *Lace Dreams* and *Show Offs* logos in curly writing on the side and it carried the wedding dress, clothes for bridesmaids, pageboys and flower girls and some items of food that couldn't be found in Italy.

Sam pulled more things from the back of the van. "Your bloody boyfriend! I drive him all this way, he spends the entire journey talking about himself and then he can't even be bothered to help me unload."

"Yes, well, that's Jake."

Dante came out of the house. "Is there much more to carry in? I can go and get one of the staff if you like. Unless your…er…boyfriend is coming back."

"Not much. Here, take these boxes." Eloise loaded him up. Then, as an afterthought, said, "Heavens, I'm so sorry. This is Samantha Kirk, my partner. Sammy, this is Dante de Rufina, who owns the castle."

"How do you do?" Dante replied, his voice muffled. "I think we'd better save the hand-shaking till later." He set off towards the house and Sammy, her eyes wide, turned to Eloise.

"Darling, he's gorgeous! Absolutely stunning."

Eloise slammed the doors of the van. "Hmm. Well, to quote a trite old saying, handsome is as handsome does."

"Really? Do tell…"

"Later. Oh, hello."

Jessica had come round the side of the house and it appeared that this time, she was going to notice Eloise, even if she couldn't quite remember her name.

"Hello, er…hi. Have you seen Dante?"

"Yes, he's just gone into the hotel. He's carrying some boxes to the little room by the office — you'll probably find him there."

Jessica nodded and went off towards the entrance. Sam's eyes were even wider. "That's Jessica Anthony!"

"I'm afraid it is."

"Gracious, this job is suddenly becoming a lot more interesting."

"Frankly, I could do with it being much *less* interesting."

The day passed in a whirl, with most of Eloise's time taken up by final dress fittings, negotiations with florists and the task of pacifying Gianni after Lady Connaught had visited the kitchens. A pizza supper had been laid on for the young people, with the Connaughts and most of the older guests eating in the restaurant. Much alcohol was consumed and Eloise was relieved to see Tamsin excuse herself early. "Got to be beautiful for tomorrow."

Eloise wasn't far behind her. She and Samantha sat in her bedroom with a bottle of Pinot Grigio and finally, her tongue loosened by the wine, she told the full and unexpurgated story of her Italian adventures.

Sammy was wide-eyed with astonishment. "But all this is so unlike you, Ellie, darling. There must be something in this Tuscan air. And you really let him…fuck you in front of all those men?"

"I didn't see what else I could do," Eloise said, trying to sound reasonable, but inwardly squirming — partly in embarrassment and partly because the now-familiar feelings of excitement were building up as she talked about the dungeon incident.

"No wonder he looks at you like that."

"Like what?"

"Like a hungry wolf."

Despite the brazenness of her revelations, now, for the first time, Eloise found herself blushing. "Oh, that's just because he wants to go to bed with me. I mean properly. Privately."

"Yes! I knew it! He's fallen for you."

"No, no, nothing like that," Eloise responded hastily. "I mean, for a start, he wants to sleep with every woman he meets. And in this case, he just wants to savour the experience properly. Because he thinks we were good together, sexually. No ties, no significance. He keeps saying that. It wouldn't mean anything. He wants it for his collection — his One-Hundred Great Sexual Moments."

"And how do you feel?"

Eloise tried to make her voice sound casual. "Oh, I've been around long enough to know it's a bad idea to get involved with a man like that. Apart from anything else, he's still seeing Jessica Anthony. I hardly think he's going to dump one of the most beautiful women in the world for me."

"You've no idea how gorgeous you are, have you?"

"Don't be silly, Sammy. Anyhow, Dante de Rufina is rude and fickle and juvenile. And he's probably a criminal. So I'm keeping well away."

"And the sex?"

"The sex..." She hesitated, but finally felt compelled to tell the truth. "The sex was out of this world. Like nothing I've ever experienced before. Sensational. Bliss."

At that moment, there was a tap on the door and one of the hotel maids came in. "Scusi, Signorina Lambert, but I have a note for you."

Eloise unfolded the sheet of hotel paper. "It's from Tamsin. She wants to see me urgently. Oh dear..." She hadn't told Sammy about the incident with Alistair and

Fred, believing it should remain private. But now she realised with dread that Alistair had done what she'd asked him and told his fiancé about his predilections. And no doubt she was distraught. "I'd better go at once."

On the way to the keep, Eloise made swift calculations about what could be salvaged when the wedding was cancelled. They might just about break even — so long as they were paid for the work done so far, but without the expected boost that a successful commission would have brought, she thought the firm would inevitably go under. And would they pay her, without complaint, for what she'd already spent? They would, wouldn't they? With a woman like Bryony Connaught, one could never tell.

She was gripped by a feeling of rising panic and when she reached the bench where she and Dante had sat that morning, she sank onto it, taking in deep draughts of air to calm herself down. The part of the wall opposite her, running from the gatehouse to the north tower was in excellent condition and the walkway along the top was lit at intervals by lights crafted to resemble flaming torches. Two people were walking along the battlements and as she watched, they stopped and faced each other. The light nearest to them flared and she drew in a breath. Dante de Rufina and Jessica Anthony. He was holding his arms out, palms upwards as if in supplication and after some animated conversation, Eloise saw Jessica nod. Dante drew her into his arms and they kissed, two beautiful people silhouetted against the night sky. With a heavy heart, Eloise got up and resumed her journey.

Chapter Twenty-Two

She entered Tamsin's luxurious room in the keep in trepidation, dreading the anticipated scene. Tamsin lay on the big four-poster, propped up on pillows and wearing a lacy negligee in a sheer black material.

"Darling, thank you so much for coming. I have to talk to you. About Alistair…"

"Yes? He told you?"

"He did." Tamsin's voice was sombre. "Come over here and sit on the bed, Ellie, please."

When she was settled, her friend went on falteringly. "He told me…he told me you found him…with Fred."

Eloise stayed silent, but when Tamsin thrust out her hands, she extended her own and took them.

"He said you saw him… Oh God! Saw him being buggered by Fred. Is that true?"

She bowed her head, feeling the increased pressure on her hands.

"Tell me, Ellie, did you see them? Fucking?"

"Oh, Tamsin… I'm so sorry. But I couldn't just leave it."

"But don't you understand it's over? Everything's changed—the wedding's off. How will I ever get over this?"

"Tamsin, what can I say? I can't bear to see you so unhappy." There were tears in Eloise's eyes as she contemplated her friend's misery and reflected that, indirectly, she had caused it. Perhaps, if she'd let it go…

"Ellie, darling, don't cry. It's not your fault."

"But I got involved. I feel so dreadful."

Tamsin pulled on her hands and she was drawn forwards. "Please, darling, don't feel bad. Kiss me."

Suddenly, Tamsin's lips were on hers, her tongue in her mouth. Eloise was so surprised that she let it go on for a while before wrenching away.

"Tamsin, you mustn't do this. You're still in shock."

Tamsin laid back on her pillows, her face suddenly wreathed in smiles. "And so are you, darling. God, Ellie, you are absolutely fabulous. How you can have lived so long and still be so innocent, I do not know."

Eloise put her hands to her face. "Stop it, Tamsin, I don't understand."

"No, I know you don't. But you soon will." She raised her voice a little. "Sweetheart, will you bring the champagne in now?"

The door of the bathroom swung open and from it emerged Arno de Vries. He was carrying a tray containing a bottle of champagne and three glasses and was clad in nothing but a towelling bathrobe.

"I think we'll start with this and then move on to my own special cocktail." He set down the tray and opened the champagne with ease. "Here you are, Eloise, you can drink to a very successful operation."

She took the glass reflexively. "Tamsin, you'd better tell me what all this is about."

Arno came and sat next to her on the bed, so she was wedged between them. "Don't be angry, little one. It spoils your allure."

Eloise ignored him. "Tamsin!"

"Well, it's a long story."

"I've got all night."

"Good. That's good, isn't it, Arno?" Eloise saw them exchange laughing glances. "Look, Ellie, you know what mother is like. She's been pushing me and nagging me to get married—to make a good match. It's been going on for years now. You've no idea what a bore it's been—eligible young men being thrust at me all the time."

"But surely, the answer was simple. Leave home and get away from her."

"Oh, Mummy made it plain very early on—no contact, no money. She wanted me in the house and under her control. And I do like my creature comforts, as you know, Ellie. Not to mention the huge expense of keeping the horses. Even if I could have got away and found a job, I'd never have earned enough for the outrageous prices Arno charges for just one of them, let alone three."

Arno put his hand on Eloise's upper arm, bare under a jacket thrown over her shoulders, and stroked it soothingly. "Drink your champagne, Eloise, it will help you to relax."

"Mummy wanted me to live my life like she had—coming out, the season, balls, grand dinners. Well, you can't come out any more, thank God, but you know the kind of thing. But, rather unfortunately for someone trying to fit into such a conventional household I had become attracted to a…slightly different life-style." Her eyes flickered over Arno's long fingers as they continued their soothing motion. "Tell me, Ellie, have you ever heard of BDSM?"

"Of course I have. I'm not a child, Tamsin."

"No, darling, but you are very innocent. Well, up until a few years ago, I had only the vaguest idea what it was myself. Then one day I was looking for new accommodation for the horses and I went out to see some stables that had been recommended to me. And there he was, this crazy Dutchman." She smiled reminiscently. "He took one look at me and led me into an empty stall. I had no idea what was going on. He bent me over a saddle and smacked my bottom through the material of my jeans. Then he hauled them down and used a flat paddle on my panties. I was wetter than I'd ever been. Finally, he pulled the panties down — very, very slowly — and spanked my bare buttocks until I howled. He shoved a whip handle up inside me and pushed saddle-grease into my bum and then he buggered me, hard. I'd never even had a man there before."

Eloise made a slight sound as she fought a feeling of intense arousal. She was only too aware of Arno behind her, so close she could feel his breath on her neck. "But I don't see what this has to do with Alistair. With the wedding."

"Oh, yes. Mummy finally got round to introducing me to Alistair. She was really keen on having him for a son-in-law and his parents wanted a match as well. It turned out they were worried about him. As well they might be. He was coming under the same sort of pressure as I was. He's sort of bisexual, though it's really men he likes. He's got this long-term thing with Fred and the thought of being stuck in a conventional marriage appalled him. But he was still being told he had to get married, have kids, provide them with an heir."

"Aaahh..." This sound was drawn from Eloise, partly because all was becoming clear to her and partly because Arno's hand had moved from her arm to slip inside her thin cotton dress and was stroking a nipple through the silky fabric of her bra.

"It was Arno who thought of it, of course. The perfect solution. We'll get married, have a few kids... I mean, Ali doesn't mind doing it. Fucking women. We had a scene all together, the four of us, it was...wow! Anyhow, we'll have the heir and the spare and we can go on living our lives as we want. The parents are happy, we're happy, Arno's happy. I don't see what's wrong with that."

Eloise drew in another long breath. Arno pulled at her skirt.

"So that's the story. Don't be cross with us, Ellie, I couldn't have told you before. You're so very straight and I was afraid you'd be terribly shocked."

Arno's fingers smoothed the flesh of Eloise's inner thigh. "I'm not sure she's as innocent as you think actually, Tamsin. Not from what I've been hearing."

Eloise wrenched round to look at him. "What do you mean?"

"Oh, the little matter of letting the Conte fuck you in every orifice in front of a crowd of about forty men."

"Oh God!" Her hands went to her face. "Who told you?"

"Let's say it was a member of the family. Don't worry, Eloise, it isn't generally known. But I always hear about these things."

"Good grief, Ellie!" Tamsin was genuinely shocked. "I don't believe it. What the hell was that all about?"

"Relax, Eloise, lie back. You can tell us all about it during the night." He had taken the glass away from her and was now pushing her shoulders gently back onto the bed.

She wriggled, trying to get away. "No, please, I don't want..."

"Oh, come on, Ellie." Now Tamsin was smoothing her arm. "You've been working so hard. Have a bit of fun. Please. It would give me so much pleasure. After all, it is my last night as a single woman."

Abandoning her unequal struggle with Arno, Eloise lay back on the bed. She was thoroughly confused. First, because the whole basis of the wedding that had been the focus of her attention for so long, had been revealed as a lie. But a second and much deeper cause of distress was the behaviour of Dante de Rufina. When he had spoken to her in the lobby that morning, she had half believed he really wanted her. But not only had she since seen him making love to Jessica, but now it transpired he had been bragging to Arno about what he'd done to her in the dungeon.

But whatever she thought about the Conte, the memory of what they had done together made her sex tingle. And she'd experienced a quite uncharacteristic glow of pleasure at Tamsin's astonished reaction to the news of her debauch. Now, Arno's hand had reached her panties and was stroking her mons. For a moment, the prying fingers reached between her legs, creating a delicious frisson in her sex.

"She soaking wet," he informed Tamsin.

"All right then, Ellie? You want to play?"

She couldn't bear to acknowledge how turned on she was, but she kept quiet, no longer attempting to resist the two pairs of hands that stroked and touched her. She felt

Arno pulling her upwards and allowed him to remove her jacket and lift the dress over her head. As if in a dream, she was aware of Tamsin's hands snaking round behind her to undo her bra. Then her friend clambered off the bed to kneel on the floor between her legs. "Time for the panties, darling. Lift your bottom up a bit."

As Tamsin drew the flimsy knickers off, she whistled. "Shaven, Ellie? Whatever next?"

Eloise gave a convulsive shudder as she remembered the act of depilation and Tamsin said soothingly, "Don't worry, darling, I know you haven't been made love to by a woman before. Apart from last time."

"Not true, actually," Eloise replied, languorously. At least, she thought, she was going to kill off the image of sweet, innocent Ellie once and for all. "Dante sent a tart to my room. She made me come..."

"There you are, you see," Arno said. "That's why she's so perfect. She looks and acts so pure, but she's a thoroughly bad girl."

This roused Eloise to say, "You're not going to hit me, are you? I don't think I'd like that."

"No," he said soothingly. "We're just going to love you. I think we'll leave your indoctrination into the other stuff to the Conte."

Tamsin was interested. "To the Count? Is he into that sort of thing?"

"Oh, I should think our dear Conte is into most things."

The thought of Dante spanking her started Eloise shaking again and when she felt a soft tongue on her sex, she started to convulse at once.

"Oh you're a very eager little beaver," Arno said, laughing at his own joke. He ran his long fingers around her breasts, flicking the nipples before lowering his mouth and sucking them, one after the other. Between her legs, Tamsin worked away, running the tip of her tongue around the swollen flesh of her outer lips. Then there were fingers entering her, one, two in her vagina and one insinuating itself into her anus. The soft pulling on her breasts was relentless and her back arched while mewling sounds burst from her as she teetered on the edge of orgasm.

As if on cue, her two lovers stopped, making her screech with frustration. They repositioned themselves and she felt Arno moving down her body, licking at her stomach, twirling his tongue around her navel. There was a pause and she could hear them whispering over her naked form. Then fingers entered her again and they seemed to be coming from two directions. Arno pulled gently with his teeth at the fleshy lips where they met her clitoris, pulling and sucking. Meanwhile, a soft tongue circled her anus. And the fingers plunged into her vagina, stretching her.

With astonishing precision, they moved together—Arno finally running his tongue around her swollen clit then sucking it into his mouth, Tamsin thrusting her tongue into the stretching hole of her anus. About eight fingers spiralled inside her. She grunted and pushed her hips upwards, trying to get away from the intrusive digits while urging them deeper inside her. The tongue in her anal passage was joined by a finger and that was the trigger that set off a massive orgasm of flashing lights and rippling skin and bubbling liquids, leaving her limp and exhausted.

She lay sated for some time and was aware of Tamsin and Arno reaching out through her spread legs and kissing, their faces touching her mons. Then Tamsin got up from her kneeling position on the floor and crawled onto the bed, lying flat with her head on the pillow so she was at right angles to where Eloise still sprawled.

"Right, Ellie, my turn now. Get licking!"

Eloise sat up. "Oh, God, I've never even…"

"Come on, Ellie, now it turns out you're so sophisticated! You ought to try…"

And Eloise, spurred on by a hazy notion that she ought to repay Tamsin the pleasure she had just experienced, rolled over and contemplated the parted legs of her old school-friend. The blonde hair glistened in the overhead lights and the puffy mons was swollen and pink. Tamsin drew her knees up, opening herself out, revealing a juicy, pink expanse of flesh.

Eloise took a deep breath and lowered her head, starting by simply nuzzling around the soft thighs. Tamsin thrust her hips upwards and with a strange detachment, Eloise saw that the area around her vagina pulsed and throbbed with a life of its own.

"I've wanted you to do this since we were at school together," Tamsin said, breathlessly. Reflecting how little she knew about the people around her, Eloise extended her tongue and began to run it around the fleshy lips.

It was fine, the taste wasn't repulsive, and Tamsin's breathy sounds of pleasure urged her on. She hardened her tongue and forced it into the pulsating hole, surprised at the vigour of Tamsin's response and the pleasure it gave her. She remembered that lesbians thought women were better at oral sex because they knew what buttons to press and she tried to imagine what she'd like herself. She put the tip of her tongue on the exposed nub of Tamsin's clitoris, noticing in passing how much bigger it was than her own.

She began to lap experimentally, remembering how she liked to be pleasured in this way and before long, Tamsin began to arch and groan. She was very wet and Eloise felt an extraordinary sense of achievement for having got her into this state. She wondered if this was how men felt when they gave a woman an orgasm.

She lay there, her cheek on Tamsin's abdomen, feeling the soft rise and fall of her body as she regained her breath. There was a pulling at her hips and she realised fingers were entering her, both vagina and anus. Arno. She was more than ready for his attentions and when he pulled her into a crawling position and entered her smoothly, she pushed back hard against him, wanting to feel the friction on her swollen clit. His hands caressed her breasts, pulling at her nipples. Then she was aware of something else, a tickling sensation on her tummy and then the feeling of wetness. Tamsin had scooted underneath her and was licking at her clit as Arno drove into her cunt. It was quite unlike anything she'd ever experienced before and the orgasm that struck her was sensational, radiating out from two centres, with a warmth and impact which left her weak and sobbing.

It was the first of many climaxes that night and of sexual positions and combinations of which she had never dreamt. It was well after midnight before the three of them fell into the sleep of utter satiety.

Chapter Twenty-Three

The sun filtered around the edges of the thick brocade curtains when Eloise awoke. She lay for a while, unsure where she was, knowing only she was on a bed and, for some reason, her feet were on the pillows. Next to her, someone slept, a hand thrown carelessly across her naked breasts. A feeling of great unease overtook her as she raised her head slightly and saw an unfamiliar white-blonde head. As her vision began to clear and her recollection returned, she recognised Arno de Vries. This was bad enough, but she was fairly sure there was more. A little, contented early morning sigh alerted her to the fact there was someone else on the bed and she turned over gingerly to see Tamsin, lying on her back and facing the other way, arms stretched above her head.

"Morning, Ellie, darling. Looks as if we've got a nice day for it!"

Eloise was saved from having to formulate a reply by the intervention of a gentle knock at the door.

"Come in!" Tamsin sang out.

"No!" Eloise said immediately and reached out in an attempt to grab something to cover herself. Too late; the door opened. A small serving trolley came into view and, pushing it, the unmistakeable figure of Dante de Rufina. He took in the sight of the tangled bodies on the bed without reaction.

"Miss Connaught, I've brought you some breakfast. And some flowers, in honour of your big day, with the compliments of Castel Rufina." He indicated a vase, in which a glorious bouquet of lilies was arranged,

"How very kind," Tamsin said, apparently unembarrassed.

"I'm afraid I didn't bring enough food for three..." Dante added, pulling back the curtains. "But I can go back to the kitchens if you like."

Arno had woken up now. "Nothing for me, thanks," he said, stretching. "I must go back to my room and shower." He stood up and began searching for his clothes. Eloise, not having found anything to cover her nakedness and quite unable to think of anything to say to Dante, rolled over on her stomach and, ostrich-like, buried her head in the crumpled sheets.

"No, that's fine, thank you, Conte," Tamsin said, in her best home-counties voice. He wheeled the trolley over to her side of the bed and turned to go.

"Thank you so much — for the breakfast and the flowers. But why on earth are you acting as chambermaid? Surely you don't usually do such menial tasks?"

"Oh, I do whatever's required. But on this occasion, I thought you might prefer not to have one of the...um...less discreet members of staff in your room. It occurred to me that you might not be alone."

Tamsin giggled. "I do like your Jeeves impression, Conte. And what a pity you didn't come a bit earlier. You could have joined us."

"A missed opportunity, Miss Connaught." His eyes were cool and amused, his expression hardening only when he glanced at Eloise's pink rump. At the door, he added, "Incidentally, I met Lady Connaught when I was on the way up here — she told me she'd be with you shortly."

He shut the door silently as Eloise leapt from the bed and began scrabbling around on the floor for her dress.

* * * *

When Eloise thought afterwards about the day of the wedding, she visualised it as a giant white swan, gliding on the waters of a beautiful lake. Underneath that effortless elegance, legs paddled frantically and it felt as if most of the propulsion was coming from Eloise herself.

Of course, she hadn't had the best of starts and she cursed her own stupidity for allowing herself to be seduced, literally, by Tamsin and Arno. It didn't help that as she moved around the Castel Rufina, she was frequently aware of the sardonic glances of Dante de Rufina. Her head ached and she felt empty and unhappy. Today was the culmination of her plan to save the business and she should have been on top form. But the knowledge that Dante had seen her degradation — that he'd been laughing at her weakness of character, ogling her bare bottom — ate away at her enjoyment, and she pursued her duties with a grim determination.

The first part of the day went fairly smoothly. Eloise spent some time with Tamsin as she dressed, but the room was crowded, with Lady Connaught and most of the bridesmaids in attendance and after a while she left them to it. The civil ceremony should have been a short, dry episode, but predictably it grew and took on a life of its own. In the ancient town hall, an official read the questions in Italian and Eloise translated, rendering the English responses back into the language. It seemed to go on for a very long time and there was a moment of hilarity when it transpired that Italian law required the details of the birth-dates, not only of the bride and groom, but also of the witnesses — causing much comic outrage.

As they emerged from the town hall, Eloise sighed with relief. At least they were married. Whatever else went wrong, she had managed to get the right couple together. As they posed for pictures on the steps, she saw a familiar face in the crowd of mostly women and children. Tom Sherwin was there, looking at her rather oddly. She waved and after a slight hesitation he returned the gesture before turning to disappear back towards the inn.

Now came the blessing, which, because it was replacing the church aspect of the wedding, had assumed a greater importance than the actual exchange of vows. Eloise suffered a little pang when she saw Tamsin, dressed in white, processing down towards the keep, just as she had herself a few days earlier. She looked absolutely stunning. The dress was very different from that worn by the unfortunate Isabella. In rich cream satin, it had a rigid bodice, thick with brocade, which displayed Tamsin's generous breasts to their full advantage. Ruched, off-the-shoulder sleeves were decorated with white rosebuds and from the waist, a full skirt swirled into a heavy train. She wore a veil of old lace, secured by what her mother insisted on calling 'the Connaught tiara' — which of course it was, having been purchased from Asprey's a few months earlier.

The journey to the chapel passed smoothly, with the guests exclaiming at the rose arches on the path down from the keep and charmed by the concept of having the pages and small bridesmaids throwing rose petals as Tamsin approached — something which Eloise missed, as she had cut on ahead to make sure everything was all right in the chapel. It looked good, except...she moved to the front and accosted Francis Carew-Wright, Alistair's uncle, who'd been excused the procession on the grounds of having gout. "Where's Alistair?"

Francis was wheezy and cheerful. From the redness of his face, Eloise deduced he had already helped himself liberally to the hospitality. "Oh, he went outside with Fred. Last minute nerves, I think."

"Where did they go?" she asked, urgently. It was only a matter of minutes before the bride's procession arrived.

Francis gestured vaguely and she raced out of the door and walked swiftly around the chapel. At the back, she found her quarry. As she rounded the corner, she saw that Alistair and Fred were locked in an embrace and Fred was patting his friend on the back. In booming tones he was saying, "It's all right, old chap, it's going to be fine."

"Shit, Freddy, I can't do it. I can't. It's all been a terrible mistake."

"Got to, Ali. Gets us all off the hook." Relief was etched on Freddy's face as he saw Eloise. "Look, here comes the boss lady. She'll sort you out."

"Alistair, I need you in the church. Tamsin will be there in a minute."

He turned towards her, his face contorted. "Can't go on. Should never have... Sorry, Ellie."

Visions of an outraged Lady Connaught flitted in front of Eloise's eyes and she felt rising panic, but faced with Alistair's obvious distress, she curbed her tongue.

"Look, Alistair, don't worry about me. Don't worry about anyone else. This is important—it's your life. Take your time, think about it."

"But Mother... Lady C..."

"Yes, well that's the problem, isn't it? They've been putting you under so much pressure. And if I understand the situation, you have to decide if you're prepared to tie yourself to Tamsin in a...um...fairly unorthodox arrangement which means you'll be free of all that interference."

"Yes, that's..."

"And you'll have what you want—a respectable family life, a society wife and yet you'll be free to be with Fred."

He nodded.

"Well, it's taken me a while to understand it, but now I think it's probably a good deal. For you, at least. Frankly, I'm not sure about Tamsin. I mean, someone else might come along, someone a little less—kinky than Arno and she might want a normal marriage. But what the hell? If that happens, you'll just be a divorcee, presumably with children. And you'll still be able to live as you want. But if you dodge out now then you've been through all this for nothing."

"Yes, but it's so final."

"True." She had her arm around him now, feeling him shaking. "But try not to think of it as losing your liberty." She had a flash of inspiration. "Really, what you're doing is committing yourself to Fred here. Only most of the people here won't know that. But that's what it is."

Alistair looked up, his face clearing.

"And there's another thing, Ali. You've done the difficult bit. Exchanged the vows. You are actually married. Everything else, all this, is just play-acting. More stuff to please the mothers."

He straightened. "Bloody hell, yes, of course. It's done, isn't it?"

Fred slapped him on the shoulders. "Nothing left now but to face the music, old chap."

Alistair gave them both a watery smile. "Absolutely. Sorry, sorry, sorry." He squared his shoulders. "Okay, I'm ready now."

They got round the chapel just as the procession arrived at the last rose arch and Eloise hustled them back inside in time for her to turn and greet the bride's party.

The ceremony was short and touching. Eloise suspected the chaplain had also been at the wedding sherry, but he got through it, his flowery language going down conspicuously well with the mothers of the bride and groom.

Alistair seemed to have conquered his nerves and he looked every inch the proud bridegroom as he emerged from the chapel beneath an arch of six lavatory brushes held aloft by his rugby chums. Eloise, anticipating Lady Connaught's anguish, clapped her hands, laughing, "Very funny, chaps. Absolutely hilarious! Now, for the sake of posterity, can we do the exit again, this time without the embellishments? Thanks a lot, boys."

Thus, two sets of photographs showed two very different accounts of the same event and Eloise reflected that this was probably a metaphor for the marriage as a whole. She was still uneasy about the deception, but somehow had got used to it, and having seen both sets of parents in operation—or to be exact, both mothers—she found herself in a greater degree of sympathy with the couple than she'd expected.

The rest of the day passed smoothly, a buffet lunch spilling out onto the terrace, after which there was a rest period before the serious business of the day — the formal dinner and speeches. With much ribaldry, Tamsin and Alistair were serenaded to their room — Tamsin's, which had become their bridal chamber — and were forced to spend the next two hours extricating whoopee cushions from the bed and hidden alarm clocks planted by his rugby companions.

At the dinner, although she was seated at the end of the top table, Eloise spent much of the meal flitting about making sure things were going smoothly. About halfway through, she was coming back from the kitchen after pursuing an enquiry about a vegetarian meal when she ran into Dante close to the big stone fireplace.

"Well, are you happy?"

"Happy is too strong a word. Ask me again when it's over."

"I thought you were keeping your spirits up very effectively. I must say, your devotion to the bride seems to me to be above and beyond the call of duty."

"Damn you, Dante, leave me alone. And by the way, I don't appreciate you telling Arno about what you...what we did...I thought it was private."

"As private as sex in front of nearly fifty people ever is." She made a sound of distress and he shrugged his shoulders. "You're very selective about what embarrasses you. But as it happens, I haven't spoken about our...er...coming together to a soul. I've maintained a gentlemanly silence throughout."

Heatedly, she responded, "But he said a member of the family told him."

"So? It sounds like Ugo to me. They're two of a kind, if you ask me. Both slavering over your debauchery."

She turned her head away, face burning, and he went on. "Oh and, Eloise...don't forget our conversation. About our unfinished business."

She had thought of very little else, but wanted to conceal it from him at all costs, so she replied coolly, "I'm afraid I can't concentrate on anything apart from the business in hand at the moment."

"Oh? Then make this the business in hand." Without warning he grabbed her arm and pulled her into the great fireplace. It was of heavy granite like the rest of that part of the building and between the massive square lintel and the fire itself was a niche, bearing on either side a small, carved bench. He dragged her in until they were out of view and thrust her against the hard stone between the seats and the fire. "Now will you think about it?"

She was scandalised. "Dante, not now!"

"Yes, now!" he retorted, his voice dark with menace. He pressed her up against the stone, his face looming over hers. "You can't just flit around the place like this, leaping into bed with all and sundry, without giving me an answer. Will you come to me tonight?"

"No, not tonight. There's still a lot to do before tomorrow. And I'm very tired."

"Too tired for this?" He put his hands on her shoulders and kissed her hard—a potent reminder of the extraordinary coda to their performance as Rodolfo and Isabella. At first, she tried to push him away before the seductive pull of his mouth, of his magnetism of his masculinity, drew her in. His hand scooped up her skirt and wrenched at her underwear. Fingers penetrated her as she tried to writhe away from him. He thrust his hand inside her, his lips not moving from her mouth, tongue probing.

Little sounds emanated from her — of resistance, of entreaty, of surrender. At last she managed to pull away and brought one hand up sharply against his cheek.

"This is not the time or the place! For God's sake, Dante, people might see us."

"Good! It'll be the closest thing to true passion they get at this wedding." He withdrew his hand. "Unless you want me to take you here, in the fireplace, you'll give me an answer. Tonight?"

Looking up into his dark eyes, she tried to rationalise their situation. "Let me make sure I've got this right. You want us to make love because you think we didn't quite get it out of our systems the other day — is that it? A sort of inoculation?"

He gave a twisted grin. "You could describe it like that, if you like. It would certainly involve an injection."

"But that's it? No love, no emotion, just a fuck?"

"Not how I would have put it, but if that suits you, then fine."

"What about Jessica?"

"What about the bore in the village, or your new lesbian lover, or the extraordinarily self-absorbed young man from London? This is outside relationships, Lola, darling — it's just about sex.

She shook her head. "I can't operate like this, Dante, it's so cold. Like a business arrangement."

He stared down at her, his face dark, eyes unfathomable. Then he gave his head a little shake. "I understand. Well, we can dress it up a bit. Make it respectable. Tell you what, tomorrow — no, that's the musical evening — the night after. Why don't you come to dinner? I'll get the children out of the way and we can have a proper talk."

"But why should I bother to come at all?"

He pushed her back onto the stone, pressing himself against her, hands either side of her head. "Because I think you're just as interested as I am in seeing how far we can go. Because if you don't, you'll wonder about it for the rest of your life."

She nodded, knowing she would have agreed to anything to remove the present danger of his body pressed against hers, his hardness firm against her.

"Yes, all right. The day after tomorrow. To talk."

"Good. Oh and, Lola. That flamingo pink really looks good on your bottom. Later on you must tell me what they did to you to get it such a lovely colour."

With that he released her and she slipped from the chimney, flushed and shaking, and went back to the woman who had queried the food. She was congratulating herself on having got away without being seen, but after the dinner, when the dancing had started, Sammy came up to her. "All well?"

"I think so. One more day of this and we'll be clear. I feel like a sheepdog with a particularly difficult flock."

"I know what you mean. But today's been brilliant. I've given away at least a dozen *Lace Dreams* brochures. People seem really impressed."

"Well, thank God for that."

"Actually," Sammy said, "I'm pretty impressed as well. So are you going to tell me what you were doing with the handsome Conte in the fireplace of all places?"

"What?"

"I saw him pull you into the fireplace and you were both gone for rather a long time. When you came out, you were very pink and ruffled and then he emerged looking wolf-like and pleased with himself."

"He always looks like that."

"So, give. What's going on?"

Eloise found she was so unsure herself about Dante that she was quite unable to discuss it, even with her best friend. "Nothing. We were talking about...vegetarian meals."

"Vegetarian meals? Well, if it makes you look that sexy, I must try it myself some time. Come off it, Ellie."

Eloise blushed. "He asked me again to sleep with him."

"That's more like it. And you accepted, several times over?"

"No. I mean... I can't go on like this, Sammy. What with..." Just in time, she remembered the secret of her tryst with Tamsin and Arno would open up a whole lot of other issues.

"What is it, Eloise? Falling in love with the enigmatic Count?"

"He isn't enigmatic at all and no, I'm not. He just...winds me up, that's all."

Chapter Twenty-Four

Later that evening, when Eloise finally got to her room, she sighed with relief. Things had gone smoothly — potential rows and scandals had been avoided. And glancing at the sheaf of papers she carried with her, she saw with pleasure that the small exhibition of paintings which she'd persuaded Matt to mount in a room off the lobby had been a huge success — already nine had sold. She smiled to herself. When they'd set it up, she'd told Matt, "I bet you sell them all."

"I bet I don't sell any at all."

"Tell you what, if we find buyers for more than — what, ten? — will you reconsider going to art school?"

He'd laughed at her. "If there are enough people sufficiently demented to buy five, I'll book myself in for next term."

She undressed, wrapped herself in a dressing gown and flung herself on the bed. What a day! Now, all she wanted to do was sleep.

There was a knock at the door and she scowled. "Who is it?"

"It's me, babe." Jake was already in the room.

She shot up. "Jake! How did you get here?"

"I walked," he said reasonably. "That guy on the desk told me where you were."

"Guy on the desk?"

He moved towards the bed, tearing off his tie and removing his jacket.

"The receptionist. Big, black-haired bloke. He's weird. Tried to make me go away, said you'd be too tired to see me. Bloody cheek!"

She sat up, sighing. "That's the Conte de Rufina. He owns this place."

"Well? He's still just a hotelier, isn't he?" Jake had now removed his trousers and was hopping from foot to foot, taking off underpants and socks.

"What are you doing?"

He toppled over onto the bed next to her, white boxers tangled around his ankles, his beautiful cock at half-mast. "Getting ready to make love to you, sweetheart. It's been a long time."

To her shame, Eloise realised that her agonising about her new adventurous love life hadn't featured Jake at all.

"Jake, I'm terribly tired and busy."

"Not too tired to take care of this, though?" He waggled his erection at her, smiling boyishly.

"Oh, Jake." With sharp comprehension, Eloise realised she would have to talk to him seriously, to ease him away, detach him. It was over — there was no doubt about it. But at the same time, she acknowledged to herself that she was too tired for a scene. And so there was only one thing she could do.

She undid the belt on her dressing gown and opened her arms to him.

* * * *

The next day was much more relaxed. No formal ceremonies or appointments were planned during the day, but in the evening a barbecue around the pool was to be followed by a musical entertainment. With some misgiving, Eloise had accepted Lady Connaught's instructions and hired a string quartet. As the days went on and she came to know the guests better, she knew this wasn't the right choice, but at this stage, she hoped that most of them would be so mellowed by the lavish food and alcohol that the choice of music wouldn't matter.

In the early afternoon, Eloise, passing through the lobby, was alarmed to find Lady Connaught haranguing the unfortunate desk clerk about the absence of that day's London papers. She was moving on to mount the stairs for her own office, when Dante emerged from his, frowning. "Ah, Lola, I just took a call from your musicians. They've been involved in a car accident."

"How dreadful! Are they all right?"

"A broken ankle, one sprained wrist and a smashed double bass, apparently. But they won't be able to appear this evening."

"Oh dear, Eloise, this is a disaster! A disaster. I knew it was a mistake to allow them to travel on the day." Lady Connaught's eyes glittered and she had the triumphant look of one who had been waiting for something to go wrong. "We can't possibly replace them at this short notice."

Eloise refrained from saying her suggestion that the musicians should stay in the hotel had been vetoed by her ladyship on the grounds of cost. "Don't worry, Bryony, I'm sure we can find someone else. Dante, can you think of anyone local who might fit the bill?"

He shook his head. "Not off-hand. I could ask Ugo. Of course…"

Lady Connaught swept on. "Well, I don't know what you intend to do about this, Eloise, because it's the set piece of the second day. Everyone was looking forward to it."

Dante held up his hand to stop her. "I'll go and talk to Ugo. But all I wanted to say was that if no one else is available, I'll perform myself. Not as good as a string quartet, but something, at least."

Lady Connaught gave him a withering stare. "Well, that's very sweet of you, young man. But I think our guests are entitled to something a bit more than amateur night."

Eloise choked down a laugh. "Bryony, you know this is the Conte de Rufina? The owner of the castle?"

The older woman looked slightly more interested, holding out her hand. Dante, with a mocking glance at Eloise, took it and brought it to his lips.

"And that he is an internationally renowned jazz pianist."

"Jazz?" She said it like Lady Bracknell speaking of the handbag.

"Yes, well I'm afraid I can't rise to the level of Mozart. But should you need me, I'll run through my modest repertoire. Let me know, will you, Lola?"

By the evening, Lady Connaught had finessed the story into a desperate crisis during which she had persuaded the reluctant genius to grant them an audience. Frankly, by the time the meal was over, Eloise thought they could have played the greatest hits of Chas and Dave and no one would have objected or even noticed.

The grand piano had been brought from the bar and set up on the deck. Dusk was well advanced and the fairy lights were on, illuminating the whole of the rear of the hotel. Dante arrived in full evening dress and bowed to a smattering of applause. Alistair's mother, oblivious to the drama that had gone on before, leaned over to Lady Connaught.

"Gracious, Bryony, however did you get Dan Rufin to perform? Mags Gabriel tried to get him for Janine's wedding and his people refused point-blank."

Dante went through a repertoire of light songs — jazz standards, pop classics and material from musicals. It was finely judged and after a while, most of the guests were on the dance floor.

His voice was deep, husky, sexy and his performance compelling. Eloise watched from the bar, her face glowing. This was Dante in a different light — he was professional, almost serious, and irresistibly charming. As his set drew to an end, she walked around the outskirts of the gathering, noticing with pleasure that people were really enjoying themselves. On the edge of the party, near the private area of the grounds, she discovered Matt, Laura and Marco, the latter clutching a sleepy Charlie.

"Hope it's all right for us to be here," Laura whispered. "But we never hear him perform in public. He won't let us go to the club."

"It's fine." Eloise made sure they had drinks and something to eat before moving on.

The evening was drawing to an end and Sir Lyndo, who apart from his speech the previous day, had been very restrained until now, stood up and gave a rambling address, praising everyone, and finished off, "I'd like to make a final vote of thanks for little Eloise, who's been with us all along, planning this happy event, taking the rough with the smooth. She's been wonderful and I think everyone who's enjoyed this great party would agree. Ladies and gentlemen, Eloise!"

He raised his glass, the gesture echoed by all the guests and Dante, still at the piano, struck up and started to sing. "Lola, Lo-Lo-La-La Lola…"

When she went up to thank him for saving the day, she found he was being mobbed by Bryony's society friends, all demanding he play at this function or that party. He fended them off with easy charm.

"No, no really, I'm terribly flattered, but I'm afraid I can't do individual commissions just now. I'm so tied up with this place and *The Inferno* and my own little family. I'm just doing this as a favour to Ms Lambert. But if you're interested in the whole package, let me recommend *Lace Dreams*. It's a first-class events agency. I think you'll find some brochures at reception."

He closed the lid of the piano with finality and got up, putting his arm around Eloise and drawing her away to indicate a polite end to the conversation.

"Come along," he insisted, moving her firmly through the house. "Save me from the harpies. Let's take a turn around the walls. I get all hyper when I've been performing."

They climbed up onto the battlements without speaking and walked around to where the stairs descended, near the keep. Here they stopped to gaze out at the view, brightly illuminated beneath them.

It was a perfect night, the moon hung low over the Tuscan countryside and the air, still warm, held the sweet odour of roses.

"Thank you for giving the plug for *Lace Dreams*, that was very kind," she said and then, with a twinge of alarm, realising they hadn't discussed money. "And of course, you must submit your invoice…"

He laughed then. "My darling, you couldn't afford me. Let's say I'll do it for a kiss." And without warning, he pulled her into an embrace, his strong arms tight around her. As their lips met, Eloise experienced that electric feeling of excitement she had felt before, compounded because she knew their behaviour was inappropriate. But she let it go, melting, blending into him.

When she finally brought herself to pull away, his voice was husky. "Bring our rendezvous forward a day? Tonight! Please?"

She wasn't ready for this. "No, there's still so much to do. And there's Jessica…"

He straightened up. "Ah yes, Jessica. She's still here, you're right, but she'll be gone tomorrow. And of course, I forgot that you've got a strict timetable with your favours. It was the vapid youth last night, who is tonight's favoured bedfellow? Not the man from the town, surely? Oh, I guess it must be the strange Dutchman — presumably your friends will manage to spend at least the wedding nights together?"

It was like a slap and she pulled away. She could have retorted that the newlyweds were indeed spending this honeymoon night together, but that it seemed to be an event open to friends. Even she had received an invitation to join them. His sarcasm had broken a spell and she pulled away and made for nearest flight of stone steps leading downwards, Dante following. Halfway down she stopped, frozen. On the inside of the walls here it was dark, but someone below them had opened a door and yellow electric light spilled out across the gravel path and the grass.

A beautifully modulated voice, with the slightest overtones of inebriation, said, "Well, are you coming in?" Eloise indicated to Dante that he should stay where he was and be quiet. With a shock, she realised exactly where they were, at the north wall, at the far end of the castle, to which Dante had exiled Jake.

Jake himself now stepped into the spotlight his opened bedroom door had created. He held out his hand to someone in the darkness.

"Come here!" he commanded, in a voice rough with lust. "I want you, now. Will your husband miss you?"

"No, of course not. By now he's probably fast asleep. Lyndo never could hold his drink. Kiss me." And Bryony Connaught stepped into the beam of light and into a very steamy embrace. Above her on the stairs, Eloise heard a choking sound which she thought was Dante trying not to laugh and she gave him a reproving glare. The kiss finished and Jake shepherded his guest into the lighted doorway. "And now I'm going to make love to you as you deserve. All night," he declaimed grandly, as the door closed on his little playlet.

They walked down the remaining steps and headed back to the house. "Well, that rules out one of your options for tonight," Dante remarked, "unless you fancy a threesome with Lady Connaught and I don't think you're really sunk sufficiently low in depravity for that."

She made a sound and he gave her a sharp look. "You're upset? This was the proper boyfriend, wasn't it?"

"No, I'm not upset. A bit miffed, I suppose. And astonished."

"Yes, it isn't one of the most obvious pairings is it? But perfect. I mean, if ever two people deserved each other…"

They rejoined the party and Dante was immediately claimed by a London acquaintance in a stunning gold gown. Eloise walked through to the top terrace, where she ran straight into Jessica Anthony. The model clutched a glass of champagne, her eyes glittering like the bubbles in the drink.

"Ah, the little organiser. A tour de force, my dear."

Eloise thought the model was drunk or high or possibly both. "Thank you."

"Oh, and I wish you joy of him. Though I doubt you have the stamina to cope. Physically or mentally."

Chapter Twenty-Five

For Eloise, the following day was chaotic. For some reason, winding things down was almost more difficult than setting them up in the first place. Her frame of mind wasn't helped by the receipt of a note from Dante, which merely said, "I'll see you tonight at eight."

Tamsin and Alistair left at midday in a glorious vintage Rolls-Royce — their destination Venice as the first part of a lengthy honeymoon. A second car, departing discreetly afterwards, carried Arno and Fred.

By the evening, most of the necessary issues had been addressed, bills had been paid and thanks distributed. Sir Lyndo and Lady Connaught departed for a trip to Rome before their return to London. Samantha went off with the van, stuffed with the detritus of the wedding and, to Eloise's intense relief, carrying Jake.

As the evening drew near she grew increasingly nervous. But she prepared for her dinner with Dante with care, dressing in a green shift dress and her green mules.

Underneath, after some hesitation, she put on the grape bra and panties. She brushed her auburn hair until it shone and decided not to put it up, but left it hanging in a silky veil down her back. She walked slowly through the garden, thinking that she had never before gone to a man's apartment with the sole and single purpose of going to bed with him. But this visit to Dante was purely about sex — although she doubted if purity would have much to do with it. Her breasts felt heavy and tender and she was aware of a dull, aching throb between her legs and that the flimsy new knickers were already wet.

Dante responded immediately to her knock on the cold glass of the French window. He wore black slacks and a dark red cashmere jumper, which accentuated his dark hair and pale skin.

If Eloise, thinking about this rendezvous, had decided to face full-on the fact it was just about sex, Dante seemed to have gone in the other direction altogether. He welcomed her in with a chaste kiss on the cheek, got her a drink and some antipasti, behaving as if this were a normal dinner party.

"Where are the children?" she asked.

"Laura and Marco are staying with school-friends. Matt's gone to Florence. Charlie's in bed — out like a light. I didn't tell him you were coming or he'd never have agreed to settle down."

"Jessica got off all right?"

Her voice had a slight edge to it and so did his when he replied, "Yes. How about Jake?"

They ate simply and well, salad and a pasta dish — which he'd made himself — washed down by Castel Rufina wine. Conversation was relaxed and easy and after they'd finished Dante cleared away the first course and came back with a dish containing a magnificent tiramisu.

"I wish I could say this was all my own work as well but I cannot tell a lie—Maria made it."

He placed a green and gold china bowl in front of her and spooned some of the trifle into it. The lush cream ran slowly across the patterned surface and the rich smell of chocolate was heavy and sensual.

The pace of their conversation had slowed. Eloise took one delicious mouthful and then glanced up to see Dante watching her with unwavering attention. She looked down at her plate. "I can't eat any more," she whispered.

"Neither can I." He pushed the untasted dessert away. "Come to bed."

After they deposited the tiramisu in the kitchen he held his hand out to her and led her to the bedroom. At the door, he stood back, letting her walk into the centre of the room. He leaned on the lintel, his eyes dark and intense.

"Lola." He said no more, just stared at her. Then he moved towards her with a feline grace that was almost menacing. "Would you like to know what I'm going to do to you?"

She made a sound that emerged as a whimper.

Standing right in front of her now he ran his fingers through her hair, letting it fall back onto her bare shoulder. "I like your hair like this. But we don't really need the dress, do we?" He reached behind her, finding the zip with practiced ease and drawing it down. He pulled the garment over her head, his mouth forming a soundless whistle as he saw the underwear. "At last, I get to see the famous bra and panties. Very nice. Turn round for me."

She revolved slowly on her high green heels.

There was an audible intake of breath. "Altogether delightful. I rather missed the subtleties last time. Mmmm. And do I take it this outfit is still...virgin?"

"Yes." The word came out as little more than a breath. He ran a finger between her legs, not saying anything, then held it up between them, the moisture on it clearly apparent.

"Well, I want to get the full benefit from this lovely lingerie before I take it off you. Then I'm going to masturbate you until you come. And watch you. Because I want to see that moment, that glorious instant, when your cool, well-mannered, good-girl expression gets chased away. The moment you realise you can't hold out against your baser instincts any longer and your eyes suddenly glaze over with lust and the knowledge of dark and dirty things to come."

She swayed on her heels, her eyes closed. She was so aroused she thought the throbbing of her vulva must be visible to him.

He curved his hands around her breasts, running his thumbs across the straining nipples. Scooping one globe out of its lacy nest he lowered his tongue to her overheated flesh. She shook as he drew the hard bud into his mouth and repeated the action with her other breast.

He began to kiss her throat, nuzzling her long neck as his hands worked expertly to unfasten the bra.

"You smell of honey," he said, then stepped back, glancing at the scrap of green and purple lace in his hand. "I love this. You must have been thinking about me when you bought it."

He gave her a wicked grin, but she was too far gone to care. He reached for the bows that held the little panties in position.

"I've dreamed about this," he said.

"And so have I."

The lacy knickers fell to the floor.

His finger smoothed very gently along her naked slit. "Oh, Lola, darling, this is getting a little bit bristly. You'll have to do something about it, or you'll have trouble walking." His hand pressed forward and the finger entered her wet, warm channel. "After tonight, you're going to have trouble walking anyway."

He started to move his hand, his fingers curving inside her. His eyes were fixed on a point at the other side of the room.

"Now then, my darling, I want to tell you what's going to happen next. After I've made you come for the first time, I'm going to get you to lie down on the bed and I'm going to examine you. Because during our rather unconventional first date, I missed the finer points. So I'm going to open your legs and spread those fleshy little lips, the ones where the hair is growing back, and I'm going to scrutinise the pink folds and whorls and I'm going to jab my tongue as far up your cunt as it will go until you come again. Then I'm going to fuck you without mercy until you scream for me to go on and scream for me to stop and climax over and over again. And afterwards, when you're still writhing and sore and throbbing, I'm going to turn you over and work my fingers into your secret place, that orifice you shouldn't allow anything to enter. Then I'm going to bugger you, very, very hard. And I know you'll like it, because I saw what happened to you in the dungeon, when you couldn't control yourself. When you went from virginal good girl to abandoned whore in a few seconds flat, just because you had a cock inside that forbidden hole."

He thrust four fingers into her, making her gasp. Then, with his thumb, he resumed his stroking of her clitoris.

"Oh and, Lola, did you know that while I was fucking you the other night, someone was taking photographs? There's a particularly fetching one of you, as I was carrying you out. I had you over my shoulder and all you can see is your bottom. It's not a very good photograph, actually. It's a bit dark. But you can see there are two distinct patches, two trickles of white just beginning. My semen oozing from your cunt and your arse..."

That did it, as he knew it would. His head turned and his dark eyes fastened on her face. The rush of heat and sensation gathered in her sex, at the pit of her stomach. She managed to cry out, "Oh, God, Dante..."

With that, the bedroom door was flung open, crashing loudly against the wall. Dante turned swiftly, masking her from the interloper. Her heart thudded violently, the snatched-away orgasm causing her something like physical pain.

A little voice said, "Dante, I've been sick..."

Dante moved forward fast. From a chair, he seized a maroon silk dressing gown, which he flung behind him to Eloise. He went down on his haunches.

"Oh, bloody hell, Charlie, what have you done now?"

Charlie was a woebegone figure. His pyjama suit, in pale blue with appliqué teddy bears, was streaked with yellow and brown vomit, which was all over his bare feet and even in his hair.

"Sick!"

"Christ, have you messed up your bed?"

Eloise went forward, the gown wrapped around her. "Perhaps you ought to get him cleaned up first, Dante."

"Little bastard. Let me see what he's done."

Dante disappeared in the direction of Charlie's room and after a moment's hesitation, Eloise picked up the child. She felt his forehead. It was warm, but not unduly so.

"Come on, Charlie, I think what you need is a bath."

She carried him through to the big family bathroom, where she had helped Laura with her pregnancy test, and started to run the water. Charlie whinged quietly, but when she stripped the romper suit off him, he seemed to cheer up. She put the pyjamas in the hand-basin to soak and lowered him gently into the water, soaping him all over. "We'd better wash your hair as well. How on earth did you get sick up there?"

After a while she became aware of intense scrutiny from the doorway. Dante was there, leaning on the lintel.

"He's wrecked his bed. I've had to strip it and disinfect the mattress. And guess what? Most of the tiramisu has disappeared and all of the antipasti. No wonder the little bastard was so ill."

Eloise got Charlie out of the bath and dried him. Dante watched with a jaundiced eye.

"Damn it, Lola, it should be me you're running your hands up and down."

This made her laugh and she bundled the child into a towel and hoisted him into her arms. "Where shall I put him?"

"Oh f...oh, bother. He'd better go into my bed. His is uninhabitable and I suppose I ought to keep an eye on him. Foul little beast."

"I don't think he has a temperature. Do you have a thermometer?"

"Do devils have temperatures? Of course he hasn't, this is purely self-inflicted. Sheer overindulgence. It's a family trait."

She carried him through and Dante pulled back the covers of his bed. Charlie was awake, but sleepy.

"Story now," he demanded.

Dante looked at him in disbelief. "You nasty little tripe-hound! You burst in here, ruining my love-life because of your own greed and selfishness and now you think you can bamboozle me into another story?"

"Tripe-hound," Charlie echoed, pleased.

Dante looked at Eloise over the bed. "I don't know what to say. We can't go back to where we were, can we?"

"We can't do anything."

"I guess you're right. God, Charlie!" He made neck-wringing gestures at the child. "I suppose you want to go?"

"No, not really. I'll stay with you. Keep an eye on him."

"Well, that would be something. If you don't mind spending the night with someone who's likely to vomit all over you at any moment."

"No, I don't mind. I don't mind Charlie either…"

He laughed, but his eyes were dark with longing.

Eloise settled down on the bed and Charlie automatically moved towards her and curled up close. Watching Dante, she saw him grimace. He stripped off his sweater and the jeans, revealing boxer shorts that could not conceal his erection.

"This is what Charlie's depriving you of," he said, climbing into bed on the other side of the child. He reached a hand across and stroked her shoulder through the silk of his robe. "Thank you, Lola."

"For what?"

"For not storming off. For understanding about the brat."

They slept fitfully until about seven-thirty, when Charlie awoke in high spirits and began bouncing about on the bed. Eloise got up and began searching for her clothes, smoothing the soft material of the bra and pants in her hand and remembering the highly charged atmosphere in which they had been removed. She looked across to see Dante watching her while Charlie sat on his legs.

"I'm so sorry, my darling. We'll try again tonight. I'll get the brat adopted. Or perhaps the RSPCA would take the horrid little creature. Whatever the Italian equivalent is."

By now she had wriggled into her dress under cover of the silk robe. Her face tightened. "I can't."

"Why not? You said you weren't flying home until tomorrow."

"Yes, I know, but I'm leaving the hotel today."

"You're leaving the hotel…" He sat up abruptly, moving Charlie to one side. "So where are you going? Oh, don't tell me, let me guess. It's your other paramour, the one in Rufina. Yes? My God, Lola, you're ruthless with any poor devil that misses his window of opportunity, aren't you?"

She turned to face him, pale and tense. "But, Dante, you said it didn't mean anything. You told me you'd teach me that pure sex, without strings and entanglements, would be liberating. Naked, uninhibited lust, you said. That's what I understood—that there was nothing between us."

"Well, there's certainly been nothing on this occasion."

"No, no emotional ties. No obligations."

"And so?" he replied, nastily.

"And so we don't owe each other anything. This was supposed to be a transaction, that's what you said. There was to be no feeling, no emotion. No love."

"Right." His face was blank. He got out of bed and picked up Charlie. "Come on, monster, I'll get you some breakfast, if you think you can hold anything down." Then, dismissively, "Goodbye, Eloise. Thank you so much for coming. Or, as it happens, not, actually." And he turned his back on her and walked off to the kitchen.

She went to her room, devastated. She'd given him his opportunity — if he'd said one word to suggest he had any feelings for her at all, she would have abandoned her tryst with Tom Sherwin in the blink of an eye. But it was clear he regarded her only as a sexual commodity. On his side there was nothing, no love, no affection even, just animal attraction.

Chapter Twenty-Six

When she left that evening, almost the whole staff of the hotel came out to say goodbye. Ugo was there and Maria and the children, Laura almost in tears. There was no sign of Dante.

"You'll be back? " Maria asked, her face crumpled.

"I think so. We've got three definite bookings for weddings here and at least five serious enquiries. I'll be back soon!"

Tom Sherwin waited for her outside the inn and after he carried her overnight bag into his room, he kissed her with a new urgency.

They ate in the hotel and although he was courteous as always, there was an edge to his conversation, which she hadn't experienced before. After the meal, they went back to his room. Eloise was already in a strange mood after her encounter with Dante and she put her natural reticence aside to ask him, "What's the matter, Tom? You're odd. Tell me, please. I'm going home tomorrow and I'm feeling out of sorts. I'm simply not up to working my way through some complicated diplomatic route to find out what this is all about."

He put his hands on her arms, a strange light in his eyes. "Oh, it's nothing. Except I know about your performance up at the Castel."

"Oh."

"Well, something like that was hardly going to be a secret. Salvatore, the innkeeper, was there and the chief of police. I heard all about it. Oh boy, did I hear about it. In explicit detail."

"Well? I could explain that I had to do it, to protect the Conte's young sister. But I don't have to justify myself to you."

He gave a grating laugh. "Oh, that's what he told you, was it? That his sister was in danger? I guessed there was some sort of scam to get you involved."

"It wasn't a scam. Petrela took her," Eloise told him the story.

His hands gripped her tightly. "And you believed it? Eloise, my dear, Dante de Rufina and Tolka Petrela are partners. They're doing deals. You really think Petrela would risk a vendetta by kidnapping his sister?"

"But I saw Laura afterwards. She was upset and frightened."

"Laura would do what Dante told her to. And in any case, she wouldn't necessarily have known what was going on. In Dante's world and Petrela's, women are commodities, pawns to be used as they think fit."

She opened her mouth to argue, but decided it wasn't worth it. Dante's distress had been genuine, she was sure of that. And yet... She put the thought to one side and with her newfound directness said, "So, do you want me to go? There's not much point in me staying if you're just going to chastise me for being the scarlet woman of Rufina."

"Chastise," he repeated. "I like that word." He pulled her into a fierce kiss, most unlike his usual respectful approach and started biting at her neck, his hands pulling roughly at her skirt until it was up around her waist. His hands went into the top of her panties, grabbing her buttocks, squeezing them.

He backed towards the bed and sat down, holding her in front of him.

"Well, Eloise, it seems you're not the kind of girl I thought you were. And, Christ, it turns me on."

"It was something I had to do. I don't think it makes me any different..."

"I do. I think all this was just an excuse for you to misbehave. I think you acted in a thoroughly wanton way. Disgusting. Like a dirty little trollop. A whore. And now I'm going to...what was that word...chastise you." He pulled her roughly across his knee, dragging her skirt up to expose the skimpy black of her panties.

Eloise was indignant with shock. This was not her style at all — crude sex games had never featured in her lifestyle before. She tried to form words for her annoyance, prepared to wriggle to her feet with as much dignity as possible. Tom took the edges of her panties and began to draw them slowly downwards.

"I'm going to examine your naughty little bottom and then I'm going to smack you until you're sorry for what you've done."

And suddenly, a rush of excitement and lust swirled through her stomach and corkscrewed into her sex. It stopped her attempt to escape in its tracks. His hands parted her buttocks and she could feel hot breath on the delicate flesh of her anus. A finger brushed lightly across it and to her shame, she pushed upwards, trying to get him closer. But he pulled away with a laugh.

"Take your punishment." And he began a slow, rhythmic slapping on the fleshiest part of her buttocks.

Now, she thought, she should get up and leave. But each blow was sending a radiant charge through her pelvis and each time his hand smacked her flesh, the slow erotic build-up inside her became irresistible. She cried out in unmistakeable, outraged pleasure and from the hard projection which prodded at her midriff, it seemed Tom was enjoying himself as well.

He brought her just to the edge of orgasm and stopped, leaving her panting and writhing in an attempt to get him to go on, or to apply some friction to her throbbing clitoris.

"Oh no you don't," he said. "Not your turn yet. Get up."

She stood a little shakily, turning away, and started to pull down her skirt, but he stopped her.

"Don't you dare cover yourself up. Pull the skirt up. Higher. I want to see your pussy. Turn round."

Humiliated and helpless, she turned to face him, her hairless mound on display, sex lips pouting and wet. Any pretence that she was not massively aroused was hopeless now.

"Oh, I like the new look." He stroked around her slit with one extended finger. "Did your precious Count do this?"

She shook her head. Her face, already flushed from the spanking and hanging upside-down, grew even redder.

"Speak up. I want to know if Dante de Rufina used a razor on your most intimate parts."

"No," she whispered. "It was a woman."

"Aaah, a woman. Good. You can tell me all about it."

And so, falteringly, she began an account of her meeting with Rachele. When she reached the part where she had allowed a Florentine prostitute to bring her to orgasm, she shut her eyes in shame and embarrassment, but Tom's voice cut through. "Open your eyes. Look at me!"

She did so, seeing he'd unzipped his trousers to fondle a huge erection. She whimpered a little at this further seedy addition to her humiliation, but he merely growled, "Go on, go on. You've got me really hard. And yourself very wet."

Indeed, her juices flowed, and the agonising, thrilling need for release tormented her. The knowledge that this man was making her tell her disreputable story as a background to masturbation pushed her right onto the edge.

She finished her narrative at the point where she had gone out, in all her finery, to walk down to the keep. There was a silence and then she enquired in a small voice. "Tom, do you think you could just...?"

"No, not yet," he said, correctly interpreting her request. "Come with me."

He grabbed her by the arm and dragged her over to the wall, where rough stone had been plastered and painted, giving it a slightly undulating appearance. He pushed her against it, face forward.

"Keep holding your skirt up. Spread your legs."

She heard rustling and knew he was removing his trousers. At least, she thought, she'd get some relief now. Anticipation made her vagina pulse and contract and she knew that he would be able to see the movement of her muscles and outer lips, see her buttocks flexing. The knowledge made the contractions accelerate.

At last, she sensed him behind her, very close and then felt his cock, monstrously hard and warm. For one glorious moment, he swiped it along her slit, front to back, causing her to shudder and throb—then he rested its length in the cleft of her buttocks, leaning against her so it was wedged between them. She gave a little cry and he said, "No, you haven't earned it yet. Tell me what he did to you. Dante de Rufina."

"You know what he did. You said everyone told you."

"Yes, but I want to hear it from you. Tell me what happened when you got to the keep."

She told him the story, stripping it of any personal elements, but describing it as the audience would have seen it. When she got to the end, to the part where Dante had entered her anally, he gave a great sigh. He began to move against her and in a demeaning sexual panic, she feared he was going to climax without ever entering her. She thrust her bottom back against him, making noises of desperate entreaty.

"Then what happened? How did he end it? How did you get off the stage?"

She was irritated beyond endurance. "I think you know. Didn't your informants tell you? What are they called? Coppers' narks?"

He brought his hand down on the exposed part of her rump. "Don't be cheeky. Tell me."

She was silent and he reached underneath her and drew his finger very gently around the lips of her sex, at the end just touching her clitoris before pulling away. Her clit throbbed so hard it hurt. She knew if she was going to get any release from Tom, she had to pay him for it.

"He put me over his shoulder and turned so the audience could see my...my bottom. He pulled the cheeks of it, the buttocks, apart, so they could see."

"And what could they see?"

"They could see his...they could see semen."

"And where was it coming from?"

"It was coming from both my...oh God, you know. Holes."

"Yes!" Tom said and he drew back, positioned himself and pushed into her without finesse. Wet as she was, he entered her to the hilt, his balls slapping against the sensitive flesh of her perineum. He slammed into her, totally oblivious to her pleasure, intent only on getting off himself. His hands crept round her and held her breasts, which had been squashed into the rough plaster of the wall. As he approached his climax, he bent his knees and began to drive upwards into her. It was rough and uncomfortable and shaming and knowing she could do nothing about it, Eloise began to come, her muscles contracting hard on his intruding cock.

Before she had finished, he pulled out of her abruptly and she screamed in frustration and distress. But his fingers worked on her anus, thrusting into the narrow channel, smearing their combined juices on the cleft of her bottom. Then, grunting, he entered her again, easing himself into her back passage inch by inch. She shouted incoherently, at first telling him to stop, but once he was deep inside her and starting to thrust, she quietened down, able only to moan as her orgasm recommenced and she was gripped by a series of violent spasms.

Tom gave a yell, pushing into her brutally and then ejaculated frantically inside her. They stood still, quivering with the power of their climaxes and she felt him soften and withdrew. Then, in a quite different voice, he said, "Eloise? I didn't hurt you, my darling, did I? I'm so, so sorry. I don't know what came over me."

He turned her round gently and folded his arms around her, shaking.

Later, much later, when they had showered together and got into bed, he made love to her gently in the missionary position. He was still overcome with remorse at his performance earlier.

"I can't believe I did that to you. Spoke to you like that."

Eloise spoke sleepily. "I expect you've always wanted to do that sort of thing, but never been able to. The weird circumstances brought it all out."

"It was just that I couldn't bear to think of you doing...what you did...with Dante de Rufina, but it excited me as well."

She kept quiet, not comfortable with the idea of talking about Dante to Tom.

"I can't bear that you had to go through such a dreadful experience at his hands. The man's a disgrace and the sooner he's behind bars, the better."

She stiffened. "Is that likely?"

"Oh, yes it is." His voice was full of satisfaction. "And very soon. We've had a bit of a breakthrough in the case. Some information. Someone on the inside. And when the Count visits his friend Petrela's boat to pick up the next consignment, we'll be waiting for him."

"But I thought you wanted Petrela."

"I did. Now I just want to see de Rufina where he belongs."

"Tom, I still believe you're wrong. Dante's not a saint, but he isn't a criminal. I don't believe he'd compromise the welfare of those children."

He gave a short laugh. "Darling, I could give you evidence about the trafficking in drugs and women between Albania and London that would make your hair stand on end. A direct route, from Durres, via Castel Rufina to *Dante's Inferno*."

She laid back, her eyes troubled in the darkness of the room. "And when is this going to happen? I mean, when will you move against him?"

His glee was evident. "By the time you're back in London this evening, Dante de Rufina will be in prison."

* * * *

Later that morning, she said goodbye. Tom was desperately eager for her to make some kind of commitment about their future, but she refused.

"I can't, Tom. I don't know what I want. There are so many complications and I don't want to make promises I can't keep."

She drove off in the direction of the airport, but before she left the town, she pulled over and got out her mobile. After a moment's hesitation, she rang the hotel. Reception put her through to the apartment and Maria answered. She could hear Charlie laughing uproariously at something in the background.

"The Conte isn't here. He's had to go out and do some errands—he's going to be away all day. I think he was going to the coast."

"Oh dear, I really need to speak to him before I go. I don't suppose you have his mobile phone number, do you?"

"I'm sure I do somewhere. It's in the address book, I think. Hold on." There was a pause, during which

Charlie's laughter turned to screams and Maria was clearly sidetracked into sorting him out. She came back with a number.

Now, Eloise sat contemplating the phone. She knew what she proposed to do was very wrong. But she couldn't bear it if the children suffered. She thought if she could just put the fear of God into him, make him abandon any foolish criminal activities he'd been seduced into, surely that would make it morally acceptable?

She punched out the number and waited. A female voice answered, "Hello?"

"Laura? I thought this was Dante's phone."

"It is, but mine's on the blink, so I took his."

"Oh damn! Does he know?"

"Nope. He'll be pissed off when he finds out, though."

Eloise looked at her watch. It would take her an hour to get to the airport and the plane left in three.

"Do you know where he is?"

"Dunno. Oh, except he said something about going to the seaside. By the way, Ellie, I've just realised you'll miss his birthday — unless you can get back by next week."

"His birthday?"

"Yeah, remember we bought him that present? And we've got lots more surprises for him. We usually have dinner out, it's great. Well, Charlie lets the side down, of course, but that's Charlie. See if you can make it. He'd be really pleased."

She sat there a bit longer, wrestling with her conscience. But the thought of the children happily preparing for a birthday party Dante wouldn't attend wrenched at her heart. She sighed and reached for the phone again to call the airline, then turned the little purple car in the direction of Rimini.

Chapter Twenty-Seven

When Eloise got to the place where *La Donnina* was moored, she realised she hadn't the faintest idea what to do next. It was now late afternoon and she assumed, from what Maria had told her, that Dante expected to be home that night. So she thought he wouldn't be much later. She left the car on the dock, just before the private area where Dante had parked before their cruise and went to reconnoitre. Clearly, someone was in residence on the vessel. There were lights and she could see some of the staff moving around. Her fear was that Dante had already arrived, in which case she'd have to intercept him before Tom's men got to him. The dock was rectangular, surrounded on three sides by water, and she assumed the police would make their move when he was well away from Tolka Petrela. She would have to wait and watch very near to the boat.

She moved back towards *La Donnina*, looking for cover. There was a small, hut-like structure near where they'd parked before and she slipped behind it and settled down for a long watch. She'd only been there for half-an-hour, when she felt a heavy hand on her arm. Turning sharply, she saw a burly man in what she recognised as Petrela's livery. She wrenched away from him, turning to run the other way and found her route blocked by another security guard. She was trapped.

Petrela was ensconced in the big salon with several of his men. With a small sense of relief, she saw that Ugo was there too. At least, he should be a moderating influence.

Petrela beamed like a big fat cat as she stood in front of him, flanked by the guards. "Aaah, dear little Ellouse. How nice of you to come to visit me. But I thought you were leaving Italy?"

"I was, but…there was something I needed to do first."

"Oh? And that involved my boat?"

"No, it was just…" Inspiration seized her. "It was Dante. We quarrelled. A terrible row. I wanted to see him before I went, to make up. I knew he was coming here."

"That would explain it. Wouldn't it, Ugo?" Petrela turned his head and Ugo nodded. "Except, of course, that you were lurking outside. Checking out my boat and hiding."

"I was waiting for Dante. He is coming…?"

"Yes, he most certainly is."

"Oh good." Her relief was genuine.

"But first, I think you need to tell us a bit more. About your friendship with a certain British policeman, for a start."

"I… I don't know what you mean."

"Oh come on, Ellouse. Surely you haven't forgotten the man who fucked you last night."

The shock must have shown on her face and it pleased Petrela. "Oh yes, my dear Signorina. We do keep an eye on you. For your own safety. Now do tell us why a nice young lady should spend the night in bed with a policeman and then the next day dodging around near my boat. And pretending to look for the man who was fucking her the week before?"

She took refuge in icy disdain. "I really don't know what you're talking about."

"No, darling, I guess you don't." He looked at his watch and then at Ugo. "The two of you will have to get out of here. It's nearly time for my next visitor."

The guards started to hustle her away and she heard Petrela, laughing, shout out, "Put her in a room and keep her close. I don't want Ugo getting to her before I do."

In the cabin she had once shared with Dante de Rufina, she lay on the bed, trying to work out what to do next. The trouble was, she couldn't formulate a plan without knowing what Petrela intended. She thought about calling him in and telling him about the threat to Dante. But without knowing who had betrayed him from inside the organisation — if indeed, that was what had happened — she didn't know who to trust. And she was pretty sure that under no circumstances should she ever trust Petrela.

They had taken away her bag, her phone, even her watch. But incongruously, given that she was a prisoner, there was a bottle of champagne in the room and some cocktail snacks. She had something to eat and a glass of the wine. There was nothing more she could do and with the new calmness that seemed to have descended over her in the past few days, she settled herself on the padded bench under the porthole and began to watch.

Dante had taken the Castel Rufina van to the wholesalers from which the hotel bought linen and picked up a lot of new sheets and towels, an activity that appalled him. He longed to get back to his life in London, to the club and his music. Afterwards, he went into Florence to meet the architect who was supervising the extension behind the hotel—this would include an indoor pool, a gym and a spa. After a light lunch, he drove off towards Rimini.

He arrived at the quayside about half-an-hour after Eloise had been escorted to her cabin and pulled the van up close to *La Donnina,* waving cheerily at the crew. He'd already made one of these runs and he knew the routine now. One of the sailors came forward and he gave him the keys.

"Here you are, Paulo. Is Signor Petrela expecting me?"

"He is. Go ahead, Conte."

Eloise hammered on the glass, but it was too thick for her fists to make any impression. She saw Dante disappear from view and knew he had come on board.

Now, she paced helplessly around the cabin. There was absolutely nothing she could do and after a while, she lay on the bed, her body rigid with tension. She made herself relax, knowing she would need all her resources to deal with Petrela and after a while, exhausted, she slept.

Several hours later, when she awoke, it was already dark outside. She washed, tidied her hair as best she could and went to the door, meaning to bang on it, but as she got there, it opened and one of the stewards came in.

"Signor Petrela will see you now," he intoned impassively and led her through to the saloon.

Petrela was there with Ugo. "Now, Ellouse, we have time to talk to you properly. Sit." He gestured to the sofa in front of him. "We'd like to know what you were doing, skulking around the boat. Spying."

She'd done some thinking and now she said tremulously, "I've already told you, I was waiting for Dante. We had a row. I wanted to talk to him."

"But you spent the night with the Englishman? The policeman?"

She hung her head. "I did. That's what the row was about."

"He seemed fine when he came here."

"Well, that's Dante. Stiff upper lip and all that. He was brought up in England, after all."

Petrela's eyes narrowed. "I don't believe you. I think it is you and the policemen who are an item and that he told you to spy on me. On Ugo. On the Conte."

"No! No, I didn't even know he was in the police force until he told me."

"And when was that?"

"Last night," she lied.

"So you really did come here to talk to the Conte?"

"Yes, of course. It's true, believe me."

Petrela smiled, stroking the sides of his moustache. He glanced at Ugo and then said, "What a pity you missed him. Because after he left here, he was picked up by the police. I'm afraid your boyfriend has been indulging in some very reprehensible behaviour."

She took her cue. "That's what I wanted to tell him. The Englishman—the policeman—told me they were going to arrest him. I wanted to warn him."

"So why lurk on the quay? You could have come to me—I would have sorted everything out for you."

She hung her head. "Of course, that's what I should have done. But I was scared, Tolka." She looked up at him, her clear green eyes wet with tears. "I'm not used to this sort of thing—I wasn't sure how to handle it. I didn't even know if you'd understand—if you'd know what it was all about."

The idea that Tolka Petrela could be unaware in such a case was absurd, but he took her apparent naivety as a compliment, letting out a roar of laughter.

"I know about most things, my dear. Now, what are we going to do about all this? Ugo, tell me, what are we going to do?"

Ugo smiled, stretching out his long legs and for a moment looking disturbingly like his nephew. "I don't know, Tolka. What do you think?"

"I don't know either. Give her a drink, Ugo."

The other man stood up and mixed something in a tall glass. Eloise took it gratefully—some sort of a cocktail, she thought. Petrela was still looking at her quizzically.

"Mmmm. You want to help the Conte, Ellouse?"

"Of course."

"You understand that if he is convicted of what they suspect—of drug smuggling—he will go to prison for a very long time."

"I do," she said and this time the tearfulness was genuine.

"Well, there are some things I can do to help. Strings I can pull. But in return, I would expect you to do something for me."

"What...what sort of thing?" She faltered, but she knew what was coming.

"Well, I so enjoyed your performance as Isabella, I would like to act out a fantasy of my own. I would like to make love to you, Ellouse."

Despite the tight control she was exerting, this made her wince and he picked up on it.

"You shudder and look all maidenly now. But you weren't so ladylike when you let the Conte fuck you and bugger you in front of an audience."

She gave him a straight look, forgetting her attempts to flatter him. "That was the most humiliating thing I have ever had to do and I only did it to protect Laura. Because you had taken her and were holding her to ransom."

Tolka chuckled. "Oh, that's what he told you, was it?" He gave Ugo a conspiratorial wink. "The things some men will do to get a nice girl into bed."

This chimed so closely with what Tom had said that Eloise was shocked. What shocked her more, however, was that Petrela's crude words had started up the now familiar thrumming inside her. It seemed that, since she had come to Italy, her sexual responses had become so hair-trigger, so excessive, that even this rough, thuggish man was turning her on. She sat back, looking at him, eyes wide. She knew that to buy any respite for Dante — for the children — was going to require a sacrifice on her part. She would have to give herself to the brutal Petrela and probably Ugo as well. She gave a small sigh, her lips parted. She had always found Ugo attractive.

At the back of her mind, a voice murmured, *But if Dante cheated to get you to play the part of Isabella, do you really want to sink so low just to help him?* To which her conscience — at least, she thought that's what it was — replied, *I don't care about him. I'm only doing this for the children.*

And underlying all of this was a feeling of sadness. Dante really was a bad man, a villain, after all. He had tricked her into a sexual performance and he was a smuggler of drugs, something she found abhorrent. As

Petrela got up from his chair and pulled her to her feet, she gave herself permission to be as wild as she liked. Dante had used her, Tom had used her, even Jake and Arno and Tamsin had used her. This was no different.

In a clear, calm voice she said. "What do you want me to do?"

Chapter Twenty-Eight

Dante left the yacht feeling happier than he had for days. He'd finally come to a decision and although he foresaw big problems ahead, in his heart he knew he'd done the right thing. As he walked to the car, jangling his keys, he reflected that Petrela had been surprisingly good about the whole business. He shrugged his shoulders a few times, feeling the tension in them. Now if he could just sort out his love life...

Just before the place where the van was parked stood a large object, shrouded in canvas. He glanced at it, surprised. He was sure it hadn't been there when he went on board. It looked like a small car and on a whim he flicked up the corner of the cover. He was right, it was a small metallic car — an unusual purple colour. And he'd seen that colour before. It was exactly the same as the hire-car Eloise had been driving. He moved round to the back of the vehicle and looked at the number-plate. He was almost sure this was her number — he'd got used to seeing it in the guest car park. He let the canvas fall again and, puzzled, walked on to the van. Petrela's men had loaded it up with crates of the distinctive bottles for the winery. He sat for a while, pondering what he'd seen, then drove it off the quay and stopped on the harbour road.

He could think of no rational reason why the car Eloise Lambert hired was under canvas in the parking lot near Tolka Petrela's yacht. It was absurd to think the same car had been hired out immediately to someone connected to Petrela. And even if such a coincidence were possible, why would they cover up the vehicle? A growing feeling of anxiety gripped him and he reached in his pocket for his mobile phone.

After several minutes of frantic searching, he gave up. Vaguely, he remembered Laura muttering about hers being on the blink and he knew she couldn't live without a phone more or less as an extension of her hand. He growled in annoyance and put the car into gear. He'd drive to the nearest bar and use a public telephone.

Maria could only tell him Eloise had been trying to get in touch with him. After some searching, she found the phone number of the Albergo Rufina. Salvatore answered – he could hear noisy laughter and the sound of a television in the background.

"The Englishman? Signor Sherwin? He's been out most of the day. But I have his mobile number."

"Do you happen to know if the woman who was staying up at the Castel was with him last night?"

Salvatore gave a rich chuckle. "Oh, your Isabella? Yes, she was here. Lucky devil."

Dante hung up and stared at the phone, thoughtfully. He was in a small booth at the back of a quiet harbour bar – only a few elderly dockworkers sat around a far table, drinking red wine and talking cheerfully. He shook his head and then dialled the new number.

"Sherwin!"

The voice at the other end was businesslike, sharper than he'd expected the amiable Englishman to be.

"Mr Sherwin, this is Dante de Rufina."

"It's...what?" Sherwin sounded astonished.

"Dante de Rufina. I'm very sorry to bother you, but I need to know if Eloise Lambert is still with you."

"I beg your...what an earth does that have to do with you?"

Dante was taken aback by the other man's aggression. "Well, nothing, except I'm a bit concerned about her. Is she there?"

"No, she's gone back to London."

"And the car?"

"The car? You mean the hire car? She was leaving it at the airport, of course. What the hell is all this?"

"Look, I'm in Rimini. I just went to collect a delivery from Tolka Petrela's yacht. You know who Tolka Petrela is?"

"Oh yes," Sherwin replied grimly. "I know who he is."

Dante told him what he'd found on the quay. There was a long silence. Then, "Shit, shit, shit!"

"What is it? What's happened to her?"

"It's complicated. Where are you?"

"I told you — Rimini."

"No, I mean exactly."

Dante ducked out of the booth and asked the barman for the address, which he relayed to Sherwin.

"Okay, look, go and wait outside. You're in a van, right?"

"Right," Dante agreed, surprised he knew.

"Well, I'm not too far away. Wait for me."

Dante was dubious. "All right, but I'm not sure what you think we can do. I'm afraid Eloise might be in very great danger."

"Look, there may be a simple explanation. Let me phone the airline, see if she got on the plane."

"But you will let me know? I can't do anything—my blasted sister has stolen my mobile."

"Yes, I'll see you in about thirty minutes."

It was rather less than half an hour that Dante, sitting in the van and looking out over the harbour, was startled by someone rapping on the driver's door. Two armed policemen stood there and he could see others behind them.

"Conte Dante de Rufina?"

"Yes. What...?"

"Does this van belong to you?"

"Yes. Well, it belongs to the Castel Rufina."

"And you own the Castel Rufina?"

"Yes. Look, what's this..."

"Can you get out of the van, please, sir? We have a warrant to search the vehicle."

Dante got out, fighting to keep calm. "Can you please tell me what this is about? I have a very important meeting..."

One of the officers escorted him over to the sea wall, a hand ostentatiously on his holster. "We've received information you are carrying drugs. Can you tell us what your load is, please?"

Fear gripped him. "There's linen for my hotel and some bottles for the winery we run. Nothing else."

"We'll see, sir."

Dante contemplated telling the officer about Eloise. But the situation was still so vague, so nebulous. He didn't want to put her in danger by bringing the police in if it were not necessary. He waited, gnawing his lip, praying that Sherwin would arrive soon.

A shout went up. The officers crowded round one of their number who emerged, bottom first, from the passenger area. In his hands a bag of white powder. The man guarding Dante let out a breath, "Cocaine."

"Under the foot-well," the man who had found it announced with satisfaction.

"Now then, Conte, I think you'd better come to the station."

"But this is a mistake. It's nothing to do with me, nothing at all. And I have to meet someone here. It's absolutely essential. He'll be here shortly and then I'll come with you willingly."

"I'm sorry, sir, but we have to take you in. You can make a phone call from the station."

So great was Dante's concern about Eloise that he didn't really recognise the seriousness of his own position until he was being fingerprinted and photographed. He was escorted into an interrogation room and two men he hadn't seen before, in plain clothes, came in.

"Conte de Rufina? I am Inspector Luigi Alfonso. My colleague is Georgio Lomeli and we would like to ask you some questions. First, tell me, are you satisfied with your treatment here? Would you like something to drink? Some coffee?"

Dante dismissed the offer with a wave of his hand. "They told me I could make a phone call."

"Yes, of course. You wish to summon your lawyer?"

Belatedly, Dante thought he should have some sort of representation, but he was too worried about Eloise to give the idea much consideration. "No, I need to talk to the person I was supposed to meet."

Alfonso raised his eyebrows. "Indeed? Well, if you give me the number, I will dial it for you."

Dante scrabbled in his pocket for the scrap of paper on which he had written Tom Sherwin's number and handed it over. Alfonso dialled the number on the phone on the desk, his eyes never leaving his prisoner's face.

The voice at the other end was clearly audible. "Sherwin."

Alfonso's eyebrows went even higher. "Who is this?"

"This is Tom Sherwin. Who are you?"

"I am Inspector Alfonso of the Rimini Police."

"What the hell, Alfonso...?"

The inspector cut across. "I have here a prisoner, the Conte de Rufina. He's been brought in on suspicion of possessing and trafficking in drugs. He asked us to telephone you, so I am handing the phone to him now." He passed the instrument to Dante who immediately launched into speech.

"Sherwin, where are you? Christ, this is a nightmare. I was waiting for you at the bar, but then suddenly all these police piled into the van and I got arrested."

"What for?"

"Oh, God knows. They're saying they found cocaine — it's absurd. A set up. Anyway, never mind about that. I'm frantic with worry about — what we talked about. I don't know what to do — whether I should make it official. The more I think about it, the more concerned I get. What did the airline say?"

"She didn't get on the flight. The hire people say she didn't return the car. Look, I'm working on it. I'll get back to you."

"Get back to me? Christ, Sherwin, if she's on that boat... You do realise what could happen to her?"

Sherwin sounded grim. "I have a very good idea. Look, keep calm, let me make some more calls. I promise I'll get back to you."

Dante sighed, realising there was nothing he could do. "Well, I'll do my best. Thank you." He was about to hand the phone back, when he remembered his own predicament. "Oh, Sherwin, could you do me a favour? Could you phone the Castel and tell them what's happened to me? See if you can get hold of my cousin Ugo? Ask him to contact my lawyer and get him down here."

With elaborate courtesy, Alfonso asked if he would like to wait for his lawyer, but Dante insisted he had nothing to hide and so the interrogation went ahead. For over an hour it was remorseless, ranging from questions about his business affairs, his relationship with Petrela, his experience of drugs and his sex life.

At last, Alfonso sat back, his long face inscrutable. "We will take a break now, Conte. You would like some coffee?"

"Tea, please." Alfonso went to the door and spoke to someone outside. Dante could hear voices as if someone else had arrived and shortly afterwards another man entered the room.

"Sherwin, thank God!"

The Englishman held up his hand. "One moment, Conte. Before you say anything I must inform you that I am Detective Chief Inspector Tom Sherwin of the

Metropolitan Police. Here's my warrant card. I've been watching you for a very long time."

* * * *

Under instruction from Petrela, Eloise had stripped to her underwear, her back to them and now she turned around. She could almost feel the heat of their eyes on her body. In response to a new command, she undid her pale blue bra and let it fall away, her innate modesty making the action unconsciously more titillating for the watchers. Her head was down and she was shaking, but she felt a flash of defiance and when she looked up and saw the look in the men's eyes, she was suddenly, strongly aware of the power she had over them.

She knew if she gave in to her nerves, if she screamed and cried, she would lose what control she had over events. With a semblance of consent, she thought she could maintain the upper hand. In any case, the insistent throbbing of her sex and the undeniable hardening of her nipples spoke of an urgent need on her part that had to be dealt with. She looked first Ugo and then Petrela in the eye, hooked her thumbs into the sides of the panties and drew them slowly down her long legs.

Petrela literally growled. He beckoned her forward and she went to him, now so turned on she welcomed the touch of his spatulate fingers. He caressed her gently, stroking her breasts, her vulva, with something like reverence, then he buried his head between her legs and his strong tongue began probing.

Eloise felt the tension drain from her. She could do this. She would even enjoy it. It was no more than an act— something she'd managed without difficulty with Dante de Rufina. True, this man wasn't Dante. But he was male and he seemed anxious to please her. The thick moustache scratched her tender flesh as the tongue entered her and she felt another hand, another mouth, on her breast. Ugo. Petrela's tongue began to circle her clitoris, his hands caressing her buttocks, and she felt herself shuddering into an orgasm.

Sherwin began by saying, "I did telephone the Castel. Your cousin is not there, but I spoke to your brother, Matteo. He's getting on to the lawyer immediately, but I understand he's not likely to be here until tomorrow. Do you want to wait?"

"Meanwhile, God knows what Eloise is going through. No, let's get it over with so you can concentrate on her."

The questioning went on for several more hours. Dante answered wearily, but as accurately as he could, interrupting now and then to say, "You are doing something about Eloise Lambert, aren't you?"

"My men are working on it now," Sherwin said.

"I don't see why you don't just board *La Donnina*. She must be there."

"We can't just raid the yacht for no reason. Besides, this investigation is at a delicate stage. I don't want to jeopardise it."

"And while you're pussy-footing around, Eloise is probably being stripped and mauled by Petrela," Dante responded savagely. "In any case, the drugs you found in the van must have been planted while I was on board — can't you use that as an excuse to raid it?"

"I'm afraid you're out of luck there, Conte. We have a surveillance camera on the dock. It shows your van quite clearly and though Petrela's crew did load the cases of bottles into the rear, no one approached the driver or passenger doors. Only you."

"You think I put it there?"

"You carried a large bag from the yacht. And you spent some time in the van before driving off."

"I stayed in the van because I was trying to decide what to do about finding Ms Lambert's car. The bag contained glass samples for me to take back to the winery."

"But there was room in it for the cocaine as well. I think you got it from someone on the yacht and that you hid it under the passenger floor before you left."

Dante felt a pang of real fear. "It's a set-up. You must know that it's a set-up."

"I think it's a falling out among thieves."

Soon after this exchange, another officer called Sherwin from the room and Dante was taken down to a small cell. He raged about the fact that nothing seemed to be being done to help Eloise and was increasingly concerned about his own position. He sank down on the narrow metal bed and tried to think rationally.

Dante remained in the cell for several hours before being taken back to the interrogation room. Sherwin and Alfonso were there.

Sherwin began. "I want to talk about your London club. Your partner is Toby Heathersett?"

"What have you done about Eloise Lambert?"

"We're watching the boat. Please answer the question."

A thought struck Dante. "Did she know you're a policeman? She did, didn't she? I've been set up three times, once by you, once by Petrela and once by her. Damn and blast…"

"Conte, please, answer my questions. I know you're distressed. But I have new information and it's very important. It's vital to you personally and to Ms Lambert that we sort this out now. Please."

Dante settled back in his chair, his face dark with worry. "If you swear this will help Eloise."

"It will. You were going to tell me about Mr Heathersett,"

"Well, I don't see... Oh very well. Toby is my business partner. We've known each other for years. He runs the front of house and the bar side, I'm the performer and in charge of the entertainment, the band, that sort of thing."

"And Larry Sampson?"

"Larry does everything. All the admin, the ordering, employing staff and so on. He's invaluable."

"And if I told you that one of these men was providing the London end of Petrela's smuggling operation? Was using your club to move drugs and women into the West End of London?"

"I wouldn't believe you. Toby's been a friend since we were teenagers. We were at university together. He's as straight as a die. And Larry's been working for us for years. Actually before that he was managing a bar here in Italy. He was recommended by my cousin, Ugo."

There was a long pause. Eventually, Sherwin asked, "And just how far would you trust your cousin, Ugo?"

Dante's eyes narrowed suddenly. "About as far as I could throw him."

When Eloise had recovered from her orgasm, Petrela forced her, quite gently, to her knees. His cock wasn't long, but it was barrel-thick and she first put out her tongue and tentatively licked the end. It seemed to grow even wider. She paused. "If I do this, you promise you'll help Dante?"

His voice was so deep it was almost a rumble. "If you give me a good show, I'll do what I can."

She opened her jaws and took the monster in. He tasted of sweat mingled with an expensive cologne she couldn't identify and his skin had a leathery texture. It wasn't unpleasant. Behind her, unseen, Ugo pulled her hair away from her face, his hand moving round to her breasts again as she bobbed backwards and forwards, getting the massive organ deeper and deeper into her throat.

Suddenly, Petrela grunted and unleashed his semen into her mouth. She sat back and swallowed, her eyes fixed on his. He stood up, his cock still wet with her saliva and still hard, and held out his hand. "Now we go to the stateroom."

It was about five hours later that Tom Sherwin entered the holding cell in Rimini police station. Dante had been sleeping fitfully and he woke with a start. He was haggard and unshaven, his pallor visible in the pale light of dawn creeping through the small barred window.

Sherwin shut the door. "This is very irregular. I need your permission to continue this discussion without others present. But if you'll agree, we can sort this business out faster."

He was completely alert now and sitting on the bed, still fully dressed in jeans and a T-shirt. "Of course. Anything to get this over with and get to Eloise."

"Right. Look, I think you're a shit."

Dante was putting on his shoes, but at this he sat back. "Well, thanks a lot. Did you wake me up to tell me this?"

"I think you're an unprincipled, undisciplined bastard. Sexually deviant and out of control."

Dante got the other shoe on and stood up. "Tell me something I don't know. Your point?"

"I don't like you, not one little bit. But I no longer think you're a crook."

Dante sat down again abruptly. "Thank God for that. What's brought on this change of heart?"

"Look, there's no time to explain now. We're on our way to raid *La Donnina*. Want to come?"

"I'm right behind you," Dante said.

Chapter Twenty-Nine

Petrela had made Eloise walk ahead of him, naked as she was, until they reached the master cabin. Crewmembers on their route stood silently to attention, only their smiles betraying their appreciation. Ugo brought up the rear, closing the door of the room behind him.

She moved into the centre of the cabin, her body tingling. She was embarrassed and aroused in equal measure. Petrela took off his jacket.

"Ellouse, I have desired you since the moment I first saw you. And I could have taken you at any time. But it would please me more if you gave yourself to me willingly."

Ugo moved behind her. "The Conte gave you pleasure, but he's brash and young. What you need is more...finesse." He put his hands on her shoulders and began a gentle stroking, his hands moving incrementally towards her breasts. Petrela moved closer until his rounded belly rested on hers. "Ellouse?"

She let out a breath. "And you will help Dante?"

"You really care for him?"

"I'm worried about the children."

"Ah, yes, the children. Very well, Ellouse, I'll do what I can. Now come here."

He sat on the bed and beckoned her. "Lie across my knee. There's a good girl."

She walked over to him, resigned to whatever came next, and arranged herself across his lap, wondering if she was to be subjected to another spanking. But Petrela merely let his fingers wander across the contours of her bottom, gradually smoothing up and down the cleft in her buttocks. She heard his deep voice say, "Ready now, Ugo," and other fingers, cool and gentle, stroked around her anus. They were slippery with oil and gradually, the tip of one pushed into the tight confines, burrowing insistently deeper. She felt liquid being poured into the hole and more fingers being introduced. Petrela murmured soothingly in a language she didn't understand.

Eventually he said, "Give me the dildo." Something hard and cold prodded at the sensitive flesh of her opening, then it gradually bore inwards and she could sense he was twisting it as he pushed. It went deeper, deeper and she writhed on Petrela's knees, wanting the magic touch to her clit that would tip her over the edge. It failed to come and after a while, the hard shaft was removed and she was pulled upright. She was sobbing, half mad with desire and alcohol, begging for relief.

It was Ugo, now mysteriously naked, who took her in his arms and began to kiss her face and neck, running his pale, narrow hands up and down her flanks. He tipped her over onto the bed, his slender body following. And at last his fingers entered her and after his fingers, his long, thin penis. He fucked her a few times, like a man priming a pump, then rolled over so she was on top of him. He drew her face down towards his, kissing and nibbling, while his hips thrust upwards. She had just begun to wonder what had become of Petrela when something firm and warm and wet nudged insistently against her other hole, against the anus already stretched and receptive from the play with the dildo. There was a grunt and he eased himself into her.

For a moment, the three of them paused, frozen. Eloise was aware of an extraordinary sensation, of fullness, of excitement, of a radiating pleasure starting somewhere at the point where the two cocks were beginning slowly to move in and out of her. She was powerfully conscious of the smells, the raw odour of sex and of the sounds — the wet, sucking noises as their swollen organs ploughed into holes stretched to capacity. And of her own moans and the grunts of the two men, interspersing their muttered encouragements to her, coming in three different languages.

She began a shuddering, convulsive orgasm that took the two men with it, so within seconds they had filled both holes with hot, wet semen. The feel of the liquid, the sensation of utter abandon and debauchery, was so great, that almost as soon as she had recovered from the first climax, she arched her back as she was racked by a second, while the men withdrew, but continued to hold her and whisper encouragement.

The advance guard of police and paramilitaries had boarded *La Donnina* first. Not until there was a thumbs-up from the officer in charge of the raiding party, leaning over the rail near the fore gangplank, did Sherwin beckon

Dante forward and lead him onto the boat. It was still only six in the morning.

"Petrela's cabin. That's where she'll be." Dante was breathing heavily.

"Well, you know the way. Take me there."

They moved silently along *La Donnina*'s luxurious corridors. Behind them was a group of men and women dressed in combat fatigues, and as they passed each door, one or two of them would peel off to examine the room. At last they came to the end of the top corridor, where Dante indicated the entrance to the master suite. Sherwin nodded, waiting until armed men were positioned either side of the door. Then he threw it open and walked in, Dante hot on his heels.

On the big bed in the centre of the cabin, Eloise lay on her back, legs spread. She was deeply asleep, one arm flung over her eyes. On her right, Ugo also slept, but on his stomach, his head next to hers on the pillow, one hand clutching her breast. On her left, Petrela sprawled, his face buried between her legs, fleshy buttocks shuddering in sleep, legs projecting beyond the end of the bed. The room was warm and it reeked of sex.

It was Petrela who awoke first, lifting his head from Eloise's lower abdomen to look blearily at the two men who stood, horrified, at the bottom of the bed. He reached up and touched her shoulder. "Wake up, Ellouse, you have visitors. Your two young paramours and they don't look very happy."

"I think it is you who's going to be unhappy, Mr Petrela," Sherwin said. Petrela rolled over and made a swift move towards the bedside cabinet and Sherwin stood aside to reveal the men with pistols aimed at the bed. "I wouldn't do that, sir. Put your hands up."

Petrela drew back and sat up. Behind him, Eloise had woken and peered over his shoulder, shocked. Ugo sat on the other side of the bed, his hands in the air. Sherwin glanced at Dante. "You'd better cover her up. Tolka Petrela, you are under arrest on charges of drug smuggling and the illegal transportation of women. Other charges may follow." He motioned two of the men forward. "Get him dressed and take him away."

Dante grabbed at the sheet, which had fallen onto the floor, and handed it to Eloise. She wrapped it around herself, but wouldn't look at him.

"Ugo de Martino, I am arresting you for facilitating the passage of drugs and the illegal trafficking in women. Other charges may follow."

Dante and Sherwin watched as the two men dressed, Petrela complaining and threatening them with his lawyers all the while. When Ugo was escorted towards the door he stopped in front of Dante.

"This is your fault, Conte."

"My fault? How?"

"Because you came from London, from nowhere. Only an accident makes you the head of the family. And you come strolling in, with your English ideas and your middle-class perceptions. What do you know about the Castel Rufina, about anything? Your father was a disgrace to the name and so are you. If the deal with Tolka had gone through, we could have salvaged something. But when I realised you were prepared to spite me, even there, then I knew I had to move. Bourgeois!" For a moment, it looked as if he would spit at his cousin, but he merely spun on his heel and went with the police guard.

When the room had emptied, the two men remaining turned to look at Eloise, who had got up from the bed, draped in the sheet.

Dante held out his arms. "Lola, darling, are you all right? I've been so worried."

She stayed where she was.

Sherwin asked, "Did they hurt you? Do you need medical attention?"

She shook her head.

"Then get dressed, Eloise, we're going to have to take a statement from you."

"Yes. But first, I must shower."

Dante opened the door to Petrela's palatial bathroom, but Sherwin's voice cut across. "No, no shower. You need to see the medical people first."

She turned at the door, dignified now, despite the fact she was wearing nothing but the sheet. "Why? I'm not injured."

"Because we need evidence for a rape charge. DNA. A doctor will examine you."

She stared at him. "Sorry, what did you say? Rape? No, I don't think so. I didn't want to come here — in fact I was brought aboard by force. But what happened afterwards was consensual. I was paying for something. I didn't resist — if I had, there might have been a rape. But I didn't, and so we'll never know."

"Paying for something? And what was that?"

"Petrela told me he would get Dante off the hook if I let him…fuck me."

Sherwin's voice was very grim. "And that's why you came here? To warn the Conte? To help him?"

Dante reached out a hand but she ignored it. "I did. I was worried about what would happen to the children if he went to prison. I thought I could get him to stop, to realise that what he was doing was very foolish. But it went wrong."

"You thought you could get me to stop? To stop?" Dante let the hand he had extended to her fall slowly to his side. "You mean you thought I was guilty? Did you really think I would stoop so low as to be in partnership with Petrela? To smuggle drugs? To bring poor, desperate little Albanian girls to the west to be abused and maltreated?"

She shook her head, not looking at him.

"Jesus, Lola, I know you don't think very highly of me, but that's appalling. And are you saying you let Petrela...you let both of them...have their way with you just because of that? Even when you knew that Petrela had kidnapped my sister and scared the wits out of her."

"Yes," she replied, in a small voice. "And they told me you made it up about Laura. Tom said it too. So I thought...what the hell! But I was trying to help you."

Dante turned round abruptly and went to the large window that looked out onto the water of the harbour and pressed his forehead against the thick glass.

Tom's face was like thunder. "You took something I told you in confidence and came running down here with it. You could have destroyed the whole operation. You betrayed me."

Dante turned his head, looking at her over his shoulder. "You thought I was a criminal. You betrayed me too."

Eloise stood silent. Swathed in the sheet, her hair, though straggly, still piled on top of her hair, she looked like a Greek goddess.

At last, she said, "Well, fuck you both. I've had a frightening experience and an exhausting twenty-four hours. Now, I'm going to take a shower and you can interrogate me, or whatever it is you want to do. Then I'm going back to London and I never want to see or hear from either of you ever again." She swept into the bathroom and closed the door.

The questioning, charging, sorting things out went on all day and into the evening. Matt turned up with the lawyer who was breathing fire and talking about suing the police and Dante sent them away again. At about eight o' clock, Sherwin took Dante and Eloise to a small hotel overlooking the sea where he had booked rooms. They were the only guests in the small dining room and the silence was oppressive. Eloise hadn't spoken a word to either of them since that morning's conversation. Alfonso had conducted all her questioning and Sherwin had kept well away. Now she seemed calm and cool, but her conversation was monosyllabic and it was clear she wouldn't have been there if she hadn't been exhausted.

Eventually, Dante broke the silence to ask Tom about the puzzling aspects of the case. "I don't understand what made you change your mind about my involvement. It was so sudden, yet so complete."

"Yes, well I'm afraid I was absolutely convinced of your guilt. We had all sorts of evidence linking you with the chain that stretched from Durres to London. But the day we picked you up, my colleagues in the Met, working on a different case, happened to arrest Larry Sampson. It was a minor dealing charge, nothing more, but in his eagerness to save his own skin, he talked more than was strictly necessary and the plot began to unravel."

"I still can't believe Larry was a crook. And that he was setting me up. He was such a good manager—a really nice chap."

"Yes and with a weakness for cocaine which overrode his other qualities. I guess Ugo realised early on that you weren't going to play ball..."

"Well, now you mention it, there was a rather weird conversation some years ago when I felt I was being sounded out...or at least, my opinion was being sought on the drug scene. I expressed my revulsion and it was never mentioned again. At the time I thought nothing of it, it just sounded like one of Ugo's mad hypothetical schemes. Of course, I had no idea how deep in Petrela's pocket he was."

"Quite. It seems as if Ugo and Petrela had determined that your club would be an ideal end point for their various criminal activities. And when it became apparent that you wouldn't cooperate, they planted Larry Sampson. I don't think at that time there was any intention to set you up."

"But I don't understand why they needed the club."

"Well, we know now that the drugs were being smuggled in with the wine consignments."

"What, our wine? Castel Rufina wine?" Dante sounded absolutely outraged.

"Yes. The bottles you were importing from Albania have thick bases—and they're hollow. Because the glass is coloured and opaque, you can't see the powder inside."

"Ye Gods!"

"Crates of the wine ended up in the cellars of *The Inferno*. Once they were empty, Larry Sampson took them away and retrieved the drugs."

Dante was looking stunned. "Yes, he did insist on collecting the empties. Something about recycling them, keeping costs down. I was impressed. And the girls?"

"They were also coming in on the delivery lorries which brought the wine to your warehouse. Once they got to London, Sampson passed them on to various pimps. It was a very lucrative side-line."

"And this began while my father was still alive?"

"It did. I guess your father was the perfect absentee landlord. You tell me he didn't like Castel Rufina, he hardly ever went there and he wasn't at all interested in how it was run. When you inherited the title, Ugo must have thought things would go on very much as before."

"And then I suddenly turned up with all the children."

"I think even that would have been all right if you'd kept out of the running of the Castel. But you didn't, did you?"

"No, but that was because I felt guilty. I thought I should be pulling my weight."

"Ugo was very resentful, but it appears the last straw was your decision to abandon the Wedding of the Wolf scenario. He thought you were tampering with tradition."

"A very ugly tradition."

"Indeed. What a pity you didn't cancel it this year."

"I'm afraid I can't agree with you."

Both men glanced at Eloise, only the slight flush on her cheekbones betraying the fact she was listening to them at all.

"Anyway, he seems to have begun to plot your downfall from that date. And it became an obsession. I don't think Petrela was bothered one way or another, but he was focused on Eloise and getting her into his bed and Ugo used that to work against you."

Eloise was still quite impassive.

"I think Petrela would have left you alone if you hadn't done what you did yesterday afternoon."

"What...oh yes..."

At last, Eloise looked up and speaking to no one in particular asked, "What did he do?"

Dante gave her a steady look. "Petrela had been negotiating to buy the Castel Rufina. He was offering an obscene amount of money for it. It would have solved all my problems—I could have bought a nice house in the English countryside somewhere—Gloucestershire or Oxfordshire perhaps, near enough to London for me to commute, near good schools and in a place the children would be less likely to get into trouble."

"So what happened?"

"So at the last moment, I found I couldn't do it. Couldn't sell my birthright. I thought I could walk away from my de Rufina heritage, but when it came to it, I wasn't able to. I told Petrela yesterday. He was surprisingly good about it—said he understood, patted me on the shoulder. That's when everything started to go wrong."

Sherwin chipped in. "I think that was the point where Petrela gave Ugo permission to do his worst. The cocaine was already planted..."

"Yes, I meant to ask you. You told me no one approached the front of the van."

"It's true. But thank heaven for CCTV and the doubt that was sown in my mind. We retraced your steps and found some footage from outside the laundry. While you were in there, two men waltzed up, opened the van door with a key and put something inside. Easy."

"Easy if they had Ugo's key." Dante shook his head, still trying to take in the extent of his cousin's perfidy.

"I guess if you had changed your mind and told Petrela you were prepared to sell, someone would have removed it while you were still on *La Donnina*."

"But what did he hope to achieve? I'd still have been alive, still have the title."

"Yes, but in prison for a long time and utterly disgraced. I imagine the children would have been split up and fostered — although from what he says, there's a possibility he meant to hang on to Matt, with the intention of moulding him and drawing him into the criminal activities."

"Matt wouldn't have cooperated," Dante said with conviction.

"I'm sure you're right, but Ugo didn't know that. They might have kept Laura too for..." He glanced at Dante and moved on. "The point is, life at the Castel Rufina would have gone on as before, with Ugo and Petrela in an unholy partnership. And when you came out of prison, you would probably have disappeared. Been found dead in some back-alley, the victim of a never-to-be-solved mugging."

Even Eloise was drawn into the conversation. "But I don't see how Petrela expected to keep himself out of the whole business. He must know the police have been watching him for years and once you'd arrested Dante, surely he'd have been implicated."

"Yes, but strangely, Dante's very innocence was their protection. He wasn't going to spill the beans, because he genuinely didn't know anything. They'd made sure the cocaine didn't come from their usual suppliers and hadn't been planted at the boat. Ugo had been laying a trail for years connecting Dante with all sort of dodgy deals and on a superficial level it was very convincing. And of course, Petrela's got a host of clever lawyers and knows all the tricks. But some of the stuff we got at the London end from Larry Sampson is going to tie Ugo down and through him, Petrela."

"So it was really only Larry's completely accidental arrest that got me off the hook." Dante ran a hand over his face. "Phew! That's rather too close for comfort."

"Well, there was something else. The way you behaved when you we brought you in. You just didn't act like a guilty man. You were so concerned for Eloise, you scarcely thought about yourself. I witnessed the exact moment when you realised just how much trouble you were in and then dismissed it. It didn't quite ring true."

"Well, thank you for that." Dante grinned. "Sorry for depriving you of the chance of putting me away."

Sherwin grunted, but it was clear he was revising his opinion of Dante de Rufina. They had finished their meal now and Eloise stood up abruptly.

"I'm going to bed."

Dante said, "I'll come with you."

She rounded on him with a look of absolute loathing and he revised hastily, "I mean, I'll come up with you."

"I'll come and see you in a while," Tom said. "Today's been a long haul; I could do with coffee and a brandy."

He was rewarded with another savage look from Eloise.

Dante followed Eloise to her room, physically stopping her from shutting the door in his face. "Please, I have to speak to you, just for a few minutes."

She let him in, mutely moving to the bed and looking at him with absolute indifference.

"Look, I'm sorry. I'm sorry if I've upset you."

"Upset me? Upset me? I risked my life and my...my honour to help you and all you can say is, 'You betrayed me.' "

"I was shocked. To find you like that. To know just how little you think of me."

"Well, I thought enough of you to miss my plane and try to warn you. Do you really think I wanted to be there with Petrela and Ugo? That I enjoyed what I had to do? I thought I was buying you a chance."

"I know and I'm grateful. But it's just that when we came into the cabin…"

She glared at him. "Yes?"

"You looked as if you'd had a good time. You looked…sexually sated. Replete. Content…"

"So? What the hell does that have to do with you? I went there to try to save you and I did what I had to. How I coped with it is absolutely none of your business. I mean, you're the one who told me I should enjoy sex completely separated from affection or love. And that's what I did."

Dante breathed heavily, his pale face taut with anger. "Can you imagine the agonies I went through when I realised what you'd done? Don't forget I knew the plans Petrela had for you. I was desperate…"

"Well, you shouldn't have been. It's nothing to do with you. I can look after myself." Rage welled up in her. "How dare you even question my motives? If you hadn't been so stupidly naïve, it need never have come to this."

"No?" His expression was icy. "But surely, Lola, you should be grateful to me. A wonderful new sexual experience to add to your growing portfolio. Double penetration. I presume they did both enter you at once? Who got your arse? It must have been Petrela. He'd been fantasising about it long enough. Yes? And Ugo fucked you? And you really enjoyed that…?"

She stood up. "I'm not prepared to have this conversation merely to satisfy your prurience. All I wanted was for the children to be safe and happy. And they are. Or at least, they have the chance, if you don't do something else stupid. So if you don't mind, I'd like to sleep now. I've got to get back to London tomorrow, to my own life. I never want to see you again."

He was now so angry that any sense, any logic, had long gone. "Oh fine. You want me to go now. I suppose I should be grateful that with your new sexual inventiveness you're not trying it on with me and Sherwin. Or perhaps you fancy a foursome this time — I'm sure that nice young barman downstairs would be happy to join in."

Again, she could find no words, but took recourse in delivering a stinging slap to his cheek. Her face was white.

"Get out, get out of my room. Get out of my life. You've caused me nothing but trouble since the day I met you."

"It will be a pleasure." He bowed sarcastically and left the room, slamming the door behind him.

For the next hour, Dante did his best to drink his way systematically through the hotel's mini-bar. At the end of that time, feeling more sober than he had when he started, his feeling of guilt about Eloise overwhelmed him. This woman, this cool, beautiful girl, had twice broken through her natural reserve and restraint in order to help him — to help his family. She'd walked into the lion's den — she'd surrendered herself to Petrela, a man he knew she found repugnant. But he couldn't get out of his head the picture of her asleep in Petrela's bed — a woman with the unmistakeable glow of one who has just had mind-blowing sex. And he had to face the fact that the problem was it should have been him who made her look like that. He acknowledged to himself that he was jealous. He, Dante de Rufina, an advocate of free love and a man totally opposed to being tied down by the monotony of a serious relationship, was impossibly, distractedly jealous of an up-tight, difficult sexual ingénue, who, thanks to his intervention, was learning too much, too fast.

He got up and made his way back to her room. At least he could apologise for his stunning lack of gratitude. He frowned when he found the door was slightly ajar and he knocked, pushing it open as he did so. The room was empty, the bed not slept in, her belongings gone. He stood staring at the unruffled bed for a long time before turning to bang his forehead on the doorframe.

"Christ almighty!" he whispered to himself, his voice hoarse. "I've driven her into Sherwin's bed."

He went back to his room and lay on his face on the bed, raging at his own stupidity until he fell into a troubled sleep.

Chapter Thirty

The next day, having shaved with a disposable razor provided by the hotel, he went downstairs, grimly determined to fight for her. Sherwin was alone in the dining room eating croissants and scrambled eggs.

"Morning, de Rufina! Hope you feel a bit better after your ordeal. Have some of this coffee, it's very good."

Dante poured himself a cup and sat at the table, willing himself to be calm. "No sign of Eloise? She still asleep?"

"Oh no, far from it." Sherwin looked at his watch. "In fact at this moment she's probably somewhere over the Alps."

"What?"

"I gather you two had words last night. She came to my room and we talked. She decided there was no point in her hanging round here, so she drove back to Florence to see if she could get a standby seat on the early flight to London. She promised to call me if there was any problem and she hasn't, so I imagine she got away."

"She's gone..." Dante seemed to be having trouble taking it in.

"Yes, I don't know what you said to her last night, but she was pretty upset."

"And you...comforted her, did you?"

Sherwin nodded. "I did what I could, yes." He gave the other man an odd look. "You know, I should have had you locked up while I had the chance."

* * * *

Back at the Castel Rufina, Dante moved in a daze, like a man in mourning. There was plenty to be done, in the absence of Ugo, but here he had his first piece of real luck. He assembled the staff to give them a frank explanation of the situation. It was extraordinary how the atmosphere of the place had lifted without the malign presence of Petrela and his lackeys.

"The problem now is finding someone to replace Ugo," he told them. "For the time being, I'll fulfil his duties. But of course, I can't go on doing that if I'm to have any chance of continuing my career in London. So we'll advertise in the trade papers for a general manager and hope for the best."

The chef, Gianni, coughed self-deprecatingly. "Conte, if you were looking for someone who could take over at once and at least fill in on a temporary basis, my brother-in-law has been managing a big country-house hotel outside Rome. Now it's been taken over by a chain and they want to put their own managers in. He doesn't fancy it—too regimented, he says. My sister was working there too, as the housekeeping administrator. So they're both out of a job. He's bloody good and I'm not just saying that because he's family."

So it was that Pietro and Anna became ensconced in the manager's suite in the hotel, fitting in as if they had worked there forever. With relief, Maria relinquished the housekeeping keys to the younger woman and devoted herself full time to looking after the children.

Dante continued to prowl listlessly around the hotel, still dealing with the fallout from Ugo and Petrela's arrest and receiving a stream of distinguished visitors who expressed delight at Petrela being out of the way and assured him they'd never had anything to do with his nefarious activities.

One evening, Matt found him sprawled on the couch in the sitting room, a glass of whisky in his hand.

"Where are the others?"

"In bed."

"You all right?"

"I'm fine, don't worry about me."

Matt perched on the arm of the sofa.

"I've got something to tell you."

Dante sat upright, regarding his sibling warily. "Don't tell me you've got some girl pregnant. Not Ginata? Please tell me it's not Ginata?"

Matt grinned. "No, calm down, Dan, it's nothing like that. It's just…you remember when Eloise was here?"

Dante covered his face with his hand. "I wish I could forget the wretched woman."

"Well, we had a sort of a bet. About how many pictures I could sell during that wedding party."

He remembered, dimly. "Oh yes, quite a few of them went, didn't they?"

"I sold them all. Thirty of them." There was pride in Matt's voice. "And the deal with Eloise was that if the exhibition did well, I'd at least take my work to the Art School in Florence. I thought I'd got nothing to lose — they'd say it was rubbish and that would be it. But they didn't, they liked it. They've offered me a place next term. If you agree."

"Oh, Matteo!" Dante stood up and hugged his brother. "There's nothing I'd like more. I'm so very proud of you."

He poured Matt a drink, splashing more whisky into his own glass. Matt raised his eyebrows.

"Dante, if Dad were still here, you'd talk to him about anything, wouldn't you? Even very private, personal things."

Dante nodded. With a sudden rush of pain he realised how much he missed his father. "Why?" he asked, striving for a lightness of tone. "Now we get to the part where you tell me you've got some local girl up the duff?"

Matt shook his head. "It's not me, it's you. Since all that business with Ugo, you're so withdrawn and grim. Do you want to talk about it?"

Dante shook his head. He'd been sorting things out for himself for a long time now.

"It's to do with Eloise, isn't it? Talk to me, Dante. I'm not Dad, but I want you to be happy. Just tell me what went wrong."

And with a feeling of quite unexpected relief, Dante told his brother the whole story of his turbulent relationship with Eloise Lambert.

* * * *

Dante woke on the morning of his birthday after a vivid nightmare about Eloise. He dreamed of her every night, waking unrefreshed and grumpy. Now he groaned as he heard a thunderous knocking on his bedroom door. Before he could tell whoever it was to go away, the door was flung open and a little procession entered. At the front Marco bounced with a tray laden with food. Behind him, Laura supported a pile of parcels. Matt, carrying Charlie, brought up the rear. They stood at the end of his bed and sang "Happy Birthday" to him, their voices ragged and Charlie merely waving a chubby fist and shouting, "Birthday, birthday, birthday..."

After they'd finished, Marco dumped the tray on his legs. "Breakfast in bed!" he announced. "Bucks Fizz, scrambled eggs, toast and coffee. Laura cooked it."

"Well, thank you. What a treat!"

They watched him closely as he ate his meal. Charlie kept yelling, "Presents!" and Matt dropped him on the bed, causing the tray to wobble violently.

"Yes, open mine!" Marco insisted. He began scrabbling through the packages on Dante's feet, coming up with something square and flat.

Dante began to open the parcels, breaking off only when Charlie started grabbing the scrambled eggs in his hands and smearing them on his face. From Marco, there was a set of Gershwin CDs he'd wanted and a computer game he'd never play, but Marco would. From Charlie, chocolates and a bottle of his favourite scotch. Laura presented him with a small package and as he unwrapped the soft leather wallet, she said, "It's really from me and Eloise."

He stopped turning the gift in his hands and gave her a sharp look. "From Eloise?"

"That time we went shopping, you remember? I bought this and then I didn't have enough money for the leather jacket. She got it for me. So really, she contributed to the present."

His hands tightened on the wallet and Matt chipped in, "Here's my present."

As Dante pulled the paper from the large, flat parcel, it was obvious it was a painting.

"Sorry to seem like a cheapskate, but they do sell for a lot of money these days!" Matt's eyes twinkled.

The view was from the bar terrace and in the background were the vivid greens of the garden and the ochre of the town. On the left of the picture, a woman sat. She had auburn hair and was clad in a green sundress, long legs elegantly crossed. Papers were spread on the table in front of her and she held a glass of wine. She looked towards the artist, smiling, as if he'd just called her name.

"Eloise!" It was no more than a breath from Dante.

"I hope it's all right."

"It's...perfect. Perfect. Thank you so much, Matt, I shall treasure this." He looked at his family gathered round the bed and his heart swelled with a feeling of love for them. Then Matt said, "There's one more thing."

"Not more presents, surely?"

"Yes. But this isn't only from us — it's from the staff as well." He handed Dante a large envelope. "I just don't want you to take it the wrong way."

Dante opened the envelope and withdrew a narrow folder. "Plane tickets? But..."

"It's a first class ticket to London with an open-ended return date. Well, you have to come back within a month. Look at the card."

The big, gaudy birthday card had been signed by every member of the hotel staff with messages like, "Thank you for saving the hotel," and, "We owe you everything." Someone had written, "Have fun in London but come back soon."

Matt continued, "I've talked to Toby. He's giving you some sets at the end of the week. They're advertising it as Dante's Birthday Bash."

"But how can I...?"

"We'll be fine. I've got lots to do to prepare for Art College and Laura and Marc have school. Maria says she's happy to take sole charge of Charlie. Go to London and relax."

The party started to break up. Laura grabbed Charlie's hand. "Come on, monster child, I'll give you some breakfast."

Matt was the last to leave. At the door, he turned, feeling in his pocket. "Oh, there was one other thing." He moved back to the bed, holding out a business card. "You might need this."

After he'd gone, Dante looked at cursive lettering on the card. '*Lace Dreams*, Wedding Planners and Event Organisers. Eloise Lambert, Samantha Kirk.' On the other side was printed: '*Show Offs*, demonstrators, presenters and exhibitionists.' There was a phone number and an address.

He examined it for a long time before carefully tucking it into his new wallet.

* * * *

On getting back to London, Eloise had refused to go back to her usual job presiding over the wedding planning business. Samantha was astonished at her friend's uncharacteristic obduracy.

"No, I can't do it. I've changed too much. And I'm not going back to Italy, ever. You'll have to handle that side of the business."

Commissions had flooded in since the Connaught/Carew-Wright wedding, but Eloise just tossed her head. "I don't care. I can't be prim and respectable. I have to have a break from it and try to sort myself out."

So Samantha continued working on the *Lace Dreams* side of the business, while Eloise switched to *Show-Offs*. Sam tentatively suggested they leave Jamie in charge, apparently sensing her friend was in no mood for managerial responsibility, and Eloise readily agreed. She spent her days at exhibitions and outside shops, in a variety of exotic costumes, handing out literature, offering samples, demonstrating equipment. It was dull, mindless work and it suited her. She knew Sam sensed she was profoundly unhappy, but she wouldn't talk about what had happened.

Late one afternoon, Sam said, "Darling, Jamie's asked me to inveigle you into doing a rush job tonight."

"Oh, Sammy, why me? I've got an appointment with a bottle of plonk, a box of chocolates and a weepy film."

"It has to be you, Ellie, because singing is required."

"What? Firstly, I sing like a cow and secondly, I thought we agreed we wouldn't do those singing telegram things anymore."

"True, but this isn't a telegram. It's more an…um…artistic statement."

With a lot of bullying and cajoling, she got Eloise to agree and later that day the *Show Offs* van travelled the short distance to Soho.

"I hate this costume, it's so uncomfortable," Eloise moaned. "Are you sure this is what the client wants?"

"Positive. Now you do remember what to do, Ellie?"

She sighed. "Of course. I wait for the drum roll, come out, sing the silly little song. Then pose, grin, vamp my hips... God, Sammy, must I really do this?"

"Yes. After that, the manager will come forward and help you down. You go up to the mark, shimmy a bit, give him a kiss and that's it. Easiest fee you've ever earned."

Eloise slumped back in her seat, sulking.

"Come on, Ellie, do snap out of it. I've never seen you like this. You're worse than a problem teenager."

They pulled up in a dark back street and both women got out. A man waited for them in a lighted doorway. He shook hands with Sammy, raising his eyebrows humorously at Eloise. "Wow, that's some costume!"

"Well I hope your friend likes it. It hurts."

"He will. It's this way. Do you need any help with the gear?"

"I could use some muscle to get it out of the van, but after that it's on wheels."

In the cramped dressing-room, the man asked Eloise, "You're okay about the routine, are you?"

"I think so."

"And you know there's an audience out there? Lights? You might be a bit dazzled when you come out."

"Fine, thanks for warning me."

"Time to climb in, Ellie," Samantha said.

Outside on the dance floor, the music came to an end. Toby Heathersett stepped into the spotlight which illuminated the small stage.

"Ladies and Gentlemen, please take your seats. As you're all aware, tonight marks the return from exile in

Italy of *The Inferno*'s very own Dan Rufin. We've heard him sing and what a pleasure it is to have him back. At the beginning of this week, Dante also had a birthday." He held up his hand. "No, I'm not going to tell you how old he is. But to mark the occasion and to show how much we've missed him, we have a little surprise."

He held out an arm towards the side of the stage and the band struck up the chords of 'Happy Birthday' as two waiters appeared, dragging a huge cake. There were six tiers of white and pink plaster icing and the giant offering moved on wheels. When it had been positioned next to Toby in the middle of the stage the drummer began a sustained drum-roll. The top of the cake splintered and the audience gasped as a woman burst upward, hands aloft. She wore a minute basque covered in grey and silver fur-like material. It forced her breasts upwards, leaving very little to the imagination. Long legs were encased in silver fishnet stockings. Her face was made up like an animal's, whiskers drawn either side of a blackened nose. Her eyes were rimmed with kohl and on her head she wore two large furry ears. After acknowledging the cheers of the audience, she turned round, still on the tiny platform inside the cake and waggled her bushy silver tail seductively. The band struck up and she went into the song she'd been given.

"Oh how we've missed you, how we have missed you, since you have been away.

Now that you're back, I'm sure going to kiss you, hope that you're here to stay.

Wishing you love and mirth, now that we mark your birth,

Please do not leave us, will you believe us, here's what we have to say."

The words were banal in the extreme, but the tune was catchy and the audience were tapping their feet as she launched into the chorus.

"We love you, we need you, we want you. This is where you belong.

Don't stay away forever, don't be a stranger too long."

Her voice was strong, sweet and clear and when she finished, there was enthusiastic applause. Toby stepped forward and helped her step over the rim of the cake, supporting her carefully as she tottered down the wooden tiers in her three-inch heels. He led her over to the piano, where a man sat in evening dress. At her approach he stood and she moved forward and kissed him on the lips.

Then, and only then, she realised who it was. Dante de Rufina. He stared at her as if she were a ghost.

Eloise's one thought was to get out of there, to run. But as she turned, he grabbed her wrist and said, "What the fuck are you playing at?"

Chapter Thirty-One

The audience laughed nervously, not sure if this was part of the act. Dante moved over the stage, dragging Eloise behind him. Halfway across he remembered they were not alone and stopped at the microphone. "My apologies, ladies and gentlemen. I'll be back shortly, but first, I'm going to have my cake and eat it." There was more laughter as he disappeared from view, Eloise staggering after him.

In the dressing room, he flung her across the room so she ended up against the dressing table. "Now will you kindly tell me what the hell you mean by turning up in my club, *my* club, to take the piss like that?"

"I didn't know it was your club and I had no intention of making fun of you." She rubbed her wrist, scowling at him. "No need to do that when you do it so competently all by yourself."

"How could you do such a thing?" He was furious. "Leaping out of a cake like some sort of trollop."

"I thought that was exactly the kind of woman you admired. But as it happens, I'm doing my job. I've been employed to jump out of the cake and sing that annoying little song. But if I'd known it was for you I'd have turned it down. I never want to see you again."

He laughed nastily. "You're seriously expecting me to believe you didn't know it was my club?"

"How could I know? We came in the van, we arrived at the back. It's such a ludicrous coincidence, it never occurred to me."

"If you didn't know it was me, why on earth are you dressed like that?"

"Well, I'm so sorry, Dante, but you're not the only man in the world who gets turned on by high heels and cleavage."

"No, I don't mean that. I mean, why are you dressed as a wolf?"

There was a stunned pause while she looked at him, wide-eyed, then she turned abruptly and stared at herself in the mirror, nodding her head from side to side so the ears flopped about. "No, I'm supposed to be an Alsatian. A German Shepherd Dog. I asked Sammy — she told me the client liked dogs."

"Well, it has been known," he said, with sudden a grin before he recalled that he was still angry with her. "I simply refuse to believe you could have dressed up as a wolf and come to my club to jump out of a cake at me without knowing what you were doing. You've done this to get at me."

"Dante, you flatter yourself. I've got better things to do than think about you and your infantile desires."

"Oh yes, of course you have. You're too busy with your insipid men. So who's getting the benefit of your doggy-style attractions now? The idiot actor or the hunky policeman? Of course, you might still be hankering after dear old Tolka. Well, that's all right, I believe the Italian authorities allow conjugal visits these days."

It was as if he'd slapped her and tears sprang to her eyes. She pulled herself together and lunged for the door. "I don't have to take this. Not from you." She wrenched open the door and, moving as fast as she could, ran away from him. Blinded by tears, her route took her diagonally across the stage, where the band was playing, down the steps and through the dancers on the darkened floor. Behind her came Dante. He should have caught her easily—especially since the heels were slowing her down—but sprinting across the dance floor he swerved to avoid a couple in a deep embrace and ran into a table laden with drinks. He managed not to knock the whole thing over, but by the time he'd apologised and summoned a waiter to replace what had been slopped, she was out of sight.

He caught up with her in the street outside. By now it was autumn and it was a chilly evening. Even in Soho, her wolf outfit was causing comment and she'd slowed down as she realised she had no idea where to go next. He caught her by the arm and pushed her out of the way of the pedestrians, backing her up against a stone arch.

"For God's sake, Lola, don't run away from me. Don't run from me again. I'm sorry. Truly sorry. Please, I only get so angry because I love you."

He leant forward, pressing her against the stone and lowered his face to hers, kissing her brutally. It was a long time before he came up for air and when he did, she lashed out at him, slapping his face yet again. "Stop it! Don't make fun of me. I can't bear it."

His hands caught hers and forced them back against the wall above her head. Then he bent forward and kissed her again. This time, she stopped struggling and melted into the kiss. It was as if he were some potent drug, coursing around her veins. She began to respond, despite herself, pushing her hips against him, feeling his hardness. A voice interrupted them.

"Excuse me, sir, would you move away from the lady for a moment?"

Dante pulled back with some difficulty and looked over his shoulder. A burly policeman stood behind him.

"Sorry, sir, but it didn't look as if the lady was entirely happy with what you were doing. Mind if I just check?"

Dante nodded, taken aback. The policeman said, "Are you all right, Miss?"

Eloise shook, partly because of the cold, partly because of what Dante had done to her. "Yes, thank you, officer, I'm all right."

"Yes," Dante added. "It's nothing, just a lovers' tiff."

"We are *not* lovers," she countered.

"Well, are you all right? Because if not, I can see you wherever you want to go."

"No, it's fine, thank you."

"Right then. But I suggest you get off the street as soon as you can, Miss. You're not really dressed for night-time in London."

"Of course, officer," Dante answered. "I'll make sure she gets back safely. Many thanks." He grabbed Eloise's hand and started off in the direction of the club, with her trailing behind him.

Just before they got to the discreet doorway to *The Inferno*, a woman crashed into him. Pulling back, he saw it was Avril, the girl he'd rescued from an over-eager punter. She was in full tart's uniform, heavy makeup, tight leopard-skin top and a miniscule leather skirt with knee boots. She swayed slightly and he guessed she'd had a few drinks.

"Oh My God, the divine Dante! How are you, darling?" She drew him into a passionate embrace. "I didn't know you were back from Italy."

"Only temporarily, I'm afraid. I have to go back next week."

"Poor baby. Still having trouble with those wretched kids?"

"They're all right. How are you?"

"All right. Nothing changes." She ran a finger down his cheek. "You're looking mean and magnificent, as usual." Reaching down, she cupped the bulge in his trousers. "Ready for fun, I see. Look, I've got a client now. But later I've got nothing on, as they say. If you fancy another freebie, come round. Same place as before. I'll be waiting for you."

"I'm afraid I'm going to be otherwise…"

Avril surged past him, her eyes glazed. "Got to go now, darling, I'm already half an hour late, but he does like to be punished." She let her glance flicker over Eloise. "Sorry, sweetie, I didn't realise you were walking your dog."

Cursing under his breath, Dante dragged Eloise into the club and across the dance floor. He thrust her down at the table he and Toby shared, scarcely noticing that Samantha was already there. "Now we're going to talk seriously."

Toby appeared. "Oh no you're not. It's time for your next set."

"Fuck that, I must talk to Lola."

"Sorry, old boy, but you have to perform. These people have paid to hear you. You can talk to Eloise afterwards."

"Yes and you, you bastard, set me up. I'll have words to say about that as well."

Toby held up his hands in a gesture of surrender. "Not really, it was Matt's idea. Samantha and I just followed orders. Anyhow, you can do what you like to me when you've finished your set."

Grumbling, Dante walked towards the stage. Eloise leaned over to Sammy and hissed, "How could you? How could you subject me to that? I'll never forgive you."

"Sorry, darling, but I had to do something."

"Well, you can do something now and get me home."

"But Dante…"

"Fuck Dante," Eloise said, with unaccustomed crudeness. "He'll find someone else to entertain him." She turned her face towards Sam's, tears coursing down her cheeks, likely blurring the finely painted whiskers. Her voice was scarcely a whisper, "Please, Sammy, get me out of here."

They loaded the prop cake onto the van. Through the open stage door, Eloise could hear Dante's voice. He was singing, "Lola".

She got into the passenger seat and huddled there. Samantha went to give Toby their invoice. When she came out, the music had ended. *The Inferno* was closing for the night.

Sammy drove the van a little way towards Covent Garden before pulling into a parking bay. "Right, I want to know what that bastard did to you."

"He didn't do anything."

"What? He dragged you off the stage, he frightened you so much you ran away from him twice and you're crying like I haven't seen for years. What did he do to upset you?"

"He said he loved me."

"He what?"

"He pushed me up against a wall and kissed me and told me he loved me."

"The nasty brute! No wonder you're so upset."

Eloise sighed gustily.

"Okay, Ellie, spill. Why on earth should a gorgeous man saying he loves you get you so upset?"

"It's what he says when he wants to get someone into bed. He doesn't mean it."

"Why are you so hard on him, Ellie? Toby says he's been dreadfully unhappy since he got back from Italy."

"Yes, well, that's probably because he's missing his whore from the town. Or the incomparable Jessica."

"Ellie, what is the matter with you? I sense you really like this man. But you seem to be doing everything possible to push him away."

"That's because I know if I let him near me I'll be destroyed. He takes women and uses them. I don't want to be one of his victims."

"Yes, but if he says he loves you…"

"I told you, he doesn't mean it. He can't."

Samantha took another tack. "Well, forget emotion. I thought you said the sex with him was the best ever."

"Yes, but it's not worth the trouble."

"But if he just wants fun and you fancy his body, why don't you take advantage of it? Take control?"

"Why? What possible good would that do?"

Samantha started to laugh. "What good? Well, it would put the Count in his place and you'd get a decent shag out of it."

"Oh really, Sammy!"

"What's the matter with you, Ellie? Gone off sex?"

In fact, since her experience in Rimini, she hadn't made love at all. But now, something stirred.

"Look, he obviously likes you. And I mean really likes you. I don't know what happened between you two at the end, but for heaven's sake, Ellie, he's gorgeous. If he's used you, then use him back. Fuck him and leave him. But do something, because I can't bear you being so listless and depressed."

"I don't think..."

"For God's sake, Ellie, this is so unlike you. Get yourself on track again. Fight back!"

Eloise sat silent for so long that Samantha prompted, "Ellie?"

"Turn the van round. I'm going back."

Chapter Thirty-Two

At the stage door of *The Inferno*, Eloise got out of the van and leaned across to Samantha. "Don't wait."

"I think I'll just hang around for a while."

"Not necessary. I know what I'm doing."

At the door she met Toby on the way out. He looked at her in surprise. "Eloise! Have you forgotten something?"

"I think I have."

"Well, he's still in the main room. Glad you came back."

As she walked inside he did a thumbs-up in the direction of the van.

The club was dark—the staff had been sent home and the cleaners hadn't yet arrived. Dante de Rufina sat at the grand piano, a sole spotlight illuminating his face. He was playing Gershwin's *Rhapsody in Blue*, his features serious, a lock of dark hair flopping over his forehead. After about five minutes he stopped and stared at the keyboard in despair. Then he crashed his hands onto the keys, creating a loud, discordant sound. He slammed the lid of the piano shut and pitched forward, sinking his head onto his arms.

She walked lightly over to him. "Very nice. I don't remember hearing that bit at the end before."

He straightened up and swung around on the piano stool. For a long moment, he stared, eyebrows raised, then leant back, resting his elbows on the closed lid of the piano and stretching out his long legs.

"What's the matter, Lola? Forget something?"

She moved to stand directly in front of him. "Yes, I did, actually. I forgot you've got something I want."

"Oh? And what's that?"

Now, she moved even closer, straddling his outstretched legs. When she stopped, she was astride his body.

"This."

Her hand dropped onto the bulge in his trousers. She felt it stir, but his expression was quizzical.

"Let me see if I understand this. You want sex, but not me? My body but not my brain. Is that right?"

"That's exactly it."

"It's not very flattering."

"It's how you've treated hundreds of women. How you operate."

He closed his eyes. "I don't think... Lola, you did hear what I told you earlier? When we were in the street?"

"I heard it," she said steadily, her hand still massaging. "It's what you say to persuade women to do what you want."

"Not, actually." He was having trouble breathing normally. "I meant... Oh, God, Lola, you'll have to stop doing that."

"All right," she said, with unexpected reasonableness and withdrew her hand. "I'll do this instead." She bent her knees slightly, her legs still wide and astride him and began to rub the growing bulge with the tiny strip of fabric that covered her crotch. Her hips moved forward and back as she undulated.

"Stop it, Lola," he groaned. "You know that wasn't what I meant."

"Sorry. Is this better?" She dismounted as if she were getting off a bicycle and put her hands on his thighs, forcing them apart before he realised what she was doing. She knelt between them, her hands undoing the waistband fastening of his trousers and pulling down the zip.

"Lola, this is too much…"

"I'm sure you can cope." She'd got his penis free now and it sprang upwards, hardening as she watched it.

"It's beautiful," she said, approvingly.

"Lola…"

"I think we should get the trousers off. And the shoes and socks." She began working at his clothes, until he was naked from the waist down.

"Lola, please. Stop. Think about what you're doing."

"I've thought. I want this. And so do you." She pulled his penis away from his body, letting it twang back against his stomach.

"Yes, but…"

She crouched between his legs and extended her tongue, running it gently across the head of his cock. It was already red and hard and she put her tongue gently into the slit and wiggled it.

"You still want me to stop?"

"Christ, Lola, no. Not now. Don't stop. Please don't."

She laughed, the sound vibrating his cock and making him breathe even more heavily. Then she ducked her head underneath and drew her tongue from the base of the swelling balls to the straining head. Dante abandoned all attempts to stop her. He slumped back against the piano, his hips lifting involuntarily.

"God, do that again!"

"Do what?"

"Laugh, whatever you did. That vibrating sensation..."

"I'll sing the song again if you like." She put her lips over his swollen member and, barely audible, launched into the jingle she'd sung after her emergence from the cake. As she hummed, she took him, deeper and deeper into her mouth. Her hands clasped his legs, her thumbs gently caressing the sensitive flesh of his inner thighs. She could feel the thrumming of his blood, coursing through the big vein on the underside of his cock. For a moment, she pulled back, making him moan in protest. From between her legs, she pulled the furry wolf's tail and brushed it gently over the sensitive head of his penis. Then, when she could see he was on the edge, she put her lips back and took his throbbing flesh back into her mouth. Soon, his body took on a rhythm of its own, his hips thrusting forwards, until he cried out and emptied himself into her throat.

She sat back on her heels, looking like the wolf that got the cream. Dante, reviving, got up and grabbed her around the waist, swinging her around and depositing her on top of the piano. He pushed her legs upwards and outwards, positioning the high heels on the polished mahogany of the instrument and began to scrabble at her crotch.

"How do you undo this thing?"

"It's Velcro. Just find the edge, then pull."

He yanked at the suit and it parted, making a satisfactory ripping sound. As an afterthought, he asked, "Can you still wear the tail?"

She gave a throaty laugh. "The tail's separate. Strapped on by webbing."

"Mmmm." His fingers probed, feeling the wetness and the puffiness of her vulva. His finger flicked across her clitoris, then traced the contours of her lips before both hands parted them. His tongue was wet and hot as it entered her, hardening to drive inside. After a while, his mouth moved upwards again and he began to caress the tip of her swelling clit with his warm tongue. He inserted a finger, then another, then a third and — as she moaned and pressed against him — a fourth, moving his hand more firmly in response to the unequivocal appeal of her thrusting hips.

She came with incredible force, her whole pelvic area pushing forward, high heels firm on the surface of the piano. He leant forward to kiss her as she lay back, but she placed her hand over his mouth.

"No kissing."

"What do you mean, no kissing? That's what tarts say."

"You should know."

"Lola!" he said, warningly.

"All right, but I remember what happens when you kiss me. Not tonight."

"What does happen?"

"You know."

He pulled her to her feet and turned her round. "This fucking piano is the wrong height. Come with me." Holding her by the wrist he dragged her towards the bar area where solid wooden stools were spaced. "Bend over." He thrust her downwards over one of the stools, so her stomach was supported on the seat, her hands and head dangling downwards.

He tucked the flap of her costume up under the tail, which looked as if it was growing from the point where her spine met her buttocks. It was supported by a harness — one webbing strap went around her body and two others circled her thighs, holding the furry protuberance firm and incidentally providing a sort of frame for her bottom. He ran his hand from the base of the tail, down across her sensitive anus and let his fingers part the lips of her sex, which pulsed with excitement.

"Well, I've never really fancied bestiality, but there's a first time for everything." He rubbed the head of his cock up and down her slit, making her wriggle, then inserted about an inch into her warm, wet vagina. And stopped.

Eloise squealed in annoyance.

"What's the matter, Lola, want me to go further?"

"Why have you stopped?"

"I'd like to be sure you really want me."

"Oh God, Dante, just do it."

"Say please."

"Please, damn you."

"That's not very nice, is it?" But he entered her by another inch or so. "More?"

"Damn you to hell, Dante." She wriggled, trying to back onto him, but her undignified position over the stool gave her little ability to manoeuvre.

"So what do you say?"

"Fuck me. Just fuck me."

"Well, I was imagining something rather more tender, but that will have to do." He thrust his hips forward, burying himself inside her. She let out an involuntary moan of ecstasy. He started slowly, pulling out until he almost left her, then moving back in, but then he gathered pace. After a while he bent over her body, so he was curved round on top of her although his feet were still on the floor. His fingers tugged roughly at the wolf costume, liberating her breasts from the low-cut top, and his thumbs massaged her nipples as he continued to slide into her with growing speed and heat.

Eloise made noises she didn't know were in her. As the friction increased on her swollen sex, she let out a howl that was almost vulpine in its intensity. Dante kissed her neck and after a while, bit down hard, at the same time thrusting with great force and releasing himself into her. They lay, panting, before he pulled away.

"Now for the finale!" he said. He picked her up from the stool and carried her to a table, laying her flat. Her hair was dishevelled, the wolf ears lopsided. He planted the heels of her shoes on the table, spreading her legs as if he were about to conduct a gynaecological examination and looked at her with satisfaction. Her exposed vulva was red and swollen, the lips puffy, the slit open and wet.

"Not so much of the cool, perfect wedding organiser now, is there? I wish I had a camera. In fact, I think there's one in the office. Stay there."

"No, Dante…"

"Stay!"

He disappeared for a few minutes, returning with a tube of something.

"That got you going, didn't it? But even I'm not such a cad as to film a lady in such a very compromising situation. Here we go." He began applying something moist and soothing to her anus.

"What are you doing?" Her voice was low and husky.

"Getting you ready. I don't want to hurt you." He applied the stuff to his cock, still stiff and red. "You have to be this way round, because I want to see your face."

"Dante, I..."

"What's the matter? You liked it at the Castel. And I bet Tolka did this to you. Didn't he?"

She made a small noise, turning her head to one side.

"I think the wolf costume might be very appropriate for you, because if I remember rightly, it's at this point you turn into a wild animal. All right?"

His fingers, slick with gel, entered her anus, sending tremors radiating out from her pelvis. He could see the exposed flower of her vulva, pulsing as if it had independent life. He placed his cock-head on the tiny star of her anus and bore down on it, gently but firmly, until it broke through the sphincter. Then he pushed onwards while she writhed and gibbered.

Her face was red, her arms lashing out behind her, her eyelids fluttering as he drove into her over and over again. His fingers entered her cunt and his thumb worked her clit as she arched her back, crying out, until an orgasm shimmied through her like electricity. He let her calm down and then reached out to a neighbouring table for a thick beer bottle. "Now then, let's see you be all prim and proper with this inside you," he told her, inserting the neck into her as he kept up his invasion of her other hole. When the bottle was deep in, he used one hand to move it in and out of her, while with the other he alternately pinched and smoothed her breasts.

Eloise hadn't thought it possible to climax so many times, so close together. But this caused the tingling build-up to begin again. For a moment, she visualised herself, spread-eagled on a table in the middle of the detritus of a nightclub, being buggered by a louche character like Dante de Rufina while being penetrated with a bottle. And she came so hard that her breath emerged in animal grunts, her back and neck arched and her face contorted. At the height of her passion, her muscles contracted on his intruding cock and he too climaxed spectacularly, flooding her insides with warm liquid.

They stayed there for a while, panting, their sweat mingling as Dante softened and left her. He leant forward to kiss her but she turned her head abruptly and he sighed heavily and straightened up.

"My God, Lola, you're the ultimate definition of sweet and sour, aren't you?" He started to pull her upright. "Come on, sweetheart, we can't stay here. The cleaners will be in soon and I don't want to scandalise them even more than I usually do. My flat's only a short walk."

She swayed against him. "No, I have to go home. I must go now."

"Darling, Lola, come with me. You can sleep in my bed and we'll talk in the morning."

He saw her flinch. "Not a good idea, Dante. Besides, you have an appointment, if I remember rightly." Her voice had recovered some of its crisp authority.

"An appointment?"

"The...er...lady we met in the street seemed to be expecting you to call on her."

He pulled her to him, his chin on her head, his face betraying despair. "You know perfectly well she means absolutely nothing to me." He closed his eyes as if in pain. "You must do what you want, my lovely Lola. But soon, very soon, you have to come to a sensible decision about me. We can't go on like this."

She fumbled, trying to pull her ravaged costume together, her hands still shaking.

"Here, let me do that." He pulled the material up over her breasts, kissing each one before he tucked it away. Then he crouched down and pulled the Velcro edges between her legs, first planting another kiss on her vulva. He stood up again and inspected her. "Well, your ears are lopsided and your tail is crooked, but I suppose you'll pass muster at this time of night."

"Thank you." She turned and headed towards the rear door. "Goodbye, Dante."

Dante dressed at speed. "I don't think so, sweetheart. I'm coming with you."

"Not necessary."

"Very necessary. If you think I'm going to let you go out, looking so...so freshly fucked...with all those other wolves out there, you can think again."

She was too tired to argue. "All right, you can walk with me."

"We'll take a cab."

They hailed a black taxi cruising through Soho and sat silent for the short journey to Eloise's flat. Dante sent the cabbie away and watched as she got her key from the little bag she'd had with her and opened the door. "Can I come up?" he asked, hopefully, knowing what her answer would be.

"No. But thank you for bringing me home. And for...the rest of it."

"It's a pleasure," he said, with grave courtesy. "But please, please let me come upstairs, just for a few minutes. We still haven't actually talked."

"No!" She was inside the hallway of the house now, her pale, smudged face peering at him round the door. He ran his thumb over the ruined whiskers.

"I wish I understood what this is all about. Well, have a sleep. Tomorrow — later today — we've got to have a stab at sorting things out."

"Goodnight."

"Goodnight, my little Lola." He turned to go, but just before she shut the door, he spoke again. "And by the way, my darling, I meant what I said to you in the street. Every word. I do love you, you know."

He walked off into the night.

* * * *

Later that same day, in the large, bright room in Covent Garden, Samantha Kirk conducted an awkward conversation with a couple who were considering the Italian wedding option. They weren't in the first flush of youth and were happy to tell anyone who'd listen that they'd met on the Internet. They were dubious about the prospect of Castel Rufina and disposed to be suspicious about the whole business.

Samantha patiently detailed the advantages of the place and showed them photographs of the Connaught wedding.

The man, a plump, red-faced individual who was something in the city was obviously keener on the Italian idea — his fiancée, an equally well-proportioned and pretty blonde, wasn't so sure.

"But, Gary, don't you think it's a bit impersonal? I mean, very grand and all that, but where's the romance?"

Before anyone could answer, the outer door burst open and Dante de Rufina strode in.

"Where is she? Where the hell is she? I can't go on like this."

Samantha stood up, trying to radiate calm dignity. "I think you're in the wrong place, Conte. Who are you looking for?"

"Lola. That prize bitch Eloise Lambert. I've been trying to talk to her all morning, but every time I call her she slams the phone down on me. I'm not putting up with it a minute longer. Now where the fuck is she?"

At the far end of the room, the concealed door moved very slightly and Dante bounded over and wrenched it open. Eloise cowered in the doorway. His hand shot out to capture her wrist and he dragged her into the room.

Eloise was dressed in a tubular costume, green at the top, shading to white, with a fringed hem and flat white boots. Her arms were clad in green-fringed gloves up to her elbow and she had a headdress of green leafy fronds.

"Right," Dante said, gripping her shoulders. "Now we're going to settle all this nonsense once and for all. Firstly, I told you very clearly yesterday that I love you. This isn't something I say lightly — in fact I've never said it to any woman before. And secondly, this business about kissing. I'm simply not..." He broke off, having taken in her appearance for the first time. "Why do you look like a giant leek?"

"I'm not a leek," she replied crossly. "I'm a spring onion."

"Good heavens!"

"We can't talk here. Come this way."

"With pleasure. But first I'm going to kiss you, my beautiful little pickled onion."

"Spring onion!" she said, her exasperation muffled as Dante pulled her into an embrace and she backed out of the room still in his arms.

In the room they'd left, there was silence, the prospective clients staring at the closed door in astonishment.

After a while, the woman asked, "Is that the man who owns the castle?"

"Yes. He's half Italian," Samantha added, as if that explained everything.

"He's very dashing."

"That's true."

"And who was *she?*"

"That's my business partner. They're…just getting together, I think."

"It certainly looked like it." Gary laughed.

His fiancée asked, "Does the Count come with the package?"

"Well," Sammy replied dubiously, "it rather depends what you wanted to do with him."

The room into which Eloise had drawn Dante was the meeting area for *Show Offs* and served largely as a common room for the demonstrators. The force of his embrace took them across the room, still twined together, until they ran into the big central table where they were forced to come to a halt—Eloise half on her back, Dante panting with passion and exertion.

His lips swooped down onto hers again, hard and demanding and she fought him feebly and without much conviction. Finally, he pulled back, becoming aware of his surroundings for the first time. All around them loomed a selection of giant vegetables, watching their antics with interest. Two tomatoes, an ordinary onion, another spring onion, a turnip, a carrot and a parsnip looked on in amusement.

Dante looked around, blinking. "Now I really am in the soup!"

There was laughter and Jamie, the only one in ordinary clothes, said, "Yes and soup is what we're supposed to be demonstrating, so can all the vegetables go down to the mini-bus please? Eloise, if you want to...um...sort things out, we don't need you, there's another spring onion."

"Yes," she said, looking guilty. "But we're supposed to be a bunch."

"Not much of a bunch with only two of us," the other spring onion piped up. "You go with your young man, my dear. I'll jump around; they'll never know the difference."

Chapter Thirty-Three

And so, as the vegetables trooped down to the street, Dante followed Eloise up another flight of stairs and into the top-floor flat. Inside she stood a few yards away and stared, the green fronds on her head nodding and rippling slightly.

Eventually he broke the silence. "What does happen when we kiss?"

She regarded him seriously. "I almost believe you really love me."

"And…"

"I know beyond a shadow of a doubt that I love you."

"What? Oh, Lola!"

He covered the gap between them in a bound and drew her into a long kiss, his tongue probing. Again, she felt that sense of merging, of become one highly sexual entity. When he broke off, he laughed shakily. "You'll have to take that thing off, I can't propose to an onion."

"You can't propose at all."

"You watch me. How does it undo? Oh, I see." He found the zip and pulled the long shift downwards. Underneath she was naked and he laughed again as she stood before him wearing only the green headdress, gloves and furry white boots.

He tore off his jacket and flung it from him. "Come along," he said, picking her up. "We'll continue this conversation in bed."

After their earlier wild contortions this was much more conventional. They made love in the missionary position, kissing as if connected at the lips. Afterwards they lay together—Dante on his back, with Eloise curled up, her head on his shoulder.

Awkwardly she broached the subject on her mind. "Dante, I'm sorry I seemed to mistrust you. But I thought you'd been sucked into something illegal and I had to react fast. Of course I know you couldn't ever be a drug smuggler."

"It doesn't matter." He tightened his arms around her. "What I don't understand is why you withdrew from me, after that night when Charlie was sick. Things seemed to be going fine and then you started that business about it being just sex, no emotion. Rubbing in the fact we hadn't actually had sex anyway."

"I thought that's what you wanted. I didn't want to make a fool of myself."

"But surely it was clear as daylight that I was absolutely infatuated with you?"

"Not to me. Besides, on the night before the wedding, I'd seen you with Jessica..."

"With Jessica?"

"Up on the battlements. Kissing."

"Then? We'd just agreed to part. Very amicably. It'd been clear for some time that it was over. How could I be with a woman who disliked the children? I asked her if she'd put in an appearance at the wedding the next day, as you'd suggested, and when she agreed, I kissed her. That's all it was."

"Oh, Dante..." She snuggled up to him, sighing.

"Anyway, what about all your followers? The idiot actor?"

"Jake? I told him I'd seen him with Bryony. He tried to wriggle out of it, but he knew he'd blown it. He's been sponging off her ever since. He says he likes the more mature woman."

"Well, that's a bit rude. And the copper?"

"He's been more persistent. But when I put him off he told me he knew I had feelings for you. He said he'd wait for me and be there when you ran off with some — what was the phrase — tarty little model or brain-dead slapper."

"Charming!" he said and then, his voice changing as he looked at her, "Charming." His lips sought hers in a long kiss. When it ended, he demanded, "And while we're on the subject, what on earth was that about? When you wouldn't let me kiss you?"

"Just that every time we did it, I fell for you even more. After that business in the dungeon, it was devastating. So intimate and powerful. But I thought you didn't care for me and I was going to be so badly hurt."

"I wouldn't... I couldn't hurt you. I've been in despair about what happened in Durres. That bloody brothel. I behaved appallingly. But I was drunk and driven to madness. Lying next to you every night in bed... Wanting you more all the time. You were so cool, so full of disgust. After that I thought you'd hate me forever..."

"I was angry. But partly it was because the whole situation excited me."

"...and I began to realise how much I love you."

"You really do?"

"I do." He stroked her face. "You?"

"I've been falling for you since the first time I saw you. But it was so unsuitable and so... banal. You know — the respectable woman and the archetypical bad boy."

"But things aren't so simple, are they? Because you're not really respectable at all."

"And you don't have a bad molecule in your body."

"I'm not sure I'd agree with that. Let's put it to the test, shall we? On your hands and knees, I think."

* * * *

When Samantha went to the flat at lunchtime, she found Eloise, dressed in jeans and a jumper, slumped on the sofa.

"My poor darling Ellie, are you all right? That wretched man! What has he done now? Where is he?"

Dante emerged from the small hallway where the bathroom was, a dark blue towel wrapped around his waist. "The wretched man is here and very contrite about bursting into your consultation. Did you explain I'm just an amiable lunatic?"

"Good heavens!"

Eloise held out her hand to him. "I told him he'd probably lost us a contract."

"Well, no, actually. They were being very tricky, but somehow your X-rated exhibition spurred them on. Especially when they learned the Count was usually in residence during these occasions."

Dante, perched on the arm of the sofa, grinned. "Come on, Samantha, what have you committed me to?"

"Just drinks with the families on the eve of the wedding and one song at the reception."

"I think I've got off very lightly. Sorry about the outfit, by the way."

"No problem," Samantha said, eying his muscled torso. "It suits you."

From somewhere came the tinkling of a mobile phone. "Damn it, that's mine. Where the hell is it?" Dante pursued the sound, finally leaning over the back of the sofa to retrieve his jacket. Samantha's eyes widened at the revelation of shapely buttocks and the heavy sac between his legs. She winked at Eloise.

"Not a bad choice, really."

The phone had stopped ringing by the time Dante had found it in a pocket and flipped it open. "Oh, hell. It's home. The children. Do you mind?"

"Of course not," Eloise said, running her fingers down his thigh as he hit the redial.

"Hello? Oh yes, hi, Matt. You called me—anything wrong?"

A tinny voice responded.

"Good. Yes, I'm having a great time. Miss you all though." He listened. "The surprise? Oh, the cake thing. Yes, highly amusing."

Clearly the phone was being passed around. "Hi, Marco. What, Manchester United? Are you sure? They can't have *another* new strip. Possibly, if it doesn't break the bank." Then a pause. "Yes I did meet Paddington Bear, and he asked me to give his regards to Charlie!"

Finally it was Laura's turn. "At a friend's flat. Yes the shows have been going well. Toby's managing brilliantly without Larry." Before he hung up he said, "Oh by the way, Laura, I knew there was something else. I'm getting married."

They could hear the shriek. "Who to? Not Jessica?"

"Jessica? Um...no, it's not actually. Hold on, my bride-to-be is here, why don't you say hello?"

He handed the phone to Eloise.

"Hello, Laura."

The scream of joy could have been audible in the street outside. "It's Eloise. He's going to marry Eloise!"

Of course, Eloise had to speak to the others before Dante took the phone and closed it. He grinned. "Do you know, I feel quite well disposed towards those children? I think we should provide a little nephew or niece for Charlie."

"Dante! No!"

"What do you mean no? You realise you won't be allowed to disobey me once you're my Contessa?"

"Contessa? Good grief, I'm not going to be a Contessa?"

"Yes. And my first command is that we begin working on an heir. Then you've got to plan the last and best Wedding of the Wolf. So let's get started. Now!" He stretched out a hand.

Smiling, she got up and obediently followed him into the bedroom.

About the Author

Ansley Vaughan is a journalist, who has worked in print, radio and television news. She read history at university and trained as an actress.

Ansley Vaughan has lived in France, Italy and the United States. Her passion is travel, and if she can just get to Antarctica will have visited every continent. She lives in London with two extremely naughty dogs.

Ansley Vaughan loves to hear from readers. You can find her contact information, website details and author profile page at http://www.total-e-bound.com.

Total-E-Bound Publishing

www.total-e-bound.com

Take a look at our exciting range of literagasmic™
erotic romance titles and discover pure quality
at Total-E-Bound.